THE STARLIGHT IN THE SHADOWS

AMBER D. LEWIS

Print Paperback ISBN: 978-1-7370541-4-6

Print Hardback ISBN: 978-1-7370541-7-7

Ebook ISBN: 978-1-7370541-5-3

Cover Design and Formatting: Once Upon an Amber Dawn

Cover Art: Benjamin Lewis

Editor: Andi L. Gregory

For Business Inquiries visit www.amberdlewis.com or write to 4359 Wade Hampton Blvd, #282, Taylors, SC 29687

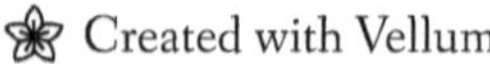 Created with Vellum

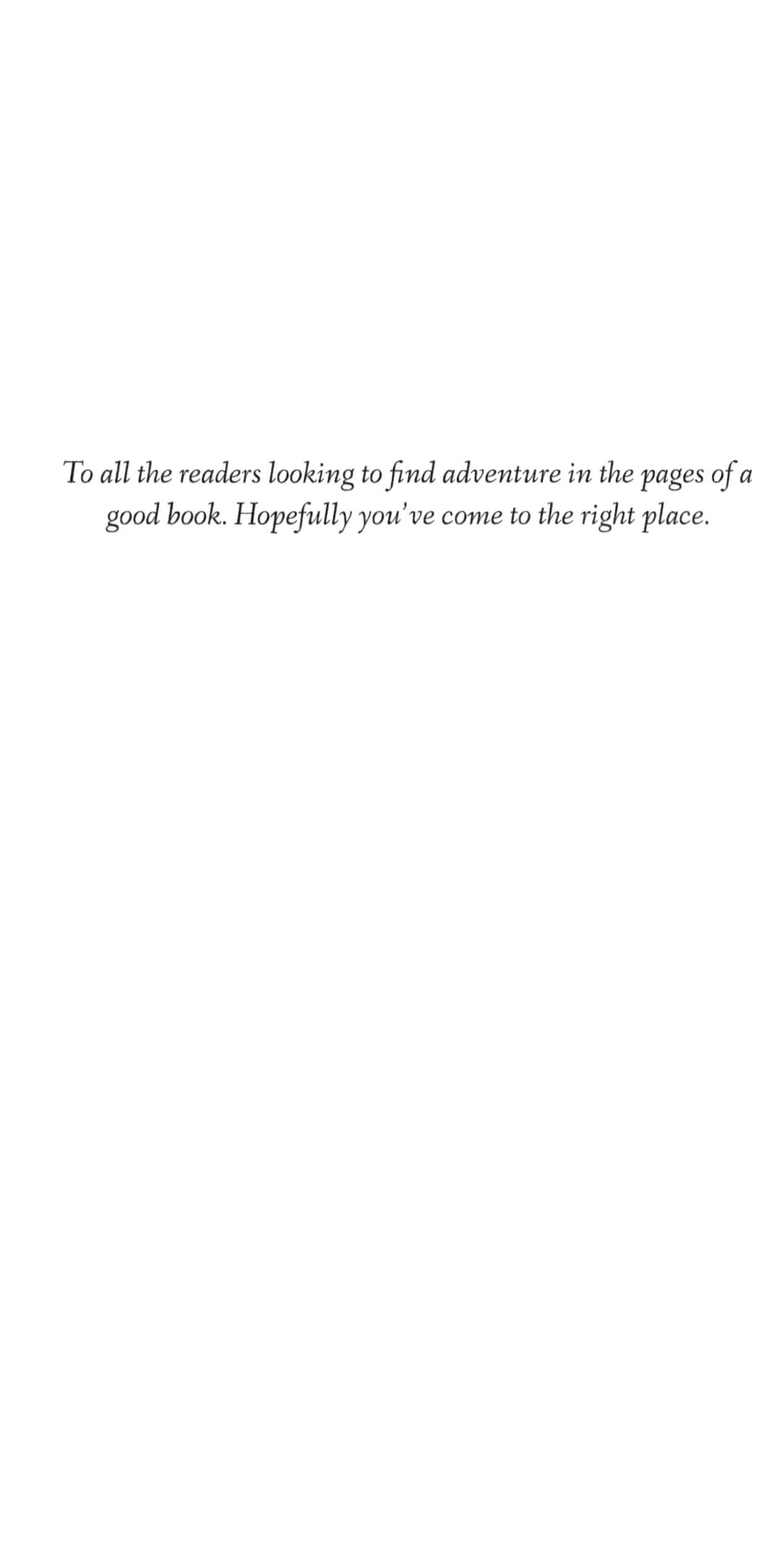

To all the readers looking to find adventure in the pages of a good book. Hopefully you've come to the right place.

ALSO BY AMBER D. LEWIS
RECOMMENDED READING ORDER

FIRE AND STARLIGHT SAGA

The Night the Stars Fell

Scars: Alak's Story

The Starlight in the Shadows

www.amberdlewis.com/fireandstarlightsaga

Ascaria
The Dark Sea
Isle of Atroxmorte
Hounddale
Callenia
Embervein
Paravlia
Athiedor
Aleahya
Brimeshore
Mythgulch Ruins
Balen
Vanaar
Gleador
Jaselstine
Koshima
PinjonMines
Heldonia
GingTa
Portia
Oyrain
Takuma
Wunlan Valley
Meldainak
Silver Mines
ArKney
Isle of Haelien
Luma

Athiedor
Dughlas
Bashmore
Brackenborough
Kensdor
Loudain
Fort Mullidain
Calleria
Gleador
Periola
Wallish
McDullun
Klahbridge
O'Brick

Character Pronunciation Guide

Aine:	än-yā (Awn-yay)
Akaash:	ā-käsh (Ae-kawsh)
Alak:	æl-ik (Al-ick)
Aoibhinn:	ā-vēn (Ae-veen)
Arcanis:	ar-kā-nis (Ar-kay-nis)
Astra:	æs-truh (Ash-truh)
Betron:	be-tron (Beh-tron)
Bram:	bræm (Bram)
Cadewynn:	kad-u-win (Kad-uh-win)
Caedios:	kā-dē-us (Kay-dee-us)
Caitlyn:	kāt-lin (Kate-lin)
Cal:	kæl (Kal)
Ehren:	eh-ruhn (Air-un)
Elidyr:	el-ē-dēr (El-ee-deer)
Felixe:	fē-liks (Fee-licks)
Finian:	fin-ē-in (Fin-ee-in)
Fionn:	fin (Fin)
Hycis:	hī-cis (High-cis)
Ian:	ē-uhn (Ee-un)
Illyas:	il-ē-us (Ill-ee-us)
Jessalynn:	jes-u-lin (Jes-uh-lin)
Kaeya:	kī-uh (Kie-uh)
Kai:	kī (Kie)
Kato:	kā-tō (Kay-toe)
Kayleigh:	kā-lē (Kay-lee)
Makin:	māk-in (Make-in)
Niall:	nī-el (Nile)
Nyco:	nī-kō (Nie-koe)
Ronan:	rō-nin (Roe-nin)
Sama:	sam-u (Sam-uh)

Clan Pronunciation Guide

Bashmore: bæš-mōr (Bash-more)
Dughlas: dug-lis (Duhg-lis)
Kensdor: kins-dōr (kinds-door)
Loudain: lü-dān (Loo-dane)
O'Brick: ō-brik (Oe-brick)
McDullun: mik-dul-lin (Mick-dul-lin)
Wallish: wäl-iš (Wahl-ish)

Place Pronunciation Guide

Kingdoms

Ascaria: æs-kâr-rē-u (Ass-scare-ree-uh)
Athiedor: æ-thē-u-dōr (A-thee-uh-door)
Callenia: ku-lin-ē-u (Kuh-len-ee-uh)
Gleador: glē-u-dōr (Glee-uh-door)
Hundan: hun-dun (Hun-done)
Naskein: næs-kēn (Nas-keen)
Portia: pōr-šu (Pour-shuh)

Key Cities

Jasaltine: jaz-ül-tēn (Jaz-ul-teen)
Klahbridge   klä-bridg (Clah-bridge)
Koshima: kō-she-mu (Koe-she-muh)
Mythgulch: mith-gûlch (mith-gulch)
Periola: pār-ē-ō-lu (Pair-ee-oe-luh)
Mullidain: mul-u-dān (Mull-uh-dain)

AUTHOR NOTE

Please note that this book may have some content that may be triggering for some readers. The story brings up topics of past abuse, suicide, PTSD, and sexual assault. For more detailed information, please view the extended author note at the end of the book after the acknowledgements or visit www.amberdlewis.com/content-warnings.

"THE NIGHT THE STARS FELL" RECAP

KEY PLOT POINTS

Part One: Kriloa

- Astra and Kato are the only twins ever born in their kingdom.
- Magic has been dead for centuries, but Astra and Kato have a power beneath their skin that hasn't quite manifested. They also communicate telepathically with each other.
- Astra discovers her father has arrived home earlier than expected with a man named Marco whom she is supposed to marry when she turns eighteen. She is disgusted by the man and Kato swears he will find a way out of the arrangement.
- Bram, the Captain of the Guard for Prince Ehren, arrives in their small village of Timerborn looking for the twins. Based on research from the prince's sister Cadewynn, aka Winnie, Prince

Ehren is desperate to help the twins and stop possible destruction.

- Bram and Astra grow closer.
- Astra and Kato discuss their fears and nightmares on the rooftop of their home while looking at the stars.
- Bram, Ehren, Astra, and Kato have a misunderstanding at first that results in Astra nearly exposing her power, but things work out and they become friendly. Together they work out a plan to control the twins' power should it manifest as expected.
- On the third night of Kriloa, Astra has a run-in with Marco and ends up killing him. A few minutes later, Astra and Kato turn eighteen and earthquakes and falling stars mark the moment. Astra and Kato burst into starlight and flames, respectively, and are taken to a Healer. Their plan works to contain the damage from their magic.

Part Two: Journey

- Astra and Kato wake at the home of Healer Heora, who has healed them using normal healing means and magical healing.
- When Bram returns a couple days after they wake, they learn that magic has returned and the king is anti-magic. Bram has been tracking magic and damage and reporting back to Ehren.
- Disowned by their father, Astra and Kato have little choice but to follow Bram back to

Embervein. They hope to find a magical instructor once they arrive that can help them understand and control their growing magic.

- Astra begins having dreams where she's visited by a dream version of herself who encourages her and gives her advice.
- Along the path to Embervein, they take a slight detour to a small village that's reporting magic. While at the village, they stumble across a traveling performer named Alak whom Bram appears to hate. Astra, however, is intrigued by Alak since he admits to having access to magic before it broke free.
- Against Bram's advice, Astra meets with Alak during the night and convinces him to join their group and teach her and Kato how to use their magic since he has knowledge and experience about using magic. She also learns that Alak has a familiar named Felixe, who happens to be an adorable magical creature called a Fae Fox.

Part Three: Embervein

- Upon arriving in Embervein, they discover that Alak also has a feud with Ehren, though it's not immediately clear why.
- During the day Astra joins Ehren's sister in the library to do research on magic. Alak tags along.
- Astra, Kato, and Alak are dragged before the king, and Bram claims that Astra has been brought to the castle as his fiancé. After the

meeting with the king, Astra agrees she would be happy to marry Bram.

- Ehren assigns two of his personal Guard to watch over and escort Astra everywhere so his father can't harm her. Cal and Makin take up the position and become quick friends with Astra and Alak.
- After another confrontation between Alak and Bram, Astra finally discovers why Bram and Ehren hate Alak. Alak had a previous relationship with Bram's sister, Isabella, and Bram blames Alak for her death, a suicide. Astra decides to continue trusting Alak, and Alak is grateful. Bram still struggles to trust Alak, but agrees to put their differences aside since they are current allies.
- While sorting through records with Alak, Astra discovers a paper written in a language she doesn't understand. Alak identifies the language as Yallik, a dialect spoken in the region of Athiedor, and is able to translate it. They discover through the records that magic didn't completely die out in some areas, including Athiedor and the Hundan Valley. Alak decides to contact his family in Athiedor.
- Cadewynn tells them about a secret room beneath the library and Alak starts using the room to train Kato and Astra in magic.
- Astra and Bram become formally engaged when he proposes to her under the stars with his mother's ring.

- One day during lunch with Cadewynn, Astra meets a cruel noble named Landis. Landis reappears at a ball and is upset when Astra refuses him a dance. Later at the ball he forces her outside with ill intentions. Astra is rescued by Alak, who wasn't even supposed to be at the ball.
- A little shaken from her experience with Landis, Astra leaves the ball a little early, escorted to her room by Bram. When she enters her room she finds Alak waiting for her. Alak confronts her, asking why she didn't use magic to take care of Landis. Astra breaks down crying and the two kiss. Alak flees her room. Astra goes to his room moments later and they agree that the kiss was a mistake and that it will be kept secret.
- Astra continues researching magic and passes her discoveries on to Ehren and Bram so they can find and save magical individuals before Ehren's father, the king, can harm anyone else. Alak receives word from his family in Athiedor inviting him to come visit.
- One day on the way back from lunch in a garden, Landis confronts Astra and threatens her. He also threatens Kato, Bram, and Ehren who are out on a mission. Astra is concerned but everyone arrives back safely. Due to the rising threat, Ehren starts putting a plan in motion.
- The king fully outlaws magic and Astra, Kato, Alak, Bram, Ehren, Cal, and Makin flee the castle. The plan is to reunite at a safe house before traveling to Alak's family in Athiedor.

Ehren is seriously wounded during their escape and Astra learns she is able to use healing magic, though it drains her quickly. Alak refills some of her magic by sharing his with her.

Part Four: Outlaws

- Traveling is extremely taxing and quickly takes its toll. Astra begins doubting herself and her magic. Alak lifts her spirits and encourages her.
- In a private conversation with Astra under the stars one night, Kato suggests eventually leaving the others behind. Astra disagrees.
- Alak and Astra combine their magic to maintain a spell that masks and hides the group from bandits and others who may wish them harm.
- When they reach Athiedor, the magic wielders in the group can feel the abundant magic in the land.
- They make several stops at pubs and inns, Ehren and Bram using alternative names so they aren't as easily recognized and turned into the king or cast out by those who don't like that Athiedor answers to the Callenian king.
- One night Astra and Alak spend a while dancing at a pub and Astra gets drunk. Most everyone else is amused, but Bram is furious and he and Alak get into a fistfight.
- When they arrive at Alak's Aunt Shannon's house, they are received with open arms. They discover that not only is magic widely accepted and flourishing in Athiedor but also is

considered the higher way of life and those without magic are considered inferior.

- The group is split up at night, Alak, Astra, and Kato staying with Alak's cousin Niall and the rest remaining at Alak's aunt's house.
- The group gets to know Alak's cousins Kayleigh and Niall, as well as Niall's finance Caitlyn and their friends Aine, Fionn, and Ian.
- Astra receives a letter from Cadewynn with an update that also includes a distressing letter from her friend, Mara, who is still back in Timberborn. Ehren receives a letter from the Order of Naskein, inviting him to visit and discuss magic.
- The group agrees in stay in Athiedor until after the upcoming festival celebrating Aoibhinn, the goddess of magic.
- One night Astra overhears Kato talking to Niall, Fionn, and Ian about how magicless people are less than those with magic. She is upset when Kato seems to agree with their stance, but she keeps everything to herself.
- When getting ready for the Festival of Aoibhinn, Astra and Alak have a moment where they nearly kiss. Bram comes in and the moment is lost. Bram becomes suspicious.
- At the festival Astra listens to a storyteller explain the full story of Aoibhinn and she realizes they may have a few things in common.
- After the festival Astra feels off and Bram escorts her back to Niall's but misunderstands her invitation to come inside. After Bram leaves,

Astra's condition worsens and she leaves Niall's house to head to a magical river nearby in the hopes the water can help heal whatever is going wrong.

- Alak follows Astra into the forest and realizes her magic has been poisoned. As Astra collapses with a scream, Alak begs her to hang on and uses his Syphon magic to drain the spell away and save her life at risk to his own.

- They wake the next morning lying together in the forest. They're both relieved that their magic seems fine. With a start they realize they've been together all night and will likely be missed. They quickly change clothes and meet up with the others at breakfast.

- Bram seems openly upset with Astra and they leave breakfast to discuss things out behind the house. Bram accuses Astra of cheating on him with Alak, citing the fact that he saw them sleeping in the forest together. Astra is furious and tells him what really happened. They're interrupted by sounds from the front of the house.

- Soldiers from the king have arrived after a tip from Niall. When Ehren refuses to surrender, the soldiers attack and Astra and Bram rush into battle. They're seriously outnumbered and Astra calls on the full force of her power to wipe out the soldiers. Using wisping, they once again flee, forced to leave all their supplies behind, and regroup.

- With nowhere else to go, Ehren leads the group on a slow, exhausting journey to the port city of Brineshore, where they will board a boat to head to the kingdom of Portia and eventually make it to the Isle of Naskein to seek refuge within the Order.
- They manage to sneak into the city without any issues, but a magical creature that sniffs magic causes them to come up with a backup plan upon entering Portia.
- The group carefully crosses Portia, making money by gambling and performing. Once in the port city of Arkney, they secure passage to the Isle of Naskein. Their plans are cut short, however, when they're attacked by a group of mercenaries. Using magic, Astra creates a bridge and they run across the water to the Isle of Naskein where the Order is waiting for them.
- The group is accepted and taken under the protection of the Order.
- While staying within the walls of the Order, they learn more about magic. Alak, Kato, and Astra learn how to better use their own magic, while the others learn general information about magic and how to use spells.
- One morning, Alak confronts Astra and asks her point blank if she still intends to marry Bram. Astra dodges the subject and doesn't want to answer. When she finally caves, she basically admits she sees no reason not to go through with the marriage. Alak accepts her decision without a fight and leaves.

- When the king sends an armada to Naskein, Master Arcanis, the head of the Order, calls a meeting. He informs the group that they will be safe inside the walls of the Order as long as they remain peaceful; if they wish to fight the king, they will need to leave. Kato insists they leave and fight, but the others seem to lean toward peace.

- Kato begs Astra to come with him, insisting they are stronger and better because of their magic. Astra refuses to leave Bram and Ehren, asking Kato to stay and reconsider. Kato refuses and they battle it out. Astra is struck by Kato's flames and wounded slightly.

- Kato is about to wisp away when Alak calls out and asks to come with him. Astra is distraught and pleads with Alak to stay. He tells her to trust him and kisses her before allowing Kato to wisp him away.

- Astra collapses, exhausted, wounded, and broken. Bram takes her to the healing rooms where she spends days lying in bed. She only finds a reason to leave the bed when Felixe, Alak's familiar, arrives with a note explaining why he left. Alak makes it clear that he does not support Kato and only left to be a spy. He also hopes to convince Kato to come back to Astra.

- With renewed purpose, Astra leaves the healing room with Ehren, ready to make a plan and take down her brother and the king.

KEY PEOPLE

- **Astra**: one of the twins; has starlight magic; 18 years old
- **Kato**: one of the twins; has fire magic; 18 years old; skilled swordsman
- **Mara**: Astra's best friend; 18 years old
- **Pax**: Kato's best friend; 19 years old
- **Bram/Captain Bramfield**: Prince Ehren's Captain of the Guard; 22 years old; best swordsman in the kingdom
- **Ehren**: Crown Prince of Callenia; 20 years old
- **Healer Heora**: Healer who helps Kato and Astra
- **Hanna**: Healer Heora's granddaughter; Healer in training
- **Alak**: performer; has Syphon magic and illusion magic; has a familiar; 20 years old
- **Felixe**: an adorable Fae Fox who can wisp at will and turn invisible; Alak's familiar
- **Cadewynn/Winnie**: Princess of Callenia; Ehren's sister; 16 years old
- **King Betron**: King of Callenia who hates magic; Ehren's father
- **Landis**: hated noble
- **Makin**: member of Ehren's Guard; close with Ehren and Bram; chosen to guard Astra
- **Cal**: member of Ehren's Guard; close with Ehren and Bram; chosen to guard Astra

- **Niall**: Alak's cousin; has shadow magic; dangerously pro-magic
- **Kayleigh**: Alak's cousin; has telekinesis; seamstress
- **Caitlyn**: Niall's fiance; an empath who can see auras
- **Ian**: Niall's friend; strong in spellwork; dangerously pro-magic
- **Aine**: Niall's friend/ Ian's sister; has metal attack magic; dangerously pro-magic; interested in Alak
- **Fionn**: Niall's friend; specializes in spellwork and potions without needing ingredients or spell books; dangerously pro-magic
- **Master Arcanis**: Head of the Order of Naskein
- **Aoibhinn**: the goddess of magic

View character profiles and art, maps, and more on my website: https://www.amberdlewis.com/storytelling

PROLOGUE

KATO

"Is everything going to plan?"

I stare down the dark figure in the corner of the room, gritting my teeth to keep my temper in check.

"Of course."

The figure glances at me over his shoulder, arching an eyebrow. "Are you so sure? Was bringing along the . . . spare completely necessary? His magic is nothing grand to speak of. There are far better allies for you to seek out."

"Astra loves him. He's an important piece in gaining her trust."

The figure scoffs and shifts his gaze out the window, the silver moonlight reflecting across his features.

"Love is weakness. I suppose it would be best to use it to my—our—advantage. I thought, however, she was in love with that *captain.*"

He spits the last word with pure disdain. A smile curves on my lips as I shake my head. "Oh, she might pretend she still loves that ridiculous, magicless nothing of a captain, but I know her. I've seen her. She loves Alak." I pause, adding thoughtfully, "He's much better suited for her, anyway. He comes from two lines of magic. Even though his magic may be weaker than ours, he's still fairly strong. With him in my possession, on my side, it's only a matter of time before she joins us."

The man nods, still not bothering to look my way. "Perhaps. But even with this Alak on your side, will that be enough pull? Your sister still seems awfully enraptured by her magicless friends."

"She and I were always meant to be together and she'll realize soon enough how weak she is tethered to them. She's going to lose to the King of Callenia. She'll be too distracted to defeat him. She'll also lose to me, should events progress that far—not that I want to go up against her. I want her by my side and I will give her another chance someday soon. One way or another she'll lose to me—either by bending her will and accepting fate, or in battle, where she will discover that I have grown stronger than she. But either way she'll eventually have to accept she's weaker without me."

The man finally deigns to glance my way, his eyes cold and challenging, lips carved into a cruel smile. "And are you really so powerful? Hiding away like you are?"

Anger roils through me and I clench my fists at my side. "I see the world for what it truly is—a place of power-hungry souls, grasping for legitimacy. I don't need to find those things. I already have them. So does she. The gods blessed us. Not only did they give us each other, they gave us unimaginable power that most people have completely forgotten ever existed. We are the weapons of the gods, put in this world to cleanse it. We ushered in a new age of magic, and we are meant to lead it. I'm not hiding; I'm waiting for the right moment to rise."

The man makes a "tsking" sound as he looks back out the window. "So full of idealistic plans. You've yet to even come into your full power."

I take a step toward him. "That's why you're here, isn't it? To guide me? To make me stronger?"

The man offers a half-shrug. "I suppose. It's one of the reasons, anyway." He turns his sharp gaze to me, fire in his eyes. "But you have to listen."

"I am listening."

"No. You might be hearing the things I'm saying but you aren't listening." He takes a step in my direction. "You have grand and mighty plans but they all revolve around your sister."

"We were meant to be together from birth until death. She is my twin, half my soul."

"She betrayed you."

His words feel like a slap and I stumble back a step. His cruel smile returns as he meets my eyes, relishing my pain.

"She made a mistake but she'll soon see sense."

"You shouldn't hold out hope. You need to let her go."

I frown and glance away. "No. I'll never leave her behind."

"You already have."

"This was only temporary! In time—"

"In time she will be worthless," he cuts me off with a careless flick of his hand. "Her power will wane. She'll never rise to her full potential. She's hiding away in the shadows. She can never realize her full power."

"Exactly. And once she realizes that—"

"Nothing. Nothing will happen. She doesn't care for power as you do; she doesn't have the taste for it. If you continue to obsess over you sister, your power will also fade."

His cold eyes meet mine once again and I feel my own power stir within me. "You claim your sister's love for the captain and Alak are her weakness? Then she is yours."

I open my mouth, willing to fight his claim, but even as the arguments form I know he's right. Astra is my weakness.

"She'll only hold you back. You don't need her. You are strong enough on your own."

I know he's right, but a piece of me won't allow me to move on. Not yet. I turn my back to him, shaking my head.

"Give her time. If, in time, your theory proves correct, then I'll continue with our plans. But for now, I will still try to draw her."

Thick silence fills the room before he finally mutters, "So be it, but do not linger too long on thoughts of unity or you will both fall."

I nod, refusing to look at him. I will find a way to convince Astra to join me. She *has* to join me. She is too important to let fall to the wayside. I know we were meant for greatness. Together we can rule Callenia.

Starlight cannot shine in the shadows, and I'm the one that must bring her out of them.

Part One: Apart

CHAPTER ONE

ASTRA

It's been thirteen days since Kato and Alak abandoned me here on the Isle of Naskein and a week since I came to my senses and realized that moping in the healing room wasn't doing me any good. Alak brought me to my senses, despite being far away. He managed to reach me when no one else could. Deep inside I know what this means, but I'm choosing to ignore it.

Alak forced me back to sanity, but Ehren is keeping me sane. Ehren's my shoulder to lean on when everything starts feeling like it's too much. The dynamic between us is shifting, and I'm beginning to realize I need him as much as he needs me.

Bram is . . . well, Bram is here. He's willing to help me, but the air between us is heavy right now. There are conversations we need to have—conversations we're both avoiding. Or, at least, conversations I'm avoiding. I've never been great at confrontation, but the days of me being passive have come to an end.

With a deep sigh, I approach the main courtyard. Makin,

Cal, Bram, and Ehren wait outside one of the main conference rooms. It's time for another meeting with the Head Mage of the Order of Naskein, Master Arcanis. He's been in direct communication with representatives from Callenia and Portia. The King of Callenia, Ehren's father, put a price on our heads. He's against magic and thinks by bringing us down that he'll somehow succeed in stamping magic out before it can grow. He's very wrong. Magic is back, whether he likes it or not, and it's already stronger than ever. While he buries his head in the sand, people like my twin, Kato, are making moves to make sure magic reigns dominant. Ehren and I are working together to make a plan to salvage the kingdom. For now, however, we have to play politics and act kind and courteous, even though there's an armada ready to whisk us back to Callenia to meet our fates.

"Is Master Arcanis ready for us yet?" I ask Ehren as I approach.

Ehren shakes his head. "Not quite, but it shouldn't be much longer." His eyes scan me for a moment. "How are you?"

"I'm good," I reply, offering him a smile.

He gives me a satisfactory nod, knowing better than to push the issue. I look past Ehren at Bram, his eyes locking onto mine, worry written on every tense feature.

The door to the room swings open and Apprentice Lia, Master Arcanis's main apprentice, smiles at us. "He's ready."

Ehren straightens his shoulders and strides into the room, the perfect picture of confidence. Bram and I walk side-by-side a couple steps behind him while Makin and Cal remain outside the room to stand guard. When we're alone or in a casual setting, we're all on equal footing, but, we've decided, it may be time to start showing open respect for

Ehren as the rightful ruler of Callenia. He's the first to walk into a room, unless it would require a Guard presence to enter first, and the rest of us will be in positions behind him according to rank.

Ehren stops in the center of the room in front of Master Arcanis, bowing slightly from the waist. Master Arcanis inclines his head in return.

"What news can you share from beyond the walls?" Ehren asks, his voice rich with authority.

"Portia and Callenia still request that we surrender you, and we are continuing to deny that request. As expected, Portia is irritated with our decision, but they respect it," Master Arcanis says evenly.

"I suppose my father is much less understanding?"

Master Arcanis nods. "His threat of war has not been rescinded."

Ehren sighs. "I'm terribly sorry for the trouble we have brought to your gate."

"We are happy to assist," Master Arcanis replies with a wave of his hand. "It is our duty as part of the Order to protect and preserve magic. Our goals are the same, though our methods may differ. We are content to house you as long as necessary. However, we will assist you in leaving discreetly when you are ready."

Ehren considers his words for a moment before replying, "I think it is best that we leave sooner rather than later. You previously mentioned that you are able to create portals between locations. How soon could you have one of those portals ready?"

"We can prepare one for you by tomorrow morning," Master Arcanis replies and Ehren's eyes widen.

"That soon?"

Master Arcanis nods. "Indeed. The portals are already in place. They simply need willing magic-wielders on both ends to open the doors. We have good relations with a few magical locations. The most beneficial to you would be Athiedor or the Hundan Valley."

"Were you able to verify the information I gave you a couple days ago?" Ehren asks.

"Yes. Your source was correct. Kato is in Athiedor." If Master Arcanis is suspicious of whom that source may be, he doesn't show it. Bram, however, frowns.

Ehren nods slowly, thinking. "Then I suppose our best option would be the Hundan Valley."

"I agree."

"And you can arrange a portal for us for tomorrow?" Ehren clarifies and Master Arcanis nods. "Thank you. We owe you our lives. Is there anything we can do for you in return?"

Master Arcanis studies Ehren for a moment. "Actually, we do have one request as well as something you may want to take into consideration as you move forward."

"Whatever you require, please, let me know."

"As I mentioned, these portals require magic and magic wielders to work properly. In times of old, there were many portals across many kingdoms, but as magic faded away, we were able to maintain only those on the small portions of land that retained significant amounts of magic. We would like to restore some of the long-lost portals and, perhaps, create some new ones. This would be beneficial to both your cause and ours."

Ehren considers Master Arcanis's request carefully. "Would having too many portals put you or the portal locations at risk?"

Master Arcanis shakes his head. "No. There are many protections in place to keep just anyone from using them. They would be secure."

Ehren glances to me for my opinion, and I nod. "I don't see any problems with helping to restore and create portals."

"Fine. I accept your terms," Ehren says, turning his attention back to a Master Arcanis. "We will gladly help you reestablish the portals. Now, what else did you wish to discuss?"

Master Arcanis smiles. It's almost unnerving.

"I'm sure you've noticed in your recent study of magical histories that it was very common in the time of magic for kings to appoint a sorcerer or sorceress as a member of his court. This individual was held in the highest esteem, second only to the king or queen. Even kingdoms that weren't particularly supportive of magic had a court mage of some sort. It was a statement of power. Those sorcerers also served as liaisons to the world of magic and orders such as ours."

"I have noticed this, and I believe I've already considered what you are about to suggest," Ehren cuts in. "It's my intention to appoint Astra as the official sorceress of my court."

My eyes go wide as my mouth drops open. Ehren gives me a side glance and smiles.

"It is very good to hear that. While in many courts the appointment by the king—or in your case, prince—is more than sufficient, there is an official ceremony that can be performed. It would publicly confirm your appointment of Astra as your Court Sorceress while also showing our support and establishing her as a liaison. We can perform the ceremony tonight, if you desire it."

Ehren shakes his head. "While I am eager to have the ceremony performed, I have not even asked." He pauses and turns to face me. "Astra, would you be willing to take up this appointment? I fully understand if you decline. You are under no obligation to accept."

His eyes meet mine, earnestness and pride shining in them. I glance over at Bram. He's tense and stiff, anger flashing in his eyes. Apparently, he had no idea this was coming, either. His reaction makes me temporarily hesitant, but when I look back at Ehren, I see something else. There's fear at my hesitation—fear I'll say no. He needs me, and, quite frankly, I need this. I need something specific to focus on. I smile.

"Of course. It would be my honor," I reply, inclining my head.

Ehren smiles and turns back to Master Arcanis. "Well, that settles that matter."

"Excellent," Master Arcanis affirms. "We will begin the preparations immediately. The ceremony will take place this evening before dinner, which we will make a feast in celebration. In the meantime, I will make the necessary arrangements for the portal to be ready at dawn."

"Thank you. Is there anything else you wish to discuss? If not, we should prepare for our departure tomorrow," Ehren says.

Master Arcanis shakes his head. "That is all for today. If you have any further questions or concerns do not hesitate to reach out to me or any of the other Masters. We are happy to assist you on your quest in whatever way we can. You have only to ask."

Ehren gives him a grateful nod and turns to exit the room. I start to follow him, but he gestures to his side.

"Please, walk side-by-side with me," Ehren requests. "From this point forward, I want us to be equals."

I open my mouth to argue but decide against it. This is too public, and I feel something like this should be discussed between the two of us without an audience. I fall into step beside him as Bram's eyes flash before he schools his features into a neutral expression. We march out of the room, Cal and Makin falling into line behind Bram. Thanks to my recent magical instruction, I've learned to wisp without physically touching my companions. As we walk, I reach out my magic, brushing it against each individual person, and wisp us directly into our room. The others stumble as they adjust to the sudden change.

"I'm never going to get used to that," Ehren mumbles under his breath.

"Me neither," Cal agrees, sinking down onto his bed, looking nauseous.

"So . . . ," Makin drawls. "How was the meeting?"

"Good," Ehren answers. "Master Arcanis confirmed Kato has gone back to Athiedor, so we'll be leaving tomorrow morning via a portal to the Hundan Valley."

"Tomorrow?" Makin asks. "That's sooner than I expected."

Ehren arches an eyebrow. "Did you want to stay longer?"

Makin shakes his head. "Not really. It's a bit nerve-wracking to have the king's armada waiting just outside the wall. I'll be happy to be far away from here. I just wasn't expecting to leave so soon."

"How will the portal work?" Cal asks, tilting his head. "It's not like wisping is it?"

Ehren shrugs, fighting a grin at Cal's grimace. "I'm not entirely sure, but if it gets us to where we need to be without weeks of traveling and dodging bounty hunters, I'm all for it. Hopefully it won't be too hard on you." Cal nods and glances off. "Regardless, we need to get everything ready to go."

"Aren't you forgetting one other detail from the meeting?" Bram says, his voice like ice as his eyes settle on me.

Makin's eyes slide from Bram's face to mine, which has gone red, before sliding them to Ehren's face.

"Ah, yes. Astra is to be appointed the official Court Sorceress. Master Arcanis is arranging an official ceremony tonight. She'll also be our official liaison with the magical world," Ehren says with a proud smile.

"Is that surprising news?" Makin says carefully, eyeing the look of displeasure on Bram's face.

Ehren shrugs, shaking his head. "It shouldn't be."

"I think it's a foolish move," Bram cuts in, not even attempting to mask his anger and frustration.

Ehren's eyes narrow at Bram and he crosses his arms. "Explain."

"You are putting a target on her back by appointing her to such a high position," Bram spits. "People see the two of you walking side-by-side, and they will want to take her down a notch."

"You mean having her picture on a wanted poster and a brother who has gone rogue hasn't already put a target on her back?" Ehren asks, his voice even and controlled.

Bram shakes his head in frustration, his fists clenched by his sides. "It is not the same. This puts her at greater risk, and you know it. Hasn't she gone through enough already?" His eyes flick momentarily to the barely noticeable scars gracing my chin and neck—scars given to me by my own brother. I fight the urge to cover them with my hand.

Ehren turns to me. "Are you concerned about becoming a greater target?"

I glance at Bram. His eyes flash. I know what he wants me to say, but I can't.

"It's a risk I'm willing to take," I reply, avoiding Bram's eyes.

Bram swears while Makin purposefully puts extra distance between them.

Ehren turns back to Bram. "I see no issue here. Astra is capable of making her own decisions."

"However," I amend, and Ehren glances back at me, arching an eyebrow.

"Yes?"

"I would prefer to walk slightly behind you—just a half-step or so, but behind you nonetheless. You are my prince, and I bow to you. I serve you."

Ehren considers my words, a slight scowl the only indication he disagrees. "All right. I can understand that, but let me be clear—I never expect you to actually bow before me. I may have final say on things, but I do not expect you to blindly bow to my will. I give you full permission to question me. For the foreseeable future, you and I are equals. Understood?"

I smile and incline my head. "I find your terms acceptable."

Bram turns and storms from the room, slamming the door behind him so hard the tapestries on the wall shudder. My heart sinks.

"I'm just going to go over here and pack," Makin says awkwardly, striding quickly toward his trunk at the opposite end of the room. "Care to help me, Cal?"

"Absolutely." Cal hops up off his bed and rushes toward Makin.

Ehren crosses the distance between us, placing his hand

on my arm. "He'll get over it."

I glance at the closed door and take a deep breath. "Do you really think so?"

Ehren smiles sadly. "He has no choice."

I shake my head and look down at my clasped hands. "He's still mad about everything that's happened. This appointment just adds to it."

Ehren places his finger under my chin and tilts my face up so my eyes meet his.

"He'll get over it." I force a weak smile, and Ehren adds, "Why don't you go talk to him? I can guarantee he hasn't left the balcony."

I nod and head outside. Sure enough, Bram stands at the edge of the balcony, leaning on the railing and looking down into the courtyard below. He hears the door and lifts his head to stare straight ahead without turning around, sunlight washing over his features. My heart skips a beat. Even with the scar on his cheek he's incredibly handsome. I quietly walk up next to him. He lowers his face to look at me.

"You can't do this."

"It's not your choice."

"Damn it, Astra! Why do you have to be so stubborn?"

"I'm the stubborn one? Seriously? You're the one who's been sulking around, glaring and snapping at everyone for the past week."

"Well, why shouldn't I? I think I have a good reason. My fiancé spends days in healing rooms and, when I go to visit her, she's missing. No one knows where the hell you are. All anyone knows is that you were last seen leaving with Ehren. Hours I searched for you. Hours, Astra." His expression shows how wounded he is, and I glance away down into the courtyard, guilt swirling in my gut.

"I already apologized for that," I mumble.

"I know, and I could forgive you, except you seem to think it is now your duty to take down your brother single-handedly."

I look up at him, hurt shining in my own eyes. His expression softens as he drags a hand down his face, sighing.

"I love you more than life itself, and the idea of you putting yourself at risk, I . . . I cannot handle it."

I reach my hand to touch his cheek, but he pulls away. "Bram . . ."

"And you think I don't know who this 'source' is?" he asks sharply.

My heart stops. Ehren and I both agreed not to tell Bram about Alak's messages. So far, I've received two letters—the initial message and one more detailing Kato's recent movements and plans. I have yet to send one back, but Ehren suggested we keep Alak equally informed. Ehren has taken the leap of faith necessary to trust Alak, but we both know Bram won't be as accepting.

"What do you mean?" I ask cautiously.

"I know you and Kato can communicate across distances." I exhale in relief as he continues. "I don't know exactly how you are working it right now, but you should not be contacting him in any way or spying on him through whatever twin bond you have. What if it backfires, and he uses it against you?"

"Once again, it's not your choice."

He swears.

"You are taking on too much, Astra," Bram states firmly. "You need to stop."

I turn away from him. "I can't. You know I can't. Ehren is depending on me now."

"Ehren can go to hell," Bram spits.

I spin to face him. "He is your prince! How can you say that? His own father and most of Callenia have turned against him. He's literally being hunted down. You, as his best friend and Captain of his Guard, should remain loyal!"

Bram takes a deep breath. "I did not mean it. Not like that." He reaches for me, but I step away from his touch. He lowers his hand, clenching it into a fist as he frowns. "Please, Astra. I know you are powerful and strong, but it does not mean you have to flaunt it. You can rein in your powers. You do not have to be this mighty sorceress at Ehren's beck and call every moment of every day."

"I'm not," I argue, cheeks flushing with anger.

"You are, or at least you will be, if you continue down this path," he insists, his voice just as angry as mine. "Becoming Ehren's Court Sorceress makes you more of a target. Whether you can see it it or not, you'll be killing yourself to prove you are strong and powerful. You're trying to make up for Kato leaving, but it wasn't your fault."

"I don't have to prove anything. I *am* strong and powerful, and I'll willingly use that power for Ehren. I support him, and I will do everything I can to assist him."

I pause and turn away from Bram. My voice grows distant.

"Kato is out there, working against us, already searching for magic wielders to bring into his ranks." I turn back to Bram. "I have to fight against him. It's my duty."

Bram's expression softens. "It is not your duty to bear all this alone. Please, let me help you. Stick to the sideline unless absolutely necessary while I lead the Guard to fight the big battles."

I shake my head. "I can't. I need to do this. I need to

embrace my power and who I am. This is my destiny. It always has been."

"Is it who you really are, though? Or are you forcing yourself to be someone you are not? The girl I met in Timberborn was wonderful and gentle and amazing, even without her power. That is the girl I fell in love with," Bram says quietly.

Tears well in my eyes as I look into his. "I'm not that girl anymore, Bram."

He grabs my hands. "Yes, you are. I know you are."

I take a deep, shuddering breath. "I'm not. A piece of me may be, but not all of me. I've changed. I'm still changing. I have the scars to prove it. And if you can't accept that . . ." I look away, unable to bear the pain in his eyes.

"What are you saying, Astra?" he asks, his voice unsteady.

I look back up at him as a tear slides down my cheek. "I can't be the girl you want me to be and that's not fair to you."

Bram shakes his head. "No, Astra, don't."

I pull my hands from his and take a step back. "I don't think I can marry you."

"Astra," Bram pleads, his voice breaking. He steps toward me, his own eyes brimming with tears. "I am still willing to marry you, no matter what. I love you. Surely you know that I love you."

"You're willing to marry me but not longing to," I reply with a weak smile.

"No, Astra. You're wrong. I love you."

"I love you, too."

I step into his arms and kiss him. I slide my hand into his as I pull away. His eyes go wide, and he looks down. In his palm lies my ring. He shakes his head, tears breaking free.

"Please, Astra, don't . . ."

"Maybe, one day, when this is all done, we can try again," I say weakly, before turning and wisping away before tears wet my cheeks.

CHAPTER TWO

ASTRA

I sink further into the hot spring, leaning my head back against the edge. This is only the second time I've gotten to use it, and I'm going to miss having access to it after we leave in the morning. It's so soothing. Despite all the troubles in my life right now, it helps calm me. It helps me think.

I hear footsteps and I jerk up. A large, long wooden divider runs through the middle of the hot spring, separating the side for men from the side for women, but I still find it unnerving that there's not much between my naked body and the naked bodies of the men on the other side. The footsteps slow, and I hear a splash as whoever it is enters the water. I decide I've been in here long enough. I leave the water, wrapping my body in a white towel. I hesitate when a familiar voice calls my name from the other side of the wall.

"Astra? Are you in here?"

I pause before answering Ehren. "Yes."

Ehren sighs. "I figured you might be."

He pauses. He knows how awkward this is. You can feel it in the air.

"I talked to Bram," he says quietly.

I release a long breath, my hand clutching the towel around me a little tighter. "Oh."

"He loves you, you know."

"I know."

"But I understand."

Tears start to well in my eyes again. "You do?"

"I do." He pauses, then adds, "Do you want to talk about it?"

I shake my head before remembering he can't actually see me. "Not right now, but I appreciate it."

"Well, I'm here if you ever want to talk." I hear him leaving the water.

"What are you doing?"

He pauses. "I was getting out. I only came in here to find you."

"No," I reply firmly. "You have a lot on your plate. You don't need to worry about me. Spend a few minutes in here to relax and reset. Stay a minimum of ten to fifteen minutes. When you're done, meet me outside. I'll wait for you."

Ehren chuckles. "I go and make you Court Sorceress and you get bossy."

I grin. "Yep. You put me in a position of authority, and I'm running with it. We'll take care of each other, you know. And right now that means you need to relax. I'll see you in a few minutes."

"Yes, Ma'am," he says, a smile in his voice as he sinks back into the water.

I make my way over to the changing area and slip into my dress. I could use magic to dry my damp hair, but I don't bother. Instead, I just wind it up into a messy bun. I head into the courtyard outside the hot spring to wait for Ehren. I lean against a tree in the center and close my eyes. Footsteps approach several minutes later.

"I leave you alone for a few minutes, and you decide it's nap time."

I open one eye and squint up at Ehren. "Well, I guess it's time to get back to work now that my almighty prince has arrived."

He laughs and offers me his hand. I open both eyes, accepting his hand, and he pulls me to my feet.

"Did you enjoy your soak?" I ask, eying his wet hair sticking up in random directions.

He smiles. "Yes, I did, actually. I'm glad you made me stay in there. It was a good chance to think." He runs his hand through his hair and scowls.

"What's wrong?"

"My hair," he mumbles, shaking his head, sending little water droplets flying through the air.

I laugh, wiping a few of the droplets from my face. "What about your hair?"

"It's never been this long before in my life, and it's starting to drive me insane," he admits with a shrug.

His hair is getting fairly long. Personally, I think the shaggy look works for him, but he does look less regal. My eyes drop to his chin. What started out as stubble has actually turned into a decent, slim beard. It suits him. He catches me taking in his appearance and his mouth quirks up into a half-grin.

"See something you like?"

I roll my eyes and shake my head, turning to lead the way out of the courtyard.

"Where are you off to now?" I ask, Ehren falling into step beside me.

"I'm going to pick up some spells and basic ingredients to take with us tomorrow," Ehren replies, kicking a small stone out of the path.

I nod. "That must mean that your spellwork is coming along well."

Ehren looks over at me and grins, eyes bright. "It is. Master Vigos says I show a lot of promise and have a natural inclination toward spells. I've learned so much. I have to admit, I really love magic."

"I'm glad you've found a way to be part of the magical world," I say earnestly. "I haven't even had my magic all that long, or at least I haven't had access to it, but I can't imagine my life without it anymore."

Ehren nods but doesn't say anything for a moment. When he does speak, he's hesitant, his eyes watching the ground beneath his feet.

"Astra, I know I kind of put you on the spot earlier, but as much as I hate to admit it, Bram wasn't entirely wrong. You've been through a lot. If you have any reservations at all about being my Court Sorceress, you only have to say the word and—"

"Ehren," I say softly, reaching out and grabbing his hand, stopping him. He looks up at me, his sea-green eyes searching my face. I offer him a smile. "I want to be your Court Sorceress. It's a terrifying thought, yes, but it's something I want."

Ehren exhales a long breath, his shoulders loosening in relief, and nods. "Good. Because I don't think I can do this without you." I drop his hand as we resume walking. "You know, most of my life I fought against my position. I wanted to have nothing to do with the crown—not in the ways my father demanded, at least. I avoided responsibility whenever I could, just wanting to be a normal boy. Not that I didn't love my kingdom—I did—but the pressures of my future were overwhelming and crushing at times. If you would've asked me even a few months ago if I would willingly step into my role early and lead a war in favor of magic against my own father, I would have laughed in your face. I'm not prepared for this. I have no idea what the right choices are anymore."

He glances at me, and I can read the uncertainty in his eyes. I offer him a small smile.

"Well," I say slowly, "I can't say I ever saw myself as anything more than a librarian or a historian until recent events changed literally everything about my life. I think we're all a little unsure about what to do. Anyone who tells you otherwise is lying. This is new ground for all of us. Even those here in Naskein who have had magic their entire lives now have to deal with a world outside their walls that's suddenly magical again. New alliances have to be formed and old ones reconsidered. Honestly, considering how you were thrust into all this, I have to say the decisions you've made so far have been more than adequate. Even if you didn't want this role, this life, you're made for it, Ehren. You can do this."

He laughs and shakes his head. "This is exactly why I need you by my side." He looks like he wants to say more but doesn't, shaking it off.

"What is it?" I press.

He opens his mouth, closing it again before finally confessing, "I really wish you would walk side-by-side with me whenever we enter a room. I understand your reasoning in wanting to walk a step behind, and I appreciate your loyalty, but I want you by my side. I'll feel less alone."

"Why?"

He glances at me and grins. "For purely selfish reasons. If I walk into a room at the head, by myself, then all eyes will be on me and only me immediately. But, if you walk in side-by-side, as my equal, you help to share that pressure."

I consider his words and nod. "All right. Fine. I'll walk by your side."

His eyes widen. "Really? You'd do that for me?"

I laugh. "Ehren, in case you haven't figured it out yet, I'm willing to help you in almost any way you need. You need me to capture a bunch of your father's soldiers in a smoky fog of my magic so you can escape? I'll do it. You need me to help create an illusion to get you out of the country? You've got it. You need me to be your Court Sorceress and walk by your side so you don't have to bear the burden of leadership alone? I'm there for you."

Ehren shakes his head, looking at me with a sense of awe. "What did I do to deserve such loyalty?"

"Well," I muse, smiling, "you did save my life in Timberborn."

He shrugs and grins. "Yeah, I guess there is that." He stops and looks up at the building in front of us. "Well, this is me." He glances back at me. "I guess I'll see you later at the ceremony."

I smile. "I guess so."

Once he's inside I wisp directly into the library. Pria glances up at me.

"I was wondering if you would actually have time to come by today. I understand you have quite the ceremony planned for this evening. Congratulations."

I incline my head. "Thank you. We're leaving in the morning, so I want to compile as much information as I can."

Pria nods. "Not a bad idea. Let me know what you need."

I thank her and get to work. I've gathered quite a collection of information during my time at Naskein, and yet I feel like I've barely scratched the surface. I can understand why people like Pria devote their entire lives to studying magical texts. I'm still scribbling away hours later when a young girl appears.

"I'm to take Mistress Astra to prepare for her ceremony," she says with a little bow.

I rise, tucking my notes away, and she takes my hand. Together, we wisp to a tiny, crowded dressing room where a small host of girls and young women wait to turn me into someone who looks worthy of my new position.

Despite having spent a good twenty minutes soaking in the hot spring earlier, I'm forced into a tub and scrubbed within an inch of my life. I can say with much surety I've never been this clean before. Once I've finished with my bath, I use magic to dry off before one of the acolytes approaches me with a robe, ushering me to a chair. Another acolyte steps forward and weaves my hair into an intricate design on top of my head. Once my hair is up, she places a thin silver tiara on my head. It sits low, just across the top of my forehead, the front dipping down into a slight point with a teardrop-shaped amethyst dangling between my eyes. Another acolyte steps in and adds touches of color to my cheeks, eyes, and lips.

Finally, it's time to put on my dress. During my stay with the Order, I've grown accustomed to wearing only shades of ivory and gold, so when they approach me with a dress made of deep purple satin, it takes my breath away. The top of the dress is so constricting I can barely breathe, but the tightness is entirely necessary in order to hold up the heavy skirt made of several thick folds of purple fabric. The dress has no sleeves, leaving my shoulders and collarbone bare. I feel a little naked and self-conscious, my fingers subconsciously drifting up to trace the exposed scars on my neck and chin. When one of the acolytes holds up the amulet I'll be wearing, I breathe a sigh of relief. It's a thick purple ribbon with an amethyst set against a shiny silver plate. Once tied, it falls perfectly above the top of the dress, helping me feel less exposed.

When they usher me in front of the mirror, I freeze. I don't recognize the girl staring back. It's not the dress or the makeup. It's not the tiara or the necklace. It's not even the silvery traces of scars against my pale skin. It's me. Somehow, since the last time I looked properly in a mirror, I've changed. I look . . . older somehow. More dignified. I'm more like the me from my dreams. It's almost terrifying.

"Are you ready?" a quiet voice asks, and I turn to find one of the acolytes offering me her hand.

I force a smile, ignoring the nerves twisting in my gut. "Sure."

I place my hand in hers and the room disappears. We reappear in a small room right off the main courtyard.

"The others should be along in a moment," the girl says with a bow before she vanishes.

Alone with my thoughts, anxiety twists like a knife in my chest. The sounds of the swelling crowd from the courtyard outside don't help. I'm willing to assume every single resident of Naskein will be in attendance—at least, everyone that can fit. All eyes are going to be on me. Suddenly, I feel very alone and lost.

Wind rushes behind me and I turn to find four acolytes wisping in the others. The acolytes disappear almost immediately. Ehren is dressed in a very prim and formal deep red tunic with his personal crest—a shield with two crossed swords over a partially coiled snake—stitched on the front in gold thread. A simple golden crown with several shining rubies sits on top of his head. Sometime after our earlier conversation, he must have found someone to trim his hair, because now it's back to its normal length, and his beard has been shaped, adding a sense of regality and age. Bram, Makin, and Cal stand behind him, dressed in sharp Guard uniforms, but instead of the typical red of Callenia, they wear the royal blue that Ehren is most known for wearing. I realize with a start that the purple of my dress is almost the exact color of the other two colors blended together.

Ehren approaches me with a nervous smile. "Are you ready for this?"

I swallow and nod. "As ready as I'll ever be."

Master Arcanis enters the room and assesses us for a moment. "Everything is prepared. In a moment, I will wisp to the dais. When the music plays, you will go on first as head guard. Go up the stairs and take a place just behind me," he says, addressing Bram first. Bram gives a sharp nod.

Master Arcanis turns his attention to me and Ehren. "Once he's gone in a few feet, Your Majesty, you will escort Astra up to the dais and take your place in the center in front of me."

I nod along with Ehren as my nerves swirl even more.

"You two follow in after they enter and take your places on either side of the stairs at the base of the dais," he says to

Makin and Cal. "When the ceremony is over, you will leave in the same order. Come back to this room and acolytes will wisp you to the celebratory feast. Any questions?"

His eyes scan us as we shake our heads. "Excellent. You may take your places outside the courtyard. The doors will open with the music."

He wisps away and we leave the room, assuming our positions. Bram steps forward to enter first. He turns, and I can see the pain still lingering in his eyes. Ehren steps aside and pretends to discuss something with Cal, who stands a few feet away. Bram takes a step closer and looks down at me.

"It is not too late. You can still stop this. You do not have to do this," Bram says quietly. His voice is even and steady, but I can hear the desperation lacing his words.

"I'm not backing down. I'm doing this."

"Astra—"

He's cut short as music begins to play inside the courtyard. Bram sighs and turns away, facing the doors as they slowly open, revealing a massive crowd. A thin ivory carpet lined with gold stretches from the door to a dais in the center of the room. Every other available space is filled with bodies. All eyes are on us as Bram takes the first regal steps onto the carpet. He's a few feet in when Ehren offers me his arm, and we take our place in the procession. I'm very grateful Ehren is there to hold me up. My legs tremble with every step, and if it weren't for his steady grip, I'm sure I would collapse.

Bram takes his place on the dais as Ehren and I turn to stand before Master Arcanis. Once Cal and Makin are in their positions, the doors shut with a boom. Master Arcanis smiles at us briefly before his voice echoes over the silent courtyard.

"Tonight, we bear witness to the anointing of the first Court Sorceress in over three hundred years. We have the privilege of uniting with Astra Downs of Timberborn, born lowly but meant for greatness. Within her swells a power that is greater than any that has been known for thousands of years. Beneath her feet, the earth quakes, and above her, the stars fall. We honor her might and her power today. Together, we acknowledge the Kingdom of Callenia, whom she serves.

"We do not acknowledge King Betron of Callenia as the rightful authority, but rather his son, Prince Ehren Andrewe Daniel Montavillier, the Crown Prince of Callenia. It is to him we give our alliance and through his court-appointed sorceress, Astra Downs, that our alliance is made firm."

Master Arcanis pauses and looks directly at Ehren. "Do you, Prince Ehren of Callenia, swear to honor magic and support our cause to unite magic and non-magic in harmony?"

Ehren nods. "I swear it."

Master Arcanis turns to me. "Astra Downs, do you swear to protect and honor magic and to be a reliable liaison for the Order while you serve the court of Callenia under the leadership of His Majesty Prince Ehren?"

His eyes study me, and my heart hammers against my ribcage. I let my eyes focus just past Master Arcanis at the throngs of people in attendance. So many witnesses. So many people supporting me. And yet, I almost feel alone. Some of the people that matter the most aren't here. Kato should be here. He should be by my side. He's always been the more sociable of the two of us. He would be a much better Court Sorcerer than I could ever be. Even if I were still the one appointed, he should be here, by my side. It seems wrong to take such an important position without him even in attendance.

Alak should be here as well. He helped me discover my power. He supported me and made me who I am. He . . . It's not right that he's away. I need him here.

I struggle to breathe, and Ehren looks down at me, moving his hand at his side so it brushes my own.

"Are you okay?" he whispers, quietly enough that no one else, not even Master Arcanis, can hear.

I can't answer. I'm frozen. I'm terrified. I glance over to Bram as subtly as possible. His eyes are fixed on me. He can tell I'm frightened. His hands are clenched at his sides. All I would have to do is give him the slightest indication I don't want this, and he would stop the ceremony. I can hide in my room. I can escape all these eyes.

No. This is what I want. It may not be happening the way I want it to, but it doesn't change the fact that this is the right decision. I take a deep breath, steadying myself.

I swallow, forcing my gaze back to Master Arcanis. "I swear it."

Master Arcanis nods. "Then before all these witnesses, we, the Order of Naskein, declare you our liaison and official sorceress of the Court of Callenia under His Majesty Prince Ehren Andrewe Daniel Montavillier. Long may you reign."

Master Arcanis and the other Masters chant in a long-forgotten language, and I gasp as the amulet around my neck slowly begins to glow, growing brighter with each word. I glance up at Ehren to find he's looking down at me, smiling. When they finish their chant, the gem's glow fades, and Master Arcanis smiles at me as the music starts again. He gives a nod to Bram who marches past us stiffly, leading us out. Ehren and I fall into step behind him, marching from the courtyard back into the small side room. Once we are safely hidden from the rest of the crowd, I can finally breathe.

"Astra," Ehren asks, his eyes studying my face with concern. "Are you okay?"

I nod, but tears start flowing down my cheeks. Bram takes a step toward me but stops short. Ehren gathers me against his chest instead.

"Hey, now," Ehren whispers, holding me tightly. "There's no need for tears."

I draw back, wiping tears from my cheeks with a trembling hand. "I'm sorry. I think it's just the nerves. I'm being ridiculous."

Ehren looks down at me, shaking his head. "It's not ridiculous to feel things strongly."

I sniff. "I just got up there and missed Kato so much. I'm not used to doing things alone." I don't mention that Alak's absence also left a hole, but I suspect Ehren can sense the unspoken words.

"That's understandable," Ehren says, brushing a tear from my cheek with his thumb, "but you don't have to feel alone. I'm here for you."

Bram finally approaches me, though he doesn't try to touch me. He just stands awkwardly nearby.

"We're all here for you," he says evenly.

I can see in his eyes that he means it. Even if he doesn't entirely agree with my decision, he supports me.

"Thanks," I say, forcing a smile. "I feel better now."

Makin cocks his head. "Good, because I say we go stuff our faces now and celebrate this alliance." He glances around at the others, grinning. "Who's with me?"

CHAPTER THREE
ASTRA

I'm already awake, staring at the ceiling, when everyone else starts to rise. Despite being the honored guests last night, none of us stayed out late. My nerves never fully settled after my breakdown following the ceremony, and I was happy to escape as soon as I could. Even after I came to bed, I hardly slept at all, nerves keeping me tossing and turning.

"Astra?" Ehren calls softly from just outside my bed curtains. "Are you awake yet?"

"I am," I answer, sitting up and pulling the bed curtain aside. I slide from my bed, already dressed in a basic linen dress. At some point in the night, I decided it wouldn't hurt to get a ready for the day. The dress is nearly as comfortable as a night dress, anyway.

"Well, look at Astra being our little overachiever," Makin laughs. "Already dressed and ready to go."

I smile as I sit on the trunk at the end of my bed and pull on my boots. "I like to be ready for anything."

Ehren scans the room as he shoulders his bag. "Do we have everything we need?"

"We're leaving with more than we came with," I point out.

The Order graciously provided us each with a bag full of supplies.

"I suspect we'll have anything else we need when we arrive in the Hundan Valley. It'll be nice to avoid the weeks of travel," Ehren muses.

"Are we ready then?" Bram asks, voice clipped. He's still mad.

Ehren nods. "I believe so."

"Do you want me to wisp us to the portal chamber or shall we walk?"

Ehren glances over at Cal, who looks uneasy at the idea of wisping, before replying. "Let's walk. We have the time."

We make our way out of the room, wandering into the maze of courtyards. Ehren and I walk side-by-side with the others trailing just behind us. Hints of dawn color the horizon as we walk. It's calm and peaceful given most of the acolytes are still sleeping. I wish that the world could stay this way for a little while longer.

When we reach the portal chamber, Master Arcanis and a couple acolytes and apprentices wait for us. Master Arcanis greets us with a bow.

"Good morning. I trust you slept well?"

Ehren inclines his head. "We did." He glances past Master Arcanis to the center of the room where the apprentices are busying themselves around a purple gem roughly the size of my palm. "Are we too early?"

Master Arcanis smiles and shakes his head. "No. You are

perfectly on time. We are securing the last pieces to ensure a smooth transfer. While we wait, we can discuss the portals you are to set up."

"Ah, yes," Ehren says with a nod. "You mentioned last night that you would give us the details this morning."

"Lia," Master Arcanis calls to his apprentice behind him. "Please, will you bring the portal stones?"

Lia nods and approaches Ehren with a wooden box. Ehren takes it and hesitantly lifts the lid, revealing a couple dozen small, clear gems no bigger than a pebble.

"What are these?" Ehren asks, looking up at Master Arcanis.

"Portal stones from the Finjon Mines."

My eyes go wide. "They're from the Finjon Mines?"

Master Arcanis nods. "You know of the mines?"

Ehren watches me with interest as I nod. "Yes. They're in Gleador. One of the many magical mines, but possibly the best known for having a vast collection of magical stones and gems. More so than any other location."

Ehren nods. "Ah, that makes sense. Gleador's main export has always been gems and other precious stones."

"I'm impressed," Master Arcanis says, eyes glowing. "You are both correct. These stones are from Gleador. They are inherently magical, but their magic needs to be activated. Without the necessary steps and conditions, they are little more than worthless rocks."

"How will we turn these into portals?" I ask, intrigued.

Lia steps forward, handing me a few folded pages of parchment. I unfold them and find spells on one and a map on the other. I look back up at Master Arcanis, waiting for his explanation.

"The map indicates locations where we need portals. Those marked with two stars show locations with existing portals that simply need to be reactivated. This can be done using the reactivation spell we provided."

"This spell," Ehren cuts in. "Is it something I could do or does it require someone born with magic?"

"You should have no difficulty performing the spell," Master Arcanis says. "Master Vigos has informed me of your progress, and I believe you will find both the activation and reactivation spells well within your scope of abilities."

Ehren nods, a glimmer of pride in his eyes.

"This other spell," I murmur, studying the paper. "It has the instructions for creating a new portal with the stones?"

Master Arcanis nods. "Yes. If you cannot locate a stone previously used for a portal or you are creating a portal in one of the new locations indicated with a single star, you will need the portal stone and the activation spell."

"How will you know when the portals are set up?" Bram asks.

Master Arcanis gestures to the purple stone behind him. "The portal stones are all linked to this stone. Whenever a new portal is created, we will know."

I eye the stone uneasily. "And you said that the portals don't cause any risk to you?"

"None at all. Even after the portal is created you need someone on both ends to open a successful portal. Think of it like a long corridor with two locked doors at either end. You can open your door and enter the corridor, but unless someone opens the door at the other end you cannot get anywhere."

"What's in between the portals?" Makin asks quietly.

Master Arcanis's face becomes very serious. "A magical void, often referred to as the 'in-between,' which I very much recommend not entering unless you have an exit."

"Master Arcanis," one of the apprentices says, stepping forward. "We are ready to open the portal."

Master Arcanis nods. "Excellent. Open it when you will."

He steps to the side as two of the apprentices step forward. They hold out their hands and chant a spell. A purple spiral of light stretches between them. It's small at first, but as they move further apart the spiral grows until it's almost the width of the room. Master Arcanis gives us a nod and we step toward the portal.

Ehren looks at me, offering his hand, which I accept with a nervous smile.

"Here goes nothing," Ehren mumbles as we step into the light.

I'm not sure what I expected the portal to feel like, but it's an experience unlike anything else. At first, it's like diving into freezing cold water, but that feeling is quickly replaced by a rush of heat prickling across my skin. I feel weightless, like I'm floating, yet, somehow I still feel heavier, like I'm filled with stones. Even though I can still vaguely feel Ehren's hand in mine, I can't see him. I'm surrounded by a white void. Just as I'm adjusting to everything, I'm sucked out into another room. I feel solid ground beneath my feet, but it takes a moment for my eyes to adjust, like I've been staring into the sun for too long.

When my eyes do finally adjust to my new surroundings, I'm in a small room, being stared down by three individuals. The one at the front is a woman not much older than I am.

Roughly a third of her long brown hair is woven into multiple, thin braids, many intertwined with colorful strings and charms. She has sharp brown eyes on a delicate, tanned face. Her body is lean but lethal, dressed in leggings and a corset top, ready to fight. Her arms are crossed as she sizes us up.

Behind her is another girl with dark skin and black hair that is entirely in small braids, also woven with colorful strings and charms. She wears tight leather leggings and a halter top that exposes most of her heavily inked skin.

And, just in case those two alone weren't intimidating enough, there's a tall, broad-shouldered man that looks made entirely of corded muscle standing next to the second girl. Most of his dark hair is shaved, save for a small, short strip down the center of his head. Black swirls of ink peek out from under his shirt up onto his neck and left side of his face.

A few additional people hover around the edges of the room, but I don't dare take my eyes off the main three.

"Hello, brother," the girl at the front drawls, her white teeth flashing at us.

My eyes go wide as I glance over at Ehren. His mouth is gaping and his brow is furrowed.

"Jessalynn?" he says slowly, his eyes narrowing as he studies her in disbelief.

She laughs, but it's not a happy, pleasant sound.

"You have another sister?" I whisper.

Jessalynn answers for him. "Well, half-sister. We have different mothers but the same father." She seems to derive pleasure from my confusion and laughs again. "Perhaps you'd like a quick history?"

"I don't think that's entirely necessary," Ehren mumbles.

"Oh, but I love to tell it! You see, the king married his

queen, but she was unable to provide a child. So, the king let his eyes stray to the beautiful young daughter of one of the Gleador ambassadors. It didn't take long at all before she was with child. Spoiler alert: that child was me. Of course, things may have gone a little smoother if the queen herself didn't conceive just a couple months later, giving the king the actual son he wanted—a proper heir to his throne. I don't think the queen was terribly happy about the king's bastard daughter being allowed in the nursery and being offered the same basic comforts as her legitimate son, but the king permitted it. When his queen gave him another daughter, well, the first daughter slowly fell more and more out of favor until the queen somehow convinced the king to banish his firstborn at only nine years old, her mother with her."

Ehren's hands clench by his sides. "You know I had nothing to do with any of that."

Jessalynn waves her hand. "Oh, I know. The way I hear it, Father wants you dead right now even more than me, so we're on pretty even ground. Wouldn't you say?"

"To put it lightly," Ehren says stiffly. He glances around briefly. "Are you the one in charge?"

"I am!" Jessalynn says, clapping her hands once. "As I'm sure you know, Gleador is divided up into provinces, each one with a ruling family. We all answer to the king, but each province has basic control over their portion of land. It so happens my mother was from the family in charge of the Hundan Valley, the smallest and most intimate province in Gleador, but still one with great power and influence. The so-called 'Melting Pot' of Gleador. Another family had stepped into her place in her absence, but it was agreed upon that I would take over when I turned twenty. I watched and observed for a while, training for my position, but I've been in charge for over a year now. Seems like we were both meant to lead, eh, brother?"

"Indeed. Well, thank you for allowing us to come," Ehren says, inclining his head.

Jessalynn laughs. "So diplomatic. Anyhow, you know me, and I know you, but everyone else is at a loss." She motions around the room. "So, let me introduce you to my friends, and you introduce me to yours. How's that sound?"

"Fine," Ehren replies, his voice strained.

Jessalynn grins, nodding to the woman behind her. "This is Kaeya, my Captain. She's in charge of ground troops, our small army, and all that sort of security. And this"—she gestures to the man—"is Brock, my Lieutenant. He's in charge of relations with the king as well as outer security."

Ehren nods. "It's a pleasure to meet you both." When they don't answer but continue staring Ehren down, he clears his throat. "This is Astra, my Court Sorceress and my equal." I incline my head slightly, unable to hide my smile at my new title. Ehren turns and gestures to Bram. "This is the Captain of my Guard, Captain Bramfield. The other two are also members of my Guard and go by Makin and Cal."

Each gives a small nod of greeting as they're introduced. Jessalynn's eyes glow as she stores away every little bit of information to use for later. After introductions are done, she turns to me, sizing me up. Her eyes focus on my hair, still done up from the night before. Her eyes linger on my scars a little longer than I care for before they travel down, taking in my appearance in general. It takes everything I have not to squirm beneath her piercing gaze.

"It seems fitting that you would have such a proper Court Sorceress. I assume she comes from a fine, fancy family. Some noblewoman, judging by her posture and appearance," Jessalynn says with a flippant wave of her hand.

Ehren's eyes light up, and he opens his mouth to speak but ends up snapping it shut. Her words have pissed me off, and he can tell. My eyes flash as I tilt my head and look at her.

"You couldn't be more wrong," I reply, trying to keep myself calm.

Her eyebrows arch. "Oh. Tell me then. How hard has your life been, little magician?"

"Shit," Makin mutters under his breath, taking a purposeful step back as Ehren tries not to laugh.

I give her a lethal smile. "Well, you did share some of your childhood with me, so why shouldn't I share my story with you?"

She shrugs, clearly amused, waiting, ready to prove me wrong.

"I was born in a little nothing town in Southern Callenia called Timberborn. The most important thing to ever happen in our town was my birth."

She huffs. "Your birth?"

She doesn't know who I am and, somehow, I find both relief and power in that.

"Yes. Well, not just my birth. The birth of me and my twin brother." Her eyes, and the eyes of her companions, widen. I continue. "But being a twin didn't provide money or food—not once our novelty wore off, anyway. My good-for-nothing father was gone most of the time, dealing in illegal business. I know what it's like to go to bed hungry, wondering if tonight is the night that the hunger and cold finally kill you. Luckily, I had my brother and good friends. We survived together.

"But then I turned eighteen and my world changed. My powers broke free, nearly killing me, and instead of trying to help, my father disowned me. He forbade the rest of my family to even visit me while I healed. I had to rely on help from strangers. When I finally woke up, yes, I was brought to the comforts of the palace, where I stayed for a couple weeks before I had to flee for my life. I've spent the majority of the months since I turned eighteen running, hiding, and barely surviving. And, in case that wasn't enough, my twin brother, the one person I could always depend on, abandoned me. So, yeah, my life has been super cozy and easy. I suspect that you had more comforts and joys in the first nine years of your life than I've had in one month of mine."

My voice is cold, and even I'm surprised by the intensity. The air in the room is thick. Ehren shifts uncomfortably next to me, getting into a position, I realize, to fight if needed. Jessalynn is lethally quiet, weighing my words. Then suddenly, she starts laughing.

"I like you. You have spirit and fire. No wonder my brother chose you as his Court Sorceress. I have no idea how much magic you have, but with that amount of energy, anyone not on your side is in trouble," she says, her eyes dancing. "Speaking of power—Sama."

Jessalynn gestures to me and I frown. A girl standing at the edge of the room steps forward. She's short, roughly my height, with soft copper skin and wearing a loose scarf around her hair that drapes over her shoulders. She slowly approaches me, searching my face with her brown eyes.

"May I have your hand?" she asks, extending her own to me.

I offer my hand hesitantly. She gently places her fingertips to my palm. I feel the familiar tingle of magic across my skin as droplets of my own magic transfer to her. Her eyes go wide and she gasps, jerking her hand back.

"You're a Syphon," I say rather than ask, my eyes widening.

"You know what a Syphon is?" she asks, her eyes bright.

"We used to have a member of our party who had Syphon blood," Ehren offers for me. Bram noticeably stiffens while Makin and Cal shift awkwardly.

"Interesting," Jessalynn says, drawing the word out as she watches our reactions. "Your Syphon companion isn't with you any longer?"

"We had to part ways," Ehren says with a shrug.

"Well, then, I'm sure you know that a Syphon can not only absorb power but can also tell exactly how much power someone has." Her eyes glint mischievously as she turns her attention to Sama. "Well, how powerful is my brother's pet magician?"

Sama turns to Jessalynn, her eyes wide. "She's by far the most powerful person or creature I've ever encountered."

Jessalynn seems to find this information disconcerting and furrows her eyebrows. "What do you mean? She's more powerful than me, Brock, or Kaeya? By how much?"

"She's more powerful than all three of you combined," Sama replies, reverent awe filling her voice. "Probably more powerful than the magic of everyone in this room combined."

Jessalynn's cocky façade fades as she pales. Ehren grins and even Bram, Cal, and Makin can't hide their smirks. I just stare her down.

"That's very intriguing," Jessalynn says at length. "I did not realize that someone with so much power could exist."

"She's not the only one with that kind of power, either," Ehren cuts in. "That's one of the reasons we're here."

Jessalynn's eyebrows arch in interest. "You aren't just here to hide out while learning about how a magical community operates?"

Ehren shakes his head. "No. While those are two reasons we have chosen to come here, there's one more. As previously stated, Astra is a twin, and her brother, Kato, has gone a bit rogue. We are seeking an alliance with you, as well as the king of Gleador, to help stand against not only my—our—father, but also her brother."

"Well, it seems those pompous religious leaders forgot a few pertinent details, but fine. We can definitely discuss all of that," Jessalynn replies with a shrug. "But not before breakfast. Breakfast is served in the dining hall for exactly one hour each morning. You miss it, and you go hungry until lunch. I never miss breakfast. So, why don't I have you shown your rooms, and we can meet back here once we've had a chance to fill our bellies? We don't have any fancy guest rooms here, so you'll be bunking with volunteers. But first, let me show you our valley."

She strides to the door behind her and throws it open. We follow her out. As soon as I see the view, I gasp. It's by far one of the most beautiful scenes I've ever had the privilege to lay eyes on. We're up on one of the mountains, looking down into the valley. Green grass stretches out below us toward the opposite end of the valley where a waterfall splashes down into a river flowing the length of the valley. There are several huts and other structures in the valley itself, but most of the dwellings and buildings are constructed directly onto the mountainside, as is the place we currently stand. The simple structures cling to the side of the mountain, seemingly by magic, with wooden rope bridges connecting them.

"You okay?" Ehren asks, his voice low. I turn to find him studying Cal with concern.

Cal looks a little green. While the rest of us are at the edge of the platform gazing down into the valley, Cal clings closely to the room we just left, looking rather uneasy.

"I don't do well with heights," Cal mutters, squeezing his eyes shut.

"Well, I suppose that means we will need to find you different accommodations. Unfortunately, the nature of our little settlement means you'll have to spend some time in the air, but the dining hall is at base level. I'm sure we can find you someone who lives in the valley itself to lend you a place to sleep during your stay," Jessalynn says. She turns to Brock. "Would you mind taking this poor fellow down and see if you can find someone to take him in?"

Brock nods as Makin steps forward. "Would it be all right if he and I stay together?"

Jessalynn raises her eyebrows. "Oh? Are you two a couple?"

Makin shakes his head while Cal glances away, the tips of his ears reddening.

"No. We're simply close friends," Makin answers with a wide grin, not bothered in the slightest by her assumption.

"I guess that's fine," she answers with a shrug. "Go with Brock."

Cal shoots her a grateful look while he and Makin follow Brock off to find a place to stay. Jessalynn turns to a tall, lean man with a short, sharp brown beard who's been standing in the shadows the whole time.

"Kai, why don't you show our prince and his captain to your place."

His cold gray eyes assess us for a moment before he slowly says, "Follow me."

As Bram and Ehren start to follow Kai in the opposite direction, Jessalynn turns to me. "You'll be staying with Sama."

Sama steps forward smiling, but Bram stops short, spinning around to face us. "What? You can't put Astra with a Syphon."

"Excuse me?" Jessalynn challenges, placing a hand on her hip.

"You can't put Astra with a Syphon," Bram repeats firmly.

Ehren places a hand on Bram's arm. "Bram . . ."

Bram shakes Ehren off and jerks away, taking a step back toward me. Sama seems to understand Bram's reaction, her eyes going wide.

"Oh, I would never try to syphon her magic without permission!" she says hurriedly, pink tinging her cheeks. "I only draw magic from the earth, magical objects, or my familiar."

"You have a familiar?" I interrupt.

Sama turns to me, grinning. "I do! He's a Shadow Hawk. He's off hunting right now, like he does most mornings, but you'll see him soon, I suspect."

I glance back over to Bram, who is still glaring at Sama. I roll my eyes.

"For gods' sake Bram, she's not going to drain my magic in my sleep. It would probably kill her if she tried. Alak told me as much."

Bram's eyes flash when I say Alak's name, and I realize I probably made a mistake. Jessalynn watches the exchange with interest, but Ehren looks wary.

"Come on, Bram," Ehren says, nudging Bram's arm.

"I'll be fine. Go. I'll meet you at breakfast," I say, waving him off.

Bram doesn't move for a moment, but finally releases me from his gaze, following Ehren and Kai away. As they disappear, Jessalynn turns back to me.

"Gods, how have you been able to put up with all that masculinity?"

Her laugh is genuine, and I can't help but smile.

"It's not always easy."

"Well, I suppose you'll be relieved to have some space from them. Anyway, Sama, now that her overprotective guard dog is gone, why don't you show Astra to your living space?"

Sama nods and motions for me to follow her. We travel along the side of the mountain, winding across several bridges. I can understand why Cal didn't like being so far from the ground, but I love it. I don't even mind the rocking of the bridge below my feet. When we finally stop, Sama pauses shyly outside a doorway.

"It's not much," she mumbles, "but it's home."

I walk through the door and find a small, comfortable room. Two hammocks hang in the corner, one above the other. There's a small trunk in the other corner next to a small table holding a lantern and a wash bowl. There's nothing else.

"We don't need much in our living spaces because there are rooms for anything else we need," Sama explains as I set my bag down near the hammocks.

"I like it," I say with a smile. Sama grins.

A screech breaks through the air and a dark gray bird sweeps into the room, landing on Sama's shoulder. The bird seems to be made of literal shadows that flow and move constantly like liquid. It fixes its onyx black eyes on me.

"Hey, Ares!" Sama cries, reaching up to stroke the hawk's back. She turns to me. "Astra, meet Ares, my Shadow Hawk."

"Hello, Ares," I say, inclining my head.

Ares tilts his head, studying me for a moment before letting out another squawk.

"I think he likes you," Sama grins.

I stare into his beady black eyes. "How can you tell?"

Sama laughs. "Trust me, I just can. Now, how about we head and get breakfast? Jess wasn't kidding when she said you're out of luck if you miss breakfast."

I nod and follow her back out onto the swaying bridges. As we bounce along, Ares hops off Sama's shoulders and soars in circles above us. I watch him fly and find myself missing Felixe.

"Hey, Sama," I say. "If I wanted to write a letter or note, is there a place I could do that?"

Sama nods. "Sure. There's a library with desks and parchment and everything you need. After breakfast I can show you the way."

By the time we make it down to the base level and find the dining hall carved into the mountain, I'm wondering if I'll ever figure out how to get back to the room. I follow Sama inside, and she shows me how the dining hall works. When you enter, you pick up a plate or bowl and then go down a line, selecting what food you want before taking it to one of the long wooden tables in the center of the room. This morning's option is oatmeal with an assortment of fruit, nuts, and other topping options. I've never actually had oatmeal before, so I follow Sama's lead and add honey and some sort of fleshy, sliced fruit. I look around but don't see Bram or Ehren anywhere in the crowd.

"Don't worry. Your friends should be here soon. You can sit with me until they arrive if you want," Sama offers with a smile.

"Sure," I grin.

We take a seat at the end of one of the tables and are soon joined by a girl with tanned skin and a long dark braid. She starts talking quickly in a language I've never heard before. Sama responds in the same language and motions to me.

"Oh, hello!" the girl says in a very thick accent. "You must be one of our new guests. I am Sasha. Pleasure to meet you."

"I'm Astra," I say with a smile. "Pleasure to meet you, too, Sasha."

I take a few tentative bites of my oatmeal and am pleasantly surprised.

"Do you like it?" Sama asks, eyeing me.

I nod. "I do."

"We eat lots of the oatmeal," Sasha says, taking a bite from her own bowl. "I like it with the honey. We raise our own bees here."

"Really?"

Sama nods. "We don't get a lot of exports from beyond the mountains because the mountain trails are rough, so we have to grow or raise most of our food in the Valley."

"That makes sense."

"Oh look!" Sama cries out, pointing past my shoulder. "Your friends are here now."

I follow her finger and see Ehren, Bram, Makin, and Cal

taking their place in the food line behind Kai. Ehren's eyes find me, and he offers a smile.

"If you want to go sit with them, we understand," Sama says with a shrug.

"No, I'm fine here. I'm almost done with my oatmeal anyway. When I'm done, I'd like to head to the library." I turn back to my food.

"Does your one friend always look so mad?" Sasha asks and I nearly choke on my oatmeal, knowing before even looking up whom she's referring to.

I glance up and, sure enough, Bram scowls in our direction. I shake my head and try to hide my smile.

"He's a very serious person," I finally manage.

"He is handsome," Sasha muses.

I feel a brief flash of jealously before I remember he's not mine anymore. I push the feeling aside and nod. "He is very handsome."

Sama eyes me, and I wonder if she can sense my unease because she quickly changes the subject. "I feel bad they have to stay with Kai."

"Why?" I look over at Kai as he crosses the room, taking a seat by himself, purposely distancing himself from everyone. He does seem to prefer being alone, but he doesn't seem bad.

Sama shrugs. "He's not all that friendly, especially with new people."

"He has a sad story. If my life were so very sad, I would be like him, too, I think," Sasha says with a sigh.

I'm tempted to ask for more details, but I have a feeling this might be another one of those stories that others can't tell. Looking at him, he wouldn't appreciate having his secrets spilled to complete strangers.

"Well, I'm done," Sama declares, pushing her bowl back. She looks over at me. "Are you ready?"

I nod. Sama bids Sasha farewell, showing me where to deposit my bowl before leading me to the library. The library is a few stories up, but it doesn't take long to reach. When we walk inside an older man with a long, braided beard greets us with a smile. He smiles and says something in another language.

"Good morning, Quin! This is Astra. She's one of our visitors, and she would like to write a letter," Sama says cheerily, switching to Callenian for my benefit.

"I can help you with that," he replies with barely any trace of an accent,

Sama turns to me. "Well, I have to be off but I'll catch up with you later. If you need anything just about anybody can help."

"Thanks, Sama," I reply. "I'll see you later."

She scampers out of the library while I follow Quin to a back corner. He gestures to a desk stacked high with parchment and ink wells with quills.

"You should have everything here you need," he says with a smile. "I'll allow you your privacy."

I thank him and take a seat at the desk.

"What do I even say?" I mumble to myself as I ready my ink and paper.

Once I start writing, the words just come. Soon, I've filled the entire page. I close my eyes and call out to Felixe. I don't expect it to work right away, but when I open my eyes he sits on the desk.

"Hey, boy!" I say, reaching out and scratching his head. "I have a feeling that the librarian wouldn't be all too happy to have you in here."

Felixe gives a quiet yip and I laugh.

I roll up the paper as best I can and offer it to Felixe. "Can you take this to Alak for me?"

Felixe gives another little yip before taking the scroll in his teeth. I smile at him sadly.

"Felixe, let Alak know I miss him. Can you do that?"

I swear Felixe nods before he spins and disappears.

CHAPTER FOUR

ALAK

It's so hot today, and the bugs are insane. I hate summer. It's a stupid time of year to be born. But that seems to be the general pattern my life takes. I sigh and swat another mosquito. Maybe hanging around the creek isn't the best place to avoid bugs, but I'm tired of being around people. I take a seat at the edge of the bridge, swinging my legs over the water.

"Alak, are you out here?" Kayleigh's voice calls through the trees.

"Aye," I call out to her. "I'm over here."

Her footsteps crunch the branches and leaves as she appears. Most of her hair is pulled up today, but strands have come down, sticking to the sweat on her face and neck.

"Do you know where Kato is?" she asks as she approaches me. "I have word from the Clans I need to get to him."

I roll my eyes. "I'm not his bloody secretary."

She puts a hand on her hip and scowls at me. "You sure act like one sometimes."

I arch my eyebrows. "Excuse me?"

"Oh, please," she says, waving me off. "Like you don't know it. You've been following him everywhere like a little lost puppy since you two turned up here a week ago, obeying his every whim."

"Oh, I'm the one kowtowing to him, eh?" I scoff. "You've been practically worshipping the ground he walks on."

Kayleigh's cheeks flush pink as she shakes her head. "I have not!"

"Right. Sorry. That must be my other cousin Kayleigh."

"Well, you saw what he did to Fionn! I don't want that to happen to me!" she cries defensively, making me wince.

The whole incident with Fionn was a horrible, bloody mess. Kato and I both suspected that Fionn had been the one to poison Astra's magic, nearly killing her, and it hadn't taken long upon returning to Brackenborough for Kato to confirm it. Fionn actually started bragging about it. The fool. Kato used magic to literally burn Fionn's tongue from his mouth. His screams were horrible. And the smell . . .

"Kato doesn't normally lash out like that," I mutter. "Fionn was an idiot. He deserved what he got."

"What?" Kayleigh gasps. "You think Fionn deserved that? No one deserves that out of the blue."

"Out of the blue?!" I snap, leaping to my feet. "He almost killed Kato's sister and had the nerve to brag about it!"

Kayleigh shakes her head. "That's right. I forgot for a moment that you're in love with that traitor."

I take a deep, steadying breath. "We've been over this."

"You can deny it as much as you want, cousin, but you can't hide the truth from me. Caitlyn told me what she saw and sensed. Even if I didn't have the proof from her, I have the proof I've seen with my own eyes."

I shake my head. "Caitlyn doesn't know everything."

"She's an empath who can see auras. I would say she's a pretty damn reliable source." Kayleigh shakes her head again, waving me off. "Whatever. I didn't come to argue with you about this again. I just don't understand why you left Astra's side for her brother if you're in love with her."

I lean on the twisted vine guardrail, staring down into the water. "Because Kato has the right idea in uniting magic. We both want to do it for her. She's smart. She'll see sense eventually. Besides, when she chose someone else over me, I knew there was no point in staying by her side."

My lie works so well because it's filled with half-truths. She did choose Bram over me. When it came down to it, she chose him. It was hard enough watching them together when I thought maybe I had a chance, albeit a small one. A Seer may have told me I would love her, but he never gave me any promise she would love me back. So, once I knew that option had officially sailed, the thought of seeing them together all the time was honestly too much to bear. It was suffocating. I needed the distance.

Eventually, I'll go back to her side, but right now, I can serve her better here. Everything I'm doing right now really is for Astra. I'm just not doing it in the way everyone here thinks I am.

"She's a fool for choosing him over you, ya know," Kayleigh says quietly.

I don't say anything for a moment. I just stare at my reflection in the water.

"Kato is at Niall's house," I finally mutter.

A pebble hits me in the head.

"Ow!" I yell, spinning to face Kayleigh as my hand flies to rub the spot the pebble hit. "What the hell was that for?"

Her face is scrunched in fury. "You've known this whole time where Kato was? And you were just going to blather on about nonsense and let me stand here?"

I can't hide my grin. "What of it?"

Oh, she's seething now. I chuckle.

"I hate you, Alak Dunne!"

I laugh again until she uses her magic to send an onslaught of pebbles and sticks my direction.

"Hey!" I yell, throwing up a shield just in time to avoid being pelted to death.

She grins at me. I'm about to say something else to her when she wisps away. I shake my head. If she does have information for Kato, he'll probably want me to be there to take notes. Damn. I am his fecking secretary. With a sigh, I wisp outside Niall's house. By the time I'm inside, Kayleigh is in front of Kato, already mid-spiel. Kato sits in a wooden chair against the far wall, watching while Ian stands nearby.

"I think that's an indication they're on board," Kayleigh is saying. Her eyes shift ever so slightly to me as I take my place in the back of the room, leaning against the wall.

"I agree," Kato muses, nodding. "How soon do you think we could get to Periola? Do we have anyone that can wisp us there?"

"I'm not sure, but I can definitely check around," Kayleigh replies enthusiastically. "I'll let you know if I find anybody."

Great. That means there's probably another Clan eager to see Kato perform, before ultimately aligning with him against the king. And Kato never disappoints. I'm sure it helps when he enters like a god in a pillar of flames. I make a note to mention this in my next letter to Astra. I want to make sure I have plenty of things to tell her so I don't waste her time.

"Good. Good. Did they say anything else?"

Kayleigh shakes her head. "Nothing of significance."

"All right. Just go ahead and—"

Kato is cut off by a young boy—one of my cousin Saran's friends, I think—rushing into the house, throwing the door open so hard it slams against the wall. His eyes dart around the room.

"Master Kato!" he cries when he spots Kato seated at the opposite end of the room. "I have news from Naskein!"

I stand straighter, pulling away from the wall, my eyes locked on the boy. Naskein? I didn't realize we had any communications set up with the Order. Kato's expression switches from frustration at being interrupted to interest.

"We've heard from Naskein? Is my sister okay?"

The boy nods. "Yes. Very okay. It seems that they performed a ceremony last night appointing her the official Court Sorceress for Prince Ehren."

I can't hide my smile. Good for her. She deserves a position of power. I lean back against the wall in an effort to appear neutral.

Kato's eyes flash literal flames, and I force my smile away. "What? Why would she tie herself down even more?"

The boy shrinks back a little, gulping. "Th-that's not all."

Kato stands and looks down at the boy. "Well? What else is there?"

"The Order officially declared her a liaison of magic with Callenia, throwing their support behind the prince."

"Shit," Kato murmurs, then he shrugs. "Not surprising, but still not good news, nonetheless."

"There's one more bit of news," the boy says timidly. "It

appears that your sister, along with the prince and his Guard, all left first thing this morning through a portal."

Kato's eyes go wide. "A portal? A portal to where?"

The boy shudders and shrugs. "Not sure. It was privileged information. Only a few people even know about the portal, and even fewer people know where the portal opened."

"But they've definitely left Naskein?"

The boy nods.

"Well, that's something at least. She's a bit further from the king's grasp."

Kato's eyes settle on me. "Alak."

I pull away from the wall, "Yes?"

"Do you know anything about portals?"

I shake my head. "Not a thing."

Kato sighs. "Pity." His cold eyes study me for a moment, trying to detect any hint of a lie, but thank the gods, for once I'm telling the complete truth. Once he seems satisfied I'm not hiding anything, he turns back to Kayleigh, who's standing by nervously. "Go ahead and see if you can find someone to wisp us to Periola, but come up with a backup plan to leave as soon we can in case we need to go on foot. Ian, help her."

Ian steps forward with a sharp nod. "Of course."

Kayleigh and Ian hurry from the room, the messenger boy tripping after them. Once the door is shut behind them, I approach Kato. He looks deep in thought.

"I didn't know we had a contact in Naskein," I say, choosing my words carefully.

Kato looks up at me. "Well, we do."

I nod. "That's handy. Too bad we don't know where they went."

"Well," Kato says, walking to look out the window. "I'm guessing portals can only go from one magical location to another. And I'm guessing they probably have to be set up ahead of time. That lowers the possibilities a good bit, wouldn't you think?"

Kato is far too smart and clever. I nod.

"You're probably right. But honestly, I have no idea how portal magic works. With magic everywhere again, who knows how many portals could be out there."

"You're right," Kato concedes. He glances sideways at me as I walk up beside him. "What do you think about Ehren making Astra Court Sorceress?"

What do I think? I think Ehren is pretty damn ballsy and smart. The boy knows how to play this game well. And I'm proud of Astra. So damn proud. But I can't tell Kato that. Instead I shrug.

"I think it was a power move on Ehren's part. The Order probably suggested it, and he jumped on board to get their permanent support against his father."

Kato's hands clench into fists. "So, you think he's using my sister as a pawn?"

No. Not what I was saying at all, mate. "It's a possibility."

Fresh anger flashes across Kato's features and I wonder for a moment if I'm making everything worse. I know I need to play the part that keeps Kato open and trusting of me, but I don't want to drive more space between them. I need to bring Kato back, not push him further away. I'm considering what I can say to smooth things over when Kato's anger cracks, hurt shining through as he turns to look at me.

"Why wouldn't she come with me, Alak?"

I meet his eyes. "I don't know, Kato."

"I have to win her over. If I can just get enough support and have all of Athiedor on my side, she'll see that I'm right. She'll understand it's with magic we can take everything back and then, once magic is established, we can bring in those without magic."

It's Kato's mantra. Prove to Astra magic can win. Prove to Astra magic is stronger. Prove to Astra magic is better. Prove. Prove. Prove. Magic. Magic. Magic.

"You know, if we can figure out where Astra is, you can still go back to her." Kato's jaw clenches tighter. I don't know why I bother. By this point it's like talking to a wall—a wall that could set me on fire with a mere thought. But I continue. For Astra. "You can talk to her some more. Make her see sense."

"No."

"Have you tried reaching out to her yet?"

He sighs and looks down, gripping the windowsill so tightly his knuckles turn white. I'm treading dangerous ground now, and I know it. But I promised.

"I can't make myself try," he says so quietly I barely hear him. "She's already told me no to my face. I don't think I could hear it again so soon. I'm going to wait until I have something to tell her—an accomplishment so big she can't ignore. Something like uniting Athiedor so I can take the crown for myself."

My heart stops. "What?"

He looks up at me as a lethal grin spreads across his face. "Once I have the support of all seven Clans, I'm going to unite Athiedor under magic. You said yourself that Athiedor wants to be its own country again. With Athiedor already so strongly imbued with magic, it only makes sense to unite them under magic. With all of Athiedor behind me, as well as a few alliances in other magical places in Callenia and other countries, we can easily overthrow the king. Once he's overthrown, I will take his place."

I struggle to keep my face neutral. Kato is more of a threat than most people realize. They know he has insanely powerful magic. People practically worship him for that. If that were all, he probably wouldn't get very far. But Kato is too damn smart. He's strategic. He was the best soldier in his village and one of the best of Ehren's Guard. He has the necessary skills to plan—and maybe even win—a war. If those two threats weren't enough, he's charismatic. He can charm almost anyone to do anything. He doesn't even need his power half the time to get people to bend to his will.

"That's quite ambitious."

"Ambition is the path to success," he replies simply. He turns back and looks out the window. "I think I need to be alone for a bit."

Without another word, he wisps away. I release a slow breath. Have I been holding it through his whole speech? It seems likely. This is bad. I need to write Astra. She needs to know what Kato's planning.

I walk up the stairs into the small guest room that Kato and I share. I sit down on my cot and am about to call out for Felixe when he appears beside me.

"Hey, boy!" I say, giving his head a scratch. I feel a small trickle of magic flow up into my fingertips in response to my Syphon powers. "How did you know I was about to call you?"

Felixe gives a little yip and I smile. I notice a scroll of paper beneath him and my heart stops. I reach a tentative hand for the paper.

"What did you bring me, Felixe?"

I carefully unroll the paper. It's from Astra. As much as I have longed to hear from her, I'm afraid to read her letter now that it has arrived.

My Dearest Alak,

I don't even know what to say. Or rather, I don't know where to start. I have many, many things to say. I've been wanting to write you for days but wasn't sure where to begin.

I suppose the first thing I need to say is thank you. And even that phrase isn't nearly sufficient enough to express how grateful I truly am for what you did, for what you're doing. I've known Kato his whole life, and I know exactly how stubborn he can be once he's made his mind up about something. If you can convince him to come back to me, it will be a small miracle. Please, do not put yourself at unnecessary risk. I need you to come back to me unharmed.

I also have some news to share. Last night, the Order performed an official ceremony confirming me as Ehren's Court Sorceress and a liaison for magic. They've officially declared an alliance with Ehren against his father, acknowledging Ehren as the rightful ruler of Callenia. He won't show it to anyone, but he's terrified of having to take down his father. It's the main reason I've become his sorceress, so he knows he's not alone in this.

While we are talking about Ehren, I think it's only fair to let you know that he is aware we are corresponding. He is the only person I told. For now, we are keeping everything between the two of us. Well, the three of us, I suppose.

One last thing worthy of note—we have left the Isle of

Naskein via a portal. We are currently residing in the Hundan Valley. Did you know Ehren has a half-sister who's a couple months older than he is? Well, he does, and apparently she's in charge here in the Valley. She's interesting, to say the least. Our goal is to get them to join us against the king and Kato, if need be, while learning about the magic that dwells here before moving on to discuss an allyship with King Naimon of Gleador.

I'm expected in an official meeting soon, so I should probably wrap up this letter. I miss you, Alak. I'm sorry about the way we left things. I truly am. I was foolish. I know that. When I was in front of all of Naskein last night, being confirmed, all I could think about was how much I wanted you to be there. You helped me get to the point where I am with my magic. You literally changed my life that night outside the Braylin Woods.

Please come back to me soon.

Forever Yours,

Astra

My heart races wildly by the end of her letter. I read it twice through to make sure I haven't missed anything. I'm sure I'm reading into the details, but she did say she missed me multiple times. I wish I could turn back time and go and see the ceremony. But no, I have a job to do here. I have a lot to share with her, too. It seems that whoever Kato knew within the Order had correct information. Thankfully, her location is still hidden.

With a sigh, I dig out everything I need to write a letter. As much as I want to read her letter again and again, I need to take advantage of Kato being gone. I need to prove my worth.

CHAPTER FIVE

ASTRA

I spent too long in the library and now I'm late. This is not a good way to start my first day as Court Sorceress. When I rush into the room, all eyes turn to me. Jessalynn sits at the head of a long table with Brock on her left and Kaeya on her right. Ehren sits at the opposite end, Bram seated on his left. Makin and Cal stand at attention directly behind Ehren against the wall.

"Sorry," I mumble. "I got a little turned around."

Jessalynn flicks her hand toward me. "It happens. Please, take a seat."

I hurry across the room and sink into the seat on Ehren's right. He offers me a weak smile.

"Everyone here now?" Jessalynn asks, scanning the room. "Okay. Let's get started."

She leans back in her chair and crosses her arms. "All right, brother. Tell me all about your plan to win our alliance."

Ehren clears his throat. "Well, as I mentioned earlier,

Astra's twin brother, Kato, is out there, recruiting magic-wielders for his own purposes."

"And what are those purposes, exactly?"

"We aren't entirely sure what his final plans are, but we know he wants to raise up an army of some sort to fight against the king," Ehren replies evenly.

"And isn't that essentially what you want? To overthrow the king and take your rightful place on the throne of Callenia? After all, from what I understand, the Order swore allegiance to you, not dearest dad."

Ehren takes a steadying breath before answering. "Honestly, I don't want the throne this way, but, as it stands, the king is doing more harm than good to Callenia. I cannot let that continue."

"Then why not support Kato?" Jessalynn asks with a shrug. "If he has as much power as you claim, his power combined with your strategic upbringing would almost guarantee victory."

"Kato thinks the kingdom can be won by magic alone. He has no need or use for those without magic. It's why he split from our group. He doesn't see a possible future with magic and non-magic side-by-side as equals. He only sees a world with or without magic."

"Now we're getting somewhere!" Jessalynn cries, a smile spreading across her face. She gestures with her hand. "Continue."

Ehren hesitates and I grab his hand under the table. A smile plays on the edges of his lips as he gives my hand a slight squeeze before continuing.

"The Callenia that I believe will be the strongest, the world I want to create, is one with magic and non-magic working together. That's how it was in days of old, when magic was alive before. There have always been those that have wanted to oppress magic and those that wished to dominate with magic, but those are not the success stories. I want my legacy to be a success story."

Jessalynn considers his words carefully before answering. "That's great for you and your legacy, but how does that help me? I mean, don't get me wrong, this Kato sounds like a potentially volatile character. Someone who can flip sides on his own sister . . . Damn, that's cold. But the fight hasn't come to Gleador yet, and it sure as hell hasn't come to the Hundan Valley. Magic still reigns freely here. And, let's just be honest, if you hadn't fled like a coward to Naskein, this war between magic and non-magic that *may* be starting in Callenia wouldn't have even left the borders."

I feel Ehren stiffen. "I didn't flee like a coward!"

Jessalynn looks pleased she got a rise out of him. Ehren notices, too, and relaxes, taking a deep breath.

"It was planned ahead of time, a calculated move."

"Right," Jessalynn says, leaning forward onto her elbows. "And what's the next step in your plan after you leave here?"

"After we hopefully convince you to join our alliance, and we learn what we can about magic, we plan to go on to the King of Gleador and enlist him as an ally."

Jessalynn's eyes go wide. "Against the King of Callenia?" She gives a short laugh and shakes her head, settling back into her seat. "You're crazier and far more ambitious than I thought. King Naimon is very unlikely to side with you against your father. He hates inter-country politics. What makes you think you can win him over? Your borrowed clothes? Your charming smile?"

Ehren smiles smugly. "You underestimate me, Jessalynn. Don't forget I was practically served politics and diplomacy for breakfast. I have people in the Gleador court already paving the way for me, just as I already have someone here."

Jessalynn goes very still. "What?"

Ehren's grin grows, and he releases my hand under the table. I smile softly. He's got this.

"When I realized my father was headed down a path that would cause me to flee Embervein, and eventually Callenia, I put a plan into place. I told you my leaving was calculated, and I meant it. A couple years ago I formed my own Guard. Those men were loyal to me first and foremost, not my father, and when push came to shove, they all chose to follow me into the shadows. Some of those men came with me." He gestures absentmindedly to Bram, Cal, and Makin. "But most of my men are spread throughout Callenia and other countries. They have their individual missions and, while I haven't been in recent contact with most of them, I have every confidence they're in place, waiting."

Pride and admiration for Ehren bubble inside me. I can't hide my smile as Jessalynn slowly rises from her seat, eyes locked on Ehren.

"So let me get this straight. You sent a spy to *my* court and now you're extending a hand of friendship, and you actually expect me to take it?"

Ehren makes a tsking sound and shakes his head, leaning back in his chair as he crosses his arms across his chest. "Not a spy. That just sounds so dirty and underhanded. A spy would indicate that I have someone gathering classified information and passing it to me. I didn't do that. My Guard has simply made a home here, made friends, become a part of your every day."

"And your Guard in Koshima, near the king, is he also just making a home?" Jessalynn asks, her voice cold.

Ehren shrugs. "He might be a little closer to what you might call a spy, but he's mostly just finding out the temperaments and leanings of the court in general. It's not my intention to sabotage, threaten, or harm anyone in any way. I simply want to know what kind of footing I have before I step on the ground. Is that so wrong?"

Jessalynn studies Ehren for a moment before a grin creeps across her face. "Well, brother, you have more of a taste for politics than I gave you credit for. But you still haven't given me a good reason to support you and your cause, nor have you have declared what *you* expect to get from our alliance."

"Right now, all I want to know is that you're behind me. Having your support will help me with King Naimon. It will add additional credibility to my cause. I'm not asking you to lend armies or anything like that. Not yet anyway. If it comes to that, we can negotiate those terms when the need arises. Right now, I simply need people in my corner. Eventually, you will have to choose sides. It's inevitable. This war will not stay within the borders of Callenia, even once I return. You might as well decide now which side you will back."

Ehren stands so they're eye to eye again.

"Do you want to be a success story, or do you want to be in the background, forever the forgotten almost princess in the shadows?" Jessalynn reacts slightly to his words, but quickly shoves her frustration under a mask of nonchalance. "Together, we could be great, Jess. We could have an amazing alliance. Father was wrong to banish you. You don't know this, but when I heard you'd been cast out, I went to father and begged him to bring you back."

Ehren's eyes lock on Jessalynn. She relaxes, her shoulders dropping.

"You what?" she asks breathlessly.

"Every day for at least a month, I went to father and pleaded with him to allow you to come back home. Our father has done many things that have been good. He's made Callenia a successful kingdom. He's kept peace during his reign. I can't deny the good he's done, but he's not perfect. He's made some big mistakes. Going against magic so force-fully is a huge mistake and shoving you to the side was another. I don't want to make the same mistakes, Jess. I want to make all new mistakes." He laughs and even Jessalynn can't quite keep a smile from playing on the corners of her lips. His eyes go serious as he adds, "I want this alliance, Jess. I wanted it before I knew it would be with you, but now that I know you're the one in charge, I want it even more."

Jessalynn takes a deep breath and exhales slowly. For a few minutes she just stares at Ehren, not speaking. Finally, she gives Ehren a slight nod. "I need some time to consider everything. Give me a few days."

Ehren nods, seemingly expecting this answer. Jessalynn motions to her companions, and they all rise. Jessalynn is halfway to the door before she turns back to Ehren, a genuine smile on her lips.

"By the way—happy birthday, brother."

Ehren's lips part in surprise but, after a moment, he laughs. "Thanks, sis."

Jessalynn grins as she leads her companions out the door. Once they're gone, Ehren collapses in his chair and releases a long breath. Makin and Cal leave their positions along the wall to take up some of the empty seats at the table.

"Well, I must say, I'm glad that's over," Ehren sighs, raking his hand through his hair.

"Do you think she'll agree to the alliance?" Bram asks, leaning forward on the table.

Ehren shrugs. "I have no idea. I sincerely hope so, but Jessalynn has always been a wild card."

"Well," I jump in, "I think you did a good job of presenting her options. If she doesn't join after everything you said, it's not your fault in the slightest." I pause, thinking before I ask, "Do you really have a member of your Guard here?"

Ehren grins, his eyes bright. "I do, actually—Nyco. His father was from Northern Gleador, so he grew up speaking the language and knowing the customs. He was a natural choice. He left Embervein before we did, so he's been here a little while. He even has some basic magic, so I had no doubt he would be accepted."

"Wait, you have a member of your Guard that has magic?" I ask, eyes wide. "Why didn't you tell me?"

Ehren sobers slightly. "He wanted it kept secret. With my father hunting down anyone with magic, I agreed that the fewer people that knew about him, the better."

"What can he do?" I ask, interest piqued.

Ehren laughs. "Honestly, I'm not entirely sure. Something to do with spiders, I think."

I shiver. "Spiders?"

"Maybe? I'm really not sure. He was kind of dodgy about it," Ehren answers with a shrug.

"Is it really your birthday?"

Ehren grins, his eyes twinkling. "I guess it is."

I laugh. "You guess?"

"I kind of lost track of the days and everything the past couple months, but it seems to track. Pretty sure today's my birthday."

"It is your birthday," Cal cuts in with a grin. Ehren cocks his head, shooting Cal a curious glance as Makin snickers. The tips of Cal's ears redden almost imperceptibly as he shrugs. "It's impossible to have been around Ehren for as long as I have and not have it burned into your brain."

Bram chuckles. "That much is true. Ehren can be a bit obsessed with his birthday."

Ehren shakes his head with a rich laugh. "I'm not that bad!" He pauses, glancing off almost wistfully. "I always imagined my twenty-first birthday would be spent with my long-lost half-sister, hiding away in a magical valley on the run from my father." Ehren sighs, shaking his head but his smile holds.

"Well, you better find a way to celebrate before Jessalynn finds you a job," Makin says, leaning back in his chair.

I scowl. "What? Why would she give Ehren a job?"

"That's right. You missed the little pre-meeting pep-talk." Makin grins.

Cal rolls his eyes and explains. "Jessalynn said part of what makes everything work smoothly here is that everyone has a job of some sort. She's allowing us today to get acquainted with everything, but she's assigning us to job details tomorrow."

"She said she will play to our strengths," Bram adds, "which means we will probably be part of the border patrol or hunting parties."

"Maybe you guys," Ehren says with a sigh. "I have a feeling Jessalynn would love nothing more than to see me doing some manual labor in the mines. She'll also probably split us all up."

I nod. "I mean, that makes sense. It could be a really good opportunity for us, too."

Ehren scowls at me. "How so?"

"Well, I have a feeling Jessalynn will make her final decision based not just on what is best for her people, but according to what they want. The more we mingle, the better a feel we can get for where others stand on this issue. If we find their support lacking, we can work from the inside to help bring them to our cause."

Ehren cocks his head. "That's brilliant."

"We can also work in our downtime to make as many connections as possible, starting with our new housemates," I add.

"Yeah, about that," Ehren counters. "Our new housemate isn't quite as friendly as yours. Getting Kai to say anything was like pulling teeth. Actually, I've never pulled teeth before, but I have a feeling it's probably easier."

"According to Sama and Sasha, he hasn't had an easy life," I say.

Ehren arches an eyebrow. "Who's Sasha? Oh, was she the other girl you were eating with this morning? She was quite pretty."

I laugh and nod. "Yes, that was Sasha. She was nice, though *you* weren't the one she seemed interested in getting to know better."

"But I'm a prince," Ehren protests, pretending to pout a bit, his eyes twinkling.

"Was she interested in you?" Makin asks, his eyes lighting up.

I roll my eyes. "No." I pause, making eye contact with Bram before adding, "She actually thought you were handsome."

I swallow my jealousy and offer Bram a weak smile. Bram stiffens, his jaw tight, while Ehren shifts uncomfortably beside me. Makin's mouth drops open and his eyes dart from me to Bram.

"I am not interested," Bram mumbles, not taking his eyes from mine.

"Did I miss something . . . ?" Makin asks. Cal elbows him, glaring and shaking his head. Makin's eyes go wide. "Well, shit."

"Well," Ehren says abruptly, rising from his seat. "I really should go find Nyco and get a status report."

I rise from my chair and everyone else joins me. As we walk toward the door I fall in step with Ehren.

"By the way, I finally responded," I whisper to Ehren, my voice low.

Ehren stops just short of the door and turns to the others. "Go on out. I'll be there in a moment."

They nod and head outside. Bram gives us a suspicious glance over his shoulder before the door shuts.

"You wrote to Alak?" Ehren confirms, turning to me.

I nod. "I did. I gave him a quick rundown. I told him about me becoming the Court Sorceress and magical liaison. I also told him we left Naskein and came here." I hesitate, trying to figure out what Ehren is thinking. "Was that okay?"

"Yes," Ehren says slowly. "I think so. I still struggle a little with trusting Alak. Our history is less than perfect, but I believe he's sincere in helping us. So, yes. I am fine with Alak knowing anything you feel comfortable telling him."

"Okay, good."

Ehren gives me a reassuring nod before we join the others outside. Cal is as far away from the edge as he can be,

Makin standing casually near his side. Bram, on the other hand, stands at the very edge, staring down into the valley.

"I know you don't care much for wisping," I offer to Cal, "but I'll happily wisp you down to the ground."

He looks up at me, gratitude shining in his eyes as he smiles weakly. "That would be nice, thank you."

CHAPTER SIX

ASTRA

I wisp Ehren, Makin, Bram, and Cal down to the base level, but I leave them to locate Nyco on their own. Instead of joining them, I decide to find someone who can help me make Ehren's birthday special. I slowly cast out my magic, sending it tumbling over the valley like an invisible net. I close my eyes as the shadowy figures and structures reveal themselves. I can sense those with magic and those without. Some of the magic I can decipher what type it is, but most of it is vague. Finally, I lock on a somewhat familiar form, glowing with a low, reddish hint of borrowed magic. I narrow in my own magic, confirming that the shadowy figure in my mind is indeed Sama. Once I'm sure, I wisp.

When I open my eyes, I find myself at the edge of a group mining minerals and stones from the river. Sama stands a few feet away, her hands stretched palm-down over a trough filled with wet rocks. She senses me approaching and turns her head.

"Oh, hello, Astra!"

I step next to her and look down at the trough. "What exactly are you doing?"

"I'm using my Syphon abilities to sort through these rocks and minerals to see if any of them give off any magical properties." As she speaks, she reaches into the trough and pulls out a dull green stone with uneven edges. "Found one!"

A young man with long brown hair falling into his eyes turns from his position on the riverbank and approaches her. He asks her a question in a language I don't understand. Sama closes her eyes for a moment, closing her fingers over the rock, holding it tight in her fist.

"Thedellite." She opens her eyes and offers the man the rock, adding more words I don't know.

The man accepts the rock with a nod. He grunts a Gleador phrase that I assume means something along the lines of "Good work." His eyes fall on me. I expect him to ask what I'm doing, but instead he shrugs and goes back to doing whatever he was doing before.

"It's used in magic-strengthening potions and fast-working medicines when ground," she explains to me with a grin, wiping her wet hands on her shirt. "What brings you down to the quarry?"

"Oh, I was just wondering if there was any way to get a cake of any kind here. Is there a bakery or someone who could help me make my own cake?"

Sama arches an eyebrow, a smile playing on her lips. "You having a sweet craving?"

I chuckle. "No, it's a friend's birthday, and I thought I might try to do something for him."

"Well, there's no bakery of any kind, but I do know a few people who have kitchens in their living quarters. Most of us do rely on the serving hall for our meals—you've seen how small my living space is—but some people, mostly families, do have traditional houses with full kitchens. One of them could maybe help you out." She pauses for a moment, thinking, and then snaps her fingers. "I bet Makenna could help you. She actually works in the kitchen to help prepare food, and I think she had family members who ran a bakery in Callenia."

"You think she'd be willing to help me?" I ask enthusiastically.

Sama gives me a half-shrug. "I don't see why not. She enjoys that sort of thing. Give me just a few minutes to wrap things up here, and then I'll take you to her."

I nod and step back, watching Sama work. It's an overall fascinating process. Most of the workers mining the rocks, gems, and minerals are using various forms of earth or water magic, making it appear almost effortless. Sama uses her Syphon magic to point out areas with the most magical objects to mine. Then, the water wielders shift the water away while earth wielders move the wanted substances into nearby troughs. Once they have a decent selection of rocks, Sama does exactly like before, using her magic to seek out the magical items. After a few minutes, she goes over and speaks with the dark-haired young man from before. The man's gaze shifts to me for a moment before he looks back at Sama and gives her a sharp nod. Sama approaches me, grinning.

"All right. I have a break now, so I can introduce you to Makenna. She should be in her house right now," Sama says, leading the way.

I expect us to wind up along the mountain bridges but, as it turns out, Makenna lives in one of the dwellings on the ground. Sama knocks on the wooden door and a girl with curly blond pigtails and bright blue eyes opens the door.

"Sama!" the girl greets with a grin.

Sama returns her grin. "Hey, Makenna! I've brought one of our visitors to meet you. She has a request I think you may be able to help her with."

I step forward. "Hello, my name is Astra."

Makenna's eyes go wide. "You're the twin!"

I shove my discomfort down and force a smile. "That I am."

"How can I help you?"

"Well," I answer, suddenly feeling a bit awkward, "I was hoping you could maybe help me bake a cake for a friend's birthday. Prince Ehren's birthday, to be exact."

"Oh! Absolutely!" Makenna cries, throwing the door open and ushering me inside. "I would love nothing more than to help!" Sama hovers just outside the door while I follow Makenna inside. Makenna looks over her shoulder at Sama. "Aren't you coming in?"

Sama shakes her head. "No, I still have a bit more work to do today. I'll catch up with you later."

Sama gives a quick parting wave, Makenna returning it as she shuts the door. She turns back to me with a grin. "Shall we get to work?"

Makenna heads over to the kitchen area of the house and starts a fire before rushing about, piling ingredients and supplies on a small counter. I've never really baked a cake before since my mother did most of the baking back home, so I'm more than happy to let Makenna take the lead. She guides me through the steps, allowing me to assist her, even though I have a feeling she could do a much better job with me out of the way, especially when I encase us in a cloud of flour from dumping it in too quickly. As we work, we chat about our lives growing up, and I learn that she actually grew up in Callenia, only moving to the Hundan Valley a couple years ago. In the end we manage to make a thick, yellow batter and pour it into a round pan. Makenna carefully places the cake on a rack above the flames to bake.

"That should be done in an hour or so," she says, wiping her hands on her dress. "While we wait, we can enjoy a cup of tea while you tell me all about your adventures with the prince, if you'd like."

I smile. "That sounds perfect."

Makenna prepares a couple cups of tea, and we take a seat at a small table by a window. I start by telling her about meeting Bram before Kriloa and share snippets of details all the way up until present. I'm a little surprised at how much story there is to tell, and, by the time I'm done, the cake is perfectly baked. Makenna removes it from the oven with a satisfactory smile, placing it onto a nearby cooling rack.

"Now it just has to cool down a bit." She turns from the cake to me. "I have some brackenberry jam here, ready for the filling, but it might be fun to collect some fresh berries from the forest while the cake cools to mix into the jam and place on top."

I rise from my seat. "Honestly, I felt a bit less than helpful with the baking, but picking berries is something I can definitely do."

Makenna grabs a basket and offers me her hand. "I can wisp us to the perfect location."

I grab her hand and the comfortable little house disappears, a lush, green forest taking its place. Makenna leads the way to bushes overflowing with bright purple-red berries, ripe and ready to pick. We quickly fill the basket to almost overflowing. I pop a few in my mouth, the perfect mix of tart and sweet serenading my tongue. Makenna assures me that their flavor will perfectly compliment the sweetness from the honey cake and the brackenberry jam filling.

Once we've gathered enough berries, we wisp back to her house. The cake is still slightly warm, but Makenna uses wind magic to cool it to the necessary temperature before slicing the cake horizontally through the middle. She places the bottom layer on a wooden plate, spreading brackenberry jam on the layer, while I use my magic to slice some of the berries in half to add to the jam for texture. Once we have a satisfactory amount of jam and berries, Makenna carefully places the other layer on top. She grabs a jar of honey from a nearby shelf and drizzles a good amount of the sticky substance over the cake. We carefully arrange some of the remaining berries on top. I stand back and admire our cake, grinning. It's not perfect, but it looks and smells delicious.

"I hope Prince Ehren likes it," Makenna whispers nervously.

I laugh. "From what I've seen of Ehren, there isn't a food he won't like. I'm sure he'll love it."

Makenna nods, not looking wholly convinced.

"I thought I might take the cake back to the woods where we picked the berries. It seems like a nice, quiet place to celebrate."

Makenna smiles. "It is a lovely area." She pauses then looks over at me. "I can let you borrow a blanket to sit on, if you like."

She's already marching off into an adjoining room before I can protest. She returns a moment later with a large brown blanket.

"Here," she says, handing the blanket off to me. "It's not

much, but I'm happy to assist Prince Ehren in whatever way I can."

I accept the blanket with a smile. "Thank you. Your help today has been much appreciated."

She gives me a nod before proclaiming she really should be off to help with her shift in the kitchen if she wants time to sneak in an early lunch before beginning her job preparing dinner. I thank her one last time before wisping into the woods. I lay the blanket out, setting the cake in the center and weighing down the corners with rocks. I cast a basic shield over everything, protecting the cake from any curious animals or bugs that might try to take a nibble or two before I return with Ehren.

I wisp back down to the base level and stretch my magic out again, closing my eyes as I search for Ehren. Shadowy figures come into view as my magic sweeps over them. It doesn't take long before my magic locks onto the familiar figures. I notice with a start that Ehren has a slight glow of magic about him, likely from all the spellwork he's been doing. With him stand three figures without any magic—Bram, Makin, and Cal—and a fourth figure that glows with a steady hum of low burning magic. I focus on their location, pulling my magic in, and I wisp. When I open my eyes Ehren and the others stand only a few feet away. The dark eyes of the fifth figure lock on me as I appear in his line of sight directly behind Ehren. He straightens from his casual relaxed position to stand tall and more alert, pushing his straight black hair out of his eyes. At his full height he's nearly as tall as Bram. Ehren notices the change in the young man's stance and spins to see what stole his attention.

"Astra!" Ehren greets me with a smile, and the young man noticeably relaxes. "Come meet Nyco!"

I approach the group and smile, inclining my head toward the young man. "You're Nyco, I assume."

"Yes, Ma'am!" Nyco grins, bowing slightly. "Nyco Seong at your service."

I grimace. "Gods, please don't call me 'Ma'am.'"

Cal's eyes sparkle as Makin laughs. "She told Cal and I the same thing when we met her."

Nyco's grin widens, his eyes taking on a mischievous twinkle. "Shall I call you our Almighty Sorceress instead?"

I laugh and give a mock bow. "If you insist."

"We were just getting ready to make our way to the dining hall for the midday meal," Ehren says. "Would you like to join us?"

"Actually, I had a slightly different plan for lunch, if you don't mind me wisping you into the woods." I glance back at Nyco. "You're more than welcome to join us."

"Color me intrigued." Nyco grins.

"But there'll be some sort of food, right?" Makin asks, scowling. "I'm a growing man, and I require constant intake of food."

I laugh. "Yes there's food."

Cal sighs, rubbing the back of his neck as he glances off. "Is wisping the only option?"

"Well, I guess you could hike up the mountain," I reply with an apologetic shrug. "Sorry."

Cal offers me a small smile. "Eh, I'm getting used to it a bit."

"Are we ready?" I ask, glancing around the group.

Everyone nods. I stretch out my magic, a small tendril touching each person, and I wisp us into the woods. Nyco's eyes go wide as the forest appears around us.

"I've never seen someone able to wisp multiple people

without them all touching in some way," Nyco mumbles in awe. "I heard your magic was impressive, but I had no idea something like that was even possible."

"If you think that was impressive, just wait until she really shows off," Makin says, grinning.

"I don't show off, do I?" I ask incredulously, scowling at Makin.

He avoids the question by glancing around. "Where's the food? I was promised food."

I grin and wave my hand, removing my protective shield, allowing the blanket and cake to come into view. Everyone turns to face the cake as I turn to Ehren.

"Happy birthday," I say quietly.

Ehren blinks at me, happy disbelief shining in eyes. "You made me a cake."

I shrug. "I had help."

"Still, you actually made me a cake." He locks his eyes with mine, and I see exactly how much he appreciates the gesture.

"Everyone should have cake on their birthday."

Behind Ehren, Bram's face falls and a shadow floods his eyes. I see a similar expression flicker momentarily on Ehren's face before he turns toward the cake.

"Well, let's celebrate me!" Ehren declares, walking over and settling down on one of the blanket's corners.

The rest of us follow his lead and seat ourselves in a circle around the cake. Once everyone is seated, Bram glances around.

"Did you happen to get anything to serve the cake with?" he asks, attempting to hide his grin. The blush rising in my cheeks is answer enough.

"Pretty sure this is why we carry daggers." Makin grins, unsheathing a dagger hidden beneath his sleeve.

"Yeah," Cal chimes in, grinning, "all that fighting and stuff is just bonus."

I roll my eyes as Makin makes the first slice. Since we also have no plates, we end up holding the sticky slices of cake in our hands. It's a bit messy, but no one seems to mind. I'm lifting my slice to take a second bite when the jam shifts and a chunk of cake and jam starts to fall. I quickly jerk up my other hand to catch it, bumping the cake into my nose which leaves behind a sticky spot of honey and jam. Ehren laughs and licks the back of his thumb, leaning over to me and swiping the sticky blob off my nose. It's a move that if done by anyone else would have been almost too intimate, but coming from Ehren, it seems perfectly casual and natural. Ehren, however, seems to realize how his action could have been perceived and awkward concern flashes across his face until I throw my head back and laugh.

"What makes you think I want your spit on my nose?" I demand, grinning and narrowing my eyes playfully.

Ehren grins and licks the jam and honey off his finger. "I think the better question is who doesn't want my spit on their nose. I am the crown prince after all. My spit is highly sought after."

I roll my eyes. "Whatever you need to tell yourself to make it easier to sleep at night."

"Hey," Makin calls to Cal, "open your mouth."

Cal scowls. "What? Why?"

"I want to see if I can toss this berry into your mouth," Makin explains, holding up a berry between his pointer finger and thumb.

"What? No!" Cal laughs, shaking his head.

"Aw! Come on!" Makin pleads with a grin. "Please, please, please?"

Cal holds up his hands in surrender. "All right! Fine!"

He opens his mouth wide and Makin takes aim. The berry arches through the air and bounces off Cal's cheek.

"You weren't even close!" Ehren laughs.

"That was just my warm up shot," Makin counters, cracking his knuckles. "I'll get the second one!"

Cal rolls his eyes and opens his mouth again. Makin shoots and misses, the second berry hitting the corner of Cal's mouth. After much insisting and begging on Makin's part, Cal allows Makin to try one last time and the third berry lands squarely on Cal's tongue.

"Yes!" Makin cries, throwing his hands in the air, victorious.

"Is that really something to be proud over?" I ask, arching an eyebrow. "Cal is sitting barely two feet away, but it took you three tries. I expect more from the Prince's Guard."

Ehren crosses his arms. "She has a point."

"Oh, so you can do better?" Makin asks, arching his eyebrows in challenge.

"Pretty sure I can." I pluck up a berry. "Who wants to be my target?"

I glance around the group and my eyes land on Bram. He's sitting across from me, making him the most direct option. I raise my eyebrows in question. He sighs, shrugging his shoulders, and opens his mouth. I toss the berry and it lands perfectly in his mouth on the first try. I turn to Makin and grin triumphantly.

"That's it," Ehren declares. "You're off my Guard, Makin. I'm replacing you with Astra."

Cal snickers and I grin. Makin shakes his head. "She cheated."

"I did not!" I protest, crossing my arms in defiance. "I just have more skill than you."

Makin rolls his eyes. "Yeah, that skill of tossing a berry into someone's mouth will come in real handy next time we're attacked."

I stick my tongue out at Makin and he laughs.

"I want to try now!" Ehren says, picking up a berry. "Cal, open up."

Cal blinks in surprise for a moment before he rolls his eyes, a grin forming on his lips. "Why me?"

"You're clearly the best target," Ehren says with a wink. Cal tilts his head curiously and Ehren laughs. "Just open up. I'll throw a berry in everyone's mouth if it makes you feel better. You should be honored, though, that you're my first choice, me being a prince and all."

Cal shakes his head, but there's no hiding his grin as he complies. Ehren makes it on his first try.

Eventually, everyone has to try their hand at berry tossing, Nyco proving to have the best aim, never missing a single target. We spend several silly minutes taking turns tossing and being targets. I'm getting ready to toss a berry in Bram's mouth when another berry flies from my right and lands on Bram's tongue before I can toss mine.

"Oh-ho!" Ehren yells, throwing his hands in the air.

Bram turns, gagging, and spits the berry out onto the grass. "You *spit* that into my mouth!" he coughs, wiping his mouth and grimacing.

"Ew, Ehren!" I yell, laughing as I playfully smack his arm. "You might as well lean over and kiss him!"

Ehren laughs and waggles his eyebrows at Bram, who just rolls his eyes.

"I want to try that!" Makin declares. "I bet I'll be a better aim that way! Who will let me spit a berry?"

We all start enthusiastically shaking our heads, but Cal pipes up, "I'll do it."

His ears and neck suddenly flush a deep red as all our gazes shift to him. Makin grins awkwardly but doesn't back down. Cal sheepishly opens his mouth as Makin spits the berry, landing it perfectly on target. Instead of spitting out the berry, Cal quickly swallows it, awkwardness washing over the group.

"So," I say quickly, turning to look at Nyco, "what exactly can you do with your magic? Ehren said something to do with spiders?"

Cal shoots me a grateful look, which I acknowledge with a quick glance and smile.

"Um, yeah," Nyco says, shifting. "I can communicate with insects and spiders, but spiders are usually the most responsive."

"You can talk to spiders?" I ask, leaning forward, my eyes wide with interest.

He shrugs. "Yeah, kind of. I mean, spiders don't really talk, but they can communicate ideas and stuff. I basically read their minds and communicate back to them when I want them to do something for me."

"What sort of things would you need a spider to do?" Makin asks, eyebrows raised. "Have them make you a really pretty web?"

Nyco grins, his eyes glinting. "No one notices spiders as long as they stay in the shadows. They see and hear a lot of things. You send them to the right spots at the right times, and you can find out all sorts of interesting information most people want to keep hidden."

I inhale. "Spider spies?"

Nyco grins, nodding.

"That's genius!"

I'm about to say more when something catches my attention out of the corner of my eye. I glance toward some bushes nearby, but don't see anything. I'm about to turn my attention back to the group when Felixe starts to slowly appear, dashing into the bushes before he's fully corporeal. I jump to my feet, Ehren shooting me a concerned look.

"It's nothing," I say quickly, waving him off. "I'll be right back."

I force my face into a casual expression and hurry after Felixe. I trudge through the bushes and past some trees until I am just out of sight of the others. That's when Felixe decides to appear. He bounds over to me and rubs against my leg.

"Were you waiting until I was alone?" I croon, scooping him up.

He gives a little happy grumble and lifts his muzzle to me, revealing a note from Alak. I take the scroll from his mouth as he climbs onto my shoulder. A nervous pit swells in my stomach as I open the letter. For Alak to have responded almost immediately is most likely not a good thing.

My Most Beloved Astra,

You have no idea how thrilled I was to receive your last letter. I am so incredibly proud of you for accepting a position as Ehren's Court Sorceress. You deserve that honor, and this action proves that Ehren is a smart and worthy prince. I am deeply sorry I was not able to attend the ceremony. I wish, however, that you had been the one to tell me, but you were not. Kato apparently has some sort of spy or connection in Naskein that informed him not only of your appointment, but also that you left Naskein. Thankfully, as of right now, Kato does not know your exact location. Be cautious with whom you trust. Kato seems to be growing his forces hourly, and that includes a spy network.

As I mentioned in my last letter, Kato wishes to unite the seven Clans here in Athiedor in favor of magic. He revealed to me today that it is his intention to gather them as an army and march against the king, along with any other allies he can make. He plans to rule Callenia himself, and he is offering Athiedor their freedom as their own country if they support his claim to the throne. As you know, this is a very appealing offer to the Clans. So far, he has heard from five of the Clans—three have already given their support and two more are requesting meetings with Kato before they decide. I do not need to tell you how charismatic Kato is. Combine that natural charisma with his skill as a soldier and his overwhelming power, and he becomes the exact leader Athiedor has been waiting for. I fear that if one more Clan throws their support behind Kato, the rest will follow suit, and Kato will have his magical army.

Kato has also hinted that he has more connections and allies brewing, but he has yet to reveal those plans to me. I tried to get him to reach out to you before he goes so far that he can't turn back, but he won't do it. He feels like he needs to accomplish something in favor of magic to prove to you he is on the right path. He was even furious that

Ehren appointed you as Court Sorceress, claiming you were little more than a pawn in Ehren's hands.

I miss you very much and hope to return to you soon. Until then, I will continue to watch over your brother and report back to you and Ehren.

Forever Yours,

Alak

P.S. Wish Ehren a happy birthday from me.

My heart goes from elation due to Alak's praise and support to sinking from the news he shares. If Kato can build his army and march against the king . . . We need to build our allies quickly and cut him off before he can do too much damage. With a sigh, I make my way back to the group. I pause and watch them through the trees for a moment. Ehren leans back on his palms, legs stretched out in front of him so his feet are practically in Cal's lap. Cal leans on one arm slightly toward Makin, who is aiming to toss a berry into Nyco's open mouth. Even Bram is sitting cross-legged, casually watching everything with a smile. Everyone is relaxed and carefree. They're laughing and happy. The news I have will make this all disappear, and I have a sinking feeling these might be the last truly happy moments we'll be able to scrape out for a while. So I wait a few minutes, watching, before I go in and ruin the day.

CHAPTER SEVEN

ALAK

’m awakened by someone near me shifting and moving around. I groan and turn over, pulling my pillow over my head. Kato is always on a soldier's schedule with a soldier's discipline. It's damn annoying. I like to sleep in. Mornings are not my friend.

"Get up," Kato commands. "You need to pack."

I roll over and crack open one eye. "Pack? What for? Are we leaving?"

Kato nods, turning away from me to shove something in his bag. "Kayleigh found someone who can guide our wisping to Periola this morning. Hopefully, we will be able to get there and negotiate everything today, so we can be home by dinner. It's better to be prepared, though, so pack a full bag. Get up. I'll meet you downstairs."

Kato flies out of the room, slamming the door behind him in his haste. I sigh and sit up, stretching with a yawn. A glance out the window tells me it's barely past dawn. How the hell did Kayleigh find someone to wisp us this early in the morning? With a groan, I rise and throw on a shirt, tossing a change of clothes and some other basic necessities into my bag. Still rubbing sleep from my eyes, I head downstairs to find the living area full of people. Niall and Caitlyn stand in the far corner, Caitlyn clinging to Niall, her eyes darting around the room. Even Ian and Aine are present, both looking as awake as I feel. In the center of the room stands Kato, facing Kayleigh and a middle-aged man who looks very uncomfortable at the attention he is receiving. I swagger to Kato's side.

"Is this the gentleman that will be guiding our way?" I ask, clapping Kato on the shoulder while grinning at the man.

Kato nods, eyeing the man. "Kayleigh says he claims to have done regular business in Periola and has a clear enough memory to guide us."

The man nods emphatically. "Aye, I have been to Periola many times. I grew up on a sheep farm just outside the city. If all I truly need to do is think clearly of the place to guide your magic, I can assist you."

His voice trembles slightly, and I can practically taste his fear. He's undoubtedly heard about Kato and is intimidated by his power. I can't say I blame him.

Kato turns and looks over at Caitlyn. "Can you tell if he speaks the truth?"

Caitlyn studies the nervous man for a moment before nodding once. She swallows hard before replying quietly, "His aura is clear. I can't detect any lying or deceit."

"Good," Kato replies, looking around the room. "Are we waiting on anyone else?"

Kayleigh glances around the group and slowly shakes her head. "No. Unless there's someone else you think should accompany us, this is everyone."

"All right, everyone gather in," Kato says, gesturing for us all to move closer together. He fixes his eyes on the man. "Now, just place a clear picture in your mind of Periola, just as you would if you were wisping yourself. I'll latch onto you magically and do the hard work. Got it?"

The man looks up at Kato and swallows, nodding.

"A-all right," the man says feebly. "I have the image."

I lean in toward the man and whisper, "You might want to close your eyes."

The man obeys just in time to avoid seeing Kato's flames surround us, pulling us from Niall's house. When Kato's flames blink out, we're in a wide green field surrounded by a chorus of bleating, frightened sheep. A quick glance behind us shows a city. Kato gives a satisfactory nod.

"All right, once we've confirmed we are where we need to be, I'll send you back to Brackenborough," Kato says to the man, leading the way toward the city gate.

"Y-you can do that?" the man gulps as the others fall in line behind Kato.

"Easily," Kato says with a dismissive wave of his hand.

The man follows the others and I fall into step beside him. He's still obviously terrified of Kato's power, so I offer him a small smile in a poor attempt to calm his nerves.

"Thank you for your help," I say. "My name's Alak."

"I'm Killian," the man says, keeping his eyes locked on Kato's back. "Is he really as powerful as people say?"

I force a laugh. "I suppose that depends on how powerful people say he is, but I expect so. I haven't seen or heard of many as powerful as Kato, save his sister."

Killian glances up at me, eyes wide with fear. "He has a sister?"

I nod and focus my gaze ahead of us. "Aye. A twin."

The man swears under his breath. "I thought the twins were a myth," he mumbles, and I nod along.

I spent most of my life believing the same, even after I'd been promised they weren't a myth. The man glances around.

"Is his sister here?"

I shake my head. "Naw, she's gone down a different path. She serves Prince Ehren of Callenia."

Kato turns his head almost imperceptibly toward me as he walks. It's the only indication that shows he's listening to every word I tell Killian. I have to tread carefully. I want to support Astra, that's my main purpose. Kato can't know. Not yet.

Killian scowls. "Why would she turn her back on her brother?"

It's all I can do to hold my tongue and not tell the man he has it wrong. He has it backwards. Kato is the one who turned his back on Astra, not the other way around. Instead, I sigh and offer a sad shrug.

"Who knows?"

I'm saved any further response as we cross through the village's main gate. It doesn't take long for Kato to find a merchant willing to confirm that we've indeed made it to Periola. With a snap, Kato sends Killian back to Bruckenborough in a flash of flame. If Killian didn't soil himself at his sudden departure, I'd be very surprised.

Periola is divided into two distinct sections. The first part is a standard city, filled with houses, merchants, and businesses of every sort. Despite it still being early morning, the streets are already bustling with people ready to sell their wares.

The second part of the city is the fortress of Clan Wallish. The fortress is a stone castle surrounded by a tall stone wall. The castle is nothing terribly grand, not even a quarter the size of the palace in Embervein, but it's a spectacle nonetheless, with towers and turrets to complete the look. As a boy I often dreamt about visiting one of the many castles of the Clans, but, under the current circumstances, the sight just makes me uneasy.

It takes little effort to make our way through the main part of the city, but the guards at the fortress gate eye us warily. Once we reach the door of the fortress, two fully armored guards stop our entry.

"What business have ye with Clan Wallish?" the larger of the guards demands.

Kato offers his most becoming smile. "If you'll tell your Lord that Kato Downs has come to fulfill his request, I would greatly appreciate it."

The guard who spoke only scowls at us, but the other guard's eyes go wide. He knows who we are. He immediately calls to a servant hidden just inside the door in the shadows and sends him off to pass the word to Lord Wallish. He turns back to us.

"Someone should be with you shortly to guide you in," he says, a slight tremor in his voice.

It does not bode well that there's already this much fear instilled. It likely guarantees a victory for Kato.

It doesn't take long for a fidgeting messenger dressed in the Clan Wallish colors of green and gold to appear in the doorway and usher us inside. He leads us down wide, winding halls filled with banners proudly displaying Clan Wallish's ram's head crest. There are few windows, but most of our way is lit by sconces on the wall, casting long shadows. The messenger pauses a moment outside double oak doors before pushing them open, a loud creak echoing around us.

As we enter, I scan the room. A few well-dressed people hover around the edges of the large space, but it's mostly empty. At the head of the room on a raised platform a man and a woman sit, both on large stone chairs that could easily be called thrones. The man is older, with reddish hair and beard that's already streaked with a decent amount of gray. His arms rest casually on the arms of his chair, but his hands are clutching the armrest a little too tightly, betraying his nerves. His eyes narrow on Kato, assessing him. The woman is roughly the same age as the man, but her long red hair, pulled back into a loose bun, shows no sign of graying. Her hands are clasped in her lap, her eyes flitting between everyone in our group.

The messenger guides us down a green carpet lined with golden weave that leads directly to the platform. At the end, he pauses and looks up at the man.

"Lord Wallish, I present Kato Downs and companions," he says, his voice lacking confidence.

Lord Wallish gives the messenger a sharp nod and he scurries off, releasing a sigh of relief as he rushes past. Lord Wallish turns his attention back to Kato, his eyes flicking to me for a brief moment.

"Thank you so much for agreeing to meet with me," Kato says, his voice ringing through the room as he bows in respect. When he raises his face to look at Lord Wallish, he's wearing his most charming grin.

"I'm pleased and a bit surprised you were able to find travel accommodations so swiftly," Lord Wallish replies, looking uneasy. "It was mere days ago we sent our reply. We expected more time to prepare."

"Ah, well, I believe you'll find I'm not one to sit around twiddling my thumbs when there's work to be done," Kato replies, his eyes gleaming. "I've always had to work hard, and I don't intend to slow my work ethic now that there's a revolution on our hands."

Lord Wallish pales and he glances around nervously. "A r-revolution? What an interesting choice of words."

Revolutions are things spoken of in whispers in pub back rooms. They're mumbles on dark street corners. They're not something you declare brazenly and openly in a grand hall where anyone can hear. Even the youngest child in Athiedor knows this. Kato's shameless declaration might just be enough to keep Clan Wallish from joining his forces. Maybe there is hope he will fail after all.

Kato nods once. "Indeed. What else should we call these times but a revolution?" He takes a bold step closer to Lord Wallish. "Athiedor is different from the rest of Callenia. It has a rich history filled with its own separate customs, languages, and celebrations. Magic never fully died out in Athiedor. You are different. And yet, the king of Callenia has ruled over you like a ruthless thug."

"I wouldn't call the king a thug," Lord Wallish argues, his voice unsteady.

Kato waves him off impatiently. "Call him what you will, but you shouldn't be forced to call him your king. Athiedor was its own country once, and it should be its own country again. For generations, you've been stuck, kowtowing to a king whose only interest in you is what power and status your land can give him. Before, you may not have had the strength or resources to fight back, but now, magic has returned to its full force. Your people have never forgotten magic, and they can wield it better than almost anyone else.

If you act quickly, you can overthrow the king and free Athiedor from his clutches."

Lord Wallish pales even more, shaking his head fervently. "What you say is treason! If word got back to the king that you've said such things, he'll have all our heads."

"The king would happily take all our heads now simply for being able to wield magic," Kato counters. "The question is whether you're going to fight back now, before he attacks, and free your people, or whether you're going to sit idly by and lose every little bit that you've managed to retain over the years."

Lord Wallish meets Kato's eyes. "And what makes you believe you are qualified to speak on such matters?" he challenges, his voice a venom-edged sword. "You're not from Athiedor. According to my sources, you didn't even step foot into Athiedor until a few weeks ago. You're from a small, nothing town at the opposite end of Callenia. Why should we risk everything to follow your words? It takes more than pretty speeches to win a war."

Kato smiles, but it's not a pleasant look. Flames flicker in his eyes as he takes another step forward.

"Surely your sources have been more complete in their tales," Kato replies, his voice hard and cold.

He flicks his hand casually and flames roar to life along the walls of the room. The people standing nearby scream and leap away from the flames, clinging to one another, their eyes wide with fear.

"After all, I'm far more than pretty speeches, Lord Wallish."

Another careless flick of his hand and a dozen or so pillars of flame spiral from the floor to the ceiling. Lord Wallish's eyes scan the room, mouth gaping. He lifts a trembling hand to wipe sweat from his brow. His wife looks at him, true terror etched in her features.

"This is what I can offer you," Kato yells above the roar of his flames as he throws his hands wide. A crown of flames appears on his head while a cape of flames drapes down his back. "I have the power to be a king, so why shouldn't I wear a crown?"

Kato snaps his fingers and the flames flicker out, leaving behind only slight traces of smoke. I release a breath that I'd been holding without realizing.

"Beyond my power I also have skill. I may be from a small village, but I'm still a lethally trained solider. My talents were impressive enough I was made a member of Prince Ehren's Guard almost instantly. I can best both the Captain of the Prince's Guard and the prince himself when it comes to nearly any weapon. I've been taught to lead an army, and I assure you, I can. Do not mistake my age for incompetence." Kato's voice is hard. "I *will* lead an army against the king, and I *will* take his crown. Callenia will bow to me and bow to magic. I ask for your support to make this path easier. I need magical allies. In exchange for your aid, I will give you the freedom you've long desired."

"And if we choose not to align with you?" Lord Wallish asks, his voice little more than a whisper.

Kato shrugs. "Then you pick the losing side and may never have your freedom. I have other allies, Lord Wallish, here in Athiedor, all over Callenia, and even in other kingdoms, and I will build more allies as I gain more power. Negotiations are already in place. But I want you, the Clans of Athiedor, by my side. I want to lead your armies to victory. I want to see your people free."

Lord Wallish studies Kato for a moment. "You're asking

us to go to war to win you a crown. You're asking my people to lay down their lives for your pursuits."

"No," Kato interjects sharply. "I'm asking them to risk their lives for freedom and for magic." Kato glances around the room, a feral grin playing on his lips. "After all, the words of revolution have already been spoken in this hall." His voice is louder now, echoing throughout the room. Lord Wallish shifts uncomfortably in his seat. "How well do you trust the people lingering at the edge of this room, Lord Wallish? What about the servants listening at the doors and windows? Do you truly believe not a whisper of revolution will leave your fortress? By allowing me to come here, you've already implicated yourself. Bystanders would see you as looking favorably upon my cause. And why wouldn't you? Our goals align. It's a logical alliance."

Lord Wallish sets his jaw, weighing Kato's words. I swallow, my throat suddenly dry. Lord Wallish knows he's being threatened, and he doesn't like it. Not one bit. But he also knows Kato is right, to an extent.

"There's a war coming, Lord Wallish, like it or not," Kato continues, his voice resonating through the hall. "If you wait too long to make a decision, you'll be forced into it, and you may not walk away with your freedom. Stand by me, support my cause, lend me your men, and I swear to you, we will win. And when we do, Athiedor will be free as the gods intended."

Lord Wallish exhales slowly. "The points you've made are valid. I won't deny you've put a voice to some of our concerns and desires. However, it is not up to me alone whether Clan Wallish will throw our full support behind you. I must consult with the Clan elders before a final decision can be made."

Kato nods. "I expected as much."

"I'll dispatch messages to the elders immediately. We will discuss everything you have told us and give you a decision as soon as possible. In the meantime, you and your companions are welcome to stay here." Lord Wallish beckons to someone behind us and a servant girl steps forward. "Are their rooms prepared?"

"Yes, Lord Wallish," the girl replies with a bow.

"Excellent."

The girl turns to us. "If you'll follow me, I'll show you to your rooms."

We nod and begin following the girl out, but Lord Wallish calls after us.

"One last question, if you don't mind."

We turn and Kato flashes Lord Wallish a grin. "Yes?"

"What of your sister?" Lord Wallish asks, standing and taking one step toward Kato.

Kato stills, a shadow crossing his features, his jaw clenching. "What about my sister?"

I take an unsteady breath. Lord Wallish is treading dangerous ground. I draw my own magic, ready to shield myself should Kato unleash his. Caitlyn inhales sharply and leans closer to Niall, who slips his arm around her protectively. Aine shoots a sharp glance to Ian, who's shifting uneasily. Even Kayleigh is readying her magic.

"My sources have informed me," Lord Wallish says, taking another bold step in our direction, "that your sister is no longer by your side."

"I should think that is obvious enough for you to see with your own eyes," Kato snaps.

Lord Wallish winces at his sharp tone. "If your sister isn't by your side, where is she? Does her power match yours?"

"My sister," Kato snarls, his body tense, "is none of your concern. She will not fight in favor of the king. Now, she is undecided on how much of an active role she wishes to take in this war. Once my armies are strong enough, once I have amassed my legions, she will join my side. We will be invincible."

Lord Wallish looks like he wants to say more, but I can feel Kato's power rising, unsteady and lethal.

"Lord Wallish," I cut in quickly, taking a step forward. "I can assure you that Astra also stands against the king." I let my accent roll thick and rich. "They may be on separate paths right now, but I cannot see her striking against her brother."

The words are a bitter betrayal, but they work. An almost sinister smile creeps onto Kato's lips as his body relaxes. Lord Wallish nods. "All right then. I will summon the elders, and we will get you a final answer soon."

Lord Wallish turns his back to us, turning to speak with one of the men that was standing near the edges earlier. The servant girl clears her throat, drawing our attention.

"Ah, yes," Kato says, offering the girl his most charming smile. "Lead the way."

The girl leads us from the hall to a winding stone staircase. The way is narrow, and we have to fall single file behind her, Kato at the lead and, much to my delight, Aine bringing up the rear. The girl veers off the staircase through a door to what I assume is the third floor if counted correctly, guiding us down a long hallway. She pauses midway down the hall.

"These four rooms have been prepared for you," she mumbles, gesturing to four wooden doors, two on each wall. "The washroom is down there, when you need it." She gives a quick nod to a door at the end of the hallway before shuf-fling off, shooting us one last glance over her shoulder before she disappears.

After a quick survey of the rooms, we find two have decent-sized single beds in them while the other two rooms each have a pair of beds. Without hesitation, Kato claims one of the single bed rooms, and, as logic follows, Caitlyn and Niall take the other. They go into their rooms, leaving me, Ian, Aine, and Kayleigh to fight over the remaining room arrangements.

"Alak and I will take this room," Aine says with a feline grin as she loops her arm through mine, pulling me toward the door on our right.

I tense under her touch and have to fight the urge to jerk from her grasp. Even my magic screams against her.

"Now, now, Aine," I reply, forcing a grin although my stomach swirls with disgust. "I'm sure your brother would prefer you not share a room with me."

"Ach! Most certainly not!" Ian growls, eyes flashing.

Aine's chilling laugh echoes down the stone hallway as she tightens her grip on my arm. I inhale sharply, gritting my teeth.

"I'm sure Alak would be a perfect gentleman," she laughs. She looks up at me through her long eyelashes. "Right, Alak, my love?"

"I will be a perfect gentleman," I reply, yanking my arm from her grasp, "in my room, which will be across the hall."

Before she can pull me back into her clutches, I take a wide step and throw open the door opposite the one she just claimed. I glance over my shoulder and casually ask, "So, are we splitting up by family or gender?"

"I am most certainly *not* sharing a room with my brother," Aine insists, crossing her arms and glaring at me.

I shrug. "Gender it is."

I stride the rest of the way into the small room and toss my bag onto the nearest bed. Ian grumbles something under his breath and slouches into the room. Aine shoots daggers at me before spinning and pulling Kayleigh after her into the room across the hall. Ian shuts our door with a huff.

"No window," he grumbles, scanning the room with a scowl as he places his bag at the foot of the other bed.

I glance around, acting like I didn't immediately notice the magic-lit chandelier in the center of the ceiling. "Huh. What do you know? There isn't window. I guess any escaping in the night for secrets trysts will have to be done via the door."

Ian just glares as I shoot him a grin. I collapse on the fully made bed, crossing my arms behind my head and closing my eyes. "Bed's comfy enough."

"What are ye up to?" Ian demands.

I crack one eye open. "What do you mean?"

He studies me a moment before continuing. "Why are ye here?"

I sit up on the bed and force my face to look as confused as possible. "I'm here for the same reason as you, mute."

"I don't believe ye are," he replies, crossing his arms.

I sigh and roll my eyes. "And what other purpose could I possibly have? You think I just wanted a nice holiday in Periola?"

"Yer up to something. I know ye are. I'm just not sure what." He eyes me closely, as if I'm suddenly going to show my hand if he stares hard enough. He shrugs after a moment. "Just know I'm watching ye."

"Okay then," I mumble, lying back down on the bed. "Noted."

Ian stands there, I'm sure wanting to say more, but there's a knock on the door. Before either of us can answer it, it's thrown open.

"Gods, Aine! What if I had been indecent?" Ian growls.

"We're going to explore a bit," Aine grins from the doorway, ignoring her brother as Kayleigh peers over her shoulder into our room. "Want to come along?"

"Naw," I reply, crossing my ankles and closing my eyes. "I'd rather rest."

"You're such a spoilsport," Aine whines.

"Leave him be," Kato's voice booms as he steps up behind the girls into the doorway. "If you push him, he'll get grumpy, and no one wants to put up with a grumpy Alak."

I chuckle. "Feck off, mate."

"See," Kato grins, his eyes twinkling. "He's getting grumpy already."

It's moments like this where Kato seems so normal. He's the casual, joking boy I met not long ago. He's the one I want to return to Astra.

I hear a door open and close further down the hall as footsteps approach.

"Are we going somewhere?" Caitlyn asks as she and Niall come into view.

"Everyone but Alak," Kayleigh answers.

Niall pokes his head in the door. "You aren't coming?"

I shake my head. "Nope." I roll over, my back facing everyone else. "If you wouldn't mind leaving me in peace, I'd appreciate it. All your chattering is giving me a headache."

Someone laughs—not sure who, but I think it's Kato—and Aine sighs, but the door closes with no further comments. I don't need to look to know that Ian shoots me a warning look before leaving. I lie still on my bed as I listen to their voices and footsteps fade down the hall. Even after I'm sure they're gone, I remain on the bed for a few minutes before easing into a sitting position. I have no idea what they're all going to get up to, but I have no desire to join them. I don't want to be a part of their group any more than necessary.

I lean down and drag my bag toward me. I reach in and dig out two items tied together with a bit of twine—a black journal and a pouch. As soon as we returned to Athiedor, I hunted down the items we had to leave behind. Astra's bag had clearly been shuffled through, but the journal from Cadewynn had remained inside. I was also pleasantly surprised to find no one had taken the medicine pouch. Of course, I have no idea what medicines were in the pouch to start with, but considering the pouch contains cures for everything from pain to restoring magic, I'm assuming nothing was taken. I tied the items together to keep them from getting scattered and lost again, with the intent of sending them back to Astra. I simply haven't found the time yet. Now seems as good of an opportunity as any.

"Felixe, where are you?" I whisper, using my magic to call for the fox. He blinks into focus on the end of the bed with a happy yip. I grin. "Hey there, boy!"

Felixe leaps into my lap and I scratch his head. Even though I've gotten much better at controlling my magic since the first time I met the Fae Fox, his presence is still soothing.

"I need you take a few things to Astra for me. Can you do that?"

Felixe looks up at me and gives a little growl. I laugh.

"Yes, I am happy to see you." Felixe barks. "And I know you're not just a messenger fox."

Felixe blinks his big blue eyes at me and gives another bark. I smile and lift the package tied with twine. Felixe shifts his gaze between me and the items.

"Can you handle it?" I ask. Felixe looks up at me and cocks his head, one of his ears flipping inside out. I laugh and pat his head. "I know you can do it. Just let me jot a quick note."

I pull a bit of parchment from my bag and something to write with. I don't make it long. A few words will suffice. When I'm done, I fold the note and tuck it into the journal, leaving enough sticking out so that Astra is sure to see it. I hold the package out to Felixe. It's as big as his head, but he doesn't hesitate to grab a bit of the twine in his teeth.

"Tell her I miss her," I say, my voice barely a whisper.

Felixe gives a small nod before he disappears. Once he's gone, an all too familiar ache fills my chest. I wish I could go with him.

CHAPTER EIGHT

ASTRA

I open my eyes to find Sama kneeling in front of me. I gasp and jerk up, my hammock swinging wildly, dumping me onto the floor.

"Oh! I'm so sorry!" Sama cries, trying unsuccessfully to hide a laugh.

Once I get over the shock of being dumped onto the floor like a discarded doll, I give a little chuckle and push up into a sitting position.

"It's all right," I laugh, rubbing my head.

Sama offers me her hand and helps me up.

"I didn't mean to make you flip," she says, grinning, "but you received a summons from Jessalynn. She wants to talk to you and your companions before breakfast."

I nod. "I suspect she's going to put us to work today."

"It's likely," Sama agrees. "Do you need help finding your way around today? If not, I promised to meet Sasha before breakfast."

I shake my head and offer Sama a smile. "No, thank you. I can find where I'm going."

"All right. If you're sure . . . ," Sama replies, stepping tentatively toward the door.

I wave her off. "Go on. I'll be fine. I swear."

Sama shoots me one last grin before she disappears out the door. I dress quickly, using magic to lace my boots and straighten my hair. I step outside and consider just wisping to the meeting room, but it's a beautiful day, so I walk instead. I take a deep breath of the fresh mountain air. It's so crisp and clear. As I walk along the swinging bridges, I glance down into the valley below. There's a decent amount of people already out and about, likely making their way toward the dining hall to snag a place near the front of the line. I love how alive everything feels here. It's so different from Naskein or even Athiedor. I could easily see myself staying here for an extended period of time. Well, that could change depending on what tasks Jessalynn finds fit to assign me. If my task is unpleasant enough, I may be ready to leave tomorrow.

When I enter the meeting room, I'm relieved to find that Jessalynn and her crew haven't arrived yet. Ehren sits at the head of the table, his head lying face down, cradled in his arms. Bram stands at near perfect attention behind him but relaxes his shoulders slightly when I enter. Cal leans against the back wall, arms crossed across his chest with Makin's head buried in his shoulder. As the door shuts behind me, Ehren raises his head just enough to look up and see who entered.

"Oh, it's just you," he mumbles, allowing his head to crash back into the comfort of his arms.

"Good morning to you, too," I jest as I plop into the chair to Ehren's right, poking his arm.

"Ow!" Ehren cries, sitting up. "Abusing a prince is basically treason."

I roll my eyes. "Lock me up."

Ehren laughs as Bram grins. I shift my eyes to Makin and Cal along the back wall.

"I know you're seldom an early bird," I say to Ehren, "but shouldn't Makin be used to rising early?"

Makin moans and mumbles some incoherent response. Cal rolls his eyes.

"Makin, here, was out late last night, gambling and drinking," Cal explains, attempting to shake Makin off his shoulder, which only makes Makin snuggle in closer.

I raise my eyebrows. "There's a tavern here?"

Cal shakes his head. "No, but leave it up to Makin to find alcohol and games wherever he goes."

At that, Makin lifts his head and shoots me a sheepish grin. "I do have my talents."

I laugh as the door swings open and Jessalynn saunters in, Kaeya at her right and new girl with dark skin and long dark braids slung over her shoulder at her left. Jessalynn's eyes scan our group, and she nods when she sees we're all present.

"All right, let's get straight to business so we can go eat breakfast," she says, not even bothering to sit. "You and you" —she points to Cal and Bram—"will both be on morning guard duty. Captain Bramfield will be on the east side with Kaeya and you, Cal, will be on the west with Britney." She gestures to the new girl on her left. "Shift change is midway through breakfast to give everyone a chance to get in a proper meal and ends midway through lunch for the same reason."

Cal and Bram each nod in turn. Jessalynn turns her attention to Ehren.

"You're going to help Quin in the library. He needs help sorting through some items written heavily in Callenian, which is not his first language. It's a lot of technical information from government meetings, so it will be right up your alley."

Ehren nods, looking less than thrilled, but Bram cuts in. "Astra is actually quite good at that sort of thing."

Jessalynn glares at Bram, and he stands a little straighter, refusing to be intimidated by her.

"I'm aware. I have another assignment for Astra."

Bram scowls. I know he wants me safely stored away in the library.

"I'm happy to do whatever you ask," I jump in before Bram can dig a deeper hole.

"Good," Jessalynn says, her smile returning. "You'll be on night guard duty with Kai." Bram inhales sharply and stiffens as Jessalynn looks to Makin. "You'll also be on night duty, but with Brock. You'll both take up your post mid-dinner. Any questions?"

Bram opens his mouth, but snaps it shut with a sharp look from me. Satisfied, Jessalynn claps her hands once.

"Excellent. Let's get to breakfast, shall we? Some of us have a busy day."

Jessalynn, Kaeya, and Britney disappear, leaving us alone again. Ehren leans back in his chair, stretching, before slowly rising to his feet. I stand with him.

"Well," he drawls, "we knew she was likely to split us up."

"She hasn't just split us up," Bram spits. "She divided us enough that we will rarely be together at all!"

"Does it really matter?" I ask with a shrug. "It's not like we need to be together all the time. We were constantly split up at Naskein."

"Naskein was different," Bram counters.

"How?" I demand, irritation lining my voice.

"Because we were safe in Naskein."

Makin laughs and Bram silences him with a curt look.

"What?" Makin says, raising his eyebrows. "Like at Naskein we weren't essentially trapped on an island with an entire armada waiting just outside the gate?"

Ehren gives a half-shrug, barely hiding his own amusement. "He has a point."

Bram shakes his head.

"Well, regardless of whether or not you like it, we have our assignments, and I don't think we're going to wiggle out of them. Now, let's get to breakfast."

I wave my hand and the room vanishes as the scene changes to the base level, just outside the dining hall. Cal, who had been leaning against the wall, stumbles forward, Ehren reacting quickly enough to catch his arm and keep him upright while Makin falls to the ground with a thud.

"Gods, a little warning, Astra!" Makin yells as Cal throws his head back, laughing.

"Sorry." I grin.

Even Bram can't hide his smile as he offers his hand to Makin. Makin accepts Bram's help, standing and brushing dirt and grass off his clothes. We join the crowd of people filtering inside and take our place in line. Despite the line being incredibly long, it moves quickly and efficiently. Breakfast this morning is a selection of scrambled eggs, bacon or sausage, fresh fruit, and toast, with the option of hot tea or juice to drink. I opt for eggs, bacon, and toast with a cup of tea. Once we have our food, we find seats at a nearby table. After a few minutes, Nyco approaches us.

"Morning! Mind if I sit with you?" he asks, sliding into the empty seat to my left before anyone can reply.

"By all means, have a seat!" Makin laughs as Nyco grins.

"I hear you got your assignments this morning," Nyco says, taking a bite of toast.

Ehren nods, washing down his eggs with juice. "That we did."

"How bad are they?" Nyco asks, scanning our faces and settling on Bram's frown. "That bad, eh?"

"No, not really bad," I say with a shrug. "Just a little more spread out than we wanted."

"Makes sense," Nyco says, his mouth full as he shovels in more food. "She likes testing people, pushing them to find their strengths and weaknesses. She'll want to see how you all survive on your own."

Ehren and I exchange a nervous glance. We expected as much, but it still makes us uneasy. I trust Jessalynn, but she's still a bit of a wildcard. I glance around and find Jessalynn standing not far off with a group of people, her arm draped affectionately around Kaeya.

"Are Jessalynn and Kaeya a couple?" I ask, looking sideways at Nyco.

"What?" Nyco asks, raising his head and looking toward Jessalynn, his mouth full. He swallows and nods. "Oh, yeah. Well, they're together, but I don't know if you can call them a couple since they're also in a relationship with Brock."

Bram chokes on his food while Ehren leans forward, eyes wide.

"What?" Ehren asks. "All three of them are together?"

Nyco nods. "It's not all that uncommon in Gleadur for

relationships to be between more than two people. There are ceremonies similar to marriage vows for such relationships, but I'm not sure if they've participated in one. Though they're serious and committed enough for it. From what I've heard, they've been together for years." Nyco shrugs and takes another bite of eggs. "Honestly, it happens a lot in other places, people just like to pretend they're committed to just one person when everyone knows they have relationships with others. At least here they're open and honest about it and treat their partners with the high level of consideration and respect they deserve."

"But you can't be in love with more than one person," Bram counters firmly.

Nyco shrugs again. "Maybe *you* can't, but some people can. Just because it works for someone else doesn't mean you have to pretend it would work for you and vice versa. I, honestly, rather like the idea."

"Hmm," Makin muses, staring off into space for a minute.

"It's nothing like what you're imagining," Cal mutters, rolling his eyes.

Makin flashes him a grin. "You don't know that."

"Oh, I'm rather sure I do," Cal counters, taking a swig of juice. "And you'd have to find willing participants first, anyway."

Ehren chuckles, shaking his head as Makin grins. Makin opens his mouth, but Cal cuts him off before he can say anything else on the subject.

"I think my guard partner might be ready to go," Cal says with a nod toward the opposite end of the dining hall.

She looks less than enthused and I wonder briefly if this assignment is some sort of punishment.

"You have fun with her," I mutter, happy that she's not the one I'll be on duty with, not that Kai seems much friendlier.

"Right," Cal mumbles, rising from his seat. "Well, I guess I'll catch up with you all at lunch."

He deposits his tray and joins Britney, who immediately wisps them from sight. Bram sighs and rises.

"I guess I'm off as well." He looks toward me and shakes his head before leaving. I turn to Ehren.

"I can show you the way to the library if you like."

Ehren feigns surprise. "Wait, you know where the library is?"

I grin. "I know it's shocking."

We make quick work of what remains of our breakfast and head to the library, Makin trailing behind us as Nyco heads off to fulfill whatever duties he normally takes care of. I offer to wisp Ehren directly to the library, but he declines, saying he would rather learn the way in case no one is around to wisp him later. When we enter the library, Quin greets us with a grin, his arms loaded with scrolls.

"Ah, young prince! I heard you would be joining me this morning to help sort through court files! Let me put these scrolls away, and I will be right with you."

He shuffles off and I turn to Ehren as he says, "Well, he seems nice enough. Much friendlier than the librarian back home."

I chuckle. "Yes, she wasn't exactly the friendliest." I pause as a thought strikes me. "You know, maybe I'll see what things I can find here in this library regarding magic. Expand my knowledge. That is, if you don't mind the company."

Ehren shrugs. "I don't mind at all."

"Well, if you don't think you'll need me hanging around, I may head back down and get a bit more sleep. I'll need it if I'm going to be on guard duty all night," Makin says, glancing over his shoulder toward wherever he's staying.

"That's fine," Ehren says with a nod. "You know, Ash, it may not be a bad idea for you to get some more sleep, too."

I start at the casual use of my nickname. Kato's the only person who's ever used it. It sounds so natural coming from Ehren, and I've honestly missed it.

"I'll rest after lunch," I reply. "I'm too awake now to go back to sleep."

Ehren nods as Makin leaves. Quin returns shortly after, ushering us to a table already stacked with pages.

"These are copies of court documents from Embervein," Quin explains, motioning to the piles. "I'm afraid I've never been much for politics, so if you could help sort the information by year and noble family, I would appreciate it. Jessalynn helps me when she can, but her duties often call her elsewhere."

Ehren studies the piles, his eyes glazing over as he nods. I stifle a laugh. Ehren is going to hate every second of this.

"Would you mind if I did some studying of my own while Ehren works?" I ask.

"Of course not! I would be most honored for you to use my library. Is there anything I can help you find?" Quin volunteers eagerly.

I pause, glancing briefly toward Ehren before replying, "Actually, I was wondering, are there records of people who had their magic appear later in life with details about how it affected them?"

Ehren's mouths opens slightly as he raises his eyebrows but doesn't speak. I avoid his gaze.

Quin nods, furrowing his brow. "Yes, yes, there are. It is not uncommon for many people to develop their magic later in life. For some, it appears literally overnight, and for others, it's a gradual process. I imagine you're interested largely in how your magic came about, am I correct?"

His eyes twinkle as I nod, forcing a weak smile. "Yes. I'd love to read some records of people who developed their magic rapidly around their coming of age."

"I have a few records I can think of immediately that I can fetch for you," he offers with a sincere smile.

"Thank you," I say, inclining my head.

Quin gives a quick bow before he rushes off to find the records I've requested. Ehren turns to the table and lets out a long breath.

"Well," he mumbles, taking a seat in front of the largest pile, "let's get this over with."

I grin and take a seat next to him. "Eh, it won't be so bad."

I pluck a paper off the top of a nearby stack and scan it. It's the notes from some sort of court trial.

"You might find this interesting," Ehren counters, frowning at a similar paper, "but I do not."

"Actually, this does look pretty dull," I confess, scanning another sheet. "Jessalynn must really hate you."

"Apparently," Ehren grumbles, and I bite my lip to keep from laughing. He glances over at me, concern shadowing his face. "What are you looking for in those records?"

I purposefully avoid his eyes and lean closer to the page in my hand.

"This looks like a record of a long-standing family feud. That sounds relatively interesting."

Ehren reaches over and pushes the paper down.

"Astra," he says, his voice thick with seriousness. I sigh and shake my head. "You're wanting to see if magic changed Kato, aren't you."

I look up into Ehren's caring sea-green eyes. "I can't help but wonder if the magic has affected him in some way. The Kato who abandoned us, he's not the Kato I've known my whole life."

Ehren places his hand on mine and gives it a little squeeze. "I believe you, Astra. I'd actually wondered the same myself but didn't feel right voicing it. I'll help you find all the answers you're looking for. If you want my help, that is."

I smile, fighting back tears. "Thank you, Ehren. I'll never turn away a helping hand." I hesitate and glance away, chewing on my lip.

"What is it?" Ehren presses, scanning my face.

"What if I don't find an answer?" I look back up into Ehren's eyes. "What if the magic isn't what changed him? What if he's willingly chosen this? What if—"

"No more what ifs," Ehren says, tightening his grip on my hand in a firm but gentle manner. "You do your research and find what you can. Then, once you have all the information, you can decide what it means. Until then, hold onto hope."

I release a long breath. "What would I do without you?"

Ehren laughs, releasing my hand, and turns back to the pile of papers in front of him. "You'd be miserable for sure." He sighs and scoots several papers closer. He stares at a few for a moment before mumbling, "Jessalynn definitely hates me."

I chuckle and help Ehren sort the papers into manageable piles until Quin comes back with the texts I requested. I offer to move to a different table, but Ehren insists I stay with him, shifting his work down so I have space for my own piles. A little over an hour later, we are both deep into our tasks when Quin comes rushing up with a large black and gold book. He drops the book onto the table, sending a few papers spiraling into the air.

"So terribly sorry for the interruption," he huffs, out of breath. "There was a story pressing against the back of my brain that I couldn't quite pull forward. But it just clicked into place." He leans forward and flips through the book, the gilded edges of the pages reflecting the light. He pauses on a page and taps his finger on the story. "Here. I thought you might find this of interest."

He turns the book toward me and I pull it closer, Ehren leaning in to read along. I quickly scan the story and inhale sharply, struggling to keep my surprise from showing. I flick my eyes up to Quin, who watches me expectantly.

"Thank you, Quin. This is exactly what I was looking for," I say, keeping my voice level and cordial.

Quin gives me a slight bow as a smile spreads across his face. "I'm glad to be of service. That story is one of the oldest tales and legends that has been passed down. I'm surprised I didn't think of it sooner." He glances toward Ehren who's scowling down at the book. "Well, I'll let you two get back to work."

Quin scuttles away and Ehren leans in and whispers, "What exactly does this say? I can tell it's Callenian, but it's not a dialect I'm familiar with."

"I'm not surprised you can't read it well. This dialect faded out of use nearly a hundred years ago. I only know it because it was part of my studies to become a historian," I explain, keeping my voice low.

"But what does it say? Does it explain anything?"

I pull the book a little closer and trace my finger along the words as I sum up the story for Ehren. "It talks about a young boy, born into poverty. He was mistreated by everyone, including his own family, who went so far as to abandon him. He was found by an old wizard who took pity on him and brought him to live in his humble home. The wizard had basic magic, and he taught the boy what he could. Since the boy had no magical heritage, however, it was mostly pointless. He also taught the boy how to read and write and treated him like his own son. The boy grew to love the wizard like the father he should have had, becoming a bright, eager pupil."

I pause to look at the gilded illustration of the wizard teaching the boy on the bottom corner of the page. They look happy.

"That doesn't sound too horrible," Ehren mutters. "But I have a feeling the story isn't over yet."

I shake my head. "No. One day, when the boy was nearly grown, the wizard made the wrong people angry when he refused to help them harm someone with his magic. They came to his house and attacked him while he was sleeping. They weren't expecting the boy, so they ran off without taking everything they had originally intended, but the wizard was hurt badly enough that he died before dawn. The boy went off seeking revenge for his slaughtered mentor and tried to attack the men. The men nearly killed him. Distraught, the boy went to the nearest temple and called upon the gods. They all ignored his pleas for help, but the boy refused to leave. He stayed for days, neither eating nor sleeping. Eventually, a forsaken god by the name of Marzoth rose up and bestowed the boy with the power of a thousand magical souls that he kept trapped in his demon realm, as well as the gift of Hellfire."

Ehren lets out a low whistle, shaking his head as I nod.

"Exactly. The boy had more power than anyone else. Having never really had any magical power before, he didn't know how to handle it. He had never learned such skills. Despite being a sweet and caring boy before, he allowed the power to taint him, drawing on his insecurities and need for revenge. His passion for vengeance soon overwhelmed his desire for good, and he destroyed not only those who had harmed him before, but anyone who got in his path. The more he killed and destroyed, the more of a taste for evil he obtained. Soon, he was too great a force to be reckoned with and people cowered in fear of him."

"Does it say how he was stopped?" Ehren asks, his voice quiet.

I shake my head, sorting the words. "Not on these pages."

I turn the page to find it covered almost entirely by a golden illustration of a woman—an angel by every appearance—standing over the body of the boy, now a man, stabbing him with a glowing sword. I trace my fingers along the inscription below the picture.

"'And thus the lady of light and hope brought forth her mighty power and slew Caedios, banishing him from our realm forevermore.'"

When I stop reading, Ehren and I just sit for a moment, staring at the page. Silence and stillness swell around us.

"Well, shit," Ehren mumbles at length. I let out a shaky breath, and he jerks his face to mine. "But just because this Caedios person let his power overwhelm him doesn't mean that will happen to Kato."

I shake my head, fighting back the tears that burn my eyes as I stare down at the image, envisioning Kato as the conquered Caedios. It's too much. A tear slides free and Ehren grabs my shoulders, turning me to face him.

"Hey," he says, his eyes scanning my face until I finally lift my eyes to meet his. "We're not going to let that happen."

His brief glance at the illustration shows he knows exactly what thoughts flicker through my brain. He lifts his hand and gently wipes a tear from my cheek with his thumb.

"Okay? We will search every book and every library and seek every solution. You understand? If there is anything—spellwork, magic, or otherwise—we will find it."

A small sob breaks from my lips as I try to nod my head. What little resolve Ehren had vanishes as his face crumbles. He pulls me close against his chest and gently strokes my back as I soak his shirt with tears.

"And don't forget about Alak," Ehren mumbles against my hair. "He's still out there, doing what he can. You're not alone in this. You will never be alone. We will always be here for you."

For a few minutes, I surrender myself to tears, allowing Ehren to hold me tightly, whispering additional comforts in my ear. Finally, I pull back, wiping my tears with my fists. Ehren lifts a hand and gently strokes my cheek.

"You okay now?" he asks gently, offering me a small smile.

I sniff and shake my head. "I don't know if I'll ever really be okay until I have answers or at least some direction, but I do feel a bit better. I just . . . I needed to get that out. I think I've been holding it in . . ."

Ehren gives an understanding nod. "We've all had moments like that in our lives." He takes a deep breath and exhales slowly, turning his attention back to the work scattered across the table. "Let's distract ourselves a bit, shall we?"

I nod, grateful to have the distraction. We decide to sort the documents first by year, then by topic. We've only been sorting for a few minutes when Felixe appears in the center of the table, scattering handfuls of papers. Ehren scowls and curses under his breath.

"Hey, Felixe!" I greet the little fox, a genuine smile flashing across my face as I reach for him. I pause when I notice he's holding a package tied together with a bit of twine. I gasp when I realize what he has, quickly scooping the items up off the table.

"What's that?" Ehren asks, looking up from the papers in his hands.

"My journal from Cadewynn!" I cry, untangling the string and freeing the items. I open the pouch and peer inside. "And all my medicines from Healer Heora! I never thought I'd see any of this again after I had to abandon it in Athiedor."

Ehren reaches over and snatches a piece of paper sticking out of the journal. I realize it must be a note form Alak and I lunge for it. Ehren grins and leans away, reaching his arm as far as he can so the note is well away from my grasp.

"Ehren!" I scold, not giving up my attempt to grab my note, practically climbing in his lap to do so.

Ehren laughs. It's a rich pleasant sound after our dismal moments not long ago, but it does little to alleviate my frustration.

"I think I should censor all communication," Ehren says,

his eyes twinkling. "I need to make sure you two stay on topic."

I let out a huff and sit back in my chair, crossing my arms as I glare at Ehren. Ehren laughs again and slowly draws in his arm, holding the paper out to me. I yank it from his hands.

"Thank you," I reply curtly as I unfold the paper.

I purposefully twist in my chair so Ehren can't read over my shoulder. Not that I expect there to be anything terribly personal in the note. I simply want to relish the words privately before I share.

My Most Beloved Astra,

I managed to salvage these items from what we had to leave behind when we fled Athiedor. I know what they meant to you. Also, know Luna is doing fine and is well cared for. All the horses are.

Forever Yours,

Alak

P.S. I miss you.

My heart thrums against my chest as I read the words. The last line is scrawled across the bottom, almost as if it were an afterthought, written hurriedly before he could change his mind. I read the note at least three times thinking about what it meant for him to risk not only finding these items, but also saving and sending them to me.

"Anything juicy?" Ehren teases, trying to peer over my shoulder.

I roll my eyes and turn to face him. I hesitate but decide to hand Ehren the note. He takes it, scanning it quickly. A soft smile plays on his lips, and I can read the relief in his eyes.

"Your horse is okay," I say quietly.

He looks up at me, eyes shining. "Dauntless," he says proudly. "My horse's name is Dauntless." He glances back at the note one last time before passing it back to me. "Alak is a good person."

I nod and tuck the note safely away inside the cover of the journal. "He is. I know you have your history, but—"

"I misjudged him," Ehren cuts me off. "I know there's more to the story than what I first believed. I didn't know Alak long before . . . it happened, but what little I did know about him never fit entirely with the narrative that was created. One day, maybe he'll tell me. Either way, I'm glad he came back into my life. *Our* lives."

Ehren gives me a steady, knowing look, and I feel heat rising on my cheeks. I swallow and focus on papers in front of me.

"We should get back to work," I distract. "If Jessalynn discovers you're not working hard enough, who knows what task she'll assign you next."

Ehren grimaces dramatically. "You're right. I don't want to imagine what she could dredge up next."

Felixe disappears from the table and reappears, curled up in my lap. I give him a couple smooth strokes as he snuggles closer. I hide a smile and reach for the journal. I grab up a pen and begin to fill in my journey, taking down my own history. It feels so normal, so calming. Somehow, even with a great distance between us, Alak has found a way to ground me yet again.

CHAPTER NINE

ASTRA

The night shift is the longest shift. According to Sama, this shift is usually run by volunteers who don't mind staying up all night. I definitely did not volunteer, but I'm not about to complain. I have a feeling Jessalynn is purposely pushing us, looking for a reason not to support our cause. If we want to win the game, we have to play by her rules.

Having just finished dinner, I lean outside the dining hall where I promised to meet Kai. The late summer sun is still setting, but it's already noticeably darker than when I entered the dining hall a little over half an hour ago. The door to the dining hall opens and laughter drifts out. I glance to the side, hoping to see Kai, but it's three teens, laughing and joking. I smile to myself as they walk past, likely heading off to carefree adventures. I envy them a bit.

I lean my head against the wall and close my eyes, inhaling deeply. What I wouldn't give to be that carefree again. Then again, I'm not willing to trade the friendships I've formed.

"Falling asleep already?" A cold voice cuts into my thoughts, making my eyes jerk open. Kai stands a few feet away, his eyebrows arched and arms crossed.

I push away from the wall. "I got bored waiting for you."

He shakes his head. "I hope you're up to this. Night shift isn't for the weak." Something in me bristles at his tone.

"Well, then I'm definitely up for the challenge," I reply, sounding a little more snappish than I mean to.

His gray eyes study me for a moment before he finally extends his hand to me. I stare at it and lift an eyebrow. He sighs.

"I assume you don't know where we are going."

Right. He'll wisp us there. Without another word I place my hand in his. He closes his warm, rough fingers around mine. The outside of the dining hall disappears, quickly replaced by trees. I peer around at my new surroundings as Kai releases my hand like it's a poisonous barb.

"This is the northeast section," Kai explains, sounding bored. "It's one of eight guarded areas."

"What are the other areas?" I ask curiously, still looking around, absorbing as many details as I can.

Kai sighs as if it's a burden to answer. "The mountainside area is divided up into four sections based on direction—North, South, East, and West. This is the northern most section of the eastern area—the part we guard. Then there are two sets of guards that patrol the valley below. The other two sections guard the cave pass."

I raise my eyebrows. "The cave pass? Like a way through the mountain without having to climb over?"

"Yes. But that's not our concern tonight. Tonight, our only concern is making sure that the eastern perimeter remains secure."

He looks past me to two figures approaching through the trees. One of them raises their hand in greeting to Kai, who returns it before the other figures wisp away.

"Were those the guards we're replacing?" I ask, still looking at the area where they stood moments before. Kai nods and walks forward. I follow him.

"So, what exactly does guard duty entail?"

He pauses, turning his head to me, glaring in response. I refuse to shrink away.

"Well?" I press, crossing my arms. "Do we just stalk through the woods glaring at trees?"

He shakes his head and starts walking again. I have to walk quickly to keep up with his long strides. He mumbles something under his breath that sounds an awful lot like swearing. I'm wondering if he's actually going to answer when he stops abruptly, and I almost crash into him.

"Just keep your eyes out for anything suspicious. We should be the only people in this area of woods. You see anyone else or sense anything amiss, you just let me know." I open my mouth to ask for clarification, but he holds up his hand, silencing me. "Just guard."

I sigh. This night is going to be dreadfully boring. Then, Kai suddenly shifts. Where he was standing moments ago, a larger than usual gray wolf now stands, blinking at me with familiar cold gray eyes. My mouth drops open.

"You're a shifter?"

The wolf cocks his head, his expression saying *Obviously*. I shake my head, unable to hide my smile. Before I can comment further, the wolf—Kai—turns and bounds away through the woods.

"Wait!" I cry, racing after him.

I run through the trees and catch him disappearing

behind more rocks and bushes. I do my best to keep up, but he's a wolf familiar with the forest, whereas I'm a simple human who has no idea where I am. After a few minutes, I stop, breathless and frustrated. I suppose guard duty with Kai will be guard duty on my own. Bram would flip. That thought, at least, makes me smile with an odd sense of satisfaction.

I sigh and resign myself to my fate. I have no idea what the perimeters of my area are, so I decide to send out my cloud of magic and sense as much area at a time as I can. As my magic tumbles out, I register all the trees, plants, and wildlife. So much of the mountain teems with magic. My scholar side wishes I'd brought along my journal to take notes and make sketches of things. My logical side reminds me that I'm not here to explore. I'm here on guard duty, whatever that entails.

I'm not sure how long I wander the woods alone. The sun sets completely, replaced by a silver crescent moon peeking out from behind deep blue clouds. The darkness makes it hard to see the uneven, rocky ground and I stumble constantly, falling at least twice, my dress getting stuck in bramble bushes both times. I expect sleepiness to creep up, but my afternoon nap seems to be enough to give me the energy I need so far. There's also something invigorating about the night air.

I keep my net of magic expanded around me as I stumble through the woods, so I'm not surprised when a large gray wolf stalks out of a nearby bush behind me.

"Decided to check up on me, Kai?" I ask, not even bothering to turn.

I feel a twinge of magic behind me when Kai shifts from a wolf back into a man.

"How did you know it was me?" he asks, his voice mostly flat, but there's a hint of curiosity there.

I turn to face him. "Because I can sense your magic."

He frowns. "How?"

Despite his somewhat demanding tone, I can sense his genuine interest.

I cock my head and raise my eyebrows. "Is that so unusual?"

"I'm not sure," he replies with a casual shrug. "Most people I've just met usually don't recognize me in my wolf form so quickly, especially when they aren't even looking at me." He pauses, glancing around, his scowl deepening before his eyes go wide, and he nods as if he's just figured out a complicated puzzle. "It's you."

It's my turn to scowl. "What's me?"

"I couldn't feel it as much in my wolf form, but as a human—the magic in the air is different. You're doing something, aren't you?"

"I guess. I'm just sensing everything around me with my magic. Staying alert. You basically abandoned me in the middle of a strange forest, so I need to be aware of my surroundings," I reply, sounding a little defensive.

He nods, crossing his arms as he surveys me. "And it doesn't exhaust your magic? To stay so alert?"

I shake my head. "No. It takes barely any of my magic at all."

"Interesting," he muses.

I shift, uneasy under his steady gaze. "Well, shouldn't we keep moving? Or does guard duty mean standing in one spot?"

Something akin to amusement flickers in his eyes, and I notice a smile playing around the edges of his lips.

"How old are you?" he asks, something unreadable on his face.

"Eighteen. What does that have to do with anything? How old are you?"

He actually chuckles as he relaxes. "I'm twenty-eight." His eyes twinkle in the moonlight. "You remind me of my sister."

And just like that, a shadow crosses his face, and he's back to the harsh Kai I've come to expect.

"How old is your sister?" I ask quietly, but somehow I already know his answer.

He turns his back to me. "She was your age when she died."

Magic swirls around him as he shifts back into his wolf form. I grit my teeth. His shifting works perfectly to avoid further conversation. He takes a few steps, but instead of bounding off to leave me alone, he turns his large head and gives it a slight jerk.

"You want me to follow you?"

The wolf nods. It's actually quite odd to see a wolf nod.

"Fine," I mumble with a shrug, "but even if you make my mauling look like an accident, Bram and Ehren will still kill you."

I swear amusement flickers in his eyes before he leads me through the forest. He still has a huge advantage over me in his wolf form, but since he isn't purposefully trying to get away this time, I manage to stay relatively by his side. When we come to a small clearing, he shifts back into a human. I study him as he changes.

"How do you do that?"

"What? Shift?" he asks, acting like I asked the dumbest question possible. "It's magic."

I roll my eyes. "I know that. But what's the process? How does your magic work?"

He crosses his arms, scrutinizing me. "What does it matter?"

"I think . . . I think I'd like to try it. See if I can shift," I confess, color rising in my cheeks.

He gives a mirthless laugh and shakes his head. "It's not something just anyone can do. You have to be born a shifter."

I jut my chin out stubbornly. "I still want to try."

"You can't," he insists. "You need to have a shifter bloodline. Do you have a shifter bloodline? No. You can't shift."

He says it so firmly and matter-of-factly I want nothing more than to prove him wrong.

"Maybe you're right," I reply, waving my hand like I couldn't care less. "But humor me. How does your magic work?"

He sighs and shakes his head, glancing off to the side. "Fine. Not that it will do you any good whatsoever, but fine." He pauses, searching for the right words. "As a shifter, there's always a part of me that is the wolf and always a part of me that is human. When I want to shift into the wolf, I simply reach inside my magic and pull that part of me forward. When I'm ready to switch back, I do the same thing, but with the human side."

I nod, taking it all in. "And does it take magic to maintain your wolf side? Does it drain you?"

He shakes his head. "No. I just need to use magic for the actual shifting. My wolf form is as natural to me as my human form, so it doesn't drain my magic. If it were even possible for you to shift, I would imagine you would have to constantly tap into your magic, making it even more impossible."

I consider him for a moment before asking quietly, "Does it hurt?"

"Not really," he says with a shrug. "There's a brief moment where it's uncomfortable, but it's not painful and it's fleeting."

I nod. "Okay." Nerves swell in my stomach. "I want to try. Can you shift again and let my magic sense how your magic works?"

He arches an eyebrow.

"Please? Just once more. Into a wolf. If it doesn't work, then nothing changes. But if it does work and I can shift . . ."

He sighs. "All right. Once. I'll shift once." He pauses, hesitating.

"What is it?" I press.

"I just don't normally shift so much so close together. I usually give my magic more time to replenish," he admits.

"If you need more time—"

He cuts me off with a wave of his hand.

"I'll be fine. I just won't shift back immediately." He narrows his eyes. "So, don't do anything stupid that would require my human form."

I scowl at him. He rolls his neck and loosens his shoulders.

"Okay, let me know when your magic is ready to sense mine," he mumbles.

I pull in my net of magic and focus it all on him. I can feel the warmth of his magic swirling inside him as he pulls it to the surface, preparing to shift. His eyes widen slightly as my magic presses in on him, realizing for the first time exactly how strong my magic may be.

"Choose a form you're most familiar with," he suggests. "If you had a familiar, I would suggest that form, but since you don't, pick an animal you can envision the clearest. I don't want to have to abandon my post to take you to a Healer because you've turned yourself into some odd hybrid creature."

I nod, taking his advice to heart.

"Here we go," he grumbles.

My magic flexes around him, and I sense the change even before he starts to physically show signs of it. I close my eyes, seeing flashes of twisting gold as his magic flips and transforms. It's electric and intense. My magic brushes against his, sensing every step and turn. The shift only takes a few seconds, but the magic it takes is intense, leaving me breathless. The magic stills, and I open to find Kai's wolf eyes locked on me.

I reach for my magic and mentally replay what I just witnessed. I swallow and lick my lips as fear and doubt start to swirl. I push my fears down. I can do this. I pull the new memory of magic forward and focus it, envisioning Felixe. He may not be my familiar, but I feel connected to him, even though he's nowhere near me right now. I guide the magic and let it take the lead. It twists around me, an ice-cold wave surging through me. I gasp. It's not painful exactly, but it's not a pleasant feeling. But I don't pull away. I forge forward, embracing the magic. Suddenly, the world shifts and changes around me. Everything feels different. I look up at Kai. *Up.* I'm below him now. I look down and realize I'm now crouched on four tiny silver paws. I turn my head and discover a silver tail, which I flick triumphantly at Kai. If a wolf can look shocked, that's exactly the expression Kai's wolf face holds.

Kai scowls before he arches his head back and howls. I give a yap. It's an odd feeling not having true words. Kai cocks his head in amusement before turning and bounding off. I race after him, leaping with ease in my Fae Fox form. I can easily see why Kai prefers to prowl the woods as a wolf. As an animal, navigating the rocky ground is a million times easier. Not to mention that all my senses are heightened. I can smell every animal, human, and plant nearby and my ears pick up every sound echoing around me. Even my eyes can see in the dark almost as clearly as they can in daylight. However, while it might not drain Kai's magic to maintain his animal form, I can feel the flow and steady depletion of mine. It's not a drastic pull—I can easily stay a Fae Fox for a decent amount of time—but it's definitely draining at a noticeable pace.

Kai constantly looks over his shoulder at me as we romp through the woods, following a trail familiar to him. I catch his scent on most of the path and can tell exactly where he's been patrolling. At first, he stays ahead of me, but eventually he seems content to let me fall into step beside him. Just like in human form, however, I have to take several steps for every one of his. Maybe next time I'll try for a larger animal.

Time passes differently as a fox, so I'm not sure how long it's been when I finally release the magic, springing back into my human form. At first, I'm afraid my clothes will be gone, leaving me standing exposed in the middle of the forest, but when I look down I'm relieved to see I'm still fully dressed.

"It's part of the magic," Kai's voice calls from behind me.

I spin to face him. I didn't even realize he changed back when I did.

"How?"

He shrugs. "No idea. It just works that way." He pauses and then his face brightens, eyes gleaming, as he asks, "So, how did you like it?"

I grin. "It was amazing! I don't know why you ever turn back into a human."

He laughs, a true genuine laugh. "Well, I don't fancy chasing squirrels for every meal."

I chuckle. "Yeah, I guess being a human has its benefits."

He watches me for a moment, his eyes bright. I feel a little self-conscious under the intensity of his gaze, and I shift uncomfortably, wrapping my arms around myself.

"What is it?" I ask, averting my gaze.

He smiles sadly. "It's just been a long time since I've been able to run through the woods like that with anyone. I didn't realize how much I missed it. How alone I've felt."

I bring my eyes up to meet his. "I didn't take you as someone who needed others." I realize how harsh that may have sounded and try to amend my statement. "Not that you're unfeeling or anything. I just—"

"No, you're right," he cuts me off. "I've never been a terribly sociable person. I've never really needed people. I lost my parents when I was a boy, and it was just my sister Leyana and I most of my life. I'm used to being alone and when I lost her . . ."

He drops off and looks away, but the pain in his expression is so clear I can almost feel it. I take a step toward him and place my hand on his arm.

"You loved your sister very much. I can see that."

He looks down at me and nods. "Losing her was the most painful day of my life."

"What happened?" I ask tentatively.

He takes a deep breath. I expect him to deflect, but he doesn't. He sits down on a nearby boulder, placing his elbows on his knees and clasping his hands together. I ease down next to him.

"You don't have to tell me if you don't want to," I say softly, my voice barely above a whisper.

He shakes his head. "No, it's all right." He looks up at me and his eyes meet mine. "She was killed by hunters." I gasp and he turns his head, fixing his gaze at the trees in front of us. "We were in our wolf forms, but we traveled too far from the Valley for our magic to allow us to transform back into humans. When the hunters found us, they just saw two large wolves. Prize pelts. Normally, we could outrun them, but there were too many. They had us surrounded. They shot her with three arrows."

His voice breaks and he takes a steadying breath, tears glistening in his eyes. I place my hand on his arm, and he gives me a grateful look.

"I got an arrow in my hip but managed to get away. I killed two of the hunters, but there were at least three more. I wanted to keep fighting for her but . . ." A tear slides down his cheek.

"But she was already gone," I finish for him, and he nods.

"I wonder every day what I could have done differently. Every day for the past six years, I've replayed her final minutes in my head. What could have changed if I'd been more alert? I should've scented a group of men that large. She shouldn't have died."

He bows his head, placing his face in his hands. We're already sitting close on the boulder, so it doesn't take much movement from me to slip my arm around him.

"Hey," I whisper, leaning my head against his arm. "You can't think like that."

He raises his swollen eyes to me and shakes his head. "How would you know?"

His voice is harsh, and it stings, but I don't break my gaze from his.

"Because I know what it's like to constantly debate what you could have done differently—to think about all the signs you should have seen and somehow missed."

"What? I thought your brother was still alive."

I pull my gaze from his and stare off into the woods. "It's a long story, but while Kato is still alive right now, he's lost to me. And I don't know if he's ever coming back. He's somehow alive and dead all at the same time. The part of him I've always known is gone." I pause and then gesture to the scars along my chin and neck. "Last time I saw him, he gave me these."

Kai frowns, studying the scars. "I'm sorry." His voice is barely above a whisper.

I take a shuddering breath. "Some scars are physical and some run deeper. Either way, we have to find a way to heal and move on, though it's not always easy."

The image of Caedios being stabbed through with the sword flashes into my mind, and I squeeze my eyes shut, pushing back the tears and the fear. Kai senses the change in my mood and sits up a little straighter.

"Well, we're quite a pair, aren't we," he says, laughing mirthlessly.

He sighs and stands, turning and offering a hand to help me up. I take it and he pulls me to my feet. "I rarely talk about Leyana. Actually, I never talk about Leyana."

I tilt my head. "Then why now?"

He smiles, but it doesn't quite go all the way to his eyes. "Because you remind me so much of her."

He shakes his head and turns away, walking through the brush. I follow him. He steps through the trees, holding back a branch for me to follow him. As I pass him, I realize we're at the edge of a cliff, looking down into the valley. I gasp at the sight. The view is perfect. It's early morning, the first hints of light on the horizon. Down below life is just starting to stir. A few candles and hearths are lit, smoke spiraling from a handful of chimneys. And yet, it's still quiet and peaceful.

"This was her favorite place to come," Kai says quietly just behind my shoulder. "She used to say she felt like a goddess looking down on her creation." He chuckles softly.

"I can understand that feeling," I breathe.

"Your spirit is so much like hers. It's a pity you didn't get to meet. You would've been fast friends. And then she would have forced you to be my friend as well. She knew I didn't care for people and was always forcing me to find friends. I think she knew, somehow, she would be gone one day and didn't want me to be alone. I feel a little guilty she failed in that aspect."

I turn my head and look at Kai's face as he stares down into the valley below.

"Why did you volunteer to house us and work guard duty with me? If you don't care for people."

He throws his head back and laughs. It's a strange sound coming from him, even more startling against the quiet of the early morning. He must read the shock in my face because he explains.

"I didn't volunteer for anything. Jessalynn forced you all on me."

My eyes are wide as I ask, "Why? Surely she knew you would hate it."

He shrugs. "Jessalynn is . . . odd. She has a natural way with people, though. She knows what people need. She can read people and situations like no one else. It's what makes her a great leader. I think she knew, in a way, that I needed to meet you, and knew I wouldn't do it unless pushed."

I grin and turn my eyes back to the waking valley. "So, I guess you don't hate me?"

Kai chuckles. "I guess not."

For a few minutes we stand in silence and watch the valley wake below. Then, on Kai's insistence, we make one more round through the forest before our replacements arrive. Kai's face returns to a blank slate, but I can see a little something glimmering in his eyes that wasn't there before. It might be happiness, but I'm not sure. I hope it is. Happiness is something we all need a little of right now.

CHAPTER TEN

ALAK

It takes a week for all of the elders of Clan Wallish to gather. They're a loud, clambering lot who drink from sunup to sundown. My people. Kato finds their lack of decorum frustrating, however, and spends most of the week sulking. The last member of the Clan to arrive is Aidan Murray, the youngest elder, and the one with connections to Clan Loudain, one of the Clans we have yet to hear from.

In the days leading up to their meeting, Kato has me researching every bit of information I can about the different members. My brain feels overloaded with facts, and most of them aren't even useful. Yet Kato has stored away every little bit of information I've been able to sneak away.

Ian has kept true to his word and has barely given me a moment's peace. Everywhere I go, his eyes follow. Once I realized he was literally trailing me every second possible, I started going to random places throughout the fortress and doing the most ridiculous things, acting as suspicious as I could. There was a lot of looking over my shoulder and pretending to hide things under my shirt. Once Ian figured out what I was doing, he was furious, but at least he let up a bit.

The elders have been locked in a room continuously for the last three days, taking both breakfast and lunch in the room and emerging right before dinner each night. No one besides the servants has come or gone while the meeting has been in session. I know for a fact. I've been stationed outside the bloody room the entire time. It's getting rather difficult to look casual when you're forced to spend your whole bloody day in the same damn courtyard watching a locked iron door. Thankfully, I brought a book along. I suppose it looks more natural to sit under the tree outside their meeting all day reading. As long as no one notices how often my eyes stray from the page or how few pages actually get turned, that is.

"That must be an awfully interesting book," Aine says, slinking toward me and taking a seat next to me on the ground.

"What do you want Aine?" I growl, scooting away from her.

"I just thought you might want some company," she huffs, crossing her arms like a petulant child.

"Well, you were wrong," I reply curtly, standing and brushing bits of dried grass from my pants.

"I was also going to ask if you wanted me to find you any food, but since my presence isn't wanted . . ."

She trails off, jerking to her feet and turning like she's about to stalk away. She pauses halfway across the courtyard and turns her head to look at me.

"I'm not going to stop you from leaving, if that's what you're waiting for," I say, grinning and crossing my arms.

She glares and stomps toward me. "What's so wrong

with me? Am I not pretty enough for you? I'm prettier than that pathetic Astra."

My eyes flash, but I grit my teeth to keep from snapping at her. I refuse to give her fuel. I will not let her bait me. I spin away from her and plop back onto the ground beneath the tree.

"Go away, Aine. There are dozens of young members of Clan Wallish that came with the elders. Surely one of them will find you acceptable for a good frolic in the sheets."

Her face turns bright red as she seethes. I grin to myself.

"Alak Dunne," she spits, "one of these days I will—"

"You'll what?" I snap, looking up at her. "Finally leave me the hell alone? Please do."

She opens her mouth with what I'm sure is a witless retort, but she's interrupted—thank the gods—by the door opening. I leap to my feet as the elders of Clan Wallish spill into the courtyard, most of them walking in pairs, chatting with one another. The last to exit is Lord Wallish. He spots me across the courtyard and beelines in my direction.

"Evenin' Lord Wallish," I greet him, inclining my head as he approaches.

"Evenin'," he returns. He shifts his eyes to Aine on my left. "I suppose you two will be running straight to Kato?"

I shrug. "It depends. Is there anything to report to him?"

Lord Wallish hesitates and then nods slowly. "Aye. We have reached a decision."

"And . . ." Aine jumps in, a little too eagerly.

I hold my breath as Lord Wallish pauses, weighing his next words carefully.

"And you can tell Master Kato that he will receive his final answer in a formal meeting tomorrow morning." His eyes shift from me to Aine and back. "There are a few terms we need drawn up to make things official. These things cannot be rushed."

I nod my head, but I can sense Aine coiling like a snake behind me.

"We understand," I say firmly without a glance toward Aine. "I will pass the information on to Kato. I know he is eager for your reply."

Lord Wallish gives us each a parting nod before following the path the other members took out of the court-yard. Once he's gone, Aine turns to me, infuriated.

"How can you let him walk away like that, not telling you a thing?" she hisses.

I brush past her, eager to leave the courtyard.

"Alak!" she calls after me, storming up to my side.

I stop abruptly, spinning to face her. She stumbles to a stop.

"Look, Aine, this is a delicate proceeding. If we push them or act rashly, it all falls apart."

She lets out a small huff and looks me directly in the eye as she sneers, "Are you sure you don't want everything to fall apart?"

I roll my eyes, shaking my head and walking away from her. "You and your brother are ridiculous. You know that?"

As expected, she chases after me. "You're the ridiculous one! Pining after a girl that wants nothing to do with you. Nothing," she spits. "You're pathetic."

My anger riles inside me, and it takes every ounce of willpower I have not to release it. I clench my fist at my side, my other other tightening around my book, but I keep walk-ing, quickening my pace.

"Admit it, Alak," Aine snaps. "You're going to continue

pathetically sitting on the sidelines forever, longing for a girl who'll never want you. It's a pathetic waste."

Unable to hold it in any longer, I spin to face her. "Want to know why I'm not interested in you? Because you're a bitch."

She recoils like I've struck her. And I don't feel the slightest bit guilty. I take another step toward her.

"You're a bitch with weak-ass magic. Astra is stronger and more powerful than you'll ever be. Not to mention she's ten times more beautiful."

Aine snarls and her magic whips through the air, sending her conjured metal spikes toward me. My Syphon magic is on full alert, so I sense her attack before she unleashes her magic, blocking her blades effortlessly with a wicked grin.

"See what I mean?" She's good and riled now, and, as horrible as it may be, I relish it. "Weak."

She goes to strike again, but before she can, I wisp to my room. I can't deal with her anymore. I'm a little concerned Ian will be in the room, but I'm happy to find it empty. I run a hand through my hair and toss the book on my bed. This whole situation is the worst. I'm ready for it to be over. I want to be away from Aine and back by Astra's side, even if she is with someone else. I want to laugh with Ehren and go back and forth with Bram.

I glance toward the bed. I long to curl up and sleep the rest of the day away, but I need to find Kato before Aine. With a sigh, I head from my room and knock on Kato's door. When he doesn't answer I wisp outside the village pub, The Crinkled Sheep. I go inside and allow my eyes to adjust to the dim light. Sure enough, Kato sits in the corner playing cards and drinking with Ian, Niall, and a couple other young men from Periola. I saunter over to them and clap Kato on the shoulder. He grins up at me.

"I take it, since you've left your post, you have good news?" he says, a thinly veiled threat lurking beneath his words.

I nod and force a grin. "They've come to a conclusion."

"Excellent!" Kato declares, starting to rise.

"But," I add quickly, "Lord Wallish said he'll give their final decision at a more formal meeting tomorrow morning."

Kato sinks back in his seat, frowning. Ian and Niall exchange concerned glances, but I grin, pulling a chair up to the table.

"Don't worry. Lord Wallish said the delay was due to needing to draw something up. Makes me think they've agreed to join and are creating an official treaty. This could be very good," I say, forcing as much cheer into my voice as I can, even though the words I say make me physically ill.

Kato nods, considering my words. "I suppose you're right. Still, this is taking longer than I was expecting."

"I know what you mean," Niall mumbles. "All this diplomacy is taking forever."

Kato and Ian nod in agreement.

"But diplomacy is the most peaceful path. We do want peace, correct?" I jump in, glancing between the three of them.

Kato nods emphatically. "Yes, naturally." He nods even more firmly. "You're right. I think this is a good sign. We should toast!"

The whole table cheers as Kato calls for the barmaid, requesting more ale for everyone on his tab, which I highly doubt he'll actually have to pay off before we leave. Once we all have fresh glasses in front of us, Kato raises his in the air.

"To a free, united Athiedor!" he says, loudly enough his voice carries across the room.

"To Athiedor!" our table echoes as we clink our mugs together. I glance around as I take a sip, taking in the other patrons watching us warily with bright, agreeing eyes. Kato does know how to win people over.

Unfortunately.

I DON'T KNOW if it's the amount of ale he consumes or the restlessness of waiting, but Kato is irritable the rest of night. When morning comes with the promise of answers, it's a relief. We start our day with a normal breakfast, then follow a servant to the room where the elders have been meeting for the past few days. Lord Wallish takes his seat at the head of the table, the other nine elders finding their respective places. After they've all taken their seats, we find ours. Kato sits opposite Lord Wallish, as expected, and I take the seat at his right with Kayleigh seated directly across from me. Aine, much to my dismay, sits to my right with Ian sitting across from her. Caitlyn and Niall opt to take a place along the back wall where Caitlyn can have a better view of everyone to read their emotions and auras. Once we're all seated, Lord Wallish motions for a servant to close the door.

"First, on behalf of the entire Clan of Wallish, we would like to thank you for your patience regarding this matter. We know you probably expected an answer with a little more haste, but we had much to weigh," Lord Wallish says, his voice confident and full of authority as it rings through the room.

"Of course!" Kato replies, inclining his head and smiling

as if he hasn't been essentially pouting for the past week, constantly complaining about the process. "We are pleased to give you whatever time you need, but you have come to decision, correct?"

Lord Wallish offers him a tight smile. "Indeed." He motions to someone on the side wall who rushes forward to Kato with a scroll. "We laid out the terms of our agreement with you."

The servant places the scroll in front of Kato and he unrolls it as the servant scurries away. Thick, curling script flows across the page. I let out a low whistle. This is an official document of the highest order, drawing on centuries of Athiedor tradition. Even Kato can sense the importance of the document before him. As he scans the words however, he scowls.

"Forgive for my ignorance, Lord Wallish," Kato says, a hint of aggravation in his voice, "but Yallik is not a language with which I am familiar."

A grin twitches around the corners of Lord Wallish's mouth. He has the upper hand, and he's enjoying every second of it.

"My apologies, Master Kato," he replies, his eyes glistening, "but Athiedor tradition begs that the document be written in Yallik. Perhaps one of your companions can translate."

Lord Wallish gestures to me and Kayleigh. Kato shifts his gaze to me.

"I can . . . ," Ian starts, leaning in toward the scroll, but Kato jerks it away, sliding it in front of me.

"Alak, if you will," Kato says as I straighten the scroll.

I nod and clear my throat, staring down at the words. It takes some effort but, thanks to all the translations I did for

Astra and Cadewynn back in Embervein, my Yallik is sharper than it has been in years.

"They agree to an alliance with you under four conditions," I translate, tracing my finger along the words. Kato raises his eyebrows in question but stays silent, so I continue.

"Condition One: they reserve the right to select which members of their Clan go to war."

Kato nods. "As long as all the ranks are properly filled, I have no objection. Next."

"Condition Two: Athiedor is to be given its freedom within a week of you being crowned king."

Kato nods again. "I swear to you that will be my first order of business as king. Athiedor has been enslaved far too long. Next."

I lick my lips and continue. "Condition Three: Clan Wallish can dissolve these terms if the approval of all seven Clans is not gained."

Kato frowns at this one and narrows his eyes.

"You cannot logically expect Clan Wallish to stand against our brother Clans," Lord Wallish states simply.

"I suppose that would be counterproductive," Kato agrees stiffly. Then he relaxes his shoulders. "Though I do not foresee it being a problem, as we already have the support of four other Clans."

Lord Wallish starts and even I'm unable to hide my surprise.

"Four? Last I heard only three had given you their full support," Lord Wallish says steadily.

Kato glances at Kayleigh and she clears her throat. "We received word from Clan O'Brick last night, and they have agreed to an alliance."

Kayleigh reaches into her pocket and withdraws a letter,

passing it down the table to Lord Wallish. He jerks it up, first examining the broken seal, and then studying the contents of the letter itself. When he's done, he shows no emotion. He only nods and passes it back to Kayleigh.

Kato grins and turns back to me. "What is the fourth condition?"

I drop my eyes back down the treaty. I read the last condition through once, immediately reading it again to be sure I've translated it correctly. My heart races.

"Well?" Kato presses impatiently.

"The fourth condition," I translate, struggling to keep my voice steady, "is that they can choose at any time to break the treaty in favor of supporting your sister, should she be able to promise Athiedor the same terms."

"What?" Kato roars, flames flickering in his eyes as he slams his fist on the table.

Lord Wallish meets Kato's eyes, completely unintimidated. "Did you think we would blindly follow you with your sister still out there? We have ears everywhere. We know she has been made the official Court Sorceress under Prince Ehren. She may be able to offer us our freedom without forcing us to go to war against the whole of Callenia. We would be fools to ignore her power."

Kato shakes his head. "Ehren is a runaway prince with no power. His court is little more than a joke. Astra cannot offer you what I can. She may have magical power, but her influence over the workings of Callenia is no greater than a court jester."

Lord Wallish shrugs. "Then our deal is secure. You have only to sign. Just be aware, should conditions change, so might our alliance."

The air around us is heavy. I eye Kato warily, expecting

him to burst into flames at any moment. After a moment of staring down Lord Wallish, he relaxes back into his seat, grinning, his fingers linked across his chest.

"So be it," Kato says. "Are there any more conditions?"

I shake my head, releasing a sigh of relief. "No, that's all."

Kato pulls the scroll in front of him and asks, "Where do I sign?"

Lord Wallish beckons to a servant who rushes forward with a pen. Without hesitation, Kato signs the treaty with a flourish.

"There," he grins, "now we are in business together."

"Assuming the remaining Clans also join the alliance," an older man further down the table says firmly.

"As to that," Aidan Murray jumps in, pulling a letter from his breast coat pocket, "I may have news on what Clan Loudain plans to do."

Lord Wallish arches his eyebrows as the letter is passed down to Kato. I glance over and catch a flash of the official green seal of Clan Loudain bearing the crest of two snakes twisting together. Kato breaks the seal and makes quick work of reading the letter. I barely dare to breathe. Kato's face breaks into a smile and my heart plummets even before he speaks.

"Clan Loudain has given me their full support!" he declares, waving the letter in triumph.

A few of the elders share his smile, but just as many look wary, almost disappointed at the turn of events. Lord Wallish forces a smile of his own.

"Then it looks like we may be in business after all. Which Clan do you have yet to hear from?"

Kato glances at Kayleigh and she answers. "Clan

McDullun. They requested a meeting around the same time you did, but we have been unable to fulfill that request due to our presence here in Periola."

My heart sinks further. Clan McDullun may play hard to get, but they're known to be relative pushovers. Once they hear the other Clans have joined Kato, they will inevitably join. I can tell by the look on Lord Wallish's face he's thinking the same thing. That condition was added as a last hope to avoid aligning with Kato. As much as Athiedor wants to be free, this isn't how they want to do it. They don't want to go to war.

"We will reach out to them immediately and finalize everything. Then, as I believe tradition dictates, we will arrange a meeting between all seven Clan leaders at Fortress Mullidain to sign a final treaty," Kato declares.

I jerk my gaze to his face, my eyes wide, and I can only imagine that Lord Wallish is doing the same. Fortress Mullidain is a sacred place among the Clans. Back when Athiedor was free, it was considered the capital. It's neutral territory. But that's not common knowledge. It's a protected secret. For Kato to know . . .

I slide my gaze to Lord Wallish, who sits very straight and still, his mouth set in a firm line. I shake my head almost imperceptibly. I'm not the one who shared this information, and I want him to know it.

"It seems you are more aware of our traditions than I thought," Lord Wallish says at length.

Kato's smile is lethal. "I would have been a fool to enter into any deals without knowing as much about the Clans as possible. I have many reliable sources, Lord Wallish. Ones that know about your ties to Clan Dughlas."

Lord Wallish blanches and several elders exchange

nervous glances. I swallow and take a steadying breath. Kato is showing just enough of his hand to let them know he truly holds the cards. He pushes away from the table and rises.

"Well, I suppose we're done here. I look forward to our future negations."

Kato turns and strides out of the room, servants shuffling quickly to open the door for him. Caitlyn and Niall follow him out as Aine, Ian, and I rise from the table. I take one last glance over my shoulder at Lord Wallish before I follow. He arches his eyebrows, and I can read his unvoiced question. I give a quick nod. I can fix this. I have to fix this.

I want to rush off and write Astra immediately, but I don't get the chance. As soon as all of us are in the courtyard, Kato wisps us away in a ring of fire to his room. I blink at the sudden change of scenery.

"Well, that went well." Kato grins.

"I don't like the extra conditions they threw in," Ian mumbles. "They're looking for an out."

Kato shrugs. "They can look all they want. We essentially have the support of all the Clans now, and there's no way Astra can get to them before a final treaty is signed."

"I say we celebrate!" Aine grins. "Let's go to the dining hall and see if we can't scrounge up something pleasant to toast with."

Kato grins. "That sounds like an excellent idea."

I try to beg off, but they won't let me. I'm forced to spend the rest of the day celebrating. With Ian eying me suspiciously, I even have to force a cheerful spirit. Damn him. They drink to celebrate, but I drink to drown my worries. I keep expecting them to finally stop drinking, but they don't. Somehow, we "celebrate" all day. I stop drinking shortly after noon but am forced to sit by, grinning and laughing. It's giving me a headache.

Finally, I manage to escape. I make my way to a lonely garden and lean against a wall, breathing in the evening air. I'm so intent on thinking up a way to unravel Kato's plans, I don't realize Aine followed me.

"Done celebrating already?" she slurs, staggering toward me. Normal Aine is bad enough, but Drunk Aine is a nightmare.

"Go away, Aine," I say, shoving her.

"No," she says sharply.

She grabs my wrist, and I feel something prick my skin.

"Shite!" I yell, yanking away, looking down at the small pinprick of red blooming on my wrist. I shoot my eyes back up to her. "What did you . . . ?"

I feel the effects of what can only be a potion, one of Ian's specialties. I feel weak, my knees giving out as the world around me swirls and tilts. I collapse on the ground and look up at Aine in disbelief.

"You're mine, Alak. All mine."

She kneels down next to me and pulls me toward her, pressing her lips to mine and forcing her tongue in my mouth. I maintain just enough control to jerk back.

"Stop," I plead, the words feeling fuzzy and thick on my tongue.

She runs a long finger down my cheek, and I try to will away the sensation, my stomach twisting.

"Don't pretend you don't like it," she purrs.

Every bit of me recoils against her touch, but the potion is in full effect, rendering me nearly helpless. She presses her lips to my neck, her hands tracing my body lower and lower. I think I'm going to be sick. I need out of this. I need to be with Astra right now more than ever to wash away the taste of Aine. I need . . .

"Felixe," I manage to choke out.

Aine pulls back, frowning. "What?"

"Felixe!" I call out, my eyes searching frantically. I need my familiar.

Felixe pops onto my shoulder, growling at Aine. Aine glares at him and reaches to touch my face. Felixe leaps forward and bites her. Hard. She screams and snaps back.

"You no-good little fox!" she snarls, clutching her bleeding finger.

"Get me away," I mutter to Felixe, holding onto what little consciousness I have left. "Get me far away. Somewhere safe."

The world twists and turns under the influence of Felixe's magic, everything turning silver and gray before fading into vague nothingness.

CHAPTER ELEVEN

ASTRA

The first morning after guard duty, I barely make it through breakfast before I go back to my room and crash. I almost sleep through lunch, but Bram comes and wakes me. Kai still acts cold when I'm with everyone else, but at night, when we resume our guard duty, he relaxes significantly. He's not what most people would consider friendly, but he doesn't abandon me again and even attempts the occasional conversation. Whenever he changes into his wolf form, I change into a Fae Fox. I consider trying a new animal, but I figure until I get used to this type of magic it's best to stick with what I know works.

On my second night of duty, I find a good balance between shifting and remaining human, so when I finish and head to breakfast I have enough energy. But, on the third morning, I remain a fox too long, and I can barely stand up straight after I return to my human form. Kai eyes me, scowling.

"Are you all right?" he asks, concern lacing his voice.

I smile. "Careful, Kai. If someone overheard they might think you care about someone other than yourself."

His shakes his head, but I catch the hint of a smile tugging at the corner of his mouth.

"I'll be fine. I just used a lot of magic. I simply need to rest," I reply, waving him off.

"At least let me wisp you down to where you're staying," he insists. "You'll kill yourself staggering down the mountain like a drunken mountain goat."

I snicker. "Fine. It's your fault I'm so drained anyway. You stayed in your wolf form too much."

"If you would have informed me your magic was draining this extensively, I would have changed back. You know that," he says, narrowing his eyes into a refined glare as only he can manage. "You just like being a fox."

I shrug, grinning. "It is rather freeing."

Two people wisp into view not far away. Our replacements. I give them a smile and a nod as Kai waves. Then, without warning, Kai places his hand on my arm and wisps me right outside Sama's dwelling.

"Thanks," I mumble, turning to go inside.

"Mistress Astra!" a voice calls.

I turn as a young boy rushes across the swinging bridgeway toward me. I arch an eyebrow.

"Yes?"

"Jessalynn has requested your presence in the meeting hall," the boy says, a little out of breath. "Immediately." Before I can ask for details, the boy wisps away.

I turn to Kai and find him scowling. "Do you think she already made her decision?"

"It has been four days," Kai replies. "But you should decline to attend. You need your sleep."

"One quick meeting won't kill me. Probably."

Kai rolls his eyes, extending his hand to me. "Well, let's get this over with."

I raise my eyebrows. "You're coming?"

"Once again, I am not letting you stagger around like a drunken mountain goat!" he cries. "Just take my hand."

"I can walk across a bridge without falling to my death," I protest, turning and taking a few steps in the direction of the meeting hall. Three steps into my independent stride, I stumble and fall against the guard rail, nearly tipping over the side.

"Damn it, Astra!" Kai yells, lunging forward and pulling me from the edge.

The next thing I know I'm outside the meeting hall, Kai's arms still holding me. I shake free.

"I tripped," I insist. "Just a normal trip."

"Well, thank goodness I was there to save you from your klutziness."

"I'm not klutzy!" I yell in exasperation.

"You're either klutzy or drained," Kai says, ticking the options off on his fingers. "Pick one."

I clench my teeth and place my hands on my hips. "You are insufferable."

"Nice to see you two are getting along pleasantly," Jessalynn cuts in.

I startle and spin around. Jessalynn stands directly behind me, eyes twinkling in amusement. Kaeya's by her side, grinning wickedly.

"Shall we go inside?" Jessalynn suggests, motioning to the door.

I open my mouth to reply, but snap it shut, nodding instead. Kai opens the door, holding it while the rest of us enter. I stomp past him and collapse into a chair near the end of the table across from Bram. Bram glances from me to Kai with a scowl. Ehren, who is leaning along the back wall talking to Cal, eyes me curiously.

"Everything okay?" Ehren asks. He leans in so he can keep his voice low, but he stays next to Cal.

I nod. "Kai's just an ass," I reply, loudly enough that I know he can hear me.

He shoots me a rude gesture, and Jessalynn grins with pure delight. Bram narrows his eyes threateningly at Kai.

"And I'm tired from being up all night." I glance at Jessalynn. "Are we starting soon?"

Jessalynn nods, still grinning. "We're just waiting on Brock and Makin to arrive."

I blush, feeling guilty that I didn't even notice they were missing. A quick glance to my left confirms Cal and Ehren are the only ones against the back wall.

"So," Jessalynn says, leaning forward in her chair and leaning on the table. "Why exactly are you so tired? What sort of physical activities have you and Kai been getting up to in my woods?"

I grit my teeth and clench my fists in my lap. Ehren shoots me a curious look, but Kai just shakes his head.

"I mean," Jessalynn says with a careless flick of her hand, "I can't imagine why someone would be this tired."

"Yes, because staying up constantly on guard for three nights in a row wouldn't make anyone irritable," I snap.

Jessalynn's feral grin grows, but she doesn't get a chance to respond before Brock wisps into the room with Makin in tow. Makin gives us a tired nod and takes his place next to Cal as Ehren takes a seat at the end of the table.

"Well, I guess that's everyone," Jessalynn says, scanning

the room. "So, I've decided to tell you my final decision, though I retain the right to change my mind at any time." Ehren nods expectantly, and I almost regret snapping at her moments earlier. "We will support your claim to the throne."

Ehren sits up straighter "Thank you. Your support means a lot."

Jessalynn shrugs. "I don't know what good the support of the bastard, banished offspring of the king will do you, but you have it, nonetheless. When you are ready for your war, let me know, and I will send volunteers. Emphasis on volunteers. I will not force my people to fight for your crown. But it seems your people"—she gestures at our whole group—"are excellent at winning over my people, so you already have several loyal allies. Even among those who were rather unexpected." I don't miss the glance toward Kai, and neither do the others.

"We will lend help wherever we can. All you need to do is ask. Of course, I can deny it if you're being ridiculous, but I am willing to help. I will even send some of my people with you to meet with King Naimon. They can guide your way, help with customs of which you may not be aware, and whatever else you require."

"Thank you, Jess," Ehren says, his eyes shining with gratitude.

Jessalynn offers him a genuine smile. "You're welcome, brother. I'll take volunteers for anyone who wants to accompany you. I'll give you time to gather your things and for those of you who require rest to get some, but we should be ready to show you to the under-mountain pass shortly after noon."

"The under-mountain pass?" Makin asks from the back wall. "You mean the caves?"

Jessalynn nods. "Yes. The pass through the caves takes a couple of days at most. If you wish to travel over the mountain, you're adding several hard days to your journey."

Makin looks uneasy but nods.

"Any more questions or comments?" Jessalynn asks, cocking her head.

"I'll go with them," Kai says from his spot on the wall.

Jessalynn's mouth drops open, her eyes going wide as she twists around in her chair. Even Kaeya and Brock can't hide their shock.

"Well now, Kai! Who would have thought you'd be among the first volunteers! Do you hate it here that much, or do you truly enjoy their company?"

Kai stands stiffly, betraying no emotion as he says, "If you don't want me to go—"

"Of course it's fine if you go," Jessalynn says with a dismissive wave of her hand. "I just enjoy being right." She pushes up from the table with both hands. "I suppose that wraps everything up. Meet me after lunch at the base of the waterfall, and we'll get you on your way."

With a wave of her hand, she blinks out of sight, Kaeya and Brock not far behind. Kai pushes off from the wall.

"Well, I'm going to grab some breakfast and then pack, I suppose," Kai says with a shrug.

He walks toward the exit, pausing, the door halfway open, and turns back and looks directly at Ehren.

"Don't let her go anywhere on her own until she's had a chance to rest," Kai says, his voice firm as he points at me. Ehren raises an eyebrow and glances sideways at me as Kai adds, "She drained too much magic last night shifting and she's weak."

With no further explanation he turns and leaves, the

door slamming shut behind him. Ehren spins to me and leans back, taking me in.

"What?" I ask sheepishly.

"Do you want to start with telling us when and how you learned to shift, or would you rather explain why you allowed your magic to drain?" Ehren asks, his eyes gleaming.

I groan. "I'm tired. Can we discuss it later?"

"Why don't we discuss it as I walk you back to your room," he suggests, standing.

I sigh and rise to my feet. "Kai is a worried old mother hen. I'm fine."

But even as I say the words, I waver slightly. Shit. I am pretty drained. Ehren tilts his head, crossing his arms and giving me knowing look.

"Fine," I concede, stifling a yawn.

"I'll come with you," Bram offers.

"Oh, yes!" Makin cries, throwing his arms in the air. "Let's all do a group escort."

I shoot him a glare but laugh as his grin turns into a yawn.

"Actually," Makin says, talking over his yawn. "I'm going to grab a bite to eat and then head to bed." He turns to Cal. "Are you going to escort Astra or come with me?"

Cal shrugs. "I've already eaten, and I really want to hear about the shifting, but if I don't go with you, you'll never be packed in time."

"What's that supposed to mean?" Makin demands, crossing his arms as he and Cal make their way out of the room.

"It means," Cal answers, doing his best not to look down as they step out onto the platform, "that your stuff is spread out everywhere, and it will take all morning to sort and pack it. I don't even know how you managed to make such a mess with what little you have."

"You're exaggerating. It's not nearly as bad as you make it sound."

The two continue arguing as they wind down the bridges and platforms leading to the base level. I shake my head, smiling as I turn to make my own way to bed.

After a few steps Ehren says, "Well, are you going to share?"

I glance from him to Bram and sigh. "There's not much to tell, really. Kai's a shifter and I was curious about his magic. I learned to shift by copying him."

"What kind of shifter is he?" Bram asks carefully.

"A wolf."

"That's . . . pretty impressive," Ehren says with a hint of awe.

"Wait, you two have been living in his home and didn't even know what he could do?" I ask, shooting them each a look of disbelief.

Ehren shrugs. "He was never really around. At night when we were actually there sleeping, he was out on patrol with you."

"That makes sense, I guess," I mumble, giving way to another yawn.

"He said you exhausted your magic. How?" Bram asks firmly.

"Well," I begin, struggling to string thoughts together. "He tends to transform into a wolf during guard duty. He's hard to keep up with as a human, so when he was a wolf, I was a fox."

"A fox?" Ehren injects.

I nod. "Yes. A Fae Fox. I chose a form I was most familiar with."

"So he was wolf and you were a Fae Fox?" Bram clarifies as we round a corner.

"Yes," I say with a nod. "He only needs to use magic when he shifts, but I have to use it the entire time to stay a fox. Last night, I used a little too much."

"That was careless, Astra," Bram scolds.

I roll my eyes. "I would have been fine if I could have just gone straight home and slept it off. I'm technically fine now, just exhausted."

I climb up one of the connecting ladders between bridge ways and Ehren places a steadying hand on my back as he follows me. A few yards down I stop in front of Sama's house.

"Well, we're here," I say, turning to Ehren and Bram. "I'll see you guys later."

I turn and head inside, but Ehren calls after me. I sigh and turn.

"Just a quick question," he promises.

"Fine. Out with it."

He meets my eyes and slowly asks, "Do you trust Kai?"

"With my life," I reply without hesitation.

Ehren cocks his head at my answer, but Bram scowls.

"You're sure? Because he's hard to read, and if he's joining us . . ."

"He's had a hard past, but I trust him. Completely. As much as I trust you," I insist.

"What exactly is your relationship?" Bram asks stiffly.

I smile softly as a welcome warmth fills my chest. "Brother and sister."

Ehren looks confused while Bram just looks completely thrown by my answer. I laugh and wave them off.

"I can explain later, but right now, I need to sleep."

Ehren nods and takes a step back. "Sweet dreams, Ash."

They turn and leave as I collapse into my hammock, falling asleep within seconds.

I'm awoken a few hours later by someone shuffling nearby. I blink my eyes open and discover Sama rushing around her room, a bag slug over her shoulder. I sit up and sling my legs over the edge of my hammock.

"I didn't mean to wake you!" Sama cries. "Though, maybe it's best as lunch is almost over and we're leaving soon."

I rub sleep from my eyes. "We?"

Sama grins. "Yes! Jessalynn said I can go with you all as far as the Koshima! I'll return here after that since I'm needed, but I get to travel with you some!"

I give her a sincere smile. "It will be nice to have another girl along." I pause. "Did you also say that lunch is almost over?"

She nods. "You should have about thirty minutes or so, but I wouldn't put it off."

I glance toward my travel bag. Pretty much everything is stuffed in it ready to go. With a wave of my hand, I tuck in the last few remaining bits and lift it to my shoulder. It's not the neatest packing job, but it will do.

"I wish I could do that," Sama sighs.

"Eh, it's handy but not everything," I reply with a shrug. "I wish I had a familiar." I nod to Ares perched on the windowsill and she follows my gaze with a grin.

"He is pretty great."

I give her one last smile, promising to meet her later at

the waterfall, before I head down to the dining hall. Most people have already filtered through the line, so I don't have to wait long to pile food on my plate. Between skipping breakfast and using so much energy on my magic, I'm starving.

"Have enough food?" a voice says from behind me as I walk toward the nearest available seat, making me almost drop my plate. I turn my head and glare at Kai.

"I didn't eat breakfast," I retort and he grins.

I sit down at a table, and he takes the seat across from me. I quickly dive into my pile of food as Kai eats silently. After a few minutes, Nyco plops down in the seat next to Kai.

"Hey! I heard you were coming with us!" Nyco grins.

"Wait, you're coming too?" I ask, washing down my food with a gulp of water.

Nyco nods. "Yeah, I never intended on staying here long term. I offered to leave with you all, and Ehren okayed it, so I'm part of the team now, I guess."

I notice his lack of plate and ask, "Did you already eat?"

"Yep! Jessalynn had the kitchen prepare a bunch of food for us to take with us, and I'm here to pick it up. I think she's already at the waterfall."

"Shit," I mumble, shoving the rest of my food in my mouth.

"Don't choke," Kai scolds, frowning. "It's not like everyone will leave without you."

My mouth is too full to answer, so I shrug instead. I gulp down the rest of my water and stand to my feet.

"Okay, I'm ready."

Nyco follows my lead and hops to his feet. "Well, I better go grab that food. I'll see you two at the waterfall."

Nyco gives us a wave and weaves his way through the

crowd toward the kitchen. Kai eases to his feet with a sigh. We place our empty plates and cups in the designated areas and head outside.

"I need to grab my bag from my house," Kai says, glancing up to the mountainside at where I assume he lives.

"I can go with you."

He shrugs. "Fine."

He extends his hand, and I place mine in his. He wisps inside a small home. I'm not sure what I was expecting, but it wasn't this. The house is small, but homey. There's one main room with two smaller side rooms along the back wall. Kai disappears into the room on the right. I realize with a start that the other room was likely Leyana's at one point. When Kai exits the room with a brown traveling pack on, I'm still staring at the second room. I glance away but it's too late. He notices.

"Yes, that was her room," he says simply. He lets out a long sigh and gives the room a long look before turning and striding past me to the door. "I have too many sad memories here. It's time to move on and find new, happy ones."

He says it with such a sense of finality it tugs at something in my chest.

"You can always come back," I whisper.

He looks at me, his gray eyes unusually bright. "Maybe. But I don't think I want to." He glances at the room and then looks down at me and smiles. "Ever since I lost Leyana, I've felt like a piece of me was missing. I've lacked purpose. Every day has been the same. But now . . . now I feel like I have purpose again. This—you are what I have been waiting for."

"Me?" I ask weakly.

"Yes. You and Ehren, I suppose, and all you stand for. I

think helping you is what Leyana would have wanted me to do with my life. She always wanted me to live, not just survive. For the last six years, I've just been surviving, and not very well at that."

I smile. "Well, let's go live."

He places his hand on my shoulder and wisps us down to the waterfall. From a distance, the waterfall was beautiful, but this close it's intimidating. The roar of water is so loud I can barely hear anything. I glance around. Jessalynn and Kaeya are present, as are Nyco with his packs of food, and Sama with Ares perched on her shoulder. The others are still missing. Kai turns and nods behind me. I turn and find Ehren, Bram, Cal, and Makin walking our way. I send out a tendril of magic and wisp them closer.

"Stop doing that!" Makin yells at me as he stumbles forward, grabbing Cal's arm to keep from crashing face first onto the ground.

"I will not," I say, flashing him grin which he returns with a gentle shake of his head.

"Well, is this everyone then?" Jessalynn yells over the roar of the crashing waterfall, ignoring our banter.

We all look around and do a quick mental tally, our heads bobbing in agreement when we realize everyone is indeed present.

"I think we're all here, unless you're expecting to send anyone else," Ehren says.

Jessalynn shakes her head. "No, this is all."

Jessalynn beckons for us to follow her inside the cave. As we pass behind the waterfall, cool droplets of water leap through the air, misting us. The farther in we go, the quieter the roar of the waterfall gets. As we step around a curve into the darkness, a couple of guards step out of the shadows, magical lights balanced on their palms. They hand Jessalynn a packet and she turns, passing it to Ehren, who accepts it cautiously.

"I know you have magic users among you who can light your way, but these candles are made with spellwork should they need a break. At the very least, light them at night while you're in the caves." She pauses and her carefree façade falters for just a moment. "Be careful." Her voice is strangely serious, sending shivers down my spine.

Ehren swallows, standing a little straighter. "We will."

Jessalynn's seriousness fades back into a feline grin. "Good, because I'd hate to have to step into your place as heir to the throne."

Ehren smiles. "There's still Cadewynn."

Jessalynn waves him off. "Psh. Like she'd care if I took your place. She'd probably rather have a sister anyway."

Ehren's laugh echoes down the dark cave. "You're probably not wrong."

"Well," I say, stepping forward, pulling on my magic and creating a floating orb of silver light above our heads. "Shall we be off, then?"

Jessalynn gives us one last nod. "You should be out of the caves in two days. Just follow the path and you'll be fine. Merry travels."

Ehren gives her a parting nod of thanks and adjusts the bag on his shoulder. He exhales and takes a step deeper into the cave.

"Let's do this."

Part Two:
Closer

CHAPTER TWELVE

ASTRA

The caves are dark and damp, with uneven floors that cause us to stumble often despite my glowing orb of silver light. When we first start, the path is wide and most of us can walk side-by-side, but the deeper into the caves we get, the narrower the pathway becomes. We attempt bits of conversation, but our voices echo too much and we ultimately surrender to traveling in silence. Nyco still tries to converse occasionally with Kai, but Kai just glowers at him until he finally gives way to his wolf form, avoiding all further conversation. I can't help but grin to myself. The ceilings are mostly high and Ares tends to spend most of our traveling soaring across the top of the passage-way. When the roof scoops down low, he settles on Sama's shoulder, screeching his dislike at the situation.

With no sun to guide our way, we have no true sense of time. We travel for what feels like several hours before we finally settle down for the night. Nyco opens his packs of food and we make quick work of a dinner of dried meats and berries before pulling out bedrolls. The men split up with

Ehren, Makin, and Cal at one end and Kai, Bram, and Nyco at the other. Sama and I sleep in the center. They claim it's for our protection, and we roll our eyes and let them have their way. I call in my magic, opting to use the candles provided by Jessalynn to give us a little light to sleep by.

My body has already adjusted to my new night schedule, so I toss and turn for a while before I finally manage to drift off to sleep. The next morning—or what we assume is morning—we rise, more than eager to be out of the darkness. The path today seems narrower, and we're forced to walk single file. Makin's breathing grows increasingly unsteady, his eyes darting anxiously at the walls as they close in tighter. I squeeze past the others between us and take up the position directly behind him.

"What's your favorite animal?" I whisper in his ear as we walk.

"What?" Makin mutters, knitting his eyebrows in confusion.

"What's your favorite animal?" I repeat, offering him a small smile.

He shakes his head. "Uh, I don't know." He swallows, pausing to think. "When I was a boy we used to go down to this river and there were all these salamanders. I used to love to catch them."

"Okay," I murmur, carefully envisioning a salamander.

"Why? What does—" Makin's voice fades as his eyes go wide.

I've created a little salamander out of silver light, and he now sits perched on Makin's shoulder. He turns his little head and looks up at Makin, blinking wide silver eyes. Makin lifts his gaze to mine, but he doesn't need to say a thing. Pure gratitude shines in his eyes.

"There, now you have your very own familiar."

"I'm naming him Sally," Makin declares, brightening up a bit. "Sally the Salamander."

Cal grins at Makin over his shoulder, rolling his eyes with affection. With Sally as his guiding light, Makin seems less concerned about the enclosed walls and unsettling darkness. His step even has more bounce to it. Of course, maintaining a life-like salamander as well as an orb of light for the rest of us does take a bit more concentration and a steady stream of magic, but I manage it well enough. Sama keeps a close eye on me, and I can tell she's monitoring my magic with her Syphon abilities.

We pause once during our second day for a quick lunch and then we're on our way again. We're considering whether or not we want to stop for another night's rest when Nyco starts grinning.

"My friends have good news," Nyco says cheerily.

I glance over at Nyco and jump at the large spider sitting on his shoulder. My eyes go even wider when I see a couple smaller spiders climbing in his hair.

"Your friends?" Makin asks in disbelief, looking increasingly uncomfortable. "You mean the spiders?"

Nyco nods, grinning. "Yes. They say the cave exit's not far away."

I'm not sure how much stock I want to put in the words of spiders but, sure enough, within the hour we see a faint light growing that eventually turns into a gaping cave exit. When we finally step out into the fresh air, I inhale deeply. The sun is setting, painting the sky with bright oranges and pinks.

"Ah, there you are," a voice calls from beside us and we all spin to find a young man with a wide grin and dark hair studying us. "My name is Posh. I'm one of the guards for this tunnel entrance. We received word that you would be arriving, and we have places prepared for you to sleep tonight."

The young man gestures behind him and we look up. There's a long wooden house of sorts built into the edge of the mountain. The make of the dwelling is very similar to the ones that graced the mountainside in the Valley.

"We've already eaten," Posh continues, "but we have plenty of food to share if you're hungry."

He motions for us to follow him. He leads us up a staircase etched into the mountain and inside the dwelling. It's essentially one long hall divided into a few rooms, the first of which is a sitting area filled with several other smiling faces. Posh ushers us past the other guards, through a kitchen and dining area to the bedrooms at the opposite end so we can deposit our bags. We then head back to the dining area where we are offered bowls of thick noodles covered in a spicy sauce with herb flatbread.

By the time we finish dinner, the sun has fully set and the weariness from our journey thus far sets in. We make our way to our beds, giving our apologies to our hosts. While they seem a little disappointed, they give us understanding nods.

I'm pleased that we get to sleep in actual beds instead of hammocks but, despite the comfort, I struggle to fall asleep. After tossing and turning for an hour, I rise and make my way outside. I step down on the top stone step and look up. The moon is a tiny silver sliver against a sea of black velvet and winking stars.

"Nothing quite like the night sky," Kai says from behind me, making me jump.

He smiles softly and settles down on the step next to me. "You couldn't sleep either?"

I shake my head.

"Don't worry," he says, gazing up at the sky with me, "eventually your body will get back on your normal sleep schedule."

For several minutes neither of us speak. We just stare up at the sky, letting the peaceful stillness of the night wrap around us.

"Back in Timberborn, where I grew up," I finally say, my voice barely above a whisper, "Kato and I used to sneak up onto our roof at night and look up at the stars. We would sit and talk about everything up on that roof."

I tear my gaze away from the stars and look at Kai, startled to find his eyes fixed on me.

"Well, if you ever need to talk and look at stars, just let me know," Kai says softly. "We can always find a roof or perhaps some stairs."

I smile and look back up at the stars. "I'd like that."

I lean my head against Kai's arm. He doesn't shift away like I half expect him to, but rather places his own head gently against mine. I'm not sure how long we sit there, but it's long enough that by the time we rise and go inside, I'm ready to sleep.

The next morning, we're all up bright and early, eager to be on our way to the capital city of Koshima. Posh is still asleep, but Cody, a middle-aged man with a shaved head, helps us find a decent breakfast before we depart.

This part of Gleador seems to be made of nothing but long stretches of hills. Used to walking over mostly flat land, my leg muscles scream at me the longer we walk, but we don't break any more than necessary. Kai shifts into his wolf form and bounds along beside us. I'm not sure if it's just easier to travel that way, or if he's avoiding conversing with anyone again. Determined to find out, I shift into a Fae Fox and bound along beside him, occasionally nipping at his feet. Kai growls and snaps at me, and I leap away, grinning as much as a fox can.

Under the recommendation of the guards at the outpost, we avoid taking the main road through towns, following instead the most direct route to Koshima. This, of course, means making our beds in the middle of a field for two nights in a row. Thankfully, by the second night, I'm able to fall asleep with little issue. Better sleep means more energy, so on the third day I decide to shift into a wolf. I've been studying Kai closely enough I feel confident I can copy his form. My wolf is made entirely of silver light and is sleeker and a little smaller than Kai's wolf, but from his expression, I've done a good job. He shifts beside me and we race off.

Running as a wolf is different than a Fae Fox. It's like the wolf form is built for speed, and I relish every moment of it. Unfortunately, maintaining a larger form drains more magic, so I'm forced to change back after only about fifteen minutes. Kai shifts with me, a wide grin on his face. We've managed to put a good amount of distance between us and the rest of our group, so we pull snacks out of our bags which, like our clothes, somehow shifted with our magic. We sit on a hillside, eating and laughing while they catch up.

It's evening when we get our first glimpse of Koshima. Even from miles away, I understand why it's called the "City of Jewels." Golden turrets spiral high above the city walls, glittering with thousands of gems and stones, each catching the sun at different angles to create an ethereal glow in a rainbow of colors. The closer we get, the more breathtaking it becomes.

The city itself is also bursting with color. Sheets of brightly dyed silk and other similar materials top almost every vendor cart packed into the crowded streets. Rugs and tapestries woven with bright yarns waft in the warm breeze and even the clothes of every villager, no matter their status, are made of bright cloth that glow in the evening light. Rich spices scent the air all around us, making my stomach growl.

As we approach the front steps of the ornate palace, a man in a sharp, deep red uniform rushes forward to greet us.

"Good evening," he says with a bow to Ehren, who inclines his head. "My name is Benick. King Naimon has been expecting you, and we have rooms prepared. We invite you to stay as our welcome guests tonight, and tomorrow we will arrange an audience with the king, if it suits you."

I breathe a sigh of relief. It's been a long day of travel and knowing I don't have to stand in front of a king looking like a vagabond is comforting. Ehren seems to share my relief.

"That is acceptable," he agrees with a nod.

Benick inclines his head and turns, heading inside. The inner palace is just as astonishing as its outside, nearly everything trimmed in gold and gems. I easily understand why Gleador is considered one of the wealthiest countries. Benick leads us up several flights of velvet-lined stairs and down a hallway with doors along one side and a balcony looking over a marbled corridor several stories down on the other. I gasp as I lean forward to take in the sight. The roof above is made of glass and the room below holds several shaped topiaries, a fountain, and multiple potted flowers.

"These three rooms have been prepared for you," Benick says, gesturing to the three nearest doors. "We were unsure how many traveling companions would be with you. If you need additional rooms prepared, we are more than willing. However, there are beds available in the barracks for any of your guards who need a place."

Ehren nods as Benick continues. "The rooms have connecting doors that you may lock or unlock according to your desires." He glances around at us, reading our weariness. "I will leave you to your resting. I'll have dinner sent up immediately."

He turns on his heel, disappearing down the hall. I turn and open the door closest to me and step inside, Sama following. The room isn't quite as large as my suite back in Embervein, but it's still bigger than I'm accustomed to. Most of the space is taken up by lavish velvet seats and couches, all trimmed in gold and stacked with tasseled pillows. There's no balcony, but a large window takes up almost the entire far wall. A few of the panels are open, a warm evening breeze twisting the semi-sheer deep red and gold curtains. Against the far right wall is a huge four-poster bed with red curtains, all tied back with golden ropes ending in tassels. Pillows are piled on the bed, taking up nearly half the surface. To the right of the bed is an open door that appears to lead to a dressing and bathing room. I step inside and confirm a wardrobe and large ivory tub, separated from the rest of the room by a bamboo folding screen.

"This is incredible," Sama breathes, looking around, eyes wide and bright as I step back into the main room. I smile.

A knock comes from a wooden door along the left wall. I cross the room and slide a large golden bolt with a click. A few seconds later, it swings open to reveal a grinning Ehren. He strides into my room, his hands on hips as he surveys everything. I peek into his room and find it practically a mirror image of my own.

"I think your room is bigger," Ehren muses, staring up at the tall ceiling bearing a large chandelier that lights the room.

I roll my eyes. "It is not."

Bram steps tentatively from Ehren's room into mine, the others trailing behind him. A few minutes later, there's a knock on the door and servants enter, bearing trays of roasted meats, mixed vegetables, flatbread, and spiced wine. We settle in different places around the room, some of us on the floor leaning against the furniture, and we relish in the heavily seasoned foods Gleador has to offer. It's decided that Sama and I will share the large bed in my room, Ehren will sleep alone in the middle room, and Kai and Bram will take the third room (though I highly doubt they will share the bed, even though I'm positive it's more than large enough). The other three will sleep in the barracks.

Once dinner is over, the men return to their respective rooms while Sama and I prepare to settle in for the night. I offer Sama the first bath and, after much protesting, she agrees. I lie down on the bed with the intention of just resting while she bathes, but exhaustion creeps in, taking hold, and I'm asleep before I know it.

CHAPTER THIRTEEN

ASTRA

I'm not entirely sure if I wake up early due to the fact I slept soundly all night, or because of the nerves wrestling inside of me. Either way, I'm wide awake at the first hints of dawn. Sama is sprawled on the opposite side of the bed with Ares nestled peacefully on the nightstand next to her. I ease from the bed and pad into the washroom and run a warm bath, filling the water with scented oils and soaps that create a mountain of bubbles.

I sink into the soothing tub and relax my head against the edge. Today will be a true test of how I'm received as Court Sorceress. Meeting Jessalynn was really just a trial run. Today, I meet an actual king. I take a deep breath and exhale slowly. I can do this.

I catch muffled sounds of Sama stirring in the room outside. The door opens and she dresses quickly, not disturbing me, before going back into the sitting room. I hear her open the door and talk briefly to someone, and I assume breakfast has arrived. It's the promise of food that eventually pulls me from the bath. I wrap in a silk robe, draining the tub, and step into the dressing room.

Most of the clothes I have are made for traveling. They're all filthy and in desperate need of a wash. However, the good people of Naskein had the forethought to pack me one dress elegant enough to meet a king. I draw the deep purple dress from my bag and hold it up, pleased immensely that the silky material didn't wrinkle in the slightest. I dress quickly, the dress slinking over my curves in a modest, yet almost seductive, way. I use magic to dry my hair, twisting it into an elegant knot on top of my head. I don't hesitate to wear the amethyst amulet provided by the Order, but I hold the tiara in my hands for several long minutes. The tiara is far more prestigious than anything I'm used to. It almost feels like a lie to wear it. And yet, I finally place it on my head. If we are to convince King Naimon to support our cause, we need to appear as regal as possible. With a sigh, I examine my reflection in the mirror. Regal is definitely the word.

When I step into the sitting room, Sama glances up from where she's seated on one of the couches, munching on some sort of bread.

"Is that what you're wearing?" she gasps, glancing down in horror at her own dress. "This is all I have."

Her dress is simple but nice. I offer her a smile.

"You look lovely."

I scan the room and quickly locate the breakfast tray. A few twists of dark, seeded bread are arranged around a bowl of cut fruit. Next to the tray is a pot of steaming coffee and a stack of mugs. I select one of the breads and take a bite as I pour a cup of coffee before taking a seat next to Sama, who still stares down at her dress.

"You look fine, I promise," I insist, bumping my shoulder

against hers. She looks up at me and gives me a weak smile. "Where's Ares off to this morning?"

She waves toward the open window. "He went out for a morning flight. Indoors aren't really his thing."

I nod. "That's understandable."

There's a knock at the door connecting my room and Ehren's. I glance up and confirm it's still unlocked from last night, so I just call out, "Come in!" There's a pause, but the door swings open and Ehren strides into the room, dressed in the sharp uniform provided by Naskein.

"Morning!" he says cheerfully, making his way to the tray of food and reaching to grab one of the breads.

"Hey!" I cry. "Don't you have your own food?"

"I do, I simply wish to compare your supply to mine."

He grins and plucks up a piece of bread, taking a big bite.

"Equally delicious," he concludes through a mouthful of crumbs. I roll my eyes but don't bother to hide my grin.

He pours himself some coffee and cups his hands around it, inhaling deeply.

"You're supposed to drink it," I mumble, my own mouth full.

Ehren rolls his eyes. "Damn. I've been doing it wrong." He grins and saunters across the room, settling into the armchair across from me. He takes a sip of his coffee and sighs in contentment. "The drink of the gods."

I chuckle and rise to grab some more breakfast. Ehren's eyes fall on me and he nods his head approvingly as his eyes travel down my frame.

"That's quite the dress. If you don't convince King Naimon to join our cause by that dress alone, it's a lost cause."

I shake my head, attempting to brush off Ehren's words,

but color creeps into my cheeks. Sama lets out a whimper and Ehren shoots her a curious glance.

"Sama is concerned her dress isn't fancy enough," I explain, plucking up a strange, brightly colored fruit slice shaped like a star.

Ehren turns to Sama, whose face has turned bright red at the attention, and surveys her dress, cocking his head. "I think your dress is more than adequate. You look lovely."

"Really?" Sama breathes, relaxing slightly.

Ehren smiles and nods. "Definitely."

"Why is this door wide open?" Bram's voice cuts sharply from Ehren's doorway. I glance over as Bram and Kai walk into the room, both their faces set in scowls. They are quite the pair. Kai closes the door with a click.

"Because Ehren's too lazy to close it," I answer with a shrug, taking a bite of the fruit. A sweet, citrusy juice fills my mouth.

Bram shoots a warning look to Ehren. "You cannot leave doors open like that."

Ehren sighs. "Really, Bram? My bedroom door is locked. I think. Maybe. I mean, I may have left it unlocked after breakfast was delivered, but the point is, I doubt anyone would break into my room just to find a way to this room, when there's a door right there they could try first." Ehren gestures to the main door of my room with a dramatic flourish.

"That's not the point, Ehren," Bram admonishes, pinching the bridge of his nose with a sigh.

"It kind of sounded like the point," I mumble and Bram glares at me.

"He's right, you know," Kai says.

"Not you, too!" I cry, laughing as I shake my head.

Kai frowns. "You're in the court of a foreign kingdom. Just because you're allies doesn't mean you're entirely safe. It's highly likely you have enemies here."

"He's right," Bram stresses with a sharp nod.

"Gods help us when those two agree," Ehren grumbles and I laugh.

There's a knock on my door and Bram stiffens, striding the distance quickly. He slowly opens the door a crack, his hand on the sword at his side.

"Can we come in or is there a secret passcode?" Makin asks, his grinning face appearing as Bram throws the door open further.

"Would it make you feel better, Bram, if we set up a secret passcode?" I tease and Ehren snickers. Even the edges of Kai's mouth threaten to turn into a smile.

Cal scans the room, his eyebrows quirked in question, but he just shakes his head. "We tried your room first, Ehren, but the door was locked."

"Ha!" Ehren cries, pointing at Bram in triumph. "I told you my door was locked!"

Bram lets out a long sigh as I bite my lip to keep from laughing.

"Hey, is that coffee?" Nyco cuts in, bounding across the room to pour a cup.

"I'm just gonna help Nyco out," Makin says, shuffling after him.

Cal sighs, and I give him a sympathetic smile as he joins the other two to grab some breakfast. I'm guessing the barracks don't have breakfast delivered on little golden trays. We all settle around and chat casually until a sharp knock on the door reveals a servant ready to take us to our audience before the king.

I stand, releasing a shaky breath as I run my hands along the front of my dress, smoothing wrinkles that don't exist. Ehren senses my nervousness and takes a step toward me, gently taking my hand. I look up into his eyes and he smiles.

"You've got this," he whispers, giving me a wink.

Sama glances anxiously toward the others and noticeably relaxes when she sees that while Ehren, Bram, Makin, and Cal are dressed in full uniform—Ehren going so far as to wear a circlet crown balanced on his head—Nyco and Kai are also dressed in normal, casual clothes.

The servant keeps a quick pace as we follow him through lavish corridors lined with rich colored tapestries and marble statues. Ehren and I take the lead, me matching him step for step. Bram follows directly behind us, the perfect Captain of the Guard, standing straight and stiff, with Makin and Cal a step behind. Even though Nyco is technically a member of the Guard, he hangs back slightly, opting to walk with Kai and Sama.

When we enter the grand hall, it's truly breathtaking. The throne room in Embervein was all darkness and foreboding, but this room is all golden light. The columns are made of pure gold, twirling and twisting to the high domed ceiling made of glass, sunlight pouring down, catching the gems embedded in the marble floor. King Naimon and his queen sit at the far end on golden thrones lined with red velvet. When Ehren and I reach the end of the red carpet leading to the thrones, it's easy to bow to their regal power.

"Welcome to my kingdom, Prince Ehren," King Naimon's voice booms, echoing off the golden walls.

We rise but Ehren inclines his head. "Thank you for meeting with us, Your Majesty."

"I won't dally about. I know why you've come," the king says. Ehren's eyes widen slightly at the bluntness.

"Your Majesty?"

"I have ears and eyes all over this continent and beyond. Callenia shares our southern border. We heard about the civil war brewing in your country almost as soon as everything was set into motion. I am well aware that your father has forbidden magic after his attempts to deny it proved unsuccessful. I know that you and your Guard fled Embervein, taking up residence in Athiedor before fleeing to the Isle of Naskein and, eventually, the Hundan Valley in my own lands. I even know about the sorceress at your side and the threat her brother is becoming."

King Naimon pauses and Ehren watches him steadily as he says, "Then Your Majesty knows how much we need your aid."

"Indeed," the king muses, tapping his fingers on the arm of his throne. "But I am afraid I cannot give you all you have to come to request."

Ehren's face falls, but he keeps his shoulders straight as the king continues.

"I have no desire to spend my citizens' lives on your civil war. Especially not when you are so young, untried, and untested. I will not allow my people's blood to be spilled for your crown. Magic returning has caused enough unrest within my own borders, and I will not further the divide between my people by going to war. As I am sure you are well aware, the kingdom of Gleador was once divided into nine separate countries, each with their own rulers and traditions. My great-great grandfather united these countries in peace and the later generations of kings, myself included, maintain that peace by allowing the former countries to retain some rights. We unite them under one crown and most choose to serve our gods, but we allow them to maintain their own culture and make many of their own decisions in governing their lands. We do not require them to fight in wars that are not our own. Of course, I will not hold back any of my people who willingly wish to serve you, but I will not force their hands either."

King Naimon pauses and eyes Ehren steadily, his gaze calculating. "Perhaps, if we had reached a marriage alliance things would be different, but as they stand, I will not step where I do not belong."

Ehren shifts uncomfortably and I don't miss the sharp look Bram sends his way.

"I do not agree with what you father is doing, however. He has never acted so unwisely before, and I can only hope he will come to his senses. Alas, I fear he will not. Therefore, I am willing to throw my support behind you. I give you my word that you, and those that ally with you, will be safe within my borders. You and your closest companions may stay here at my own palace."

The king motions to the side and four servants step forward, each holding a handle on a massive golden chest. The chest drops to the floor, a loud clank echoing through the room. With a nod from the king, one of the servants throws the lid open, revealing a pile of gold, gems, and jewels. My eyes go wide and I hear a whispered curse from Makin behind me.

"I can also support you monetarily, if you will allow," the king says, waving his hand toward the chest.

Ehren swallows, lifting his eyes slowly from the chest.

"And what must we do in exchange for your . . . patronage?" he asks, selecting his words carefully.

King Naimon smiles and gives Ehren a nod. "Good. I like to see you think like a diplomat, always wary of a catch. This money comes with no strings. We have similar goals, you and I. We both see the benefits of a society with magic and non-magic working together. I believe that in the very near future, we will be strong allies. Therefore, I give you my gems and gold so you can secure your kingdom. I simply have no desire to enter a war where there are three heads battling for one crown. Eliminate one of those threats, narrow your war fronts, and then, perhaps, we can discuss what further steps we can take."

Ehren bows his head, lowering his eyes. "Thank you, Your Majesty." He lifts his head and locks eyes with the king. "What if my father should keep the throne? What then?"

King Naimon takes a deep breath and exhales slowly. "Then, more terms may need to be negotiated. If you escape with your life, my offer to provide refuge remains. If you should perish in the fight for the crown, my home is open to your companions here, to your sorceress, and to those most loyal to you. If dealing with your father proves to be . . . more difficult than anticipated, we will adapt as necessary."

King Naimon pauses and his eyes fall on me, his gaze shifting to a harder intensity. I press my hands against my side to keep them from shaking, but I meet his eyes.

"I'm more concerned about her brother and the rumors surrounding his rise to power."

"What would you care to know, Your Majesty?" I ask, dipping my head, refusing to be intimidated.

"I simply wish to know what level of threat he may be, and what I can do to prepare my people."

"A reasonable request," I say with a nod. "Right now, much is unknown with my brother. We know for sure that his power is nothing to be trivialized. He is extraordinarily powerful, dangerously so, and right now he has plans of grandeur."

The king nods. "We have heard he plans to unite the Clans of Athiedor against the king to claim the crown for himself. Is this true?"

"Unfortunately so. According to our contact, who is close to Kato, he has not yet succeeded in uniting all the Clans, but if he does, he will build an army and take the crown with their forces."

"And how should I prepare my people, should your brother rise?" King Naimon presses.

I pause, considering his words. "That is one of those things that has yet to be seen. I do not know if my brother's quest for power will be . . . satiated, or if he will desire to expand his realm. He is volatile and potentially dangerous and will not make for a peaceful neighbor even in the best of circumstances, I'm afraid. I imagine that as long as you support magic, you will be safe from him for the time being, but if he assumes the throne . . ."

I let my voice trail off, allowing King Naimon to fill in the blank with his own fears. If I deny Kato will be a potential future threat, we may not gain an alliance in the future should Ehren win against his father.

"You give me much to consider," King Naimon replies evenly as I nod.

"There is one other matter we would wish to discuss," Ehren says, drawing the king's eyes back to him.

Ehren pulls a small object from his pocket, and I realize he brought one of the portal stones with him. He holds it up, allowing it to catch the light, sending rainbows dancing across the floor.

"The Order of Naskein has requested we use these portal stones to reestablish portals that were once in effect when magic was strong before. With your permission, we would like to activate a portal within your city." King Naimon looks on the verge of denying the request, but Ehren quickly adds, "There is no risk to you. It simply works as a door directly to Naskein that requires magic on both ends for the door to open."

The king turns his head and crooks his finger to someone off to the side. A man steps forward, and I wonder how I didn't notice him before. He's tall, easily as tall as Bram, with dark hair and bronzed skin. A bright red cloak covered in ancient magical symbols stitched on with golden thread is draped over his shoulders. I can't pinpoint his exact age, but he can't be more than a few years older than Ehren. As he steps closer, I realize he was using some sort of spell to keep himself masked and unnoticeable.

"This is Illyas," King Naimon says, gesturing to the man as he bows. "He is my official Court Mage."

"Your Court Mage?" Ehren repeats slowly, allowing the words to sink in.

King Naimon smiles. "Of course. Did you think you would be the only ruler to appoint someone with magic to their court?"

Ehren shakes his head. "Of course not. The concept is still so new. It takes time for it all to adjust." His face breaks into a smile. "Pleased to meet you, Illyas."

Illyas nods in greeting, a small smile curving his lips.

"Good. Now that you know each other, you may discuss the portals with him. Any other issues you wish to address?"

Ehren shakes his head. "No, Your Majesty. I believe we have covered everything."

"Excellent," King Naimon replies. "You and your companions are welcome to stay in the comforts of my palace as long as you like. Additionally, I would like to formally invite you all to be my honored guests at our annual Masquerade Ball in honor of Oryus, the god of festivities. My royal tailors are ready to measure you for your costumes. Everything you need shall be granted you."

"We would be most honored to attend," Ehren accepts with another bow.

"Very good. Now, if you do not mind, I have other things which require my attention this morning," King Naimon says, standing.

Ehren and I give a final bow and turn. The others part and allow us to take the lead out of the room, falling into their places behind us. Once we're all out in the corridor, Ehren gives me a nod, and I wisp us back to my room. The others stumble a little at the change, but no one complains.

"Well, I suppose that went all right," Ehren mutters, plopping into a chair.

"Is it what you expected?" I ask.

Ehren shrugs. "More or less."

There's a knock on the door and Ehren straightens, alert. Bram answers the door and reveals Illyas. He steps into the room and scans us quickly.

"Am I interrupting?" he asks, offering us a smile.

I shake my head. "No, not at all! What can we do for you?"

"I simply came to discuss the possibilities for recreating the portal. I believe I know the location of the previous portal, if that would help."

Ehren rises from the chair. "Actually, we do have a spell that can reactivate the portal stones already in place."

Ehren disappears into his room, returning a moment later with the instructions from Naskein. I let him take the lead on explaining the process to Illyas. He's more skilled at spellwork than I am. Once they've discussed everything to Illyas's satisfaction, the two of them, accompanied by Bram, depart to take care of the reactivation process. The remaining men strike up a card game in Ehren's room while Sama and I escape to be fitted for dresses for the masquerade.

I shouldn't be surprised when the seamstress asks what our costumes will be but, somehow, the question throws me. I blurt the first animal that comes to mind—a Fae Fox. Sama decides to go as a Shadow Hawk. If our selections take the seamstress by surprise, she doesn't show it. She just barks orders in broken Callenian, measuring and pinning, before shooing us away.

The next three days pass quietly. It's nice to be doted on again, being allowed to sleep in and having trays of breakfast greet me when I'm ready to rise. It's relaxing enough I can almost pretend there's not a war brewing.

I even enjoy escaping to the city outside the palace walls. The market is always so alive. I can't understand half of what the vendors are saying, but Sama, who accompanies me, translates when necessary. The foods are all rich and filling, and everything is bright and colorful. Sama and I spend almost an entire afternoon wandering from jewelry cart to jewelry cart examining the wares. We swear we won't buy anything, but by the time we wander back to the palace, we are both in possession of several new pieces.

The evening of the ball, we are presented with our

dresses. Sama's is made of several shades of gray material, with black diamonds around her waist. Her matching mask is a deep gray with black feathers near her eyes and a beak crafted of several black diamonds. Mine is flowing blue and silver silk with glittering sheer silver material laid over top. Diamonds glisten around my waistline and across the neckline, which dips far lower than I'm used to. My mask is slate blue silk, trimmed with soft white fur and more glittering diamonds. When it comes time to dress for the ball, I'm nervously excited.

Even though our faces won't show much below our masks, Sama and I put on touches of makeup, focusing on brightening our lips. Sama wraps her hair with a new deep gray headscarf trimmed in sparkling black thread while I adorn my hair with glittering pale blue gems and pearls. When we meet Ehren in the hall before heading down to the ballroom, he gives us an approving nod, his eyes sparkling with mischief.

"You both look stunning tonight," he says, grinning.

He's dressed as a firebird, his red tunic covered with swirls of bright orange. His mask is lined with rubies, coming to a point above his mouth in a beak crafted from some sort of orange gem.

"You look all right, too, I guess," I tease.

"For that, you have to give me your first dance tonight," Ehren admonishes with a laugh.

I giggle and look past Ehren to the others. Bram is presumably a black horse, dressed in a sleek, black tunic with a mask that hides most of his features. Makin has chosen a cat of some sort, his black mask curving up into glittering, pointed ears. Cal, swathed in a green tunic glittered with emeralds, has chosen a dragon. Nyco has, unsurprisingly, chosen a spider, his mask designed like a web. Kai is a . . . I pause and roll my eyes.

"A wolf, Kai? Really?"

Admittedly, he strikes a handsome figure in his crisp, gray tunic, but still . . .

Kai grins, his eyes glinting behind his dark gray, fur-lined mask. "You're a Fae Fox. How is that any different?"

I laugh. "I suppose you're right."

He offers me his arm and I accept, even if it makes Bram bristle. Ehren offers Sama his arm and she takes it, blushing a deep crimson. Ehren and Sama take the lead and Kai and I follow behind, drifting toward the bellowing, lively music. Everything in the ballroom is glowing and alive.

As promised, I give Ehren the first dance. The steps are a little different to the dances we're used to, but we adapt quickly. I follow my dance with Ehren by dancing with Bram. He's stiff and awkward the entire time. After a couple dances with foreign nobles, I excuse myself and make my way over to the side to enjoy some of the food. I'm sipping a glass of spiced wine when Kai approaches me from the dark corner where's he's been standing since we entered.

"Careful, Kai," I tease, poking his arm. "That wall might fall down without you over there holding it up."

He narrows his eyes, but his lips turn upward ever so slightly.

"It seems you're having fun," he deflects, glancing toward the dancers.

"I am," I confirm, smiling. "You look miserable, though."

He shifts his gaze back to me and shrugs. "I'm not miserable. I enjoy watching the dancing."

"Just not participating in said dancing," I clarify and he nods, his smile blooming.

"Precisely."

"Will you dance with me?" I ask and his smile vanishes.

"No," he says firmly, crossing his arms.

I tug on his arm. "Please!" I beg. "It could be fun. Just one dance."

I flutter my eyelashes up at him and he sighs. "*One* dance, but that's it. And if I step on your toes the entire time, I don't want to hear a word of complaint."

I grin, surprised he caved so easily. The music fades and the dancers shift, preparing for the next dance. I set my glass down on a nearby table and drag Kai onto the dance floor. Despite his reservations, he's actually a pretty good dancer, albeit a bit stiff. He doesn't miss a step, and even spins me on cue. I grin wildly the entire time, and Kai wears a tight smile that gradually loosens into a full grin. When the dance finishes, I skip off the dance floor, dragging Kai along with me to where Sama stands on the edges.

"Dance with Sama," I instruct.

Kai pulls away from me, shaking his head. "I agreed to one dance."

"One dance with *me*. And then once dance with Sama."

Kai narrows his eyes. "Those were not the terms."

"Please?" Sama asks, looking up at Kai with her big, brown eyes. "It'll be quick."

Kai grits his teeth. "Fine, but this is truly the last dance."

Sama bounds onto the dance floor with Kai trailing behind her. I watch them take their positions on the dance floor. Kai may act grumpy, but I can see the light shimmering in his eyes.

"It's a pity for someone as beautiful as you to be on the sidelines," a low voice says from behind me.

My heart stops as my breath catches in my throat. My

lips part and I bite my lip. I'm sure I imagined the voice, the lilt, the accent. I spin and find myself looking into a pair of emerald green eyes trimmed by a bright orange fox mask. I gasp, lifting a trembling hand to my gaping mouth.

"May I have this dance?"

CHAPTER FOURTEEN

ALAK

When I wake, the world has stopped spinning, but I have no idea where I am. I blink my eyes several times, trying to make sense of my surroundings. Nothing looks familiar. I stand and glance around. I'm in a garden, but not one of the gardens near the fortress. No, this is a place I've never been before. And it's darker here. I'm not sure if I've just traveled that far, or if I've been passed out long enough that it's night. I have a feeling it's the latter.

I slowly walk around, looking for anything that might clue me in to my new location, but I'm at a complete loss. I look up at the building the garden surrounds and come to the conclusion it's a palace of some sort. I really wish I had paid more attention to information about other countries.

Music pours out a doorway not far away, and I follow the sounds of laughter. I peer inside. Everyone is dressed in bright outfits, glittering masks covering their faces. It's a masquerade. The music is unlike any I've ever heard, but I love it instantly. I'm about to wander away when I notice a table of food laid out, and I realize how hungry I am. I don't even know how much time has passed since my last meal. With a quick wave of my hand, I create my own costume. I embrace my red hair and change my basic travel clothes into an orange-red tunic with golden buttons and craft what I hope is a bright orange fox mask. I step cautiously into the ballroom and am pleased to find that I go unnoticed. I quickly grab a few bites of food and retreat to a back corner to watch while I eat.

I scan the crowd, still trying to make sense of everything. Why the hell would Felixe bring me here? I figured he would only take me a little way away from Aine. Just far enough to get me from her clutches. I listen in on a group of chattering girls within hearing distance, paying close attention to their language and accents. I'm almost positive now I'm in Gleador. Judging by the opulence, I'm in the king's palace. I need to find Felixe and get out of here. I don't even know if I can wisp back to Periola without his help.

I turn to leave when a familiar laugh rises above the clamor of the ball, freezing me in my tracks. My eyes search wildly for the owner. When I find her, I blink several times as my heart races. She's wearing a mask, but I know the curve of those lips, the way she holds herself, that dove-white hair, her laugh, and, of course, those remarkable, amethyst eyes. And if that wasn't all familiar enough, she's dressed as a Fae Fox. I grin. She's the most beautiful Fae Fox I've ever seen.

I want to rush to Astra, but I decide to bide my time. I need her to be alone. I watch as she leaves the dance floor, bidding her partner goodbye with a nod, and makes her way toward the food. Before I can seize the opportunity, she's approached by a tall man in a sharp gray tunic wearing a gray wolf mask. By the way she grins up at him and touches him so casually, she clearly knows him well. He must be someone she's met fairly recently, because I have no idea who he is, although she's clearly comfortable with him. I push down the rising sting of jealously, reminding myself she's not mine, and even if she were, she could talk to whomever she damn well pleased.

She drags the man onto the dance the floor as a new song starts. Whoever he is, he has a scowl that could rival Bram, even with the mask covering half his face. Bram. I glance around for Bram, or even Ehren, but I can't locate them in the sea of masked strangers. I'm surprised they've left her side in a strange place. Especially Bram. I focus back on Astra as she dances, as graceful as ever.

When the dance ends, Astra drags the now-grinning man from the dance floor toward a girl dressed in a dark gray dress. Someone else she obviously knows that I don't recognize. I can tell she's somehow talking the scowling man into dancing with the girl, so I slowly begin to drift toward her, creating an illusion around myself that keeps me unnoticeable should Bram or anyone else I know spot me. Once her friends have stepped away, I take my chance.

"It's a pity for someone as beautiful as you to be on the sidelines," I say, struggling to keep my voice steady.

My heart beats wildly inside my chest so loudly I fear she can hear it. Astra goes completely still before slowly turning. Her amethyst eyes are wide with wonder and her lips part in surprise. She takes an unsteady breath, and I almost want to cry. I can't believe she's standing in front of me. It's taking every ounce of self-control I possess not to pull her into my arms.

"May I have this dance?" I ask, extending my hand, flashing my teeth in a grin.

She accepts immediately, still staring at me in disbelief. I lead her to the dance floor. Luckily, this dance is familiar enough that I manage to lead smoothly.

"You don't have to keep staring at me like that, love," I tease. "If you blink I won't disappear."

She laughs softly and shakes her head as I spin her. I pull her back closer against me, and she looks up into my eyes.

"But how are you here?" she breathes. Her eyes go wide and, for the first time since my approach, she jerks her gaze away from me, frantically scanning the other dancers. "Kato—"

I chuckle and shake my head. "He's not here, love. It's just me."

She looks back up at me. "But how?"

I pull her tightly against me and lean in, my lips brushing her ear as I whisper, "Just dance with me for now, and then I'll explain everything."

She nods, a smile finally crossing her lips. It's only then I notice the small hints of scars running along her chin and down onto her neck. I have to reign in my anger. I know those scars are where Kato struck her, but I refuse to focus on that. For the first time in weeks, I can finally be with her, hold her. I relish every moment she's wrapped in my arms. Her eyes never leave mine, and my heart feels as if it's going to burst from my chest.

When the music starts to fade, I lead her from the dance floor out the side door into the garden. I throw a simple spell around us to hide our departure so no one follows. Once outside, she turns to me.

"I can't believe you're really here," she whispers, reaching out to stroke my cheek with her fingertips, sending shivers down my spine with her delicate touch.

I smile and allow my mask illusion to fade away. I reach and slowly lift the Fae Fox mask from her face. She doesn't stop me.

"Gods, I've missed your face," I whisper, my voice unsteady as I reach up and place my hand on her warm cheek.

Her lips part as she places her hand on top of mine, closing her eyes. With a start I notice Bram's ring isn't on her finger. Her eyes flicker open, and I pull my eyes from her hand, meeting her gaze. Without warning she closes the distance between us and presses her lips to mine. I start at the unexpected touch and she jerks back.

"I'm sorry," she mumbles, her cheeks flushing pink. "I just—"

I don't let her finish. I wrap my arms around her, dropping her mask to the ground, and pull her against me, pressing my lips to hers. She returns the kiss hungrily, and I draw her closer. She slides her arms around my neck and twists her fingers into my hair. I flick my tongue across her lips, and she releases a little gasp, her lips parting against mine, giving my tongue full access. My heart surges. I crave more. But I know I can't have that. I pull back with a shuddering breath, running a hand through my hair. She looks up at me for a moment, and then laughs, leaning her forehead against my chest. I kiss the top her head with a contented sigh.

"Believe it or not," I mumble into her hair, "I did not come here for that, love."

She laughs again and lifts her face to mine, her eyes shining. "Are you sure?"

I laugh. "Why don't we sit?" I nod to a stone bench just a little way off and she nods.

She settles down next to me on the bench and leans against me. I slip my arm around and hold her close. I'm pleasantly surprised when she reaches over to my lap and links her fingers with my other hand. I pull back away from her just enough to look at her face. She looks up at me, cheeks flushed and lips swollen, but wholly content.

"So, why did you come? And how?" she asks, her voice quiet.

"Well," I reply, looking down at our hands in my lap and tightening my grip. "Felixe brought me."

I glance back up at her and catch the surprise flicker across her face. "Felixe? But how?"

How. There's the question. Deep inside I know the answer. I *know*. But I can't tell her. I simply can't put it into words. Not yet. So instead I shrug.

"He knew I needed you."

She smiles softly then slowly frowns, furrowing her eyebrows. "Is everything okay? It isn't, is it? Otherwise, why would you be here?" Fear flashes in her eyes as she asks, "Is Kato okay?"

I nod. "Yes, Kato is okay."

She relaxes. "Then what is it?"

I release a sigh. I don't want to ruin the moment, but her eyes press me into an answer.

"Kato has essentially secured all seven Clans."

Her face drops. "That's not good, is it."

I shake my head, even though it's not really a question. "No, it's not. He has an official alliance with six of the Clans, but I have no doubt the seventh Clan will join once they hear. Kato plans to officially unite them soon under an unbreakable treaty. Then he'll have his armies."

"Is there anything we can do?" she asks, her eyes swimming with worry. I hate it.

"I think you could change their minds," I admit. "Lord Wallish was less than happy aligning with Kato, so they worked an amendment into their deal with him. If you step forward and prove your power, promising them a free Athiedor like Kato offers, they may side with you."

She stares off into the night, chewing on her lip as she thinks.

"So," she says slowly, "if Ehren agrees to free Athiedor when he gets the crown, they won't follow Kato."

I nod. "Yes."

She looks back me, her eyes bright. "I think I can arrange that."

I raise my eyebrows. "You think Ehren will free Athiedor?"

It's more than I dared to hope, but if anyone could do it, Astra can.

She hesitates but then nods. "Yes, for this cause I think he will." After a moment she adds, "King Naimon is unwilling to aid in a civil war with too many battle fronts. If we can keep Kato from rising to power, Ehren has only his father to contend with. He'll make the deal."

She sounds so certain it fills me with hope.

"So, King Naimon refused an alliance?"

"Not entirely," she replies, swinging her feet. "He's given his verbal support, backed by a trunk of jewels and coins to fund our quest, but he's not willing to risk his people as soldiers yet."

"Makes sense."

She nods. "Yeah, I can't blame him." She looks up at me. "If we stop the deal with the Clans, will you come back?"

Her eyes search my face and a pressure rises in my chest. I swallow and mindlessly trace my fingers in a circle on her shoulder.

"Do you want me to?" I ask, my voice barely above a whisper.

She nods once, answering without a breath of hesitation. "Yes."

Gods, I want to kiss her again. I force myself to look away.

"I think Kato is working on something big. Something he's not telling me. If this Clan deal falls through, I think he has a backup. I think . . . I think I need to stay with him and find out what it is."

She nods but looks down. I can feel her disappointment.

"Hey," I say softly, pulling my arm from around her shoulders to turn her face back to mine. She looks up at me, tears brimming in her amethyst eyes. I brush a lock of hair from her face and tuck it behind her ear. "I'm coming back. Soon. I swear it. I just want to be as useful as I can."

She nods and tries to smile, but it's weak. "Is he . . . will Kato ever come back?"

I pause and then shake my head. "I don't know, love. Some days I think he will. He's reasonable and level headed. Other days, he's too focused on power. With each step he gets further and further away. But I'll keep trying to bring him back."

She lifts her hand and traces a finger down my cheek. "Just . . . be careful. I need at least one of you to come back to me."

I can't resist anymore. I lean down and kiss her. When I pull back, I meet her eyes. "I will."

With a sigh, I stand. I've been gone for too long. If Kato hasn't started looking for me yet, he will soon.

"You have to go," she states simply, her voice flat.

I look down at her and nod sadly.

She stands and wraps her arms around my neck. "One last dance?"

I smile and nod. "Fine, one last dance."

I pull her close, and we sway to the music drifting from the door not far away. I never want the dance to end. I could dance like this forever. But it does end. An ache rises in my chest as she takes a step back, her arms dropping to her sides. I can't put it off any longer, or I'll never leave. I call out to Felixe and he appears on my shoulder. Astra grins up at him and scratches his ears.

"Can he guide you back to Kato?"

I shrug. "I don't know. I have a feeling it won't work quite the same way," I confess. "I'll probably have to use more of my own magic."

She scowls. "Do you have enough magic for that?"

"I hope so," I reply as lightly as I can, but the truth is, I don't know. It's going to be close.

"Well, take some of mine."

And then her lips are on mine again, Felixe hopping to the ground. My heart skips a beat, but I obey, drawing a few droplets of magic. My magic swirls inside of me, eagerly accepting hers, reaching for it. I draw a little more and then pull away.

"You should get back inside," I say, my voice rough. "I'm sure people are looking for you by now."

She sighs like going back to a ball where she was clearly having fun is now the biggest burden. She glances over her shoulder.

"You're probably right. Kai is most likely pacing circles around the dance floor." Kai. That must be the man in the wolf mask. Her eyes go wide. "If he shifts into a wolf, I will kill him!"

I crack a smile. She looks up at me and laughs at my obvious confusion.

"I'll explain in a future letter," she says with a wave of her hand. "But you're right. I should go."

She turns and takes a few reluctant steps away from me. I watch her walk away and scoop up her mask, securing it across her face. She looks at me and smiles. Without warning she rushes toward me and throws her arms around my neck, drawing me into one last kiss. She pulls back grinning, and there's no mistaking the longing in her eyes.

"I've missed you," she whispers, and then she turns and skips back inside.

I stand for a moment, steadying my breath and collecting my thoughts. Felixe draws my attention with a gentle yap, popping onto my shoulder and nipping my ear. I chuckle.

"All right, let's go."

I pull all my magic to the surface, along with Astra's borrowed magic and force all my concentration into wisping. The strain is intense but, when I open my eyes, I recognize the familiar courtyard of the fortress. I'm both pleased and disappointed.

I wander around for a bit, but it doesn't take long to find Kato and crew. They're walking back from the dining hall, likely having stayed late after dinner to play some sort of card game. Kato spots me first and his face spreads into a wide, drunken grin. Aine's eyes find me next, and she glares in my direction.

"There you are!" Kato cries, slinging his arm around my shoulder. "Where have you been?"

I shrug. "Around."

"You can't just disappear like that in the middle of celebrating," Kato admonishes with a grin. Gods, how pissed is he?

"We've been dealing with him for hours," Caitlyn whispers. "It's your turn now."

The others quickly rush away, leaving us alone. Shite.

"All right, mate. Let's get you to bed," I insist, guiding him toward the stairs.

He mumbles some sort of incoherent protest, but I ignore him, dragging him along. As we stumble up the narrow stairs, Kato is forced to release me, much to my relief. I steer him to his room. He staggers inside and crashes face down on the bed, rolling over to stare at the ceiling.

"Well, goodnight, mate," I mumble, getting ready to shut the door.

"Do you think she even thinks about me?" he slurs.

I freeze.

"Who?" I ask, glancing over my shoulder at him.

"Astra. Do you think she even cares I'm gone?"

I sigh and step back into the room, closing the door behind me. Whatever is said next doesn't need to be overheard and twisted by the others.

"Of course she cares, mate. It's probably tearing her up every single day."

Kato pushes up onto his elbows and stares at me. "You think?"

"I know," I say with nod.

He narrows his eyes. "How can you know?"

I sigh and sink down onto the bed next to him.

"Because I know Astra," I reply carefully. "She'll never give up on you. She loves you."

"She loves you, too, you know," Kato drawls, dropping back on the bed and closing his eyes.

Normally I would argue but after tonight, I feel like it might be a possibility. I smile slightly.

"She tried to hide it, but I could tell," Kato mumbles, shifting and curling on his side. Good. Now, if he pukes in his sleep, he won't choke to death.

"Yeah, well, she loves you in a completely different way. You two have a bond that can't be broken. She'll forgive you if you go back—"

"No!" Kato yells, his eyes snapping open. "I'm not going back! Not when I'm on the verge of accomplishing what I set out to do."

I sigh. So much for that idea.

"No, she'll eventually come to me," he mumbles, his voice slurring more and more. He curls back up, closing his eyes. "You'll see."

He goes silent, and I wait a moment until his breath steadies before I leave, extinguishing the gas lights. I cross the hallway and open my door. I can barely contain my disdain when I see Ian sitting on the end of his bed. His eyes narrow as I enter the room.

"I'm not in the mood," I snap at him before he can say anything. I cross to my bed and pull my shirt over my head, tossing it on top of my bag.

"I just wanna know where ya were," he says, his voice low and cold.

"It's none of your damn business," I retort, sitting on the edge of my bed to remove my boots.

"It's my business when it involves my sister."

I jerk my face up and look at Ian. "You can't be serious."

"I am, mate. Deadly serious."

"Look," I reply, kicking off one boot and working the laces on the second, "she came on to me, pricking me with something I expect you gave her." I kick off the second boot with more force than necessary. "I barely got away before she did gods know what. Whatever it would have been I was *not* a willing participant. I managed to get away, passed out, and when I came to I went and found you guys."

Judging by the expression on his face, Ian knows exactly what Aine used but had no idea she was going to use it on me.

"Shite," he growls.

"Yeah. So now, if you don't mind, I would like to sleep off whatever remains in my system from your sister's little rape attempt."

Ian glowers at me from his bed but doesn't say anything. I slide under the covers, eager for sleep. My magic is drained from maintaining my illusion and wisping. I'm on the verge of crashing. Ian shuffles across the room, and it goes dark as he extinguishes the light. His bed creaks and the room goes silent. I'm almost asleep when Ian finally speaks.

"I'm sorry. I didn't know she would do that."

I don't reply. I don't need to. I have nothing more to say.

CHAPTER FIFTEEN
ALAK

When I rise the next morning, I'm half-expecting to find Kato pushing us to leave Periola, but I guess he got pissed enough last night he's sleeping in. A glance at Ian's bed confirms he's already up and gone, which is a bit of a relief.

I close my eyes and take a deep breath. I can't believe I saw Astra last night. Not just saw—held, kissed. A smile plays on my lips at the memory. But, as usual, cold, cruel reality comes crashing in around me.

"Alak, are you up yet?" Kayleigh's voice drifts through the door with a knock.

With a grunt, I sit up. "Yeah."

Kayleigh tentatively opens the door, light from the hall drifting into my otherwise dark room.

"Gods, it's dark in here with no window," she mutters, stepping inside. She quickly lights one of the lanterns with a flick of her hand and glances around with a look of satisfaction. "That's better."

I clear my throat. "I assume you have a purpose in my room besides adding light?"

"Oh! Yes! Kato is awake and he wants to leave soon."

"As completely pissed as he was last night, I'm surprised he's functioning," I admit and Kayleigh laughs.

"Well, he's down in the dining hall guzzling black coffee as fast as he can get it." She pauses, opening her mouth like she wants to say something, but then thinks better of it.

I sigh. "Out with it."

"I don't know what—"

"You want to know where I was last night, correct?"

She hesitates, and then nods.

"So would I," I lie and she raises her eyebrows. "Aine was bothering me so I wisped away and got a little turned around. It took a while for me to be able to wisp back."

The lie, once again, has just enough truth mixed in to make it believable. Kayleigh accepts my explanation without question.

"Well, regardless of where you went last night, it's time to go," she says. "Pack up and meet us downstairs."

"So bossy." I grin, and she rolls her eyes.

After she leaves, I pull on a clean shirt and slip on my boots. My bag is pretty much packed. I just double check to make I have everything before slinging it over my shoulder. I extinguish the light and step out into the hallway. I'm rounding the stairs near the second floor when I hear a quiet voice.

"Are ye Master Alak?"

I start and look around, spotting a young boy hiding in the shadows just inside the doorway leading off to the second floor, his wide eyes watching me warily.

"Aye," I answer, furrowing my brows. "What of it?"

The boy's eyes dart around before he answers. "I need ya to come with me."

I glance around. We're alone. And while I've never had a particular fear of young boys, something about this situation seems off.

"I have to meet up with my friends," I say, shaking my head and taking another step down the stairs.

"Please, Sir," the boy begs. "I need ya to come with me. It's important."

I look down at the boy's unblinking hazel eyes. He almost looks afraid. What will happen if I ignore the boy? I sigh.

"All right. Fine. Let's make it quick."

The boy grins, relief washing over his face. "Follow me."

As I step off the stairwell onto the second floor, I gather my magic, ready to use it if needed. The boy clearly knows where he's going, weaving and bobbing through the halls and past rooms. When he halts outside a large pair of carved wooden doors, I think I know where we are, though I'm not entirely sure why. Nerves twist in my stomach as the boy opens one of the doors a crack.

"I have Master Alak for ya, Sir," the boy says to someone I can't see.

Whoever it is must signal for me to come in, because the next moment the boy takes a step back and gestures for me to enter the room. I swallow and step forward, opening the door a little wider as I enter. Lord Wallish stands in the center of what I assume is his private sitting room. It's sparse, but easily the most comfortable looking room I've seen so far in the fortress. The door slams behind me and I jump at the sound, though I should have been expecting it. Gods am I on edge this morning.

"Good morning," Lord Wallish says, smiling. He motions to a nearby table bearing sausages, breakfast potatoes, and a pot of coffee. "Can I interest you in a bite to eat?"

My stomach feels uneasy, so I shake my head.

"Naw, Lord Wallish. I would prefer to get directly to why you've had a young lad sneak me here."

Lord Wallish chuckles. "Straight to the point. I like that."

He clears his throat and clasps his hands behind his back as he starts pacing the room.

"As you could probably tell, the elders and I were not fully content with signing everything away to Kato, even if it would mean a potentially free Athiedor."

I nod. "Aye. I gathered as much."

"I figured you would. You seem astute. You're different from the others. They look at Kato with blind devotion. You, however, seem to have a better grasp of what a dangerous thing it could be if he were to truly gain the power he seeks." He pauses in his pacing and looks me directly in the eye. "You aren't as staunchly committed to his cause, and yet, he clearly sees you as his right hand. Why?"

"I don't know what you mean," I say, trying to keep my face blank.

Lord Wallish smiles. "Oh, I think you know exactly why. It has to do with his sister, doesn't it?"

I don't answer. I take slow steady breaths. If this is a trap, I cannot get caught. Lord Wallish resumes his pacing.

"As I see it, Kato would want his right hand to be someone he truly trusts, which demands loyalty on your part. This means you've been close to him longer than the others. But it's more than that, though. I heard what Kato did to that boy in Brackenborough who tried to hurt his sister."

I wince at the memory but allow no more emotion to show. If Lord Wallish notices, he doesn't react.

"Kato still loves his sister and must truly not see her as a threat. There's still a piece of him that wants to protect his twin, and I surmise that, somehow, you are a link to his sister. Aren't you?"

"I'm not sure what you want me to say," I reply, my voice cold and hard. "How do I know that you won't twist my words and go to Kato with the leverage? I could tell you weren't entirely happy with the alliance. How do I know you aren't using me to get additional terms in your favor?"

Lord Wallish takes several strides toward me, stopping less than a foot away. "Quite frankly, you don't know what I will do with this information, but you are certainly correct. I am not happy with the terms. Most of the elders balked at this alliance, but we felt we had little to no choice. We cannot stand against a power like Kato's on our own."

"I suppose having a free Athiedor wasn't appealing at all?" As soon as I say the words I regret them. Lord Wallish's eyes flash and he sneers, red rising in his face.

"Look here, boy, you are from Athiedor, and you know what a free Athiedor means! Of course we want it! But not in this way! Athiedor has always been a land of peace!" He shakes his head, taking a long, calming breath. "Why should I risk the lives of my people to place the crown on the head of yet another king with no roots to Athiedor? What guarantee do we actually have that, even after a war, Athiedor will be free? My point is, if you are not loyal to Kato, but are by his side, you must be loyal to his sister, and as far as I know, she has no desire to flaunt her power to gain a crown. We need you to use your connection to give us another option."

"That's a bit of leap," I say slowly, treading carefully.

"Isn't it possible I'm just by his side because of the same fear that caused you to sign that treaty?"

Lord Wallish studies me for a moment before shaking his head. "No. I am positive you are somehow in league with his sister."

A thought strikes me, and I pale slightly, my eyes widening. "You can read minds, can't you?"

Lord Wallish's eyes brighten as the corners of his lips turn upward. "You're clever. I can't so much read thoughts, but rather read intent with the occasional flash of a memory when I concentrate my magic. I detect lies and half-truths. I know when I'm being tricked. In you I read uncertainty, but also a fierce loyalty. Having watched you around Kato, that loyalty is not for him. Somehow, you serve his sister. This information is something I could have already shared with Kato, but I have not. You can trust me. Quite frankly, I need your help. I am desperate to save the lives of the people of my Clan. It is my duty. Now, will you assist me?"

I take a deep breath. At this point there's no more avoiding.

"Yes."

Lord Wallish's lips part in delight and turn up into a toothy grin. "Do you think you can get Astra to strike against her brother?"

"Strike him physically? No. She will not strike against her brother if it brings him harm. Not yet." Lord Wallish's grin fades. "However, I believe she may be able to get Prince Ehren to agree to your terms. That condition on your treaty may come to pass."

"She is that close to the prince?" he asks, almost breathless.

I nod. "He did not make her his Court Sorceress only

because her power is unlike any ever known. He trusts her with his life and listens to her. They are friends."

Lord Wallish licks his lips and nods. "Good. Good."

He steps away from me and resumes his pacing. I can tell he's calculating what this information means. I sense his hope.

"And she has the power to rival Kato's magic?"

"Their magic is very different," I say carefully, "but she is incredibly strong and, if pressed, can rival him and possibly even beat him. However, she longs for a peaceful solution."

Lord Wallish pauses, his shoulders relaxing. He looks at me, his eyes wide with hope. "That's all we want, too—a peaceful solution."

I smile softly. "Then I swear to you, I'll do what I can. But I make no promises as to what I can accomplish."

"That's all I ask," he says simply with a half-shrug.

"Now," I say, straightening, "I need to meet up with Kato or he'll get suspicious of my disappearance."

Lord Wallish nods. "Yes. Yes. Of course. I won't keep you any longer." He strides past me and opens the door. The young boy leans against the opposite wall but jumps to attention as soon as he sees Lord Wallish.

"Ryan," Lord Wallish addresses the boy, "will you please show Alak the way to his friends?"

The boy looks up at me. "Aye. I can do that."

"They're in the dining hall," I say, smiling down at the boy.

The boy nods and steps away. I start to follow him, but Lord Wallish calls out to me. "Please, Alak, we can't do this without you."

I give him one last nod before turning and disappearing down the hall after Ryan. We wind through back halls to reach the dining hall. Once I know where I am, I give Ryan a nod and he scurries away. I step into the dining hall, and it only takes a minute to find where the others sit. I take a deep breath and approach the table. Kato looks like he's feeling normal, so the coffee in his hand must be doing the trick. Aine's still seething though.

"Well, you took your sweet time," Kayleigh scowls as I take a seat.

I shrug nonchalantly and reach across the table, loading a plate with what remains of the breakfast potatoes. "I didn't want to miss anything packing up. A book had fallen under the bed, and it took me a bit to find."

I can tell by the way she purses her lips she doesn't believe me in the slightest. I don't care. As long she doesn't suspect what I was truly doing, she can purse her lips all she wants.

"So," I say, taking a bite of potato, "are we heading home this morning?"

Kato shakes his head. "No, we're going directly to Klahbridge to meet with Clan McDullun."

I choke on my food. Kato is moving quicker than I anticipated.

"We're close to sealing the final alliance, so I would rather not dally about longer than necessary," Kato continues. "Since there are those among the elders' families with connections to Klahbridge, it's only logical to go ahead and take advantage of those connections for wisping purposes."

Kato takes a long sip of his coffee as I struggle not to let my unease show. I need to let Astra know about the developments as soon as possible. She needs to prepare. She was sure Ehren would be willing to do what was necessary to keep Kato from obtaining Athiedor's full support, but what if Ehren doesn't agree? What if he wants further compromise? Kato is moving too rapidly for alternative negotiations.

"All right," Kato says, setting his coffee down with a thump, pulling me from my thoughts. "We should probably get going."

I stuff the last few bites of potatoes in my mouth and rise along with the others. We've all brought our bags, packed and ready to go, so we head outside. A woman with hair as deep red as my own stands at the edge of the courtyard, a deep scowl on her face.

"Morning, Orla," Kato greets her as we approach.

"You said you wanted to leave first thing this morning," Orla replies, her voice cold and her eyes colder. "It's nearly mid-morning"

"Semantics," Kato says with a careless shrug.

Orla inhales sharply through her nose, setting her jaw as she shakes her head. "You're lucky I waited around for you. Most everyone else in my traveling party departed already."

"I do apologize," Kato says with a slight bow. "I sincerely did not mean to inconvenience you. My companions and I merely lost track of the time."

His voice is smooth and seems to do the trick. Orla straightens and sighs, picking casually at the waist of her dress.

"Well, I suppose as you're here now, we might as well get going," Orla shrugs, lifting her eyes from her dress.

"Indeed. If you'll just envision where we are going, just like you would with your own wisp, I'll take it from there. Let me know when you're ready," Kato instructs.

Orla narrows her eyes and looks like she has a few words to say on being told what to do, but after a moment of consideration, she just takes a deep breath and nods. She closes her eyes.

"Okay. Ready."

With a casual flick of his wrist, Kato surrounds us with a wall of fire, wisping us to Klahbridge. If Orla is surprised by the cascading flames, she doesn't show it in the slightest. She merely opens her eyes and blinks in disinterest as the wall disappears into wisps of smoke.

"So, I suppose my job is done, correct?"

Kato looks disappointed she doesn't seem more impressed by his flippant show of power, but nods.

"All right. Good luck, though I doubt you'll need it. Ronan is sure to join our cause. He's no fool."

Before any of us can reply she flicks her hand and disappears. Kato licks his lips and looks around at our new surroundings. Klahbridge may be the main residence of Lord McDullun, but it's a simple farm village at best. The whole of Clan McDullun is known for providing crops for the rest of Athiedor and parts of Callenia. This quiet town is a typical village.

Orla guided us to the outskirts of the town between two large fields. On either side of us people work off in the distance, harvesting whatever crop grows in these fields. Even as far away as they are, it's clear that at least half of them are using magic. With such unabashed wielding, it's no wonder Orla expects us to succeed easily. Magic is clearly used openly and is a common occurrence.

The village streets themselves are mostly quiet, everyone off working this time of morning, most in the fields if I had to guess. Even without the bustle of people, the streets are alive. Smoke spirals from smokestacks and chimneys, the wind carrying the remnant aroma of breakfast. A shaggy dog bounds down the road chasing chickens that scuttle and cluck. Shadows pass windows as people work inside. It's peaceful, but not dead.

The residence of Lord McDullun is far larger than any typical house, but smaller and more welcoming than the fortress of Clan Wallish. Where Clan Wallish has a large, bulky castle fortress made of towering stone turrets, Clan McDullun has a smaller fortress—if that word could even be used—that's only three stories high but wider and longer. The main wall surrounding the fortress is barely shoulder-high and made of worn, sun-paled stone. The gate is wide open and no guards stand stationed outside. However, as we approach, we warrant the attention of a thin young man with shaggy blonde hair talking to a woman laden with what appears to be a bag of laundry. When the man spots us, he eyes us for a moment before turning back to the woman. He says something else to her before smiling and nodding to her as she smiles back and turns to be on her way. He strides toward us, his long, lanky legs covering the distance quickly.

"Mornin'!" he says cheerily in an accent so thick even I can barely make out what he's saying. "What kin I do fer ya?"

Kato blinks, taking a moment to process the man's words though his accent.

"We've come to meet with Lord McDullun," Kato says at length, pulling a letter stamped with a red seal bearing a crest of a rose surrounded by a circling of twisting vines and thorns. "He agreed to meet with us at our earliest convenience."

Kato offers the man the letter, but he doesn't even begin to reach for it. Instead, he grins.

"Aye! You must that Kato lad. Lord McDullun said ya

might arrive all-a-sudden," the man says, the speed of his words mixing with his rolling accent to blur his words together. I'm not sure if the thick rumble of words is why Kato suddenly seems slightly unsettled or the fact he wanted to throw Lord McDullun off with a sudden, unexpected arrival, only to be told his appearance has been anticipated.

"Is he ready to meet with us now?" Kato says, pushing aside his discomfort in favor of his winning grin.

"Ach, naw," the man replies, shaking his head. "Lord McDullun isn't about. He's gone off huntin' boars. Perhaps with some notice he may-a been here ta greet ya but he should be back a little after noon. He has a suite prepared for ya if ya'd like to be escorted thar?"

Kato stiffens, setting his jaw, but nods. The man grins and motions for us to follow him. He leads us inside the large mouth of the front door and gestures to a servant girl off to the side in the shadows. She steps forward with a smile and the man leans in to her and says something in what sounds like pure Yallik. The girl smiles and nods and turns to face us.

"Greetings," she says, her accent so thick I almost think she's still speaking Yallik at first. "My name is Muireann. If you'll follow me, I'll be happy to take ya to yer rooms."

Thankfully, she gestures smoothly for us to follow her, so Kato doesn't have to pretend to understand a word she just said, because I doubt he caught half of it. He nods all the same and falls in step behind her as she leads us further inside.

I half expect the inside to look as dismal and dark as the fortress in Periola, but whoever designed this building created it to be bright. Tall arched windows usher in rays of bright mid-morning sun that caress the white stone walls.

The McDullun rose crest is clearly displayed through every part of the fortress, sometimes on carefully woven tapestries, sometimes worked into artwork such as paintings or vases, and occasionally even carved elegantly into the stone walls themselves. Clan McDullun is proud of who they are.

We finally come to a stop outside large double doors made of wood with large stone handles, each with a rose knot carved in the center. Muireann rattles off some information that I can tell goes right over Kato's head. Even the others seem to have trouble following her exact words. I gather enough to know that these doors lead to our rooms, and that there's a separate washroom down the hall should we need it. Once she's delivered her message to a satisfactory number of confused nods, she spins on her heel and leaves the way we came. Kato watches her go for a moment before shaking his head like he's clearing cobwebs and opens the door.

The room instantly gives off a pleasant, cozy vibe. Much of the stone floor has been covered by a large raspberry-red rug bearing the rose crest in silver thread. Five long windows along the opposite wall bathe the room in warm sunlight. Easy chairs and couches are arranged around the room near tables and small bookshelves, covered in soft, worn but not ragged material. Four doors each reveal a room bearing two beds, each large enough for two people without much extra space between them.

Once we've each claimed our rooms—much to my chagrin, I'm stuck with Ian again—we make ourselves comfortable around the room. A servant bustles in with tea and biscuits before scuttling off without saying a word. I content myself in the corner with a book, but Kato is restless, constantly fidgeting when he's seated and pacing when he's standing.

"This is ridiculous!" Kato cries after several minutes of pacing the length of the room. "It's like we've been pushed aside, out of the way."

"Well, mate," I say cautiously, "you did show up without any notice. You can't expect people to just wait at home, hoping you'll come knock on their door."

Flames flash in Kato's eyes and I swallow. I'm close to crossing a line. I need to tread carefully.

"We could see if there's a decent pub," Niall jumps in, standing from where he's been reading on a couch next to Caitlyn. "Pretty sure I saw a sign for one on our way in."

This idea seems to settle Kato a bit, and he nods in agreement. Caitlyn seems less than thrilled about going to the pub, but she follows along. We wind through the halls, getting lost only once on our way back into the village. The Jilted Sparrow is easy enough to find, even though it's a small corner pub with only a long counter and a handful of tables. The pub is empty save for a table of five older men near the back corner. They glance toward us, talking in low voices, speaking what I'm positive is Yallik. They puff on long pipes, the musky smoke filling the air with the sweet scent of Jesnick weed. I'm tempted to ask if they have a bit of Jesnick to spare, but I can tell by their hard stares they have no desire to be disturbed. Instead, I take the empty barstool next to Kato.

A barkeep with a gray hat pulled low over his eyes takes our orders of ale and offers up bowls of beef and barely stew, which we all eagerly accept. In addition to the stew and ale, we are presented with a loaf of crusty bread, which we break off into chunks and use to scoop our soup. We follow our lunch with a couple more rounds of ale before we make our way back outside in the hopes of seeing Lord McDullun returning from his hunting trip.

There are no signs of the lord, but a group of children have come out to play. Half of them are barefoot and, as we watch, one little boy sits and kicks off his brown shoes. They laugh and spin, playing a made-up game. I watch them, grinning. I look over and discover Kato doing the same, his eyes bright as he watches one of the little girls spin, creating a stream of petals that dance through the air around her, fluttering down around her giggling playmates. Without hesitation, Kato strides toward the children as if beckoned by the magic. When he's a few feet away, the children notice his approach and shrink away from him in a tight cluster, eyeing him cautiously.

"I saw your magic with the petals," Kato says gently, kneeling down on one knee to make himself eye-level with the girl. She chews on her lip, her eyes wide. "It was beautiful."

The girl's face brightens and she breaks out into a grin. "Wanna see more?"

Kato nods with a genuine smile that goes all the way to his eyes. "I'd love that."

The girl's grin widens as she holds her hands above her head, wiggling her fingers. A shower of petals in every color imaginable flow down from the sky, twisting in a warm late-summer breeze.

"That's some wonderful magic," Kato says encouragingly.

"Can you do magic?" a little boy with a smattering of freckles across his face asks tentatively.

Kato nods. "Would you like to see it?"

The children all nod eagerly and shuffle forward. I hold my breath, slightly afraid of what magic Kato might show. The only magic I've seen him display of late has been to intimidate. When Kato creates a small, life-size kitten made of flame, I release my breath and relax my shoulders, taking a few steps closer. He creates a couple more kittens and they tumble and play, chasing their fire tails. The children squeal in delight and beg for more. He replaces the kittens with a small dog and "commands" it to perform tricks such as lying down and rolling over. Soon, the giggling children chime in with their commands, each getting sillier and sillier until the pup is dancing and floating and turning somersaults in the air.

I watch in awe as Kato interacts with the children. There's nothing fearsome about him. He's kind and gentle. *This* is the Kato Astra longs to save. And he's worth saving. It gives me a bit of hope that perhaps my mission to bring Kato back to Astra may not be impossible after all.

Kato's fire pup is jumping through a carefully crafted ring of fire when the clatter of horse hooves and laughter echo on the road behind us. We turn to find the hunting party returning, heading toward the fortress.

"Well, I'm afraid I have to go," Kato says to the children, who immediately begin to protest and beg him to stay. He laughs and performs a few more simple tricks before pulling in his fire magic.

"Will ya come back?" one of the little girls asks, her eyes wide and hopeful.

Kato shrugs, his eyes bright. "Maybe. We'll see what fate has in store.

He waves to the children and turns to us, giving me a sharp nod. Playtime is over. Now it's time to get down to business. A business I bloody hate.

CHAPTER SIXTEEN

ALAK

We arrive back to the fortress shortly after Lord McDullun and his hunting party return. The servant from earlier leads us to the library. It's yet another cozy room that makes me feel immediately at home. A large stained-glass window takes up a decent portion of one wall, its geometric shapes crafted into the McDullun crest. Smaller windows run in a straight line down the rest of the wall, bathing the library in natural light. An ornate wooden writing desk sits almost perfectly centered under the stained-glass. Beneath the short windows are comfortable armchairs and short wooden shelves. The remaining walls are filled with varnished wooden shelves, most of which reach from the floor to ceiling, lined with books of every shape and size. Scattered around the room are several pieces of furniture matching the ones in our suite.

"So sorry to keep you waiting," a voice calls from the doorway, and we all turn to look at the man striding into the room.

I try to reign in my shock when I notice how young he is.

He can't be much more than thirty, which is extremely young to be the leader of a Clan. Despite his younger age, he uses a wooden walking cane with a bronze rose for the grip, using it to support his left leg. His short reddish-brown hair is still wind-whipped from riding his horse and his clothes are neat and sharp, yet relatively casual. The only thing that might mark him as a Clan Lord is the proper way he stands—his shoulders straight back and his chin high—and the golden stitching of the McDullun crest on his green riding tunic.

"Lord McDullun?" Kato asks, arching an eyebrow in polite disbelief.

"Aye," Lord McDullun laughs. "I am the one you seek."

His accent is thick and rich, but he speaks very clearly.

Kato bows his head in recognition of the man's title. "It's a pleasure to meet you. I just wasn't expecting someone so . . ."

Lord McDullun laughs as Kato searches for words.

"Young?" Lord McDullun finishes for him, his eyes sparkling mischievously.

Kato nods stiffly and Lord McDullun laughs again. I bite my lip to hold back the smile threatening to break free. Kato meant to come and surprise Lord McDullun, throwing him off his feet, but the tables have turned. Kato is now the one uneasy and unsteady. Things could go very wrong, very quickly but, for once, it's nice to see Kato not get the upper hand so easily. He's going to have work a little harder. Maybe Clan McDullun wasn't such a given after all.

"Yes, I'm afraid you get a young Clan Lord when his father, the old, respectable Lord is killed unexpectedly." Lord McDullun still smiles, but the joyful spark that was there a moment ago has faded. "Please, let's take our seats and make ourselves comfortable."

Lord McDullun leads us toward a cluster of chairs and couches near the center of the room. He pauses at a drink cart beside the armchair facing the other pieces of furniture in the grouping.

"Anyone care for a bit of cherry mead? It's made within the borders of my Clan and some of the best you'll find anywhere," Lord McDullun offers, pouring a thick red liquid into a glass. When we all shake our heads, he shrugs. "More for me then."

He eases into the armchair, resting his cane against his leg, and gestures for us to sit on the couches and remaining chair. We settle into an awkward silence as we take our places, aware of Lord McDullun's assessing gaze as he sits in the armchair, legs crossed, absentmindedly swirling the mead in his glass.

"Well, do you want to start with whatever spiel I'm sure you've rehearsed, or shall we just jump straight to the part where I share my intentions?" Lord McDullun asks, all traces of humor vanishing.

Kato straightens, tense. "I suppose if you know why I'm here, I'd just be wasting both your time and mine explaining."

"Quite right. I heard you were clever. Good to know those rumors were true." He pauses, taking a sip of his mead. "Well, you want me to join the little alliance you're forming with the other Clans. You promise to unite Athiedor under your rule, lead us into war to win you a crown, and, in return, you will allow Athiedor to become a kingdom of its own again, ruled by the Clans. And you do all this in the name of magic. Do I have the sum of it?"

Lord McDullun takes another long sip of his drink while Kato nods. "You have the essentials."

"And, from what I hear, you're not a bad choice to lead us. Your magic—which, by the way, I would prefer for you not to use in my library as I like books whole and not piles of ashes—is some of the most powerful ever seen or recorded. You have experience as a soldier and even worked side-by-side with the prince. You also have the charisma most want in a leader. And yet . . ."

He lets his words hang in the air. Kato shifts, annoyance flashing on his face. The air around us feels suddenly warmer, and I realize Kato is close to unleashing his magic. Lord McDullun glances briefly at Kato, sensing the magic, but only grins and tips his glass in Kato's direction.

"Are you sure you won't have any mead? It is quite delicious."

Kato seethes and shakes his head, his mouth a tight, thin line. I wonder if Lord McDullun knows the dangerous path he treads right now. He's watching Kato steadily, which makes me believe he understands the risk, but his gaze is calculating. He has a plan.

"So be it." Lord McDullun tips the glass back, draining the contents, and smacks his lips contentedly. "Now, where was I? Ah, yes. Your alliance. You see, I'm not sure I'm interested."

Red rises on Kato's face, but he keeps his voice controlled as he asks, "And why not?"

"Well, the incentive you offer is a free Athiedor, but I'm not sure that is enough for me and my Clan. I don't care if Athiedor is free or not."

Lord McDullun's words have a stilling effect over our entire group. His response is unexpected, to say the very least.

"What do ye mean?" Ian asks, his voice thick with anger.

I glance over at him, eyes wide with shock. Normally in meetings such as this, he's a quiet little mouse, always nodding along but never speaking.

"How can you not want a free Athiedor?" he spits, fists clenching by his side.

"It's not that I don't want a free Athiedor," Lord McDullun answers with a dismissive flick of his hand. "It simply isn't a priority for me."

"May I ask why not?" Kato says, his frustration no longer masked. "The rest of the Clans all seem eager to be free. All six have agreed to join me. Why are you so different?"

Lord McDullun grins like he knows a great secret, and I wonder for a moment how much he *does* know. Is he aware this will all likely fall apart if he refuses? He must. He's certainly acting like someone who holds all the cards. He knows Kato needs him but, it appears, he doesn't need Kato.

"Have you ever really paid attention to a map of Athiedor?" Lord McDullun asks, gesturing down the wall to where a large, colorful map hangs between towering bookshelves. "My Clan resides in the farthest corner, with no piece of our land touching the border of Athiedor and Callenia. While the king does demand his taxes and tithes, he doesn't bother us much up here. We can operate things as we wish. Most of Athiedor wants to be out from under the king's thumb because it presses against them, but the king doesn't seem to care about reaching out to control land filled with poor farms, not when other parts of Callenia much closer to him can provide him with all the crops he needs."

"I don't only offer Athiedor freedom," Kato counters. "I offer power as well. The king may not be bothering you yet, but he wants nothing more than to wipe out magic. Eventually, his hand will reach you. If you side against me, you will have no protection against him."

Lord McDullun cocks his head, considering Kato's words.

"Perhaps," he replies with a shrug. "I'll openly admit that I have no desire to fight against my brother Clans, but I don't want war. For one, I have no soldiers to offer you. Members of my Clan are farmers, not soldiers. Most can barely hold a weapon correctly, let alone wield one effectively. How are my people supposed to help you fight your war?"

"With magic," Kato says simply, relaxing now that he's able to get his words in. Words are as much his weapons as swords and arrows. "Our war will be fought on two fronts, and only one of those will be fought with physical weapons. The other will be magic. When we arrived, I saw the workers in the fields wielding their magic. I know it's rampant here. Any soldiers you send won't be fighting on a battlefield with swords, but safely behind our line with magic."

Lord McDullun nods, weighing Kato's words. "That sounds reasonable enough, but even then I cannot spare my people." Kato's jaw tightens again and his eyes flash. "Magic or no, we rely on our farms for food, for living. If I send off everyone with strong magic to fight for your cause, the crops will not be reaped in time, and my people will go hungry. They will have no money to clothe their families or buy other necessaries. What kind of leader would I be to let my people fall to such a fate, for a cause I don't wholly believe in?"

Kato leans back in his seat and assesses Lord McDullun.

"What if all we require of your Clan is food? Armies aren't cheap to feed and having a constant source of food would be very useful to the cause," Kato replies after several moments of thought, a triumphant gleam in his eyes.

Lord McDullun sets his jaw and taps his index finger against his chin in thought. "That is a reasonable compromise, perhaps. Though, what additional compensation would we receive for our food? We cannot simply be expected to hand over our crops for free."

Kato waves his hand as if this is a non-issue. "Once the coffers of the king are at my disposal, I can be sure you are reimbursed appropriately."

"I'm not sure that is enough," Lord McDullun says, gripping his cane with both hands, one hand on top of the other, and leaning forward to match Kato's glare. "While it may be entirely possible you will succeed against the king, there are no guarantees. You're asking me to risk the fate of my people on a chance."

Kato frowns, a tight "v" forming between his eyes as he shifts uncomfortably under Lord McDullun's sharp gaze. He recovers quickly, however, and opens his mouth to speak, but Lord McDullun waves him off. A deep crimson flushes Kato's cheeks.

"I'm not saying I will outright refuse an alliance. You've given me much to consider, but I do not feel that I can make a decision in this moment. Please, allow me time to reach out to my people and trusted advisors, as well as the leaders of the other Clans. Then, once I have all the information, I can give you a firm answer."

"And how long will that take?" Kato asks stiffly, his anger and frustration barely contained.

"Hmm," Lord McDullun ponders, looking off to the side as if he's calculating a series of invisible numbers. "Give me two weeks."

"Two weeks?" Kato roars, leaping from his seat.

Lord McDullun glances up at Kato, arching his eyebrows. While he looks a little surprised at Kato's outburst, he doesn't look intimidated in the slightest. In fact, he's entirely composed, appearing almost bored.

"Yes. Two weeks. These things take time."

"One week," Kato counters, reigning in his temper.

"No," Lord McDullun replies without even pausing to consider Kato's offer.

Kato tenses, gritting his teeth. "Ten days. I want this alliance sealed in no less than ten days."

This time, Lord McDullun raises his chin slightly, tilting his head as he considers Kato's offer. Finally, he nods.

"I can do ten days."

Kato's teeth flash into a toothy grin. "Then, ten days from today we will expect your presence at Fortress Mullidain."

If Kato expected Lord McDullun to act shocked at his knowledge of Fortress Mullidain in the same way Clan Wallish did, he's disappointed. Lord McDullun barely reacts to the name with more than a passive nod, standing in one smooth motion, pushing up with his cane.

"Fine. In ten days I will meet you at Fortress Mullidain and give you my final answer."

"Wait," Kato says, his eyebrows knitting in confusion. "You have no intention of letting me know before I form the meeting?"

Lord McDullun shrugs. "You won't allow me a full two weeks, so I must take every day you've allowed. You will have your answer, but you will not get it for ten days."

Kato inhales a long breath through his nose, exhaling it

slowly. "So be it." He extends his hand. "Then, do we have a deal?"

Lord McDullun grasps Kato's hand and gives it a firm, assertive shake. "We do."

Niall rises first with Caitlyn and the rest of us all follow suit. Lord McDullun glances at us each in turn, a smile playing on his lips.

"As you already know, we have a suite prepared for you, so you are welcome to stay the night if you desire. I will have dinner sent to your room so you can dine in peace. Please, let me know if you require anything before your departure in the morning."

His words are given with a warm smile in a pleasant, cheerful voice, but their intent is clear—our presence is no longer needed or wanted. Kato stiffens at the words but offers a smile in exchange.

"Thank you for your hospitality," Kato replies, his voice tight as he inclines his head.

Kato turns and strides out of the room, Niall, Ian, Aine, Caitlyn, and Kayleigh close on his heels, but I hesitate for a moment. I glance at Lord McDullun, and he meets my eyes, his lips curving into a knowing smile before I join the others in the hall.

"He's stuffing us in a corner to be forgotten," Niall growls in a low voice.

"But we are not so easily discarded," Kato replies. His voice is oddly even, diplomatic. "He can try to pretend we aren't here, but he cannot truly ignore us. He will come to our side."

"If you want, I can go back in and talk to him one on one," I offer as Ian shoots me a suspicious glance. "Perhaps talking with someone who has lived in Athiedor and other parts of Callenia and has experienced the wrath of the king more closely may have a chance of swaying his opinion a little."

It's a gamble, I know. My stomach twists in knots as Kato tilts his head, considering my offer. If he suspects my true motives, not only are all my efforts up to this point potentially worthless, but I could literally be endangering myself. It's a risk I'm willing to take.

"It can't hurt to try," Kato says at last. "We don't have anything to lose."

Ian shoots Kato a look of disbelief, but my shoulders almost sag with relief. Somehow, I manage to keep my composure as I nod, turning back toward the door.

"I'll do what I can," I promise before I slip back into the library.

Lord McDullun looks up at me from where he stands at the drink cart, pouring more mead into his glass.

"Ah, I figured Kato would send one of you back in here to chat some more one on one. I have to say, I'm rather glad it's you." He gives me a flirtatious grin, and I have to admit he's a very handsome man. In another life, under different circumstances . . .

The corners of my lips twitch into a smile. "Flattered, truly, but my heart is taken."

Lord McDullun winks. "Never hurts to try." He takes a long sip of his mead. "Would you care for a glass? I promise, it is excellent."

I shrug, walking over to him. "Sure."

With a grin, Lord McDullun pours a glass and offers it to me. I take a quick swig. It's as delicious as he promised and more. Lord McDullun registers my delight and his eyes twinkle.

"I never tell a lie." He pauses and then gestures to a pair of armchairs angled toward each other in the far corner of the room beneath the windows. "If we're going to have another conversation, let's make ourselves comfortable at the very least."

I nod, following him to the chairs. I ease down into mine and take another sip of my mead.

"Now then," Lord McDullun says, stretching his legs out in front of him as he leans back comfortably in the chair, one hand swirling his mead while the other absentmindedly taps the head of the cane resting against his leg. "What have you returned to say? Are you here to convince me to throw everything I have behind Kato, or are you going to try to sway me away from Kato and to his sister instead?"

His eyes gleam as my face openly registers my shock.

"I don't know what you mean," I say carefully, tearing my gaze from him and focusing on the drink in my hand.

"Oh, I think you do," he replies, his voice low.

I raise my eyes to him, and I see the feral delight flashing in his eyes. He knows far more information than he let on. He may be a young lord but he's a crafty one. I open my mouth hesitantly but close it quickly, shaking my head. If Kato is still standing outside the library, there's no telling what he might overhear or how he will perceive it. Even if he has gone, I highly doubt Ian will trust me alone with Lord McDullun.

"Ah," Lord McDullun says, understanding dawning. He lifts his hand above his head and turns it slowly. As he does, I feel a curtain of magic cascade around the room. "There. A silencing spell. Simple, but completely effective. No one outside this room will be able to hear a word we speak."

I reach out tentatively with my magic, allowing my

Syphon senses to feel the spell. The spell is what he claims. I settle back in my chair, draping my arm causally over the armrest.

"That's all well and good, but how do I know that even within this room my words are safe and will not be used or twisted against me?" I lock my eyes with Lord McDullun, challenging him. He throws back his head, rich laughter flooding the room.

"You are clever! I love that!" he cries cheerfully. His laugh quiets and he sobers, a slight twinkle remaining in his eye. "I swear to you, whatever you say will not leave this room unless you will it. But I want the honest truth. If I'm to bargain the lives of my people, the truth is no great thing to ask."

I nod slowly, taking a moment to gather my thoughts by sipping more mead from my glass.

"Fine," I reply, "ask what you want, and I'll answer as honestly as I can."

I expect him to smile at my offer, but his face is still and serious. A leader's face.

"If you were me, would you join your Clan in support of Kato?" he asks bluntly.

Damn. He doesn't mess around. He went straight for the throat of the issue.

"No."

He smiles slightly, as if he expected my answer and the question was a test.

"What would you do?"

I hesitate barely a moment before answering, "I would align with Astra."

"His twin?" Lord McDullun asks, his eyebrows arching.

"Is she truly an option?" His voice is nearly breathless, filled with hope.

"Yes. She has already presented Prince Ehren with the idea of freeing Athiedor once he takes his rightful place as king. I do not know Ehren's exact thoughts on the matter, but Astra assures me he is willing to compromise. He's a reasonable man and a good friend."

"Well, that definitely sheds a new light on things," Lord McDullun muses, taking a deep sip of his mead, his eyes staring unfocused toward the window. "I know the entire alliance with Clan Wallish falls apart without my support, and I suspect others would back out as well. Yes, joining with Astra may be a better option, if she can truly deliver what she promises."

"I truly believe she can and will. Even if she can't give a one hundred percent guarantee of a free Athiedor with no war or involvement in the war against the king, the world she offers is a better one," I say firmly.

Lord McDullun meets my eyes, arching his eyebrows at my words. "How so?"

I take a deep breath. "Kato wants to rule in magic, fight in magic, and make everything about magic. He doesn't really care about everyone else who may not have magic to their name. That's why he and Astra split. Astra believes that magic and non-magic people should work together, side-by-side, to build a new world. Ehren firmly believes this as well. The world they want leaves no one behind. Astra is even engaged to a man who holds no magic in the slightest." Or at least she was engaged. My heart skips a beat recalling the lack of ring on her finger.

Lord Mcdullun rises slowly, not speaking, and walks to the window, staring out into whatever view there is to behold. He stands for a moment, one hand clasped tightly on his cane, the other lifting his mead to his lips.

"My father was killed in a hunting accident," he says at length, his voice low and quiet as he continues to stare out the window. "He was mauled by a boar and there was no helping him. If we had healing magic back then, he likely would have lived."

"You had no healing magic?" I ask, my voice quiet as well.

Lord McDullun shakes his head. "No. This section of Athiedor did not have magic until it returned other places." He pauses and adds with a shrug, "Well, we had people with affinities beyond that of a normal person that were likely tied to magic. Farmers who could tame unruly land into flourishing crops and Seers who got strong enough feelings to be of use, but no real magic. Not like it is now."

He pulls his gaze away from the window and locks his eyes with mine. "My people may have long bloodlines of magical heritage, but our magic is still new and raw. Every day more and more people discover they have magic, but there are still many in my Clan that do not wield any magic. I will not have them separated from their friends and family or thought less of because the gods did not see fit to gift them with magic. I do not wish to align with Kato, but I will consider an alliance with Astra, should you be able to arrange it."

My heart seizes in my chest. This is the first true alliance I have been able to secure for her.

"Of course," Lord McDullun adds, "I still wish to reach out to my people in the ten days I have before I formally reject Kato's offer. When I came to my position, I was young and untried. My father taught me what he could while he lived, but learning about leading and actually leading are two very different things. I tried, and failed, to lead on my own. It was only by reaching out to members of my Clan, respecting their thoughts and wishes and truly listening to them, that I have been able to lead. Even though I truly desire to throw my support behind Astra, assuming she comes through as you promise, I still wish to make sure my people are on the same page."

I smile and nod. "You are a good leader, Lord McDullun."

He grins. "Oh, please, call me Ronan. We're barely ten years apart in age, possibly less. If we're going forward in this alliance, it's best to be on friendly terms, anyway."

I laugh. "Fine, Ronan." I stand and drain the rest of my mead, feeling a rush. I lick my lips and nod toward the desk. "Do you mind if I write a quick letter to Astra?"

Ronan shakes his head and gestures to the desk. "Write away! There should be parchment in the top drawer."

I saunter over to the desk and find the paper exactly where he says, with ink and pens on the top. As I write, Ronan remains in the library but gives me a semblance of privacy, refilling his glass and then standing in front of the map of Athiedor, staring at it like he's unraveling a great puzzle. When I finish my letter, I call to Felixe, and he appears on my shoulder.

"Bloody hell!" Ronan laughs, striding toward me, his eyes fixed on Felixe. "Is that a Fae Fox?"

I nod proudly. "Aye. His name is Felixe. He's my familiar."

Felixe stretches out toward Ronan, his little black nose sniffing wildly. He seems content with whatever he finds and pulls back, blinking up at me with his wide blue eyes. I fold the letter and lift it to him.

"You know what to do," I whisper as he grasps it in his teeth.

He gives me one last blink before vanishing. I look over at Ronan whose face is scrunched with confusion.

"You're using him as a messenger? How . . ." Realization dawns on his face and his eyes widen as his mouth gapes open. "He's not just your familiar. He's hers as well. You're soul-bonded to Kato's twin!"

I wince at the words as he says them out loud. I've barely admitted to myself what Astra's obvious connection to Felixe means and having a man who's essentially a stranger declare it with abandon is unsettling.

"No wonder you're supporting her cause," he mumbles in awe as he sinks into the nearest armchair. "You can speak with confidence as to her character because your souls know and understand each other. Your magic is bonded."

I glance away, but I can feel his assessing gaze fixed on me.

"But why is Kato allowing you to remain by his side, allowing you to complete his negotiations, if you are soul-bonded to his sister?" He pauses and then slowly adds, "He doesn't know, does he."

I shake my head and meet his eyes. "No. No one knows. No one besides me, you, and Felixe, though I think a few people might suspect," I admit weakly, my stomach turning.

"Wait. Even Astra doesn't know? You haven't completed the soul bond ceremony?" His eyes are wide with disbelief as he scans my face, looking for any indication he's wrong. "Why? A soul bond is one of the strongest feats of magic! It's sacred and rare. Why wouldn't you want to secure the bond?"

I shift uncomfortably and avert my gaze, shoving my hands in my pockets. "I can't bring myself to tell her. I'm afraid . . . I'm afraid it will mess everything up."

"You care deeply for her, don't you." He says it not as a question, but as a statement, as the fact it is. I nod anyway.

"I love her more than life itself," I admit, my chest aching with a sense of longing.

"And you're afraid that if she accepts the soul bond, and you complete the ceremony, that your feelings for her will grow more intense, but she'll still love someone else? She'll still want the fiancé you mentioned?"

His eyes hold a sad understanding. But he's wrong. That's not what worries me the most. Yes, there's a piece of me that wonders if she'll always love Bram but, no, that's not it. I remember the way she rushed into my arms barely a night ago. I remember the light that shines in her eyes when she looks my way. I even remember the way she returned those first truly hungry kisses in her room following the ball in Embervein. I don't fear enacting the soul bond would leave her in a relationship with Bram, if she even is still in that relationship.

"No," I say slowly shaking my head and taking a steadying breath. "I fear the opposite." I meet Ronan's eyes as I put a voice to my fears, my voice tight with emotion. "I fear that she will love me *because* of the bond. I fear the bond will force her emotions to be greater for me, even if it's not a path she would have chosen herself. I don't want that. I want her to love me for me and nothing more. I don't want to manipulate her into feeling something for me."

"That's a reasonable desire," Ronan says quietly, "but

enacting the soul bond, or even admitting to her it exists between you, doesn't guarantee she'll fall in love with you. From what I understand, a soul bond connects you based on compatibility of several different factors, feelings and emotions only being one. There are examples throughout history of soul-bonded pairs who were not in romantic relationships with one another. Some even had relationships with other people while keeping their soul bond intact."

His words are comforting, and I manage a weak smile. "It's just . . . I believe she does care for me. I'm just not sure she cares for me as greatly as I care for her. Once the bond is enacted, everything between us will be felt more keenly." With a heavy sigh I drop into a chair across from Ronan. "I want a relationship with her. For years before I even met her, she was no more than a name on my lips from a crazy man I was only half-convinced was a Seer. Then I met her and my world shifted. I didn't love her immediately. I was more cautious than that, but she was instantly more important to me than anyone else in my life. Now I love her, and I cannot imagine life without her. I want her to feel the same, regardless of the soul bond."

"Well, mate," Ronan says, offering me a sympathetic grin, "I can't say I blame you for wanting sincere feelings, but you're essentially lying to her by keeping the bond to yourself. It isn't fair to her."

I sigh and run a hand through my hair. "I know. I know. I just can't bring myself to tell her."

"Well," Ronan says, pushing up from his chair and strolling toward the drink cart, "why don't you drown your sorrows in more excellent mead? It's what I do every day."

He gives me a sad smile as I rise and join him by the cart.

"What problems does a handsome young lord like your-self have that requires the constant drowning of sorrows?"

Ronan leans his cane against the cart and pours a glass of mead. "Love, of course." He hands me the glass. "As the only true heir in my father's line, I'm of course expected to marry and produce an heir, but since women hold no interest for me . . ."

His voice trails off and he shrugs, pouring his own glass full nearly to the rim. He lifts his glass, careful not spill any of the deep red liquid.

"Here's to being in love and hoping one day true love can conquer all."

I lift my glass in agreement and we each take a swig. Ronan tips his glass back and gulps the contents down, wiping his lips before slamming the empty cup down on the tray. His cheeks are tinged pink from all the mead. He lifts his eyes to me as I take another small sip.

"So, when you go back to play your part with Kato, what will you tell him we discussed?"

I grin. "I'll tell him the truth." Ronan's eyebrows quirk up. "We discussed love and politics."

Ronan laughs. "You're clever. Too clever. It's a pity your heart is so stoutly taken because you and I would make quite the couple."

I laugh, eyes shining. My cleverness has been my saving grace over the years, but it's also been my downfall. Here's to hoping this time it helps me to succeed.

CHAPTER SEVENTEEN

ASTRA

I'm wide awake, staring up at the red velvet canopy above my bed. Thoughts of the masquerade swirl through my mind, a smile playing on my lips. Well, not so much thoughts of the ball itself, but rather thoughts of Alak. I subconsciously raise my fingertips to trace my lips at the memory of his mouth on mine. Heat rises in my cheeks as I remember the way he held me, recalling every gentle touch and caress. I sigh and turn over in bed, snuggling the blanket. I'm still not exactly sure why I reacted the way I did when we walked into the garden. Something about seeing him there in front of me overwhelmed my senses and I gave in, craving his touch.

I wish he could have stayed longer, but he was correct in his assumption that I was missed from the ball. Kai was in a nervous, fidgety state when I returned. Alak must have used some sort of magic to mask our departure and make sure no one cared if I was missing, because Kai had only just realized I had been gone for several minutes. I brushed him off when he demanded to know where I had been and continued to dance. No one else said anything beyond Sama inquiring after my handsome fox dance partner and Ehren shooting me a knowing glance across the dance floor.

A huff from the floor draws my attention and I let my gaze drift to the giant sleeping wolf. Kai may have relented his scolding last night, but he refused to leave my room after the ball. Bram had been indignant at the suggestion that Kai stay in my room but had ceased his arguing when Kai transformed into a giant, snarling wolf. I chuckle slightly at the memory of Bram shrinking away from Kai, his hands raised in surrender.

Unable to drift back to sleep despite feeling a little tired from dancing all night, I sit up. It's still early, but the sun has risen enough to cast its warm rays through the nearly sheer red curtains over the window, casting the room in a glowing red light. I feel like I'm inside a ruby itself, which, given that I'm in the City of Gems, is probably exactly the effect they wanted.

As I slide from the bed, Sama doesn't stir in the slightest. I quickly cross into the dressing room and change from my night dress into a simple day dress. When I re-enter the room, I step cautiously over the sleeping wolf in my way and stride over to the door connecting my room to Ehren's. I knock quietly but, as expected, he doesn't answer. I try the handle and, when I discover it isn't locked, I carefully creep into his room, shutting my door behind me.

Ehren's room is bathed in the same ruby light, though it somehow looks more regal as it casts across his sleeping features. I feel awkward as I watch his bare chest rise and fall, only barely obscured by maroon and gold blankets. As I cross the room, he stirs, his eyes blinking open. When he spots me, he forces away the haze of sleep, pushing up into a sitting position, rubbing his eyes with one palm while propping himself on his elbow.

"Morning, sunshine," I say with a grin.

He just blinks at me in reply and I laugh. He shakes his head, a smile crossing his lips.

"And what exactly are you so eager to discuss this early in the morning?" he asks, fighting back a yawn.

Before I can answer, a memory dawns, his lips parting as he nods. "That *was* Alak I saw last night, wasn't it?"

I bite my lip and nod.

"But how . . . ?"

I shrug. "I have no idea. Somehow, he managed to get here, and he had some important information to share."

Ehren groans. "All right, if I have to listen to bad news so early in the morning, I need coffee first."

He goes to get out of bed, but I cry out, "Wait! Are you even wearing pants?"

Heat blooms on my cheeks as he grins. "Let's find out."

I squint, holding up my hands between my face and Ehren as he throws back the blanket and swings his legs out of the bed. Much to my relief, he's still wearing his pants from the night before. I release a sigh of relief and relax my hands by my side.

"Seeing me without pants would be an honor and a delight," Ehren teases with a laugh as he stands, crossing the room to ring for breakfast.

I laugh, shaking my head. "I'm not sure it's an honor I want."

Ehren chuckles again as he pulls the long, tasseled rope that will beckon a servant before taking a seat on a nearby couch, his arm slung casually over the back. I sit down across from him, my hands folded in my lap.

"How long was Alak here last night? I have a feeling he used some sort of manipulation to hide his presence, seeing as how I only remembered seeing you dance with him *after* he left."

"He wasn't here long," I admit with a shrug. "Three, maybe four dances."

Ehren cocks an eyebrow as he smirks. "And yet I only recall you dancing one. What, pray tell, did you do for the remaining dances?"

Color rises in my cheeks as I recall the heated kisses. Ehren waggles his eyebrows as his grin grows. The servant knocking on the door to deliver breakfast is a welcome distraction.

"Thank the gods for coffee," Ehren declares, pouring a cup full of the steaming brew as the servant exits the room. He takes a careful sip, sighing in contentment. He leans against the table and lifts the coffee again, taking a longer sip.

"All right," he says. "I'm ready. Tell me all Alak had to say."

As Ehren drinks his coffee, I share the details of Kato's coup. The longer I talk, the deeper the "v" between Ehren's furrowed eyebrows grows. When I finish, Ehren lets out a long sigh and refills his cup.

"So in order to stop Kato, I have to give up Athiedor?"

I nod and fill a cup of my own. "It seems that way." I take a sip of coffee and raise my eyes to meet Ehren's. "But you'll do it, won't you?"

He sighs and runs a hand through his tousled bed hair. "It's not that easy, Ash. I can't just wave my hand and make Athiedor its own country. And if Kato thinks he can, he's gravely mistaken. There are all sorts of regulations and rules in place that make it . . . complicated. Not to mention that the lands of Athiedor are technically owned by different nobles. Athiedor has been a part of Callenia since my great-grandfather reigned. I can't just undo it."

I nod, sipping my coffee, my stomach twisting. It seemed like such an easy solution. Too easy, it seems.

"But," Ehren continues, shaking his head, "it makes sense to do it. Kato has to be stopped, and while this may not stop him entirely, it may stall him long enough for us to gain a better foothold against my father. Like King Naimon said, we are fighting a war on two fronts. If I can narrow those fronts to just one, I stand a better chance. You know what? Damn the regulations to hell!" he yells suddenly, slamming his cup on the table, coffee sloshing around the sides of his cup. "I'm doing it."

My eyes brighten, and I feel like a weight has been lifted. "You will? You'll really give Athiedor their freedom?"

Ehren nods confidently. "I will. After having seen Athiedor firsthand, they deserve to be their own country. It's only right. And if Alak says it will turn the tide in our favor, then all the more reason to do it."

"What?" a cold voice snaps from the corner of the room, startling me so much I spill my coffee, hot liquid splashing onto my hand.

"Ow!" I hiss, switching my cup to my other hand and shaking the coffee off as I glare to where Bram stands in the doorway of his connecting room. "You scared me, Bram! You shouldn't sneak up on people like that."

I try to keep my voice light and carefree, but Bram's cold glare is like hard stone. His hands are clenched at his side and his mouth is set in a tight, thin line.

"So your 'contact' all this time has been Alak?" Bram

demands, stomping toward us, his voice loud and venom-laced.

"Shh! Quiet!" I whisper sharply, my eyes darting to the closed door leading to my room where Sama and Kai sleep.

"No!" Bram yells, his voice gaining volume. "I will not be quiet! You have been keeping this from me!" His voice does drop, however, as he adds in a broken whisper, "How could you?"

Pain lines every inch of his face as he shifts his eyes from me to Ehren. Ehren's shoulders drop in guilt.

"Look, Bram, we didn't think it would be right to tell you —" Ehren starts, but Bram cuts him off with a curt wave.

"No. You don't get to talk your way out of this. First of all, I cannot believe you kept something this big a secret from me. I thought I was your most trusted Guard, by your side to help you, but I guess that job has passed to Astra." I wince at the way he spits my name. "Secondly, I can't believe you're trusting Alak! You can't believe a word that lying bastard says. After all he's done, how can you trust him? Tell me Ehren. How?"

Bram's voice trembles as emotions overtake him. He's more hurt now than angry, and it breaks something inside of me. I take a step toward him, reaching my hand to touch his arm, but he jerks away.

"What's going on?" a voice drawls from behind me.

I turn to find Kai standing in the connecting doorway, leaning lazily against the doorpost. He's still wearing his suit from the night before, albeit wrinkled and lopsided.

"Bram is a little upset that he didn't have as much information as he wanted," Ehren says, selecting his words carefully.

"No," Bram cuts in. "I am furious you went behind my back and lied to me. You cannot trust Alak, and you know it."

"What I know," Ehren says firmly, standing at his full height, "is that Alak is risking is life to get us information."

"You cannot trust that information," Bram insists through clenched teeth.

"Who exactly is Alak?" Kai asks slowly, his eyes shifting from Bram to me.

"Alak is a liar who cares about no one but himself and doesn't care who he hurts or kills," Bram snarls, his face red with answer. "He's the man responsible for my sister's death."

At Bram's last words, Kai snaps upright into a standing position, his face colder than usual. Bram has no idea why his words have had the effect they did, but I do, and it hurts my heart to see the hints of pain in Kai's eyes.

"What?" Kai says, his voice quiet but sharp.

"Alak is the reason my sister is dead and they"—Bram gestures at me and Ehren—"know this." He points directly at Ehren. "He was there! He witnessed it, and yet, for some unknown reason, he still trusts the bastard!"

"You trusted him, too," I whisper on the verge of tears. "You said you trusted him."

I hate this. I hate that both Kai and Bram are hurting. I hate that it's because of me.

Bram sees the tears threatening to spill and his shoulders drop. "I had to trust him," he says defensively, his voice finally lowering to a normal volume and staying there. "I didn't have a choice. We needed him. *You* needed him. I thought he was finally gone, only to find out that you've been communicating in secret and lying to me about it. How can I trust him—or you for that matter—when I have been betrayed so thoroughly?"

He stops, his voice breaking, tears reflecting in his own eyes.

"Bram," I whisper, my voice trembling as I reach for him.

Once again, he jerks away. "I need to get out of here."

He turns and beelines for the door, slamming it behind him as he leaves. My heart shatters, and I look to Ehren, desperate for his help. Ehren runs a shaky hand through his hair.

"I . . . I'll fix this," Ehren mutters.

"It's my fault," I whisper as tears slide free.

Kai crosses the room toward me in three solid strides, but Ehren pulls me into his arms before Kai reaches me. I think he needs to be comforted as much as I do.

"No, it's not," Ehren whispers into my hair as I wrap my arms around him, holding him close. "I'm as much to blame as you, if not more so. I told you not to tell him."

He releases me with a sigh and looks down at me as I pull back, my arms dropping to my sides. "You going to be okay?"

I nod and force a half-smile. "Yeah." I glance toward the door. "Maybe I should go find him."

Ehren shakes his head. "No, I'll do it."

He takes another deep sigh before striding to the door, shooting me a weak smile over his shoulder before he leaves. Once's he's gone I turn to Kai and find his eyebrows knitted in worry as he watches me.

"Do I get to know what's going on, or is it classified?" he asks, his voice hard.

"I'll tell you whatever you want to know," I admit with a shrug.

"All this has something to do with your missing minutes from the ball last night, I assume?"

I nod and he grunts, crossing his arms.

"I knew you were up to something."

Even though his voice is laced with aggravation, a smile plays on his lips and there's a twinkle in his eyes. It makes me feel lighter.

"I'm not sure exactly where to start," I confess as I meet his eyes.

"Well," Kai says, uncrossing his arms and walking to the table to pour a cup of coffee. "Why don't you start with who Alak is?"

"Okay," I say with a nod. "That's easy enough, I suppose. Alak is the first person I met who truly understood magic. He helped me learn how to access my power and control it before it could consume me." I pause, smiling as an image of Alak's emerald eyes flashes in my mind.

"He's someone who keeps me grounded and has always had faith in my power, even when I lose faith myself. When Kato abandoned me, Alak went with him, to keep Kato safe and try to bring him back to me. He's been in contact, letting me know what Kato has been doing."

Kai nods as he sips his coffee. "He sounds helpful. So, why doesn't Bram trust him?"

I glance away at the unspoken words: *How did he kill Bram's sister?*

"Ehren and Bram knew Alak years ago, long before I did and, while I don't have all the details, Alak somehow hurt Bram's sister and she committed suicide." My voice is a low whisper, and if it weren't for Kai's sharp intake of breath I would wonder if he even heard me.

"So," Kai clarifies, his voice even, "Alak didn't actually kill Bram's sister, but he blames him for her death?"

I nod.

"And Ehren was there?"

I nod again.

"But Ehren trusts Alak, even though he knows the story?"

"Yes. Alak has been an asset to Ehren, both before he left with Kato and after," I say, more defensively than I intend.

"And you love him?"

Kai's question catches me completely off guard, and I actually stumble back a step.

"Wh-what makes you say that?" I stutter, my cheeks flushing against my will.

Kai smiles and lets out a huff that easily could be a laugh.

"Just because I don't personally feel romantic attraction to others myself, doesn't mean I don't recognize the signs in other people."

"But you've never even really seen us together," I mumble in protest.

He smiles, the corners of his eyes crinkling. "I've seen enough. I saw the way you looked at him while you were dancing and your face just now as you talked about him. Even if it's not quite full-blown romantic love, you care for him a great deal." His face grows more serious as he furrows his brow. "But are you sure you can trust him? Bram seems adamantly set against him. And he did sneak you away from the dance, putting up some sort of spell to keep anyone from finding you."

"I trust him completely and you can, too," I assure him. "My feelings aside, whatever they may be, Alak has proven himself trustworthy and invaluable. Despite Bram's reservations, Alak has been very helpful, and the information he's given us may be what we need to keep Kato from gaining too much power." I pause and take a deep breath. "As to why he pulled me away at the dance and covered it with a spell, well, he was giving me information in person he didn't want overheard. And, as you can clearly tell, Bram didn't know about what he was doing for us, and neither do any of the others besides Ehren, so he had to conceal himself from anyone who might recognize him."

Kai nods, sipping his coffee. "That's reasonable enough. I assume he has illusion magic?"

I nod. "And Syphon magic."

Kai chokes on his coffee. At his initial reaction, I assume Kai is upset like Bram was when he discovered Sama was a Syphon, but when he speaks, his voice is full of something closer to awe than fear.

"He's a Syphon? They're relatively rare." He pauses, thinking for a moment and then adds, "I vaguely recall you mentioning a Syphon when you first arrived in the Valley. I just never expected you to be so . . . close."

"Both his illusion magic and his Syphon abilities have saved us multiple times. Honestly, it's largely thanks to his magic we're all alive."

"Yes, I can see how that would come in handy when you're on the run," Kai says with a gentle smile.

"Oh, there you are," Sama says, stepping into Ehren's room from ours. "I woke up and wondered where everyone had gone." Her eyes fall on the coffee and her face lights up. "Is that coffee?"

"It sure is," I grin at her. "Help yourself."

She pads across the room and pours a cup, taking a deep

breath of it before gulping down several mouthfuls. After several sips, her eyes scan the room.

"Where's everyone else?" she asks, cupping her hands around the coffee.

"Bram is throwing a fit, and Ehren went to calm him down," Kai says nonchalantly, and I choke on a laugh.

"Okay," Sama says, drawing the word out, clearly sensing there's much more to the situation, but deciding to leave it alone.

Kai clears his throat. "So, it seemed everyone had fun at the masquerade last night." His eyes twinkle, flicking momentarily to me before settling on Sama.

"Oh, yes!" Sama replies, glowing. "It was lovely."

"It was your first ball, right?" I ask and she nods.

"Yes. I mean, I've been to festivals with dancing before, but never an official ball, let alone one at a palace," she says, her voice and eyes bright.

"Did you have a good time?" I ask, addressing Kai.

He shrugs. "It wasn't bad. The food was decent. A pesky girl somehow tricked me into multiple dances, but I survived."

I grin. "Yes, you did survive. And you're not a bad dancer,"

"You're really not," Sama offers enthusiastically. "You danced just as fine as any of the other young men I danced with last night."

Kai tries to look irritated by our proclamations, but beneath his scowl I can see the smile he's trying to hide. The door opens, drawing my attention away from Kai as Ehren waltzes into the room, looking weary. I look behind him but there's no Bram. Ehren shakes his head, shutting the door with a sigh.

"He needs more time to adjust," he says slowly and my face falls. "He didn't like being kept in the dark, but he'll come around eventually."

"I can't blame him," Kai says simply with a shrug.

Ehren flashes him a look of annoyance but doesn't argue.

"Well, what now?" I ask.

"Now," Ehren says, straightening his shoulders, "we use what information we have to come up with a plan, and then we act on it." He pauses, tilting his head in thought. "I'm supposed to meet with Illyas in the garden where we reactivated the portal stone. Would you like to come with me?"

"Hmm . . . ," I muse, furrowing my brow in feigned consideration. "Do I want to come along with you on your secret rendezvous? I don't know . . . ."

Ehren laughs and nudges my shoulder with his, though I catch a little pink tinging his cheeks. "It's nothing like what you are insinuating. We need to make sure it's still working as is it should before we leave."

"Fine." I laugh. "I am a little interested to see where you put it."

"All right. Just give me a moment to change and we can go."

"I'd like to accompany you, if that's all right," Kai offers and Ehren nods.

"Sure. Why not." He turns to Sama. "You're welcome to come along too. Hell, we'll swing by the barracks and drag the others with us. We'll make it a whole group outing."

Sama grins. "Okay, I need to change first as well."

"I should probably change too, and then we'll head down," I say. "Meet in the hall in ten minutes?"

Everyone nods as we return to our own rooms.

CHAPTER EIGHTEEN

ASTRA

When we get to the barracks, we find Cal easily. He's wide awake and dressed for the day. Nyco and Makin, however, are still fast asleep. Ehren and Cal insist the barracks are no place for ladies such as me and Sama despite the fact that Gleador employs several female soldiers. However, we don't argue and leave Cal and Ehren to go and fetch Nyco and Makin. They return several minutes later with two disgruntled, scowling guards, Nyco's mouth opened wide in a yawn.

"You three need more respect for sleep," Makin moans, fighting off a yawn of his own. His eyes scan the hall. "Wait, where's Bram?"

"He's busy," Ehren says, his voice short.

Makin opens his mouth to ask more but snaps it shut, shaking his head.

"So, I was dragged from bed to see a garden?" Nyco asks, eyeing Ehren with distaste.

"And because it's time to get up," I scold.

Nyco rolls his eyes. "You sure know how to live."

I roll my own eyes in response as we turn and follow Ehren to the garden. It's a different garden than the one Alak and I visited last night, but it looks similar. The paths, made of smooth bright stone, weave between masterfully carved bushes, marble statues, fountains, and brightly colored flowers and plants. Ehren leads us down a path past a fountain of a dragon with emerald wings that catch the sunlight, glowing. He pauses at an arch made of twisting vines speckled with bright purple flowers.

"Well, here it is," he says, gesturing to the arch.

"The stone is in the arch?" I ask, knitting my eyebrows in confusion.

Ehren chuckles. "It's in the ground, but when the portal opens it should be contained within the arch."

My eyes widen. "That's amazing!"

"I agree," a voice with a slight Gleador accent says from behind us.

I turn to find Illyas walking down the path toward us, his hands shoved in his pockets and his mage cape billowing behind him.

"There are several different types of vines growing on this arch," he explains, standing in front of it and looking up. "That way flowers will always be blooming, regardless of the season."

He pulls his gaze from the arch and his eyes settle on me, his grin widening. "You know, you've been here at the palace for a few days now, yet this is the first time we've actually met in an informal setting."

"I suppose that's true," I muse. "I apologize if I've offended you in any way. This whole 'Court Sorceress' thing is a bit new."

He laughs, waving a hand. "You haven't offended me in

the slightest. You prince has been friendly and quite . . . accommodating."

I glance to Ehren, who ducks his head to hide a sheepish grin. "I'm sure he's been very diplomatic."

Illyas's eyes shine. "Indeed. Our time together has been well-spent. However, I would like to get to know you better. As official Court Mage and Sorceress, it's likely we will be interacting often in the future. We might as well start off on as good of terms as we possibly can."

"I agree," I reply with a sincere smile.

He cocks his head, his finger on his chin as he studies me for a minute, as if he's weighing his next words carefully.

"I don't suppose you would care to join me in the village today to celebrate the continuation of Oryus's festival?" he finally asks.

"There's more than the masquerade ball?" I ask, my eyebrows rising slightly.

Illyas laughs. "He's the god of festivities! One masquerade ball would hardly suit!"

The corner of my mouth quirks up. "I would absolutely love to see how the city celebrates."

"Excellent!" He turns his attention back to Ehren. "Of course, everyone is welcome. It would be my honor to show you all around the celebrations."

Ehren shakes his head, smiling. "Thank you, but I'm afraid I have to decline, at least for now. I should really make some preparations for continuing our journey. I may meet up with you later, however."

Illyas gives Ehren an understanding nod, but I catch a hint of disappointment in his eyes.

"I'd love to go into the city," Sama says softly, her eyes

bright. "I'd like to see how the celebration here compares to the Valley."

"I'd kind of like to see it myself," Makin says with a shrug as Nyco and Cal nod along.

"Unless, of course, you need me to stay behind and assist you with whatever you need," Cal adds quickly, glancing to Ehren.

Ehren offers Cal a small smile. "No, you go and enjoy the city. I'll be fine on my own for a bit."

"Well then," Illyas grins, "let me show you how we celebrate in Koshima. Though, once you see a true festival, you may never want to leave." A twinkle gleams in his eye.

Nyco laughs and claps Illyas on his shoulder. "Consider us warned."

Grinning, Illyas escorts us through a side gate that leads into the city. If I thought everything was bright and colorful before, it has nothing on today. Banners and brightly colored ribbons and bits of fabric wave in the warm breeze, and people stroll through the streets dressed in vibrant outfits, many equipped with matching masks. Some of the masks are crudely crafted from basic materials, while others are nearly as elegant as the ones we wore last night. Regardless of make, they're all cheerful and add to the beauty of the celebration. Anyone without a mask has plenty of chances to purchase one; almost every other vendor cart crowded into the street is selling a wide variety, their ribbons twirling in the breeze created by the shuffling crowd.

As we pass by one such cart, I turn to Illyas. "Why are masks associated with Oryus? I understand he's the god of festivities, but there's definitely an emphasis on the masks." I make a sweeping gesture at the masks around us and Illyas grins.

"Because Oryus is not only the god of festivities," Illyas says in a low voice, leaning down close to my ear as we walk. "He's also the god of secrets."

I glance over at him, and he gives me a smile that indeed looks full of secrets. I wonder briefly if he knows something I don't.

"Oh, Balka cakes!" he says, pulling his gaze from me as he directs me toward a cart selling small oval-shaped cakes rolled in sugar and spices.

He pulls out a few coins, exchanging them for several of the cakes wrapped in paper. We step out of the way, and I tentatively take one in my fingers.

"Go on," Illyas encourages me with a nod. "You'll love them. I promise."

I take a bite and the sweet dough practically melts in my mouth.

"This is delicious," I declare, shoving the rest of the ball in my mouth and reaching for a second.

"Told you," Illyas grins, popping one in his own mouth.

I hear Makin swear in delight and turn to see him holding a packet of the cakes as well. Nyco reaches to take one, but Makin swats his hand away.

"Get your own!" Makin cries, pulling the cakes out of Nyco's reach.

Cal sneaks around behind Makin and plucks up a cake, grinning at Makin as he takes a bite.

"Hey!" Makin laughs, making to grab the last bit of the cake from Cal's fingers.

Cal's grin widens as he pops the rest of the cake in his mouth. "I'm stealthier than you."

Illyas laughs and looks down at me. "Are they always like this?"

I nod and laugh. "Unfortunately so."

As we wind through the crowd, it's easy to get caught up in all the performances, something new to see every few yards. Somewhere along the way, our group gets separated, and I end up wandering the crowded streets alone with Illyas, which I really don't mind. For several minutes, I find myself captivated by a group of female dancers. Their skirts are made of two long strips of fabric tied cleverly around their waists, leaving their long, tanned legs almost fully exposed. Their tops are tightly bound strips of matching cloth across their breasts with small golden tassels across the bottom that shimmer with every movement. Each dancer also wears a short, sheer veil that covers their eyes and stops at the tip of their nose. The tiny bells they wear on their wrists and ankles tinkle pleasantly as they dance, moving as smooth as liquid. I can't tear my eyes away until the music stops and the girls turn, smiling, to the watching crowd that cheers and tosses coins at their feet.

The next bit of entertainment that draws my attention is a group of fire dancers. Three men wearing only tight black leather pants stand on a bright carpet, their strong, tanned chests bare and oiled. The man front and center twists two batons, each with both ends on fire, cleverly through the air, making it appear as four flawless lines of fire. As he twists them between his legs, the crowd, including myself, draws its breath. The men standing slightly behind him are juggling six flaming objects each.

Once we leave the fire dancers, we head toward performers that appear to be different storytellers. An older woman sits, leaning up against a building, surrounded by wide-eyed children. She holds out her hand and golden images flicker to life, small gasps coming from her attentive crowd. I smile, remembering the similar reactions to the storyteller in Athiedor. Just behind the woman is a small booth with a red curtain where two puppets dance before a giggling crowd of children. I'm so captivated watching the children react in pure glee, I don't even realize Illyas has slipped away until he returns, offering me a stick speared through chunks of seasoned meat and vegetables.

"What's this?" I ask, pulling my gaze from the children and accepting the food.

"Seasoned lamb kabobs," he replies.

I take a bite and almost lose my breath at the unexpected heat from the spices. Illyas laughs.

"You need Hulluh juice," he says, nodding his head toward another nearby booth offering some sort of bright green liquid.

Unable to say anything, let alone argue due to my mouth feeling like it's on fire, I simply nod and follow him. I don't know exactly where Hulluh juice comes from, but it immediately soothes the burn, filling my mouth with a delightfully sweet, sticky juice. Illyas and I take a seat on the edge of the crowd to finish our food.

"So," he says, as I finish the last few gulps of my juice, "what is your honest opinion of Koshima?"

I can't help but smile as I let my eyes drift around the energetic streets. "I absolutely love it," I breathe, a warm glow on my face. "I really love it."

When I look back at Illyas, pride shines in his eyes.

"I do, too," he says softly as we rise from our seated positions and begin walking again.

"You know," Illyas says conversationally, linking his hands behind his back as he walks, "I didn't actually grow up in Koshima. I didn't even really grow up in Gleador."

I widen my eyes. "What? I assumed in order for you to be the Court Mage . . ."

Illyas shakes his head. "No. My mother was from Koshima, but my father was an ambassador from Naskein. He met my mother on one of his assignments. After a few trips to Koshima, he convinced her to return with him through the very portal you used. She was hesitant, but eventually agreed. I was born on Naskein and lived there, learning magic, until I was fifteen."

"What happened when you turned fifteen?" I ask, genuinely curious.

"My father resigned his position as ambassador, and we moved to the Hundan Valley for a couple years. When he passed away, my mother moved back here to be close to her family, me with her."

"You grew up with magic? But Koshima didn't have magic at that time, so what did you do?"

Illyas smiles tightly at the memory. "I felt like a limb had been ripped from my body. I complained every day until I turned eighteen and returned to the Hundan Valley."

I cock my head. "What brought you back to Koshima?"

"A year ago my mother fell ill. She's fine now," he rushes to add when he registers my concern, "but she needed my help. After that, I just couldn't leave her. It scared me being so far away from her. Had it been more serious than it was, I might never have seen her again."

My face falls as I think of my own mother, far away in Timberborn, forced by my father to disown me. Illyas doesn't seem to notice the shift in my mood and continues.

"It was in the middle of the night this past spring when I woke up suddenly. At first, I couldn't figure out what had woken me. I felt like I had been pricked by something sharp.

That's when I realized I had my magic back. I couldn't believe it. The next day, I rushed into the city to see if anyone else noticed magic returning. It was slow, but little by little magic began to spread through the city.

"About a week after magic returned, emissaries from the Hundan Valley arrived at the king's request. He had no real idea what to do with all the circulating magic and needed guidance. One of the emissaries was a good friend of mine and introduced me to the king. With the recommendations from the Hundan Valley, my magical training and experience, and my father's name being known, King Naimon didn't even hesitate to offer me my position."

"That's quite the story," I muse, pausing to examine a pretty green mask.

"I think that mask would look lovely on you," Illyas says with a nod to a purple, blue, and silver mask with long, thin ribbons.

"Really?" I ask, picking up the mask and lifting it to my face. "What do you think?"

Illyas grins. "I think you cannot live without it."

Before I can protest, he pulls coins from his pocket, handing them to the vendor, who smiles and nods.

"If you're buying me a mask, then I will buy you"—my eyes drift over the selection, settling on a black and red mask—"this one."

I pluck up the mask and offer it to Illyas after handing the lady my coins. Illyas grins, sliding his mask on as I secure my own.

"Now we'll blend right into the crowd," he says with a grin.

I grin in return as we begin weaving through the crowd once again.

"You know, you're not at all what I was expecting," Illyas says, choosing his words with care.

I look up at him. "What do you mean?"

"When we first received word of you, all we heard of was your power. How you unleashed a powerful silver light that rendered you unconscious. How you took down fifty of the king's men almost single-handedly. How you escaped a band of mercenaries by running across water."

I frown. "I didn't take down the king's men single-handedly at all. I had a lot of help."

Illyas shrugged. "Perhaps, but the description we received of how your power radiated over them—strangling and crushing, killing at least two dozen men in ruthless abandon, eyes glowing and twin blades crafted from silver light in your hands—painted a more vicious picture of you."

I pale at his words, my stomach dropping.

"The soldiers died?" I whisper, my voice barely audible over the noise of the crowd.

Illyas notices my discomfort and quickly backtracks. "I can't say for sure, but that's what our sources relayed." His voice softens as he adds, "In a time of war, some things become necessary, no matter how awful they may be."

I nod, looking down at my feet. "I suppose. I hope I never get used to it."

"I hope you don't either."

Illyas stops abruptly and looks up. "Ah, we're here."

I hadn't realized we were headed anywhere specific, but apparently Illyas had other plans. I follow him inside a small, cluttered shop. Beautiful, crafted jewelry is displayed everywhere. A middle-aged woman in a red headscarf stands behind a thin counter lined with stones. Upon seeing Illyas, her face lights up and she rambles something off in Gleador.

"I'm most delighted to see you as well," Illyas says in Callenian for my benefit. The woman gives an understanding nod. He gestures to me. "This is Astra, the one I had the cuff prepared for."

"A pleasure to meet you, Astra," the woman says in a thick, rolling accent as she inclines her head. Before I can respond, she looks back at Illyas. "I will go get them."

She turns and shuffles from the room, disappearing behind a wall of colorful, swaying curtains at the back of the shop. I look up at Illyas, his dark eyes glinting mischievously behind his mask.

"What is she getting?" I ask, my brow furrowed.

"You'll see," he grins, stepping closer to the counter as the woman returns holding two pieces of velvet.

"Here is hers," the woman says, placing the larger of the two packages on the counter with a nod.

"Well, go on," Illyas says, nodding to the purple velvet. "I know you're curious."

I reach out tentatively and peel back the folds of fabric, revealing a silver cuff bracelet. I lift it, gasping at the beauty. It's simply made, but it's still well crafted. The bulk of the bracelet is made from thin silver, thinner at the bottom but growing wider as it circles around to a large oval stone set in the center. The stone itself is marbled blues and purples with a soft, opal sheen. Illyas gently takes it from my hands and secures it around my wrist.

"It's beautiful," I gasp, admiring at the way it sits so perfectly on my arm. I look up at Illyas. "Thank you. Now I feel bad I have nothing for you."

Illyas throws his head back and laughs. "I expect nothing from you. It is a tradition in our kingdom that the Court Mage gives any other Court Mage, Sorcerer, Sorceress, or whatever titles they may be given, a gift to show that an alliance has been struck. As you are on the run from the king of your kingdom, I clearly expect nothing in return, save a favorable alliance."

I nod, a smile on my lips. "That I can give you." My eyes shift to the second package still in the woman's hands. "What's that?"

"This," he says, accepting the black velvet from the woman, "is for Ehren."

He unfolds the velvet and a small golden ring with a similar stone appears.

"Do you recognize these stones?" Illyas asks, eyeing me curiously. I shake my head. "I'm not terribly surprised. They haven't really been used in centuries. They're Syphon Stones."

"Syphon Stones?" I repeat, arching my eyebrows in interest.

Illyas nods. "Yes. From the Finjon Mines."

"They absorb magic?"

"They can, but they won't just steal your magic. They draw it in and reserve it for later. To fill it with magic, simply use a spell or allow the transfer of magic into the stone. It's a good idea to have a little magic in your stone at all times to guarantee you never completely drain your magic. In Ehren's case, he can store a little magic and use it for spell casting. Of course, his stone is small, only holding enough magic for a couple spells."

"That could be very helpful in battle," I say in awe, eyes wide in appreciation.

"Indeed. The stones can also help to channel magic and help you control it better."

I trace my fingers along the top of the stone on my wrist. "I don't even know how to thank you."

"Win the war," Illyas says, not hint of jest in his voice.

I smile. "I intend to."

Illyas straightens and glances toward the door. "Now, I'm afraid I actually have business elsewhere I should attend to, so I must take my leave." He looks back at me and holds Ehren's ring out. "Would you mind passing this on to Ehren? I'm not sure when you're departing for Callenia, and I want to make sure he gets it."

I nod, accepting the ring and slipping it in my pocket.

"Do you need help finding your way back to the others?" Illyas asks, stepping forward to hold the door open for me.

I shake my head, glancing toward the towering palace. "No, I'll be fine."

"If you're sure?"

I nod and he smiles.

"All right. Hopefully, I will see you again, but just in case I don't, may your travels be pleasant and may we meet again soon."

He lifts my hand to his lips and brushes a quick kiss against my skin before he disappears into the throngs of people. For several minutes I wander aimlessly, winding through the streets, taking in all the sights and smells. I treat myself to another round of Balka cakes. As I nibble the delicious treat, I spot Sama and Nyco across the crowd. I start to walk their way, but when I notice the bright way that Sama looks up at Nyco and how gently he looks down at her, I decide to let them be. Even though they're surrounded by a sea of people, it would still feel like I'm intruding.

Licking sugar dust off my fingers, I weave around the edge of the crowd, making my way back toward the palace. I'm paused at the edge of the fire dancers' performance when I spot a lazy Fae Fox flopped on his side in the shadows of a tall building. Even before he turns his large, crystal blue eyes to me, giving me a knowing blink, I recognize him as Felixe. At least, my magic does. I smile and cross over to him. He stretches out his legs and gives a dramatic yawn before popping up onto my shoulder.

"Is it exhausting being a Fae Fox?" I tease, lifting my hand to stroke his ears.

Felixe gives a sharp yip, a piece of folded paper falling into my hand. I furrow my brow and turn to look at the fox.

"Where were you hiding this?"

Felixe just blinks his eyes in response as if he doesn't understand why he should have to answer such a ridiculous question. I chuckle and unfold the paper, my heart leaping at the familiar scrawl.

My Most Beloved Astra,

Words cannot begin to describe how much I enjoyed dancing with you at the masquerade. These past few weeks have been dark and dreary. Seeing your face reminded me that everything will be worth it. Leaving you at that dance was extremely difficult—far more difficult than the first time I left—but I still have things to do here at Kato's side.

It will please you to know that I recently saw glimpses of the Kato you grew up with. He has not fully surrendered to power and domination. The Kato you love is still in there. He spent nearly half an hour this morning playing with children and showing them his magic. It reminded me exactly why you want your brother returned to you. I will not give up on him.

I also have good news on the Clans. Clan McDullun is not as easily persuaded as I first thought. While the other six Clans have tentatively signed on to your brother's alliance, it may easily fall apart without Clan McDullun. Lord McDullun is young, but clever and wise. He has no desire for a war and told Kato as much. He isn't so easily bought like the older Lords. I was given an opportunity to talk to him one on one, and he has more or less agreed to throw his cards in with you. Without his support, Clan Wallish will likely back out, followed by additional Clans. If you can truly offer a free Athiedor, I believe you can win the Clans.

Kato has given Lord McDullun ten days to make his final decision before his presence is required along with the other Clan leaders at Fortress Mullidain—a sacred fortress to the Clans on neutral territory where important documents are always signed when they involve multiple Clans. I'm not sure how your brother knew the fortress existed, but his knowledge of Athiedor affairs definitely rattled the Clans.

If you present yourself to the Clans, you must offer more than a free Athiedor, however. You will have to prove that you can match Kato's power and even protect them if need be. They are afraid and intimidated by your brother's power. But you are strong, perhaps even stronger than Kato, and your power is more controlled. I have every confidence that you can win them over.

As to how you can actually meet the Clans in time, I have an idea. When I found you at the masquerade, I had no idea how I got to you or even where I was. Ainc, in a desperate attempt to make me hers, pricked me with something covered in a potion from her brother, and I was quickly losing consciousness. I called out to Felixe and he drew me away from her, bringing me to you. I believe that the connection between us that has allowed Felixe to pass these letters can also draw us to each other physically when we need it to. Once the Clans have arrived at Fortress Mullidain, I will let you know, and I will get you the exact time of meeting, if possible. You will likely only get one chance to address the Clans, so it will be best if you can be there when all the leaders are assembled together. When the time comes, call Felixe, and he can bring you to me. You can halt the negations and final signing of the treaty, stopping Kato.

I will not be able to openly assist you when you appear, but know I am on your side, as always. You are amazing and powerful, and you can do this. Do not for a moment doubt yourself. I believe in you.

Forever Yours,

Alak

Anger roils through me as I read about Aine, but the rest of his letter fills me with warm hope. Nerves twist as I read back over Alak's plan, but his faith in me is grounding, despite the intimidating task. I have to make this work.

I fold the letter and slip it in my pocket, my fingers brushing against Ehren's ring. Ehren. I should find him as soon as I can. It's time to formulate a plan, and few are better at crafting one than Ehren.

CHAPTER NINETEEN

ASTRA

When I share the latest developments with Ehren, he remains quiet and nods along. We share the information with Bram in an attempt to smooth things over and keep him in the loop, but it only backfires.

"You can't be serious!" he yells, throwing his hands in the air. "You'd be going into the lion's den, completely unprotected!"

"Unprotected?" I snap back. "Maybe you missed the part where I have magic?" I take a deep breath. "See, this is why we didn't tell you to start with."

Red rises on Bram's face as fury flashes in his eyes. "Why? Because you didn't want someone pointing out the obvious?"

"I don't suppose there's a way for any of us to go with you," Kai muses calmly from the couch where he sits next to Ehren.

Since Bram is now fully informed, Ehren and I agreed it wouldn't hurt to bring Kai in as well for additional support.

Kai sat quietly absorbing all the information while I talked, weighing my words.

"No, I don't think so. If I knew where I was going on my own, maybe I could wisp others with me, but I think Felixe can only direct me."

Bram shakes his head more firmly. "No. You cannot do this."

"What if you go on your own, and then come back and get one or two of us once you know where you are?" Kai suggests.

"I think I need to do it on my own. Even if I could get you there I couldn't guarantee I'd have enough magic left to get you out. I wouldn't want everyone at risk."

"Oh!" Bram snaps. "So, it is fine for you to put yourself at risk, but the rest of us—"

"Shut up, Bram!" Ehren cuts in, his voice harsh. He takes a deep breath and runs a hand through his hair, continuing in a calmer voice. "For gods' sake, just shut up. It's been decided. Astra is doing this. Alone."

Bram crosses his arms. "What was the point, then, of including me if you don't want to consider what I have to say?" he growls through gritted teeth

I sigh in response and collapse on the couch on Kai's other side.

"We want you involved, Bram, but we won't re-plan everything simply because you don't like it." I look up at Kai. "What do you think?"

He arches an eyebrow. "Does it matter?"

I nod.

"Fine. I don't like it, but I think it's necessary. As long as you're careful and don't do anything stupid, I think it will work."

Bram lets out a frustrated huff, opening his mouth but snapping it shut without speaking. He waves us all off and storms out of the room. Ehren watches him go, shaking his head sadly.

"This doesn't change anything," I say firmly.

"No, it doesn't," Ehren agrees with a sigh. "I wish he would get on board but we'll just move on without him."

"What do you need help with?" Kai asks. "Let me know and I'll do what I can."

"Well, we don't have much planned beyond what we've already told you," I reply with a small shrug. "There's a lot we need to work out."

Ehren nods, chewing on the inside of his cheek as he thinks. He leaps from the couch a moment later so abruptly I startle but he doesn't seem to notice.

"I think I need to speak with Illyas."

I laugh as he slides across the room to ring for a servant.

"You do, do you?"

Ehren shoots me a sheepish grin over his shoulder as he pulls the tasseled rope. "I'm sure I have no idea what you mean or why you're using that tone."

I stand, crossing my arms. "Right."

Ehren's grin grows. "Is it true that Illyas and I . . . connected? Yes. He's a rather handsome man with wit and wiles. I'd be a fool to ignore all of that. But I can assure you that nothing of import happened between us."

"Nothing?" I ask, arching an eyebrow.

Ehren chuckles. "Nearly nothing. A few kisses beneath a magical archway. Nothing more."

I'm inclined to ask for a bit more clarification, but a knock on the door stops my inquiries. Ehren answers and the servant scampers off moments later to find Illyas.

Barely a minute passes before Illyas himself is outside our door.

"I hope we didn't interrupt any important business," Ehren says once Illyas is inside the room.

Illyas shakes his head. "Not at all. You actually caught me between assignments." His gaze shifts around the three of us. "What can I do for you?"

Ehren slowly unveils his plan, giving Illyas just enough details to know what's going on without showing our full hand. Illyas listens attentively, absorbing the information with an occasional nod.

"So," Illyas says once Ehren falls silent, "you need a dress for Astra that commands a room, official treaties drawn up, and a bit of help setting up additional portals? Am I missing anything?"

Ehren nods. "I think that about sums it all up."

"It's all very doable and I'm happy to help make all the necessary arrangements. Perhaps you could come by my rooms later and we can figure out what needs to be done with the portals."

A smile snakes onto Ehren's lips as he nods. "That shouldn't be a problem."

I roll my eyes.

"I feel the need to point out that King Naimon won't like you leaving behind a portion of the money he's offered. He'll likely see it as an insult of sorts."

"I considered that, but I'd rather not have all our funds in one place. It's only logical to spread it out."

Illyas nods. "Well, I can't argue with that." He grins and claps a hand to Ehren's shoulder. "I'll get on everything right away and keep you posted."

There's something almost seductive about Ehren's smile as he replies, "I expect nothing less."

"It shouldn't take more than a couple days to make the necessary arrangements," Illyas says as Ehren escorts him to the door.

"Very good. I can meet you in your rooms in an hour?"

Illyas grins, cocking his head as he surveys Ehren. "Make it two."

"Excellent."

Illyas starts out the door but pauses halfway through the frame, glancing over his shoulder at me. "If I were you, I would start filling your Syphon Stone with magic now. The more magic you have stored when you go to fulfill these plans, the better."

I nod and Illyas disappears. Ehren glances from me to Kai and releases a long breath.

"I suppose all we do now is wait."

"Are you sure you don't want to follow Illyas right now and squeeze in some quality time together before your official meeting later?"

Ehren's laugh is thick and rich. "No, I'm quite fine." He sobers, a shadow crossing his features. "I learned long ago not to get too close to people who are tied to my kingdom in significant ways. It doesn't make for good long term results."

"Surely that doesn't keep you from the occasional fling," Kai says, lifting an eyebrow.

Ehren smiles but it's a bit forced. "No, not entirely. There are other reasons for that." Ehren waves his hand as if clearing the air. "But let's not discuss it. Instead, let's find a map and plan out the next stage of our journey and then I need to check in with my Guard that I have stationed here. I do want to have everything in place when I meet with Illyas."

Ehren's plan is efficient and we run into few problems sorting everything out. He invites me along to his meeting with Illyas and, while I am a tad hesitant to interfere with their relationship, Illyas doesn't seem to mind in the slightest. Together we sort out the finer details of the portal stones. Naskein has requested four additional portals in Gleador, and Illyas volunteers to distribute three of them accordingly. The fourth we will take with us as the location is near the border between Callenia and Gleador.

The morning we go to leave, Sama receives word from Jessalynn encouraging her to continue traveling with us. Thrilled but nervous, Sama is provided with a horse and other supplies. As predicted, King Naimon is slightly ruffled by Ehren's suggestion to leave some of the funds behind, but in the end he consents. He seems eager to make up for it, however, by providing us with an excess of supplies.

"We're very grateful for everything," Ehren says, eyeing the small caravan of horses and provisions. "I'm not sure if all of this is necessary, however."

I don't say anything, but given that the king not only supplied Ehren and I with tents larger than necessary but also with travel beds that raise off the ground, I'm inclined to agree with Ehren.

King Naimon waves his hand. "Nothing is too much for an ally of Gleador. You and your Sorceress deserve the best and I would be amiss not to provide it."

Ehren inclines his head. "As you wish, Your Majesty. Your kindness is greatly appreciated."

King Naimon puffs up a bit and motions to a couple of his personal guards standing off to the side. "Please also accept some of my most-trusted soldiers to accompany you to the border. They will ensure your safety while in my kingdom and make sure you are able to cross the border with no difficulty."

Ehren thanks the king again, but we both know that the true danger lies beyond the Gleador border. After a bit more filling of supplies and exchanging of farewells, we're on our way.

If we took a straight line to the Gleador border, we would reach Callenia in three days with good weather, but since we are making a slight detour to place a portal stone, a day or two is added to our journey. Thanks to the lavish tents and bedding supplied by King Naimon, we don't need to seek out inns along the way, but comfortably camp at night. I feel a bit awkward to receive such honors and happily share my tent with Sama. It's nice to finally have another girl around.

The location with the portal stone is an abandoned city, once known for a mine that produced a magical mineral called Luvgim. According to Illyas, Jasaltine was a flourishing city back when magic was alive, but after magic faded, so did the city. Without the magical minerals to mine, the city struggled to provide for its citizens. People began to claim that the city was cursed. It was plagued by earthquake after earthquake until the ruined city was abandoned. Part of our mission at Jasaltine is not only to reactivate their portal stone, but also to see if the mine is producing Luvgim again.

As we round the top of a hill on our third day of travel, we get our first glimpse down into the ruined city below. Even in ruins, it's breathtaking. The sun is still hours from truly setting, but a golden evening light illuminates the tumbled remains with an ethereal glow. As we make our way down the hill, I can feel a pull from somewhere in the city. Something is beckoning to me, or at least, to my magic. I'm not sure if it's the remnants of magical objects, such as the portal stone we've come to reactivate, or if it's a sign that the mine is truly alive with magic again. A quick glance at my magical companions tells me they, too, can feel the draw of magic.

We're nearly at the edge of the crumbled buildings outlining the edge of Jasaltine when we're bombarded by a fluffle of fat wild rabbits. Makin is the first to recognize their dinner potential, deftly striking one down. Not to be outdone, Nyco, Ehren, and I can't resist flicking our own weapons, striking down three more of the plump creatures. Kai shifts into his wolf form and chases a fifth rabbit, bringing it back in his teeth.

Bearing our rabbits, we stumble over the remains of the deserted city, walking down well-worn but overgrown and forgotten roads past broken bits of buildings, some with their remains jutting up at awkward angles, and other rotted remnants of a place that once was. Though the people have been long-gone, their presence is not forgotten, haunting the tumbled village.

Once we find a good place to rest for the night, Ehren and Cal volunteer to gather wood to strike up a fire while Makin, Kai, and I make quick work of skinning and readying the rabbits for dinner. Soon, the rabbits are roasting on a spit while we lounge around. After nearly an hour of switching between watching the rabbits turn and the card game that has been struck, I rise, eager to stretch my legs and go off in search of whatever magic is drawing me. Ehren is the first to notice and arches an eyebrow, silently asking if I want company. I smile and shake my head.

"I'm just going to look around a bit," I mouth, gesturing vaguely to the village around us.

Ehren gives me a half-shrug and a nod that I take to essentially mean "do whatever you want" before he turns his focus back on the cards in his hand. I step away from the flickering fire and wander through the village. I don't take the main road, or what I'm sure used to be the main road, but instead step directly over the cluttered, shambled wreckage of the buildings. Which were homes? Was there a bakery? An apothecary? What hints are buried beneath these crumbled stones that shed some light on the lives that used to swarm Jasaltine?

I step up onto a chunk of stone jutting out of the ground, balancing precariously on the balls of my feet. The setting sun casts a deep orange haze over the shadowy remains that make the stones appear on fire. I'm so caught up in the breathtaking view I almost don't hear the footsteps behind me.

"Sad, isn't it?" Kai's voice says quietly as he steps up behind me. "This used to be a flourishing city back when the mine was active."

I nod solemnly, not bothering to turn and look at him. "Maybe it will flourish again."

"If it's not cursed."

At this, I turn my head and look down at Kai. "Do you really think it's cursed?"

Looking at the shambles around me it's easy enough to believe, but it doesn't feel cursed. It feels . . . alive.

"I'm not sure." Kai shrugs. I shift on my awkward perch, stretching my toes, and Kai eyes my feet warily. "Maybe you should get down before you fall."

I roll my eyes but hop down anyway. Not because of Kai's

suggestion as much as the fact my feet are starting to cramp in the odd position. I spin to face Kai and am a little surprised to see a second figure picking his way over the remains toward us.

"Were you losing at cards?" I tease Bram when he's a few steps closer.

Bram grins, stopping just behind Kai. "Actually, I won my last hand. I was tired of sitting and was curious to see what you were up to." His gaze slides past me, taking in the broken village around me. "What *are* you up to?"

I shrug. "Exploring?"

Bram's eyebrow quirks up. "You are not even sure? It is almost dark, so it is probably not a great idea to wander around alone, especially with the footing so unsure."

I flash Bram a grin. "Well, it's lucky you two came to accompany me."

Bram scowls. "That's not what I—"

"Come on!" I say, gesturing for Kai and Bram to follow me as I stride forward. "Let's see what there is to see before it does get too dark."

Bram and Kai fall into step behind me. Bram grumbles under his breath but doesn't argue, and Kai is his normal stoic self. I have a feeling the reason Kai isn't protesting my adventure in the slightest is because he, too, is being drawn by the same magic calling to me.

It doesn't take us long to find what I'm looking for. The old mine is situated against the edge of the town. The mine is buried into a sad lump of a hill, most of it seemingly underground. Broken pieces of stone that once held the mine open are now sunken into the earth, sticking up like broken bones. I squat down and press my hand against the stone blocking the entrance to the mine. It hums with magical warmth.

"Is there Luvgim inside?" Kai asks, kneeling beside me.

I swallow and close my eyes, trying to get a read on the magic, but it's useless. Perhaps Sama could tell us, but she's still back at the campsite.

"I don't know for sure. Help me move these stones."

I lean forward, working my fingers into the cracks in an attempt to loosen the rubble, but I can't get a decent grip.

"Careful," Kai says slowly, looking up at the stones towering just above the level of his head. "Removing the wrong stone will bring the rest down."

"He is right, Astra," Bram insists, stepping forward. "We can come back tomorrow with everyone else."

I shake my head. They don't understand. The magic inside this mine is like a song I can't get out of my head. I have to see it and touch it. Tonight.

"If I can just free one bit . . ."

The stone in my hand shifts slightly and is followed by a threatening groan. I lose my balance and tumble back with a thud.

"Gods, Astra," Kai swears under his breath. "You'll kill yourself doing that. And me along with you."

"Then help me!" I say, motioning wildly to the mine.

With sighs, Bram and Kai step forward and begin working at the rock. After several long minutes, a chunk breaks free, a stale whiff of magic-filled air puffing out. My heart races with excitement. They've cleared a way.

"I'm going in," I say, more to myself than Kai or Bram.

Bram scowls. "How exactly? That hole is barely big enough for a mouse."

I grin and Kai shakes his head, clearly already guessing what I'm about to do. Before either can argue, I shift, turning into a tiny silver mouse. Bram swears, and if I could grin in mouse form, I would. I leap into the opening.

"Be careful," Kai says sternly as I'm engulfed by the darkness.

I scamper over the uneven path that's been left behind, my whiskers trembling. Even as a mouse, the stale air makes it difficult to catch a decent breath. I'm wondering how far I'll have to go before I find a place to shift back into human, if I find a place at all. I'm debating if I can even turn around with what little space I have when I tumble from my tiny hole into an opening. I unfold into my human form and find myself in a space about a yard wide between crumbled walls from the mine caving in. My head is mere inches from the ceiling. I had expected to use my light once inside, but I don't need it. On the wall in front of me is exactly what we've come to find, what has been calling to me—Luvgim. A thick, blueish silver vein of the Luvgim runs from the ceiling down to the ground, starting as a single, crooked line at the top and then dividing midway into thinner veins like a strike of lightning. I reach out trembling fingers and stroke the glowing mineral, my breath catching at the power.

"Astra," Kai's voice drifts through the darkness, "are you okay?"

"I'm fine," I call back. The mine shudders around me.

"Hurry back," Bram's voice comes next.

I don't respond. Instead, I study the wall. There has to be a way to take some of the Luvgim with me. I scan the small space, hoping to find a pickax or similar tool, but there is none. I take a deep breath and summon my magic. I'll have to be precise. I place my fingers directly above the portion where the vein of Luvgim splits and begin to carve. My magic cuts the rock surprisingly well, but the mineral itself fights back. Sweat droplets form on my head and my muscles flex as I force my magic to slice through. Finally, the wall surrenders a chunk of rock with a great, threatening rumble, specks of dirt breaking free and tumbling onto my head.

"Don't push it, Astra!" Kai demands, fear ringing in his voice.

I should respond, but I'm staring in awe at the rock in my hand. The uneven back is marbled with the Luvgim. It's stunning. I look back at the hole I've made. I can spot two more pieces that could easily be removed. Dropping the first rock into my pocket, I reach out again with my magic and force it to cut away additional pieces of solid Luvgim. As they fall into my outstretched palm, the mine roars around me.

"Shit," I whisper, shoving the Luvgim into my pocket before shifting back into mouse form.

This time as I race through the tunnel, I can feel it threatening to cave in around me. When I get to the exit, I leap out, shifting mid-jump so I land in a tousled heap on the ground.

"Gods' sake, Astra!" Bram chides. I look up, sheepishly meeting his gaze. His eyes flash with worry-fueled anger. "That was incredibly stupid!"

Bram steps forward, offering me his hand. I take it and he pulls me to my feet.

"Did you at least find something?" Kai asks with a scowl.

I grin and reach into my pocket, withdrawing the stones. "I did."

I hold out the Luvgim toward them on my open palm. Kai's eyes go wide, letting out a low whistle as he tentatively picks up the largest chunk.

"That is what you went in after?" Bram says, looking

from Kai to me, trying to gauge our reactions. He reaches toward the larger of the two remaining pieces, a solid silver-blue rock the size of my thumbnail. "What's the big—" He drops off and his eyes shoot wide the moment his skin comes into contact with the Luvgim.

"What is this, exactly?" Bram asks, his voice full of awe and wonder as he lifts the stone to eye level, examining it.

"Luvgim, of course," I reply with a smile.

"Why can I feel the magic?" he asks, his voice barely above a whisper.

"Because Luvgim isn't like most magical gems and stones that channel magic or enhance magic," Kai explains, turning his rock over in his hand. "Luvgim is pure magic, places where the gods touched the earth, if you believe the lore."

Bram lifts his eyes to meet mine. "Can *I* perform magic with this?"

"It's possible," I reply, my eyes bright. "Of course, it's not as easy as simply performing magic. It's not quite like the magic Kai or I have but, with the right spell or situation, even those without the slightest trace of magic in their bloodline can wield some magic."

Bram holds the stone for a moment more before dropping back in my hand so abruptly it's almost as if the stone burned him.

"Should King Naimon have this kind of power?" Bram asks, his eyes narrowed on the Luvgim.

"I believe we can trust him," Kai replies firmly, handing me his rock as well.

I slip all three pieces back into my pocket.

"Of course *you* trust him," Bram challenges, crossing his arms. "He is *your* king, but he isn't ours."

"But he is our ally," I point out quickly before Kai can

retort. "I believe at this point we have to trust him. If we can't be honest and trusting with our allies, we've already lost the war."

Bram lets out a long sigh. "So be it."

"We should get back to the others," Kai suggests, his voice steady and cold.

Bram and I nod in agreement. We silently trek back toward the faint glow of firelight in the distance. By the time we reach camp, the sun has fully set and the rabbits are ready to eat. We stuff our faces until we're almost too full to move. We don't bother breaking out the tents. It's a warm enough night with decent weather, so we make ourselves comfortable on our bed rolls, situated around the flickering flames to ward off the cooler night temperatures. Personally, I like falling asleep out in the open. That way, the last thing I see before I drift to sleep are the stars winking down at me.

CHAPTER TWENTY

ASTRA

When morning breaks, we're all eager to complete our tasks and get on the road. Over breakfast, I share my find at the mine with Ehren and King Naimon's men. I give the men the largest chunk but keep the smaller pieces a secret. Neither Bram nor Kai let on I have more.

After breakfast, we make our way through the remains in search of the portal stone. According to the records Ehren accessed with Illyas's help before leaving Koshima, the portal stone should be in the center of town. It doesn't take long to find. Not only does the center of town have less rubble, but it's cleared and raised. It appears that this area was once set up like a stage. The platform itself is made of carefully carved tiles made from soft stones, fitted together perfectly. In the city's prime, it must have been glorious to behold, but now its colors are faded by the sun, the stones cracked with plants peeking through.

We step up onto the raised ground and cross to the center. There, the portal stone gleams, catching the early morning light. It's positioned in the dead center of the plat-form with strange, ancient symbols encircling the stone. Despite the many cracks in the other tiles, this one is perfectly intact, albeit faded. I'm not sure if it's by luck or magic.

Ehren squats in front of the stone, tracing the symbols with his finger. "These are the symbols I traced into the dirt when I placed the first stone."

"You traced symbols?" I ask curiously, kneeling beside him to get a better look.

Ehren nods. "Illyas told me they're actually words from an ancient magical tongue. They're the words I say in my spell."

Ehren rolls his neck and rubs his hands tighter. "All right. Let's do this."

He pulls a journal from his pocket and opens it to an ear-marked page where he's copied down the spell. He inhales deeply and recites each word carefully while tracing the corresponding etched symbol. With each word, I think I see the stone brighten slightly and then dim, but I assume it's a trick of light. When Ehren whispers the last word, however, the symbols all light up. Ehren jumps to his feet, pulling me up with him. The stone glows, followed by a bright, blinding flash of light. I slam my eyes shut. When I open them, the stone and symbols are back to normal.

"So," Makin drawls, blinking away the dots spotting his vision. "Did it work?"

Ehren mumbles an "I think so" while those of us with magic give an emphatic "yes." For us, the hum of magic now flowing from the stone is undeniable.

"So, what now?" Bram asks.

Ehren shrugs. "We continue our journey."

Everything is packed back onto our horses and we're on our way within the hour. The king's men seem eager to return to Koshima but keep their promise to escort us to the border, which works well when we do run into border patrol. A flash of the king's official seal probably goes further from men dressed in official Gleador guard uniforms. Once we clear the border patrol and cross into Callenia, the men bid us goodbye and disappear into the hills.

We travel for about an hour before stopping for lunch. Something about being back in Callenia has us all on edge, nervous and jumping at every little sound. We eat quickly, eager to be back on our path.

A few hours later we near our next destination, which is another abandoned city. The city of Mythgulch was once a great and mighty magical city that was the home to druids with religious practices akin to the Order of Naskein. Unlike Naskein, the druids worshipped all the gods of the pantheon, even the ones that are minor or often forgotten due to their limited powers. The druids' worship, however, included mostly magical practices and rites. When magic faded, the religion faltered. For decades, druids remained behind in an attempt to maintain Mythgulch, but, eventually, it was abandoned.

Mythgulch is surrounded by a high wall guarded by two rock giants. We can see the giants miles away. From a distance they're foreboding, but up close they're too cracked, broken, and covered with vines to truly strike fear. For some reason, the dilapidation fills me with sadness. The city itself isn't much better off than its giants. It's nowhere near the same amount of disarray as Jasaltine, but everything is faded, cracked, and empty.

The portal stone, according to Naskein, is inside a

temple. Since Mythgulch boasts no less than fifteen separate temples, the one we require takes a little while to find. The temple we need is made from white stone, or what was white before ages of neglect turned it dusty and dirty. Tall columns hold up an entryway. They're cracked but sturdy. Inside is a wide room with stained-glass windows picturing gods. Two of the windows are cracked and broken to the point the pictures are no longer clear, but the remaining four look almost perfectly intact, casting their rainbow light around the room. At the far end sits a large white stone altar, stained dark on top by what I assume is blood. Towering behind the altar on the wall is a large mural that closely resembles the picture I saw of Caedios. My heart stills and I'm so fixed on the picture I don't even notice the arched doorway below leading to a shallow alcove until Ehren steps next to me staring up at it.

"That's it," Ehren mumbles, nodding to a stone embedded at the top point of the arch in the center of a star.

I drag my eyes from the picture, focusing on the stone, my hands on my hips. On either side of the stone are the same symbols we saw etched in a circle around the previous stone, but they aren't the only symbols, though they are the largest. Carved all over the frame of the arch are additional symbols and words, seemingly in every known language. I only recognize a third at best.

"Do you have to trace the symbols to reactivate it?" I ask.

Ehren chews on his lip. "Gods. I hope not. I'm tall, but not *that* tall."

"I'll hoist you up on my shoulders," Cal offers with a lopsided grin and Ehren laughs.

"Thanks, but I'll just try saying the words and hope it

works." He pauses, adding with a wink, "But that can be our backup plan."

He takes a deep breath and places his palms on the sides of the arch. He closes his eyes and whispers the ancient words. In the dark of the temple it's more obvious when each symbol brightens, the stone glowing and dimming with each word. This time, we're expecting the blast of light and properly shield our eyes. Once he's done, Ehren places his hands on his hips and looks up at the stone with satisfaction.

We temporarily debate whether we want to make camp in Mythgulch or continue, and ultimately decide to make use of the last couple hours of daylight to travel as far as we can. The entrance to the city we came through was guarded by stone giants and the way we exit is guarded by gods. The main path leading out of the city is surrounded by tall walls stretching four stories high covered in murals of the gods defeating their foes and bestowing favors to their worshipers.

We're nearly halfway down the passage when Nyco suddenly goes stiff, scowling. I wonder why until I notice a spider in his hair near his left ear. I shiver and wonder if I'll ever get used to his magic. Whatever the spider says spurs Nyco to action. He presses his horse forward, coming up beside Ehren.

"We should hurry," he says in a low voice, his eyes darting around nervously.

"Wh—"

Before he can finish the question, Ehren has his answer. Arrows rain down on us from the tops of the walls trapping us. I instinctively throw up a shield as someone yells, "Archers!'

"Press forward!" Ehren commands, spurring his horse into a gallop only to have to abruptly halt as soldiers start swarming through the exit, weapons drawn. "Go back! Go back!" Ehren cries, but he's too late. Soldiers pour in from behind us as well. How they remained hidden all this time, I have no idea.

"We have to fight," Bram says, his jaw set as he draws his sword, the other guards following suit.

Ehren swallows nervously and gives a nod to his comrades. "Let's do this!"

They charge forward, clashing against the attacking soldiers. I throw up a wall of protection behind us so we only have one front to worry about. Kai is the first to use his magic in attack. He shifts into his wolf form and plunges into the onslaught of soldiers, grabbing one by his neck and jerking him to the ground, blood dripping down Kai's maw.

Nyco follows shortly with his own magic. At first, I wonder what he's doing. He leaps from his horse and stands in the center of the passage, closing his eyes, hands outstretched. Suddenly, his eyes flash open and I startle—his eyes are solid black. Then I hear them—millions of scuttling insects crawling out of every crack and crevice, swarming the soldiers. The soldiers scream and swat at the bugs, many dropping their weapons. My skin crawls as I watch in wide-eyed horror. Some of the insects must be venomous, because several soldiers fall to the ground, twitching and convulsing.

Nyco's attack is short-lived, however. His magic flickers out and he blinks, his eyes returning to normal. He's weak but not drained. He draws his sword and rushes forward to join the fray without hesitation.

No sooner has Nyco's magic faded than I hear Ares screech. I turn my head and see Sama ready to strike, her eyes clouded gray and smokey as she draws magic from her Shadow Hawk. She creates misty shadows, surrounding the attacking soldiers at the front, thickest near Nyco. I'm sure she can sense he's weakest from using his magic. All the guards quickly strike down as many soldiers as they can while the shadows hold.

At this point, I join them. I leap from my horse, my twin blades of light drawn. I rush forward, but I freeze mere feet away as Illyas's words in the market come flooding back. I remember all the men I killed before. I swallow. I don't want to be a killer. These men probably have families—little children waiting for their dads to come home, lovers waiting with hopes and dreams. I cut those dreams to shreds.

"Astra!" Bram's commanding voice cuts into my thoughts, rimmed with panic. I look up and find his chestnut brown eyes locked on me. "Fight!"

I take a deep breath and rush in. My blades find their marks, striking down soldier after solider. I swing my blade and slice a man's throat, hot blood spraying my face. Disgust roils through me, but there's no time to stop and wipe it off or to dwell on my actions. I can't spare a moment of hesitation. I swap my swords for daggers and take out several men further up with practiced flicks of my wrists.

We're pushing forward, but it's too slow. My arms already ache, and even the footwork of the well-trained soldiers in our group start to falter. My heart sinks into my stomach when I realize my shields are no longer being attacked from above or behind. A quick glance confirms the soldiers are rallying in front of us, leaving just enough men behind to deter us from turning around. Even the archers are climbing down the walls to join the fight.

"The archers!" I cry desperately.

"I've got them," Sama calls back.

Out of the corner of my eye I see her squat down and dig

her hand into the earth. She throws her head back as her eyes flash a muddy green. The walls and earth begin to tremble. Most of the archers plunge to their deaths while many of the foot soldiers stumble back.

It helps, but it's not enough. I'm going to need to use the full force of my magic. Fighting with my swords and daggers seems . . . fair. Magic seems cruel. I swallow. I don't want to use magic. I don't want to kill. Ehren shoots me a desperate look, his sea-green eyes pleading. I hear a sharp yelp and realize Kai has been struck. Sama cries out, and I spin to see that a solider has stabbed her horse to distract her from her earth magic, too afraid to strike her directly.

"Astra!" Bram calls out, his voice a command. "Unleash your magic!"

His face is firm and set. He's not requesting. For once, he's not holding me back. He's a commander of a ragtag army, and he's calling in his soldier. He needs me. They all need me.

I take a deep breath and summon my magic. It purrs beneath my skin, a vicious animal ready to be let loose to hunt its prey. As the power flows through me, I let it take control. I rise above the ground, my body glowing like liquid silver. Several of the soldiers look up at me, eyes wide in terror. I smile, relishing their fear. I stretch out my fingers and long silver tendrils weave through the soldiers, winding around their necks. I don't even know how many I have ensnared as they clutch pointlessly at their throats. They can't touch my magic. With a jerk of my wrist, I snap their necks in unison, a crack echoing around us as their bodies fall limp and useless.

Ehren takes advantage of the space now surrounding him and pulls something from his pocket. It's a powder of some sort. He throws it forward and shouts a spell. A blast shatters the air, pushing the soldiers farther back. We're nearly out of the passage.

I reach out more tendrils of magic. This time, some of the soldiers have the good sense to try to evade them. Their efforts are useless, however. My magic finds them. My magic kills them. My magic clears the way.

Ehren sends out another blast of magic, this time a spell harnessed in his ring from Illyas. There are less than fifty soldiers in our way now. We need them gone before their reinforcements come. I craft a silver mist rising from the ground, surrounding our attackers in a thick fog. As they breathe in my magic, I take hold of their life force. They sense it. I feel their struggle as they fight to regain control. I make a fist and pull, tugging their lives through their gaping mouths. When my mist fades, nothing but dead bodies line our path.

But we know it won't last.

"Go!" Ehren commands, leaping on his horse.

We all follow suit. I snap out of my magical state and jump on my horse. Nyco pulls Sama onto his horse as Kai leaps from the ground in wolf form, landing in human form on his horse. We ride fast and hard, clearing the edge of the walls, the riderless horses carrying our supplies thankfully falling in line with us. Behind us, ranks are reforming. There's probably less than a hundred men, but we're tired and worn. We can't take another battle. In desperation, I look for a place to wisp us. About two miles in the distance is a forest. Wisping to an unknown location where I can't see is dangerous, potentially deadly. I could wisp us on top of a tree or underwater, but I have to risk it. I reach out what remains of my magic, drawing heavily from the Syphon

Stone on my wrist. I link us together, horses and all, and we wisp.

It's an unsteady change and it jolts the entire group. We reign in our horses, blinking as we adjust to our new surroundings. We survived. Everyone looks as shocked as I feel.

We take a few minutes to assess our wounds. Thankfully, none of us is deeply injured. I dig through my bag of medicines from Healer Heora and go about doing what I can to help the others. I stumble across the small bottle of oil meant to replenish magic and put a few sticky, bitter drops on my tongue. It's not enough to immediately refill my magic, but it helps keep me steady and upright while allowing me enough magic to heal a couple minor injuries.

Once everyone is bandaged, we make our way through the forest. There's no way the soldiers can know where we went, but we still want to put as much distance between us and our attackers as possible. We travel along the path of a babbling brook, making camp once it's fully dark. Dinner is quick—bits of flatbread, dried meat, and cheese.

My tent is one of the first erected. Sama crashes on the bed and falls asleep almost instantly. I try to help with the other tents, but I'm forced into my tent by Bram. I collapse on the bed, but I can't sleep. I try—gods, I try. Every time I close my eyes I see the soldiers fall. I feel them die. I see their weeping wives and lovers. I hear the cries of their children. I taste their blood. Pain courses through me. I can't breathe. I sit on the edge of my bed, clutching my dress above my aching heart. I gasp for breath as tears stream down my cheeks. I need air. Fresh air.

I rise on unsteady legs and step outside. It's quiet. Everyone else has gone to bed. It's just chirping crickets, rustling leaves, and babbling water. Water. That's what I need. I need to clean away the blood that's still sticky on my cheek and crusted in my hair. I need to wash.

I practically run to the edge of the water, flinging off my clothes and plunging in. I wade to the center which, thankfully, isn't terribly deep, and I sink down, letting the now shoulder-high water wash over me. I duck my head under, using my fingers to pry free everything trapped in my locks. I claw at my skin, wondering if I'll ever feel clean again. Once I scrub off as much blood as possible, I lose what little control I've managed to maintain. Sobs wrack my body as I draw my knees up and clasp them against my chest. I lean my forehead onto my knees and I weep. I don't even notice anyone else is there until Ehren calls my name. I jerk my red, swollen eyes to his. Even in the dim moonlight, I see the worry etching every line of his face.

"I killed them," I choke out, my voice almost lost to the water. "I killed them. They had families and friends, and they'll never see them again because I killed them." I shake my head. "They're dead because of me."

"Oh, Ash," Ehren says softly. "It's not your fault."

"Yes, it is!" I yell, much louder than I mean to, my voice hoarse with emotion. "I felt their lives in my hands as I pulled it from them!"

Ehren hesitates for a moment, and I'm scared he's afraid of me. I'm terrified he'll run. But it's not fear in his eyes, I realize. It's concern.

"Damn it," he mutters, yanking his shirt over his head and kicking off his boots. "I'm coming in."

He splashes through the water and kneels behind me, wrapping his arms around me, his hands clasped over my own as he clutches me tightly against his chest.

"You saved us, Ash," he whispers in my hair, his voice wrought with an emotion I can't quite place. "You saved us all. We'd all be dead right now if not for you."

"But I killed them," I whisper, horror still swelling in my chest.

Ehren traces his fingers along my arm in a smooth, comforting motion. "And you saved us. They attacked. They were wrong. You saved us. You're a hero."

"I don't think I want to be this kind of hero."

His hand stills and he presses his forehead against the back of my head. "Me neither, but sometimes we have to step into the roles provided for us, whether we like it or not."

"I see their faces every time I close my eyes," I confess, my voice barely above a whisper. I'm not sure he heard me until he whispers back, "Me too."

We both fall silent as he holds me. I realize he needs the comfort as much as I do. We're in this together. I don't have to be alone and neither does he. Finally, after I don't know how long, I feel a little better. It's then the heat rushes into my cheeks as realization strikes.

"Um, Ehren," I mutter. "I'm . . . naked."

Ehren chuckles into my hair. "I know. It's why I hesitated to join you, but hell if I was going to leave you in the water crying by yourself."

"Thank you," I reply, loosing a long breath. I pause and glance toward the shore. "Should I get out first? Or you?"

"Doesn't matter to me," Ehren mumbles. "You go first. I'll close my eyes."

I nod and wait a moment before rising. Water trickles down my body as I rush to shore, small pebbles and sticks stabbing my feet. I use a quick brush of magic to dry before dressing as quickly as possible. When I'm done, I call to

Ehren. He emerges from the water and I use my magic to dry him as well. Once we're both dressed my initial embarrassment starts to fade.

"Thank you," I say, placing my hand on Ehren's arm. "I really needed you there for me tonight. Even if I was . . . you know." My cheeks turn pink and Ehren laughs, brushing a hand on my cheek.

"You're not the first naked girl I've ever seen," he teases.

My cheeks grow redder, and he throws his head back and laughs. Even though it's at my expense, it's a beautiful sound and I smile.

"Yeah, but I'm assuming the girls you saw naked were girls you were involved with." I pause, afraid of the answer to my next question. "You don't think of me in that way, do you?"

"As a lover?" Ehren asks, waggling his eyebrows as he grins wickedly.

I shake my head and turn away, embarrassment rushing in with fresh waves. "Never mind."

"Wait," Ehren says, all teasing gone from his voice.

He reaches out, catching my elbow, and pulls me back to face him. I look up into his sea-green eyes. He reaches out and tucks a loose strand of hair behind my ear.

"I think I could have fallen in love with you, hard and fast had the situation been different," he confesses, his voice soft.

"What do you mean?" I ask, my voice catching slightly.

"Well, there are a couple reasons, but the first one is that Bram met you first," he answers simply with a shrug. "And Bram had already fallen in love with you, even though you barely knew each other. That was so opposite of anything I expected of Bram, so immediately in my mind and heart you were off limits. Our relationship has grown and formed in such a way that it cannot be undone. I love you, Astra, but not in a romantic way. My love for you is deeper, richer somehow. I'd die for you without a moment of hesitation, but I don't want you as a lover."

His confession rocks me to my core. I know exactly what he's describing because it's exactly how I feel. I relax and breathe a sigh of relief, I press my forehead against his chest as giggles overwhelm me.

"I'm not quite sure how to take this reaction," Ehren mumbles.

I pull back and smile up at him, stifling my giggles the best I can.

"I'm sorry. I'm just relieved, I guess."

Ehren laughs. "Oh. Fine. I'll have you know, *most* girls want the prince."

I grin. "Believe me, I know." I slip my hand into his and give it a squeeze. "I like what we have better. I'm relieved because I feel the exact same about you. I love you, Ehren, but not romantically."

Ehren releases a long breath and runs his free hand through his hair. "Thank the gods! After your reaction, I was afraid I had broken you!"

I throw my head back and laugh. "I might be broken, but it wasn't you that did it."

I grow quiet as the seriousness swarms back in.

"You know," Ehren says at length, "I'm pretty sure I have a spell in one of my books that will allow you to sleep peacefully with no dreams. I can put you under, if you'd like, so you can get some proper rest."

I knit my eyebrows. "Is that a good idea? What if we have to run in the middle of the night?"

"There's almost definitely a counter spell, so I'll be able to wake you at any moment." He pauses. "Why don't you come back to my tent? I'll find the spells and then you can sleep near me. I'll watch over you, keep *you* safe for once." His eyes lock with mine. "I'll protect you, if you'll let me."

I smile weakly and nod. "All right."

He squeezes my hand and I expect him to release it, but instead he just tightens his grip and leads me back through the trees to his tent. Once inside, I sit awkwardly at the edge of his bed while he sifts through a book.

"Ah, here it is," he says, tracing his finger along the words. "It seems pretty straightforward and only takes a few very basic ingredients. I can do this."

I lean over and peer at the book. "And there's a counter spell?"

He nods and points to a few additional lines of text. "Right here. You'll automatically wake on your own when the spell is spent if we don't need to use the counter spell. The length of the spell depends on the amount of ingredients used. I'll start with six hours."

Nerves twist in my stomach. "All right. What do I need to do?"

Ehren gives me a half smile and gestures to the bed. "Lie down and make yourself comfortable."

Heat rises in my cheeks, but I feel instantly better when I notice pink tinging Ehren's as well. This is just as awkward for him. Once I'm relaxed, Ehren kneels on the floor next to me. He carefully measures a few ingredients, mostly dried bits of leaves and plants, and grinds them. Once the mixture is done, he dips in his thumb and traces a symbol between my eyes whispering a simple phrase. He smiles and leans away from me, studying me almost nervously.

"How do you feel?"

I blink as the world around me starts to blur.

"Sleepy," I manage to murmur.

The last things I see are Ehren's bright eyes and confident smile before I'm pulled into the peaceful arms of sleep.

CHAPTER TWENTY-ONE

ALAK

If Kato's confidence is shaken in the slightest by Ronan not signing on immediately like the other Clans, he doesn't show it. Kato's practically glowing this morning as we prepare to leave. He swaggers down the hall and makes a show of thanking Ronan for his hospitality. Ronan plays the part of a gracious lord perfectly, smiling and thanking Kato for his visit, though the invitation to come again is a blaring missing component to their final conversation. Thankfully, no one else notices the parting wink Ronan shoots me the moment before we wisp away.

Once back in Brackenborough, Kato goes into full-on strategy mode. He has Kayleigh researching and digging up as much information as possible about how everything will work at Fortress Mullidain. He wants to make sure that when the Clans arrive they have rooms prepared, servants to do their bidding, and meals worthy of a king.

After only a few hours, Kayleigh has enough information gathered for Kato to call a counsel. He sits in a chair against one wall like a king surveying a room of peasants. I lean against the wall to his right, wishing I could be anywhere else.

"So," Kayleigh says, glancing up at Kato over the stack of papers in her hands, scribbled with notes. "The village of Klangdale usually maintains the fortress. They have people who look over it and keep the grounds mostly in good repair, but no one actually lives in the fortress itself."

"How far is the village from the fortress?" Kato asks, leaning back in his chair.

"Um," Kayleigh mumbles, shifting through the papers. One flutters to floor, and I step forward and whip it up. It's a diagram layout of the fortress.

"Oh, thanks," Kayleigh says, extending her hand expectantly. I nod and place the paper in her hand, resuming my position along the wall.

"Well?" Kato presses, his voice tinged with irritation at the delay.

"Sorry!" Kayleigh replies, red rising in her cheeks. "Oh, here it is. Um, the village is roughly a thirty-minute walk from the fortress."

Kato nods like this is the exact information he was looking for. "And there are people ready to step into service and make sure everything is prepared? And others available to wait on guests as they arrive?"

Kayleigh nods. "They haven't had to host in a while, but there are families in place. We may need to add a bit more staff, though, and some of the rooms will need work." Kayleigh pauses, tilting her head and biting the inside of her cheek.

"What aren't you saying?" Kato asks, sitting straighter, his eyes boring into Kayleigh.

She hesitates and glances at me. I know exactly what

she's not saying. There are people to staff the fortress and people that care for it, but they're not likely to step in for just anyone without proper compensation. They don't care about Kato's plans. If Klangdale is that close to Fortress Mullidain, chances are they're in neutral territory. They don't answer to a Clan and, therefore, have no Clan to disappoint.

"It's just a matter of the . . . the payment," Kayleigh stammers, her eyes darting away from Kato's prying gaze.

"Ah," Kato says, grinning as he settles back comfortably in his seat. He waves a hand. "That's not an issue."

I arch an eyebrow. "It's not?"

Kato's grin turns feral, sending shivers down my spine. "Not even almost an issue." He turns his attention back to Kayleigh. "Assure the people of Klangdale that they will be properly compensated for their assistance."

Kato rises from his seat so abruptly it makes Kayleigh jump. I bite back a smile.

"Also, let them know that anyone who goes above and beyond will receive extra compensation." His expression goes dark and something even darker flashes in his eyes as he adds, "And make it clear that anyone who refuses to do a decent job will face dire consequences."

I inhale sharply and hope Kato doesn't notice. Kayleigh shoots me a worried look, but I avert my eyes.

"Y-yes, I'll do that," Kayleigh stutters, bowing her head. "Is there anything else you need from me?"

Kato shakes his head. "Not right now. Let them know we will arrive soon to begin preparation of the grounds, and I expect everything to be set in motion."

Kayleigh nods and scurries away at a motion of Kato's hand. Kato strides across the room, his hands linked behind his back. His eyes lock on Ian in the far corner. Ian straightens from a slouch and takes a deep breath.

"Have you found appropriate guardsmen?" Kato asks sharply, stopping a few feet from Ian.

I raise my eyebrows. I had no idea he was already building any sort of army or guard.

Ian licks his lips. "Aye. I have more than a few decent volunteers."

Kato grins and turns away from Ian. "Excellent. Tell them to be ready to leave at a moment's notice."

Ian nods, even though Kato isn't looking at him, and hurries from the room even quicker than Kayleigh did.

"Do you need anything from me?" Niall asks tentatively from his spot along the same wall, his arms wrapped almost protectively around Caitlyn.

Kato looks over his shoulder at Niall, considering him. "No more than I've already requested."

Niall nods, his shoulders relaxing. I can't help but wonder what Niall's already doing and not knowing makes me uncomfortable.

Kato's shifts his gaze around the room, taking in the few of us that remain.

"You can all go. Get everything prepared. We leave tomorrow."

Everyone else nods and shuffles off, but I take a step toward Kato.

"Tomorrow? But you told Kayleigh to tell them we would arrive in a couple days," I point out carefully.

Kato flashes his teeth in a wicked grin and his eyes spark. "Indeed. I have a feeling they'll work faster under a watchful eye, and I won't leave it to chance everything will be ready in time if I'm not there."

I nod and take a deep breath. "I guess that's logical enough."

Kato cocks his head. "Something you're concerned about?"

Yes. A thousand things. But I shake my head.

"Not really." I pause. "What is 'proper compensation'? Are there funds I don't know about?"

Kato's grin widens. "We have several very generous benefactors giving us their support."

My heart stops. This is . . . not good news.

"In Athiedor?"

Kato shrugs. "From all over." Something otherworldly flashes on his face as he purrs, "I have allies beyond the walls of Athiedor, you know. My influence is ever-growing. Athiedor is only the first step of many."

I feel as if all the air has been sucked from the room and cold settles over me. I struggle to keep my features neutral as I press my hands to my sides to keep them from shaking. I bob my head in seeming agreement, unable to find or form any words. I don't know exactly who these benefactors are or how he found them, but there's something off. Something . . . dark.

"Anyway, don't worry about the money," Kato says with a careless wave.

"I just," I manage to get to get out, my voice uneven, "well, I just don't understand why you didn't mention these . . . benefactors to Ro—Lord McDullun."

"Have you ever seen me lose a game of cards?" Kato asks, a smile playing on his lips as he takes a few steps toward me.

I pause, thinking before slowly shaking my head. "No, I don't believe I have."

"That's because I know how to play the game. I know

how to use the cards I'm dealt. I know when not to show my hand."

He claps his hand to my shoulder and my magic lurches. He squeezes my shoulder tightly enough that it's borderline painful, but I keep my expression controlled as he adds, "Don't question how I play the game. Just know I'm going to win."

His eyes lock on mine and my magic screams and roils. I feel like I'm going to be sick. Very, very violently sick. I long to pull from his grasp, but the second I start to draw away his hand heats and I flinch, the scent of burning flesh filling my nostrils. His eyes gleam and he knows he's made his point. He releases my shoulder with a jerk, and I tumble back with a sharp gasp. He turns his back to me and walks across the room, pausing at the door.

"Alak," he says, his voice cold, not bothering to turn. "I wouldn't question me again if I were you."

I don't need to respond because he's gone the next second. I stumble over to the chair Kato vacated and collapse into it. I tenderly peel back the neckline of my shirt and look at my shoulder. There, right along the curve of my shoulder is a pink burn mark in the shape of Kato's hand. By some twist of magic, my shirt is still perfectly intact. I reach up with my other hand and tentatively touch the raw skin. I hiss and swear, yanking my hand away. It's painful and hot to the touch.

I take a deep breath and look to where Kato disappeared moments ago. Things are not going well. At all.

A short yip brings my attention to my feet. Felixe sits between my boots, blinking up at me, his head cocked in curiosity.

"Hey, Felixe."

Felixe barks his response and leaps up into my lap. He raises up, placing his paws on my chest as he stretches his muzzle toward my shoulder, sniffing. When his cold nose brushes against the hot skin, I start and Felixe drops back, growling in the direction of the burnt flesh. I pull my shirt back over my shoulder and wince at the feeling of the rough material against the raw skin.

"Yeah, I know," I sigh as I scratch Felixe behind his ear.

Felixe glances back up at my shoulder and whimpers. I force a smile.

"I'm fine. Gods know I've survived worse." I glance around and make sure I'm alone before I lean forward and whisper, "Just tell Astra her brother is turning into a bit of an arsehole."

At Astra's name, Felixe gives an affirmative bark and spins, a folded piece of paper appearing grasped in his teeth. I stare at him, puzzled as I take the paper.

"Where the hell were you hiding this?"

Felixe simply cocks his head and looks at me like he has better things to do than answer obvious questions. With a chuckle, I unfold the paper and read.

My Dearest Alak,

I apologize that I did not write back immediately, but Ehren and I have been formulating a plan on our end. While I am nervous about wisping to a place I've never been, I trust you. I think your plan will work. Ehren is making as many necessary arrangements as possible. I think we have come up with something that will win the Clans to our side.

On another note, Bram overheard Ehren and I talking, so we've let him in on our plans. He's not happy in the slightest, but I think he appreciates not being lied to anymore. We've also filled Kai in on our plan. Kai is a shifter we met in the Hundan Valley. I know you don't know him, but I assure you he can be trusted. I trust him with my life. I'd say you two would get along, but I don't think anyone gets along with Kai besides me.

Please, please be careful. I know Kato and he will not be happy to lose. If we are successful, which I pray we will be, things may become very dangerous for you. Don't put your life at risk. I need you to be back by my side. I didn't realize how much I truly missed you until you showed up at the masquerade. Now, I am sure I cannot live without you. So, please, be careful. Come back to me in one piece.

Forever Yours,

Astra

My heart skips at least two beats as I read the last few lines of her letter. She misses me. She can't live without me. I take a deep breath and try to still my racing heart. It's likely just the soul bond. The bond she doesn't even know exists. Guilt surges through me.

"Should I tell her?" I mumble, half to myself and half to the Fae Fox curled in my lap. I absentmindedly rub Felixe's head. "She deserves to know." I sigh and shake my head. "But I can't do that in a letter. It's not fair to her."

I lift Felixe to my unburned shoulder and he grumbles as he adjusts. I stand and slowly walk toward the door, stuffing the letter in my pocket. I need to prepare to leave and make sure everything is ready for Astra to make her entrance. Whatever she and Ehren have planned needs to work. If we fail . . . I shudder. I don't want to think of what might happen if Kato wins.

CHAPTER TWENTY-TWO

ALAK

Morning comes early. Well, I guess morning always comes early, but this morning seems to come extraordinarily early. Kato is like a dog chasing a rabbit. He's wild and irritable, eager to be on our way. I shove what I need in my travel bag and escape to the woods to get away from the insanity and preparations. Honestly, I almost wish he'd just leave me behind. But I guess in order for my plan with Astra to work, I need to be there.

The morning is cooler than it has been, finally feeling like autumn may be right around the corner. I stand on the bridge and watch a golden leaf flutter down from the trees, landing on the crystal surface of the water, disturbing its previous stillness with a circle of ripples.

"There you are!" Kayleigh yells from the shore behind me, making me jump. "Are you even ready?"

I turn and glare at her, gesturing to the bag at my feet. "Packed and ready to go."

"Well, come on, then!" she snaps. "Kato is ready to leave, and he's not happy at all that you went missing."

Kayleigh bites her lip and glances off, her eyebrows knit in a worried scowl. I sling my bag over my shoulder and walk toward her.

"You know, Kayleigh," I start slowly, cautiously, "if you're having second thoughts about following Kato—"

Her eyes snap to mine and flash. "I'm not having doubts," she bites.

I hold my hands up defensively. "Fine. Noted."

She spins away from me. "Just hurry up."

She wisps away and I sigh, running a hand through my hair. Shite. Oh well, what's said is said. Taking a deep breath, I wisp to Niall's house and discover everyone gathered out front. Kato's eyes fall on me and he smiles.

"Now that we're all here"—he glances pointedly in my direction—"we can get going."

I shrug and mouth "sorry" as I step in line next to Kayleigh. I glance around and notice no one new to guide us to Fortress Mullidain.

"Who's guiding the wisp?" I ask, scowling.

"I am," Kayleigh says proudly.

"How . . . ?"

"Does it really matter?" she challenges, her voice cold. I really can't risk pissing her off.

I shake my head. "I guess not."

Kato scans the group. "Everyone ready?" We nod. "All right. Here we go."

The all-too-familiar wall of flames surrounds us as we're pulled away from the familiarity of our village to the outskirts of the fortress. When the flames fade, we're standing at the edge of a forest. I turn and find the fortress behind me, not far off. From this distance, it looks like a worn castle from a fairy tale or legend, lost but not forgotten. The closer we get, the more I'm impressed with how well it's held up over the years. It's worn, there's no doubt about that. The stones, likely once bright and smooth, have been dulled by the sun and years of dust and dirt. Vines climb the walls in several places, adding to the storybook effect, but otherwise everything is well kept. No weeds poke through the stone pathway leading up to the front gate. In fact, many portions of the stones look freshly laid. The plants and bushes in the front courtyard are all trimmed and pruned and the knockers and handles on the front door appear freshly polished.

Kato seems to notice all these little details, looking around and smiling like a cat who's just cornered his prey. His look of pleasure is shared by the others, so I force a contented smile on my face as well.

We enter the dark front hall and are almost immediately greeted by a young man around our age with shockingly bright orange hair and a face covered in freckles.

"Ah, hello there, mates," the man says awkwardly, surveying us with caution. His eyes fall on Kayleigh and then Kato, recognition sparking as his eyes go wide.

"Oh, uh, you must be Master Kato," he fumbles, falling into a bow. "We weren't expecting ya quite yet."

Kato flashes his most charming grin and the man relaxes a bit. "That's all right. We are early. I simply wanted to be here to make sure everything goes smoothly."

The man swallows and nods. "Aye. Makes sense."

He pauses, his eyes darting nervously from face to face. Kato seems to relish his discomfort. The arsehole.

"My name is Alak," I offer, stepping forward.

The man smiles weakly. "Nice to meetcha. My name is

Eamon. My sister, Siobhan, is here as well. She's prepping the rooms."

"Is it just you two?" Kato questions, arching an eyebrow.

Eamon shakes his head furiously. "Naw. Though it is mostly our family. The McClines have always been the keepers of the fortress." His voice rings with pride as he stands a little straighter. "My cousins Brannon and Conan are here as well, doing much of the manual labor, while my other cousin, Eabha, is helping Siobhan."

Kato nods approvingly, glancing around. "I'll admit the fortress is in better shape than I expected." His gaze falls back on Eamon and hardens. "We'll need more people to make everything go smoothly."

Eamon gulps and nods at the unspoken threat in Kato's voice. "Aye. And there will be more. It's early in the day yet. Many that will be here later this week have, uh, other duties and jobs to attend right now."

Translation: the world here doesn't revolve around Kato's whims. Kato stiffens but keeps a smile plastered on his face as he nods. Eamon senses Kato's irritation, however.

"I'll send my brother Kellan into the village," Eamon amends. "He can bring back anyone who is available."

As if summoned, a little boy no more than seven years old with the same shocking orange hair stumbles around the corner. When he sees us, his eyes go wide. Kato relaxes and drops to his knees to be eye level with the boy.

"Hey, there. What's your name?" Kato asks gently.

The boy takes a step back and glances up at Eamon nervously. When Eamon gives him a reassuring nod, the boy replies, "Kellan."

"Ah, Kellan!" Kato says cheerfully. "Your brother was just telling us how helpful you are."

Kellan's eyes light up and he grins, glancing sideways at his brother in wonder. "He did?"

Kato nods. "He sure did!"

Eamon offers Kellan a smile. "Course I did, Kells."

Kellan turns his wide eyes to Kato's face. "I try my hardest to help! I'm little but I'm mighty! That's what Papa always says!"

Kato chuckles, and I marvel at how different Kato is with children.

"Well, I think we have a mission just for you if you're up to it," Kato says slowly and the boy nods eagerly.

Eamon quickly explains to his brother what we need and suggests a few people to get, more cousins by the sound of it. Kellan's head bobs along enthusiastically the entire time. When Eamon is finished with the instructions, Kellan races off, promising to return in "three shakes of a lamb's tail."

Once Kellan is gone, Eamon leads us off to find his sister who, he assures us, can lead us to a prepared room. We find his sister and cousin laughing and chatting in the laundry room as they sort piles of sheets and blankets. Eamon clears his throat as he steps into the room. Their laughter stops when they see Kato just behind Eamon.

"Siobhan, Master Kato has arrived early," Eamon says carefully.

The older of the two girls jumps to her feet, her face pale and eyes wide. "Master Kato," she mumbles with a stiff bow. "We weren't expecting you yet. I'm afraid we only have one room ready. The rest are still airing out, but a few more can be ready by the end of the day."

"That's fine. We know we're early and we do apologize," Kato replies in a voice that doesn't sound apologetic in the slightest. "Show us the room you have."

Siobhan steps out into the hall, motioning for us to follow. We wind through dusty corridors lined with statues and busts. All of the Clans are represented in the decor. Vases bear symbols and crests, as does artwork hanging on the walls. One long hall is lined with colorful tapestries alternating the crests. Despite the layers of dust, it's a warm feeling to be around so much Athiedor history.

When we finally come to a halt, Siobhan throws open a door to a reasonably-sized room. The room has a slight musty smell to it, but the fresh air wafting in the window and twirling the sheer blue curtains helps. The large bed against one wall has been recently made and adorned with a deep blue comforter and gray pillows. There's not much furniture beyond the bed. Just a small writing desk, a bedside table, and a loveseat. Judging by the size of the room, it once held more furniture, but the years of disuse have taken their toll. Kato, however, doesn't seem put off by the sparse room and nods approvingly. Siobhan relaxes.

"Eabha and I will prepare rooms for your companions straight away," Siobhan promises with a bow before she leaves.

Once she's gone, we deposit our bags on the floor near Kato's bed and leave to explore the grounds. The fortress is larger than I expected. It's nearly the size of the fortress held by Clan Wallish but has the comfortable familiarity of Clan McDullun. I suppose if I were more familiar with the other clans and their main residences, I would see even more touches from each. After all, Mullidain was always meant as a neutral meeting ground where everyone would feel comfortable and welcome.

Kellan does his job well, and within the hour people are crawling like busy ants all over the fortress. Tapestries are brought down and the dust is beaten out. Lanterns are filled and lit. Every surface is dusted and cleaned until it shines. Even little details like chipped paint and wobbling chairs are quickly fixed. A cook arrives in the kitchen a little before lunch to prepare some simple sandwiches, promising a better dinner.

Kato saunters around the fortress like a king, a sloppy grin on his face. Whenever he walks in a room, people scuttle out of his way, terror in their eyes. With a sinking feeling, I wonder how many of these villagers are here because of promised "compensation" or because they fear for their lives and the lives of everyone in their village. How many businesses are empty today because their workers are here? No matter their reasons, however, the results are undeniable. The efforts of the villagers pay off, and when the Clan leaders begin arriving a couple of days before the meeting, the fortress almost looks like a completely different place.

Lord O'Brick is the first to arrive during the mid-morning hours three days before the meeting is set to start. At nearly seventy years of age, he's among the oldest of the Clan leaders with a stout belly and gray hair and beard. He was quick to sing about the glory days of a free Athiedor as if he were old enough to remember, despite not having been born yet. He was the second Clan leader to sign on with Kato with very little convincing.

Lord O'Brick doesn't arrive alone, but brings along his wife and oldest son, as well as a handful of servants. Lady O'Brick looks like she's swallowed a lemon and smells nothing but spoiled trout. Her cold eyes scan every room, weighing and judging, and she almost seems disappointed when she finds nothing to scoff at. Once she's led away to her room, we don't see her for the majority the time. His son, however, is much more agreeable and falls into easy conversation with anyone who will talk to him.

Lord Dughlas is the next to arrive, wisping outside the gate just before noon. He's a stodgy old man who claimed he left his wife behind because she doesn't care for politics, but his true reasoning is evident when his mistress, a woman a good thirty years younger than he, arrives that evening. He and Lord O'Brick drink ale and toast to the old days, celebrating the future of a free Athiedor.

Lord Bashmore arrives early afternoon. While he's not exactly young for a Clan leader, being in his mid-forties, he looks very youthful compared to Lord Dughlas and Lord O'Brick. He is aged up a bit by the fact he brought along his twenty-something son, Cillian, and daughter, Eire. His wife, however, opted to stay behind with their younger children.

On the one previous occasion I met Lord Bashmore, he never stopped watching and observing. This occasion is no different. He takes in every movement, storing information away for later. His son, while more relaxed and less obvious, seems to be doing the same. It's no wonder Clan Bashmore is known for its spymasters.

Lord Bashmore and his heirs join the other Lords around pints of ale and continue to laugh and chat through dinner. Aine and Ian latch onto his children like charming leeches, winning them over—much to my chagrin. I stick to the edges, taking note of each conversation and movement. The only one who seems to notice my presence is Eire. Her gaze is locked on me every time I glance her way. She doesn't shy away when our eyes meet. Instead, she holds my gaze for a moment or two, a smile playing on her lips before she finally blinks slowly and turns her attention to someone else. She acts as if there are deep secrets between us, a history full and rich. But the fact is I've never met her before, and her gaze is both unwelcome and unsettling.

I manage to escape from the Clan leaders and their families, seeking sanctuary and peace outside. The gardens have been well kept and tended over the years, flourishing with late-summer flowers. I trace my fingers along the golden petals of a rose-like flower. *Blythian Rose,* my magic whispers. *Useful for those wishing to see or understand visions.* I feel drawn to a small cluster of bright reddish-orange mushrooms not far away. *Devil's Kiss—deadly poison.* My magic begins pulling in every direction, dozens of voices echoing in my head. There are too many magical plants here. I take a deep breath, concentrating, and reel my magic in. I still sense the hum of magic, but it's softer and less overwhelming.

I turn to go back inside when suddenly the ground feels like it's shifting. My head spins and the world swirls. With a gasp, I stumble backward, leaning my weight against a smooth stone wall. I sink down to the dirt and lift a shaking hand to my pounding head. I squeeze my eyes shut, trying to sort out what's happening. Something isn't right. Something is . . . off. But it's not my magic. At least, I don't think it is, but my magic does seem affected.

"Are you okay?"

I open my eyes to find Eire squatting in front of me, her eyes swimming with concern. I try to force a smile and nod.

"Aye, I'm fine. I'm just a bit weary from all the preparations." Another wave of unease rushes over me, and I inhale sharply, closing my eyes. When I open them again, her face is set in a firm scowl.

"You are most definitely not all right," she insists,

reaching a hand out to wipe beads of sweat from my forehead.

I shift away from her touch. "I only need a moment." She remains skeptical so I add, "A bit of water might help."

She stands, her hands on her hips. "Fine. I'll get you some water, but if it doesn't help, I'm finding you a Healer."

I manage a nod as she shuffles off. I lean against the wall and breathe in and out slowly. Little by little the feeling fades. By the time Eire returns with a cup of water, I'm able to stand and even offer a semi-genuine smile.

"See," I say with a grin. "I'm fine."

Eire doesn't seem convinced but doesn't bother me again and even leaves me alone in the garden for a bit. I know she hovers nearby just out of sight for a while but eventually, she does rejoin the others.

Lord Loudain makes his appearance mid-morning the next day. He's very stern and his thick eyebrows seem set in a permanent scowl. He also comes alone. He's one of the only Clans to have thrown support behind Kato sight unseen, so Kato is eager to please him and obliges his every request and whim. Lord Loudain is more than happy to take advantage of that fact, requesting everything from the largest room to the best ale and the most respectable seats. While Kato smiles and appeases him in public, behind closed doors he's aggravated. It's only when Aine steps in to use her feminine graces that Lord Loudain seems satiated, although his scowl never completely fades.

That evening, Lord Kensdor arrives with several servants and his heir. Lord Kensdor himself is well into his sixties and his son in his forties. Both are heavyset men with boisterous personalities. When they arrive their cheeks are already pink with drink, and they don't hesitate to indulge in the ale and meads provided by Kato. By the time dinner is served, they're both pissed.

Kato takes everything in stride. He's a perfect host. I can tell that even the Clans who are less than eager to support Kato are becoming more relaxed in his presence. When he clears his throat at dinner and proposes a toast, all eyes turn to him, intrigue and delight on their faces.

"Good evening, friends, for I feel that we very much are friends and not only allies," Kato begins, his voice booming through the dining hall. The Clan leaders respond with general grunts and nods of agreement. "I hope that you are all enjoying your stay here, gathered together. Soon, Athiedor will be free once again and this fort will be yours to use for negotiations amongst yourselves. For now, we gather to garner support for magic, to work together to create a new and wonderful world where magic reigns. At the center of that power are all of you." Kato gestures to the Clan leaders and offers them a winning smile. They tip their heads in appreciation. "In celebration of our alliance, I have arranged a hunt for the morning followed by a bit of a party in the evening."

Rumbles of excitement erupt from the table of Clan leaders and Lord Kensdor cheers loudly. Kato's smile grows.

"Of course," he continues, "I was hoping all seven Clans would be in attendance, but perhaps they will arrive in the morning before our hunt. Either way, here's to a wonderful future together."

He raises his glass and everyone else follows suit.

"To a free Athiedor!" he declares before tipping the glass against his lips.

"To a free Athiedor!" everyone echoes, drinking from

their own glasses. My mead, which tasted sweet before, now seems bitter on my tongue.

Kato takes his seat and surveys the eager faces of his guests, a wicked smile curling on his lips. He thinks he's won and, to be honest, everything seems to be falling in his favor. Lord Wallish and Ronan have yet to arrive. I hope that when they do, they'll have the influence to sway things in Astra's favor so when she appears she will win the others over.

I let my eyes drift over the Clan members and find Eire's eyes back on me. Her lips turn upward into a smile. She lifts her glass in a cheers motion, and I force a smile and do the same. Aine notices and sends me a steely glare. I'm not entirely sure what sort of alliance Eire seeks, but if it pisses Aine off it might be a bit fun to pursue.

CHAPTER TWENTY-THREE

ALAK

Kato couldn't have picked a better day for a hunt. The cool kiss of autumn winds blend perfectly with the warmth of summer sun.

Everyone is up early and eager for the hunt. They pile into the dining hall for a quick breakfast of pastries and fruit and cream before spilling into the courtyard to wait for Kato. I have firmly decided not to join them. Hunting has never appealed to me, and no one needs to know exactly how unskilled I am with weapons. I lean against the doorframe and watch the jittery crowd assembled.

Aine has managed to find an outfit that is not only suitable for hunting, but also somewhat seductive, the material tight, slinking over her curves. She's currently using her looks to her advantage, holding the attention of several of the men. Ian stands nearby glaring at them.

"Aren't you joining us?" Eire asks, stepping out of the door behind me.

I turn toward her. She's wearing a simple riding dress, her strawberry blond hair braided over her shoulder.

"Believe you me, love, it's safer for everyone if I stay here."

She laughs, her eyes sparkling. "I'm not much one for hunting myself," she admits. "However, I do enjoy riding, and I've heard Kato has provided some excellent mounts."

I push away from the doorway and offer her a smile. "Well, I hope you enjoy yourself. Knowing Kato, everything will be spectacular."

She nods absentmindedly and lets her eyes drift toward the larger group before falling back on me.

"I can stay here and keep you company, if you'd like."

Her gentle blue eyes meet mine, and she blinks up at me through long eyelashes. For the first time I notice a sprinkling of freckles across her nose and cheekbones. She is very pretty in a simple way. I swallow and purposefully take a step to the side, dragging my eyes from hers.

"I actually have a lot to get done while you're hunting, or I'd appreciate the company," I lie.

"Oh," she says, disappointment ringing in her voice. "I don't suppose there's any of your duties with which I could assist?"

I look back at her and smile. "Unfortunately, no. Lots of boring things to do and not many tasks meant for two."

She dips her head. "Ah, I see."

For whatever reason, guilt swells in my chest. She's a lovely girl, and I hate disappointing her. I sigh and run a hand through my hair.

"Trust me," I insist, "you're sure to have much more fun on the hunt."

She raises her eyes and smiles weakly. "I'm not sure you know me well enough to assess what I find fun."

She takes a step toward me, closing the distance between

us. Her face is mere inches from mine. My cheeks warm as my pulse quickens.

"However," she continues, her voice low and sultry, "I would love to get to know you more . . . personally, so you could assess such things."

I swallow. Why do I feel like a cornered mouse?

"I—"

"Eire, are you joining us?" her brother calls from the group in the center of the courtyard, bringing a welcome interruption.

Eire snaps her head in her brother's direction and shoots him a deathly glare. "I will in a moment."

Cillian grins and saunters our way. Eire sighs and mutters something under her breath. I bite my lip to hold back a grin. When Cillian reaches Eire, he throws his arm around her shoulders.

"My sister isn't bothering you too much, is she?" Cillian teases, grinning like a lark.

"I wasn't," Eire grumbles, ducking out from under his arm. "I was merely wondering why Alak wasn't joining us for the hunt."

"Huh," Cillian replies, glancing up and down at my very non-hunting-friendly attire. "No good at hunting?"

I shake my head. "No. Never had much opportunity to develop the skill."

"Well, then you should definitely join. That way Eire and I won't be the worst ones." Cillian laughs, his grin growing.

"Speak for yourself," Eire hisses, smacking her brother in the chest. "I may not be exceptionally skilled, but I'm better than you!"

Cillian laughs harder and I smile.

"I'm sure you're both excellent enough."

Before either of them can reply, Kato strides into the courtyard, drawing all eyes to him.

"Well, shall we be off?" Kato asks cheerily as he makes his way across the courtyard. He's met with several hardy greetings.

The group begins shuffling from the courtyard toward the stables.

"Come on, Eire," Cillian says, tugging on his sister's arm. "You don't want to miss the best mounts."

Eire shrugs her brother off. "Go on. I'll follow in a moment."

Cillian shrugs and follows the others as Eire turns back to me.

"Are you sure you won't come?"

I shake my head. "There really wouldn't be any point. I really do have things to do."

"And I can't be of *any* help?"

Once again I shake my head, taking a step back. "No, but you really should enjoy the hunt."

With a deep, dramatic sigh of resignation, she turns and begins the short trek to the stables, shooting me one last longing glance before turning the corner. At one point in my life, I would have readily welcomed the advances of such a pretty girl, most definitely taking the opportunity to get to know her better while her father and brother were occupied with a hunt. Now, however, I have very different aspirations. With a sigh of relief, I head inside to find Kayleigh.

The servants and staff seem much more relaxed without Kato around, and the fortress has a more natural air to it. It's almost enjoyable. Even Kayleigh seems more relaxed when I find her in the library, examining the long list of tasks in her hand.

"Oh, Alak! There you are!" she cries, looking up from her paper as I enter the room. "I was afraid you might have gone on the hunt, and I'd have to do all this on my own."

"I have no desire to hunt. What do you need?"

She sighs and glances down her list. "If you could take care of these things"—she points to several items, all dealing with food—"that would be very helpful."

I nod, committing the tasks to memory. "Got it."

"Okay, good." She looks up from the list and glances around, gathering her thoughts. "Now, I just have to make sure everything else is ready."

She walks out of the room, staring at her list and mumbling to herself. I shake my head. Kato has her overworked, but she'll never admit it. I start to leave the library but pause at the door, looking over my shoulder at the writing desk. I wonder if it's stocked. Knowing Kato, he probably made sure it was. I cross the room and open a drawer to find everything I need. I glance around before settling in at the desk. I can hear people shuffling around in the halls. I don't have long, but I feel the need to update Astra. Quickly, without any more hesitation, I make quick work of a letter. Nothing fancy or detailed, just enough to keep Astra informed. I'm almost done writing when Felixe appears on the desktop and begins batting at the corner of the paper.

"Did you show up to cause trouble?" I ask, rubbing his ears.

He gives a quiet yap as I sign my name. I roll the paper into a scroll and hold it out to him. Felixe sighs (if a Fae Fox can sigh) and takes it.

"One day soon you won't be just our messenger fox," I assure him, giving his ears more scratches. "I promise."

Felixe blinks up at me, clearly not believing a word I said, then disappears. With a sigh of my own, I rise and go off to complete the tasks bestowed upon me by my cousin.

Most of my assigned duties have me in the kitchen sorting and arranging, so I'm among the first to hear about the return of the hunting party. Even though it's not quite noon, they've returned with a large boar and buck for tonight's feast. I help the scrambling kitchen servants throw together a quick lunch before heading into the dining hall to finish sorting out goblets. The Clan leaders and their heirs are gathered around a table drinking ale, but Kato and his crew have disappeared. I'm nearly done with my chores when the dining hall doors are thrown open with a burst of wind.

"Ach!" Lord O'Brick yells, startling so hard he splashes ale down the front of his shirt as all eyes turn to see who's made such a raucous entrance.

Lord Wallish bounds through the door, a jovial bounce in his step and wide smile stretching across his face.

"Morning, lads," he greets everyone with a tip of his head as he plops down in a seat.

"Morning?" Lord Dughlas huffs. "It's after noon already. And who are you callin' lads? You're little more than a lad yourself."

Lord Bashmore chokes on his ale trying to hide a laugh.

"True enough when compared to an old cock like yerself." Lord Wallish chuckles. His eyes travel down the table to the jug of ale and empty mugs. "Perhaps I should have a drink then, eh?"

"Ya missed a good hunt this mornin'," Lord Dughlas says

pointedly as Lord Kensdor pours a mug of ale, passing it to Lord Wallish.

"Perhaps," Lord Wallish concedes with a carefree shrug. "But I have a good bit of news that may just interest everyone. Somethin' that may change our fate in this game."

Lord Loudain scowls and crosses his arms. "About what?"

"While you've all been holed up here kissing Kato's arse"—several Clan leaders wince but Cillian grins—"his sister has been making her mark." Lord Wallish pauses and chugs down a good bit of ale, smacking his lips with pleasure when he's done. "That's right good ale, there."

"Yes it is," Lord Loudain agrees. "But what about Kato's sister?" He pauses and turns his head slightly in my direction as he adds, "And in present company, is it a good idea to discuss such things?"

I try to focus intently on the goblet in front of me, throwing up an illusion spell to mask my presence and make the others forget I was ever here. I can sense Lord Wallish scan the room.

"Naw, we're all good," he says with bubbly reassurance before taking another sip of ale. "That is most excellent."

"What about the twin?" Lord Bashmore growls in exasperation.

I turn my head enough to catch the twinkle in Lord Wallish's eye as he replies, "It bothers ya that I know something your spies don't."

Lord Loudain huffs and shakes his head. "I doubt you have any news that hasn't reached my ears."

"Is that so?" Lord Wallish challenges, grinning.

"Out with it!" Lord Dughlas yells, slamming a fist on the

table. "Some of us don't have years to sit around and babble. If ya have news, share it."

Lord Wallish takes another long sip of his ale before finally answering. "So, I suppose it's reached everyone by now that Mistress Astra has been ordained Prince Ehren's official Court Sorceress."

Lord Bashmore waves his hand. "That's old news."

"Aye, I know. 'Tis why I said it's probably reached everyone. That's not my news."

"Then what *is* your bloody news?" Lord Bashmore demands through gritted teeth.

"Well," Lord Wallish begins, relishing the attention, "Mistress Astra, Prince Ehren, and their group of misfits left the Isle of Naskein after she was made official Court Sorceress and they went to Gleador. Appeared before the king."

"That's a fairly logical step," Lord Kensdor says with an approving nod as Lord Wallish drains his ale.

"Aye, but that's not the news either. The news is what happened *after* they left the king." He pauses and nods to the ale. "Can I get a refill?"

"For gods' sake! Finish your tale!" Lord Loudain snaps.

Lord Wallish arches an eyebrow but sighs and pushes his mug back. "Fine." He leans in, placing his elbows on the table. "So, Mistress Astra and the prince left King Naimon on relatively good terms. He even had a couple guards escort them to the border. After they crossed into Callenia, they went through the abandoned druid city of Mythgulch. Everything was going smoothly until they were ambushed on their way out of the city."

My heart stops and my breath catches. My brain reels as I struggle to form thoughts. That strange feeling I had in the garden must have been Astra. It had to be our bond, our link reaching out to me. I panic. Surely I would know if she were dead. I'd know. I'd have to know. I try to calm my racing heart and thoughts, concentrating on Lord Wallish.

"At least six-hundred of the king's men surrounded them. They were trapped on both sides by high walls lined with archers with troops of soldiers coming in behind and in front of them."

Oh gods. Oh gods. Oh gods.

Someone lets out a low whistle and several others swear.

"So that's it, then," Lord Dughlas says, not bothering to hide his delight. "His twin is out of the running. No need to worry."

I swallow. No. No. *NO.*

Lord Wallish chuckles and I sit straighter. He wouldn't laugh if something bad had happened. He wants Astra to win.

"Hardly. Someone with magic, likely Astra herself, immediately threw up a shield above them protecting from the archers and a shield behind them narrowing their attack to one front."

"Still," Lord Dughlas presses with a scowl, "a handful of magical imps couldn't stand against six-hundred of the king's soldiers."

"Wait, did you say it was most likely that Astra put up the shield? Does that mean more people with magical talents accompanied the prince?" Lord Kensdor asks slowly.

"Aye," Lord Wallish replies with a nod. "There were reports of a girl who used earth magic to make the walls tumble. Another boy with them called forth insects that bit and stung, incapacitating several soldiers and killing more. There was also a powerful shifter among them that turned into a great wolf that leapt up on the horses, tearing out throats. The prince himself even seemed to call forth spells, blasting men out of his way. There are also vague reports of shadow magic. All of that magic was separate from what Astra performed."

More cursing. I breathe a little easier, but my hands still shake.

"Still, surely against six-hundred men—"

"The soldiers with the prince are well trained and held their own at their prince's side, too. Might as well have been magic."

"You're not telling us," Lord Loudain cuts in, "that somehow they escaped?"

"They not only escaped. They won."

The silence in the room is so heavy I'm not even sure anyone is breathing. I know I hold my breath for a moment.

"That's . . . that's not possible," Lord Dughlas whispers.

"Possible or not, it happened."

"How?"

"Astra."

My heart swells, and I bow my head to hide my smile.

"Astra?"

"Yes. Reports say she jumped from her horse and crafted two perfect twin blades of silver light and plunged into the fray without hesitation, wielding all the talent of the most skilled soldiers. Then, she put away her twin blades and crafted similar daggers and took out more soldiers. With those blades alone she struck down over two dozen men."

Lord Wallish's voice is low and quiet, but I can still hear everything he is saying. The men are hanging on Lord Wallish's every word.

"And when it became evident that swords alone

wouldn't win this battle, she harnessed the might of her power. Her skin glowed silver, her eyes flashed with pure starlight, and she rose into the air like a specter. She stretched out her hand and snapped the necks of dozens of men without touching them. Next, she stretched out her magic in a great, silver fog and reached down into the soldiers' throats, pulling life directly from their bodies with naught but a twist of her hand. All in all, she brought down well over two hundred men all on her own."

"Gods," Lord Loudain mutters in awe, his face pale as freshly fallen snow.

"And that's not all," Lord Wallish continues.

"What more could there be?" Lord Bashmore grunts in disbelief.

Lord Wallish smiles slowly. "After she cleared a path, she wisped them away. Made them all disappear. Horses and all. No one knows how far she took them, but they couldn't be seen for miles."

I can't hide my grin as pride swells in my chest. I didn't feel her defeat. No, I felt her might, her victory.

"Naw," Lord O'Brick denies, shaking his head vigorously. "Naw. That's just not possible."

"He's right," Lord Bashmore agrees. "I would have heard. How did any of this reach your ears, anyway?"

"I have my sources," Lord Wallish says with a sly grin. He waves his hand. "Go on and check with your own spies. See if they can't confirm every detail."

Lord Bashmore jumps to his feet. "I will. Right now."

He storms from the room and the others erupt into careless, nervous whispers, so chaotic I can't catch most of what they're saying. When Lord Bashmore returns, his wide eyes and pale face are enough to confirm the story.

"Six-hundred men," Lord Bashmore mutters, sinking down at the table. "390 are confirmed dead. Another 70 wounded." He reaches across the table and pours himself more ale and chugs it as dissent erupts across the table.

"I knew it! I bloody knew it!" Lord Loudain yells, standing and pressing his palms down on the table.

"Knew what?" Lord O'Brick challenges. "Are you going to pretend to know something we didn't?"

"Naw, but that's just it, isn't it? We knew Kato was a twin, and yet we all threw our support blindly behind him. And here's his twin—just as bloody powerful, if not more so!" Lord Loudain snaps.

"She gave no indication of her power," Lord Dughlas counters.

"Didn't she, though?" Lord Kensdor cuts in. "Didn't she go up against the kings's men before, plus magic users in your own territory, and came out the victor?"

"That's entirely different!" Lord Dughlas sputters, his face red. "That was fifty men at most!"

"Still," Lord Wallish grins, leaning back his chair, "perhaps we didn't give her enough credit. She's shown her power now, and I doubt that's all she has."

"Well, it's too late now," Lord Loudain moans.

Lord Kensdor arches an eyebrow. "Is it, though?"

Lord Bashmore's eyes go wide with shock. "Surely you're not suggesting what I think you are?"

Lord Kensdor shrugs. "I'm not saying I'm going to run to find the twin right now, but perhaps she's someone we should seriously consider."

"The treaty signing is tomorrow!" Lord Dughlas hisses. "You're out of time to decide!"

Several more men yell at once, debating pros and cons of

putting off the treaty meeting. I slink from the hall unnoticed, a delighted smirk playing on my lips.

By the time everyone gathers for the evening feast, dissension seems to be set aside, but I still catch the doubtful glances cast in Kato's direction. Thankfully he seems oblivious, eating the finest foods and drinking the finest ales.

The next morning, however, his mood has severely soured. I find him pacing in his room like a caged animal. At first I'm afraid word has reached him of Astra's victory and of the possible coup.

"Where is he?" Kato roars when his eyes settle on me as I shut the door.

"Who?" I ask slowly, knitting my eyebrows.

"Lord McDullun!" Kato spits, throwing his hands in the air.

Somehow, with everything going on, I'd almost forgotten Ronan was even a part of this equation.

"He's supposed to be here by now! Today is the tenth day! He agreed to be here!"

I nod slowly. "I'm sure he'll stay true to his word. He'll come."

Kato stops his pacing, releasing a long breath. "He better."

I swallow hard and pray Ronan arrives soon. It's a little after noon when he finally appears. He doesn't bring any bags with him. He's just dressed in a fine emerald-green tunic with a golden crest on the pocket. He saunters in the front door, a sloppy grin on his face. He catches my eye and his grin widens.

"Ah! Alak!" he greets me, making his way in my direction.

I turn to the nearest servant and instruct him to go let Kato know Lord McDullun has arrived.

"Kato isn't happy with you," I mutter when he's close enough.

Ronan's eyes twinkle mischievously. "I would hope not."

Kato wisps next to me and I jump.

"Where have you been?" he demands, his voice tight.

Ronan meets Kato's eyes without fear. The only indication of nerves is the tapping of his forefinger on the head of his cane.

"I requested two weeks, and you gave me ten days. I used every second of my time wisely," Ronan says evenly.

Kato trembles with barely contained rage. I can feel his magic thick in the air.

"We meet in one hour. Exactly. Not a minute later. Understood?" Kato demands through gritted teeth.

Ronan cocks his head like he's considering making a counteroffer but ends up nodding. "Aye. One hour."

Kato wisps away and Ronan winks at me before sauntering past me to find the other lords. I release a long breath and sneak into the first empty room I can. I find a scrap of paper and ink and jot a quick note. Felixe is there before I've even finished, ready to take my message to Astra. It's almost time.

I take a shaky breath and lean against the wall. Gods help us all.

CHAPTER TWENTY-FOUR

ASTRA

When I first wake up it takes me a minute to remember where I am. I turn over, blinking away sleep, and startle at the sight of a shirtless Ehren sleeping inches away. I take a deep breath, sitting up as the memories from the night before come flooding back. I ease back down onto the bed, realizing I'm not quite ready to rise. Listening to Ehren's easy breathing, I drift in and out of sleep until he starts to stir. I roll over and face him, finding his sleepy sea-green eyes fixed on me.

"Good morning," he mumbles, smiling softly.

"Good morning," I reply, awkwardness washing over me.

Ehren props himself up on his elbow, his hand on his cheek. "I suppose the spell worked? You seemed to sleep well."

"Yes, I feel rested and don't remember dreaming," I answer, rising into a sitting position. I glance toward the closed tent flap. "I suppose I should go get ready for the day."

"I already had your bag brought in," Ehren says, easing up with a groan.

"What?" I ask, my eyes drifting around the tent until they land on my bag lying on the ground to my right. "You didn't have to do that."

Ehren shrugs as he stands and stretches, his muscles tight. He glances over his shoulder and catches me staring. I blush as he laughs.

"Don't worry," he teases. "I'm used to people basking in my glory."

I roll my eyes and smile as he leans down and pulls a shirt from his own bag, slipping it over his head. I slide out of the bed and start sorting through my things to find a new dress. When I glance back over at Ehren, he's sitting cross-legged on the floor putting on his boots.

"Ehren," I say quietly, "can I ask you something?"

He raises his eyes to me and shoots me a curious look. "Ash, after all we've been through together, I'd think you'd know by now you can ask me anything."

I swallow and nod. "Last night, you said there were a couple reasons why you've never been interested in me romantically, but you only told me one."

"Ah. I thought perhaps your curiosity was satiated last night, but I don't mind sharing," Ehren mutters, turning his focus back to lacing and tying his boots. "Well, the other reason is because I simply refuse to let myself care for anyone in that way. That part of my heart has been closed off since I realized that any marriage I have will likely be political, part of some treaty, or a ploy for peace or better trade. I don't see the point in falling in love only to have to cast that person aside."

When he lifts his eyes back to mine, I can see the deep sadness there. I cross the tent and place my hand on his cheek.

"You should still open your heart to love," I say, my voice barely audible.

Ehren smiles sadly and places his hand over mine, leaning into my touch. After a moment he sighs and pulls away.

"It wouldn't be fair to me or the person I love. I won't be one of those kings married to one person for the public eye and having an affair with another in the shadows. I will be loyal and devoted to my spouse, even if I don't love them," he says with a determination I've never heard in his voice before.

I nod and bite my lip. "I guess I can understand that. Only . . . wouldn't it be worse to be able to marry for love one day, but not find that love because you're too closed off? Love makes you stronger, even if you have to give it up. Surely you've loved someone at least a little to know how powerful love is?"

Ehren stares off toward the tent entrance, his eyes unfocused. "I have, and it would be so easy . . ." He sighs shaking his head. "But I can't. Even if I wanted to, there is no way my choice would be accepted. For many reasons." He meets my eyes and I can feel the heartbreaking sadness he radiates. "I refuse to let myself hope, even if some days I really wish I could find a way."

"Maybe after we change the world, love will be easier."

"You still love Bram, don't you?" Ehren asks softly.

I fight not to pull my gaze form his as I nod. "I'll always love him. He was my first love. But I don't think we're meant to be, so I let him go. And it hurt. It still hurts. But I don't regret a single moment with him. And I think if you opened your heart you wouldn't regret it either."

Ehren sighs, looking away from me as he runs a hand

through his hair. I'm afraid I might have crossed a line, but when he turns back to me, a smile plays on his lips.

"You know, you would make an excellent queen."

A surprised laugh bubbles out of my throat. "I thought we established that we don't feel that way about each other."

Ehren grins, his eyes twinkling. "Who cares?" I laugh and shake my head. Ehren takes both my hands in his and meets my eyes. "Okay, then, how's this—if neither of us find our perfect match in ten years, we'll marry each other. You'll be my sorceress queen, my best friend by my side."

I laugh and shake my head. "Fine. I'll agree to your ridiculous proposal, but only because it doesn't matter."

"Oh?" he replies, arching an eyebrow. "Why not?"

"Because," I grin, "I foresee love and happy matches for both of us in the near future."

Ehren releases my hands and throws his head back, laughing. My grin widens.

"You're a Seer, now, are you?"

"I don't need to be a Seer to believe in love," I insist, my eyes meeting his.

He smiles softly, a new light shining in his eyes. "Let's hope you're right. It'd be a nice change to be truly happy." He breaks his gaze and strides to the exit, calling over his shoulder, "Hurry and dress. I'll make coffee."

When the tent flap closes behind him, I quickly shed my dress from the previous day, which I realize is terribly stained with blood, and slip into new clothes. When I exit the tent, I feel several pairs of eyes shift to me. Instead of sinking into the awkwardness of being seen leaving Ehren's tent, I straighten my shoulders and walk confidentially to the smoldering fire and take a seat between Ehren and Nyco.

"Is that coffee?" I ask, pointing to the kettle nestled in the hot ashes.

"Sure is," Ehren replies, reaching behind him to grab a cup. "Here, have some."

I take the cup and fill it, all eyes still watching every interaction between me and Ehren. I purposefully ignore them, concentrating on my coffee.

"We should probably leave soon," Ehren says before taking a long of sip of his coffee.

"So, we're ignoring it," Nyco mutters under his breath, shaking his head. "That's fine. It's not like I was curious."

Ehren hides his grin by lifting his coffee to his mouth. I make the mistake of making eye contact with Makin, who flashes me a wicked grin and an exaggerated wink. I shake my head and roll my eyes, letting my gaze drift over the others. Sama's attention is piqued, but she has the decency to at least look a bit ashamed by her curiosity and glances away. Cal's steady gaze is fixed on Ehren more than me, his mouth a tight line before he opts to ignore us both, fixating on his hands folded in his lap. Kai seems completely unaffected, and I realize he probably knows the true nature of why I was in Ehren's tent. When my gaze falls on Bram, standing off to the side, I no longer find humor in the situation. His gaze is hard as steel, his jaw set. Ehren shifts and pushes to his feet, draining his coffee.

"We need to pack up camp and get on the road," he commands. "And you can all wipe those smirks off your faces. If you want to know why Astra was in my tent, ask her. Stop jumping to conclusions."

His eyes fall on Bram, who shakes the words off and stomps away to begin disassembling tents. I hurriedly finish my coffee and help Sama pack our tent before dousing the fire with my magic. As I attach my bag to my horse, I see Ehren and Bram talking not far off. I can't hear what they're saying, but I see Bram's shoulders relax as Ehren claps a hand to his shoulder. I release a sigh of relief.

"So," Cal says, startling me. I spin to him and the corner of his mouth turns up slightly. "Sorry."

I smile shaking my head. "It's fine. Did you need something?"

Cal rubs the back of his neck and glances off as I finish securing my supplies.

"I, well, I don't want to assume, and you probably think I'm a fool for asking . . ."

"You want to know why I was in Ehren's tent?"

Cal glances back to me and nods. "I know it's none of my business, but, well, it's just . . . Makin won't stop coming up with theories. So I thought . . ." He sighs and turns away. "Never mind. It's really none of my business. Forget I asked."

"I couldn't sleep and he gave me a spell."

Cal stops and turns back to me, cocking his head. "A spell?"

I nod. "Yes. One that would leave me a bit vulnerable so I couldn't really be left alone."

"Oh." A hint of a smile plays on Cal's lips as he nods. He forces the smile away and straightens. "So I suppose it may become a regular thing?" I arch an eyebrow and he hurries to add, "For security purposes it helps to know how many people are in his tent. He's careless enough with his previous . . . relationships that, as his Guard, we're used to adjusting."

"In that case, I suppose I might be in there more often."

"Very well, then I—"

"Are you all packed up?" Ehren's voice cuts our conversation short.

I smile and nod as Cal jerks back.

"I should go help Makin sort out what to do about our lack of horses."

Ehren sighs, running a hand through his hair. "Indeed. We are one short now. I'll join you."

Cal smiles and nods. They join Makin and Bram to discuss the horse situation while the rest of us finish packing up the camp. In the end, Kai volunteers to stay in wolf form, freeing his horse for Sama.

As we travel, I occasionally place droplets of magic into my Syphon Stone in an attempt to refill a portion of the magic I used against the king's soldiers, but I have to be careful. I'll need my magic as full as possible when I go to face the Clans. If I put too much into the stone, I won't be able to reach my full potential.

When we stop for lunch, Kai shifts into his human form and takes a seat beside me.

"I've noticed you scowling at your Syphon Stone," he whispers. "You drained it, didn't you?"

I sigh and nod. "Near enough. I was really hoping to have more magic stored for when I have to meet the Clans."

He fixes his eyes on the stone for a moment and then lifts his gray eyes to mine. "Will it hold my magic?"

I startle at his question. "I think so."

"And you could use it?"

I nod slowly. "As far as I know."

"The Syphon Stone?" Sama cuts in, taking a seat on my other side.

I turn to her and nod.

"It will hold any kind of magic—spells, shifter magic,

whatever you have. You'd also be able to wield any of the magic in it as long as you wear the stone. If you use the magic in its original form, it will last longer and be more powerful, but you can also transfer it into whatever magic you're familiar with. It just won't be worth as much."

"So," I clarify, "if Kai transferred some of his magic into the stone, I could use it? If I shifted it would last longer, but if I used it to, let's say, create a shield, it would work, but just wouldn't be as strong."

Sama nods. "Exactly. Though," she pauses with a thoughtful look, "you could also use the magic for wisping and anything Kai can do with his magic."

Before I can ask any further questions, Kai is reaching his hand toward my bracelet. I jerk back, holding my wrist against my chest protectively, covering the bracelet with my other hand.

"What are you doing?"

His eyes meet mine. "I'm giving you some of my magic."

I shake my head. "You need your magic."

"You know it doesn't take me much magic to shift. You need it more than I do," he says evenly. I hesitate. "Come on, Astra. Let me do this. You saved us all yesterday. The least I can do is share my magic."

I relent and lower my wrist. He reaches out and closes his large hand over the cuff. He closes his eyes and I feel the warmth of his magic channel into the stone. After a few moments I pull away.

"That's enough for now." I raise my eyes to Kai's. "Thank you."

He gives a half nod. "Always."

When we're done with lunch, Kai shifts back into a wolf and we start on our way. Every so often, Sama stops me to transfer bits of earth magic into the stone. Some of it comes from plants, like little golden tipped flowers and strange, sparkling clovers. Other parts come from stones and the earth itself. Kai shifts back into human form after a couple hours and transfers more magic. By the time we stop for the night, my stone is humming with magic.

"I'm trying to decide if I should be offended," Nyco says, tilting his head and grinning at me over our dinner of dried meat.

"What are you talking about?" I ask, a smile twitching at the corners of my lips.

"Well," Nyco says with a shrug, "I can't help but notice that you've been accepting magic from Kai and Sama all day to fill up that stone there. And, while I can't pretend I know exactly what your mission is, I wonder why you haven't asked for *my* magic."

I grin. "Because bugs are creepy."

Nyco slams his hand on his chest like I just shot him with an arrow. "Straight through my ever-beating heart!"

"She's right," Makin agrees, his mouth full. "Bugs are creepy."

"Creepy, maybe," Nyco's counters, holding up a finger, "but damn useful."

"To be fair, she didn't ask us for our magic. We volunteered it," Kai points out.

"Fine. Well, consider this me volunteering." Nyco meets my eyes with a wicked grin. "Would you care for some of my magic?"

I survey him for a moment. "I don't want to take it from you if you'll need it."

Nyco laughs, his eyes sparkling. "I think I have plenty to spare. The bugs aren't terribly chatty today."

I find myself smiling. "All right."

With a grin, Nyco crosses over to me. Sama scoots over a bit as Nyco squeezes between us. He rubs his palms together and then pauses, looking up at me.

"Um, what exactly do I need to do?"

I laugh. "Just touch the stone and will some of your magic into it."

He starts to reach out his hand, then pulls it back. "Will it hurt?"

"It's extremely painful," Kai says before I can answer.

Nyco's eyes go wide. "Seriously?"

He turns and looks at Sama who is doing her best to hide a smile.

"Oh, yes," she replies with a barely convincing nod. "It hurts. A lot."

Nyco's wide, terrified eyes turn back to me as Sama covers her mouth, shaking with silent laughter.

"You're part of Ehren's Guard, though, so you can probably handle pain pretty well, right?" Kai says.

Nyco schools his features as he swallows and nods. "O-of course."

"Well, go on then," Ehren encourages, nodding to my stone as his eyes glisten mischievously. "Show them what you can withstand as a member of my illustrious Guard."

Nyco straightens and takes a deep breath. "Right."

He reaches toward my bracelet slowly and closes his eyes, wincing slightly as his fingertips graze the stone. After a moment, his eyes shoot open as his magic trickles into the stone.

"You're all liars!" he yells. We burst out laughing. "This doesn't hurt at all!"

"Careful," I warn through my grin. "It may not hurt, but you don't want to drain too much magic."

He nods and keeps his fingers pressed against the stone for a few more moments before pulling his hand back.

"Can you sense my magic?" he asks, studying my face.

I nod. "A bit."

"You know," Ehren says, leaning forward and picking up a long stick, "I think I may know a spell or two I can add to your Syphon Stone arsenal."

My eyebrows shoot up in interest. "Really? How exactly would that work?"

"Well"—Ehren pokes at the fire with the stick, sending little sparks flickering into the air—"I remember a section in one of my books with specific spells that could be put into certain magical objects. Most just use basic incantations. I can put one or two of those spells in your Syphon Stone, and if you need them, you're covered." He raises his eyes to mine. "Interested in trying?"

I nod eagerly. "Absolutely."

Ehren smiles and nods. "Good." He tosses the stick into the flames and stands, brushing his hands down his shirt to wipe off dirt. "Let's get camp set up for the night, and then I'll see what spells I can find."

Everyone takes Ehren's words to heart, and the camp is soon ready for the night. I don't even pretend I'm going to share a tent with Sama and instead go straight to Ehren's. When I duck inside he's sitting cross-legged next to the bed, flipping through a small, brown book. I take a seat on the bed and grab a green journal from his pile of books and begin thumbing through.

After a few minutes Ehren mumbles, "I think this might work."

I lean over and peer at the page of text. "What is it?"

Ehren shifts so I can see the page. "It's an unlocking spell."

"An unlocking spell?"

He nods and looks over at me. "I'm not sure how exactly you would use it but you never know." He looks back down at the page. "It's a simple enough spell and a good one to try. If it works, I'll add another one."

"Okay, what do we do first?"

His eyes scan the page. "Not much. I basically say the words and transfer them into the stone." He holds his hand out to me, palm up. "Give me your hand with the stone."

I swallow nervously and place my wrist on his palm. He takes a deep breath and looks at the page one last time before focusing on the stone. He places his other hand on top of my wrist, his palm pressing against the stone, my small hand devoured by his larger hands. He closes his eyes and mumbles ancient words, repeating a phrase over and over. I'm wondering if it's working in the slightest when I feel the stone hum with warmth. When he opens his eyes and releases my hand, the stone is glowing more steadily than before.

"I guess it worked," he grins. "Now, all you have to do to use the spell is find it and will it into being. Can you sense it?"

I close my eyes and focus on the magic ebbing from the stone. I startle when I realize I can tell the spell apart from the other magic swirling inside. It's like oil on water—there with the other magic, but still separate. I open my eyes and smile.

"I can definitely feel it." My eyes meet his and my heart warms. "Thank you."

He nods awkwardly and glances away. "I wish I had more to offer you beyond a weak, potentially useless spell."

I scowl. "Ehren—"

"No," he says firmly, lifting his eyes and holding up his hand. "Don't try to console me. You're ready and willing to risk your life for me, prepared to go against your own brother, and I can't even help you refill your magic."

I reach out and grab his hand, giving it a gentle squeeze. "You support me in other ways."

He smiles weakly, but I can tell it's forced. "I want to give you the world, Ash."

"Well, get the crown, save the kingdom, and then we'll discuss payment."

Ehren laughs, a rich genuine laugh. "Deal." His eyes shift to the bed behind me. "Are you—do you want to sleep in here again tonight?"

I look down to avoid his gaze and nod. "If that's okay."

"Always."

Ehren turns away, and I make myself comfortable in the bed while he mixes up the spell.

"I made it a little stronger this time," he says as he kneels overs me. "I figure you might need a little extra sleep the next couple of nights to make sure your magic restores to its peak before you have to go . . . you know."

I swallow and nod. He presses his thumb gently to my forehead and whispers the spell. He follows the motion with a gentle kiss on my cheek.

CHAPTER TWENTY-FIVE

ASTRA

Everything about the day is foreboding. From the moment I wake next to Ehren to the moment we leave, I feel uneasy. The knowledge that at any moment I could receive word to go meet Alak hangs over me like an ominous cloud.

We haven't been traveling long when Felixe appears in my lap atop my horse. I take a little scroll from his mouth, giving his ears a scratch.

My Most Beloved Astra,

I'm afraid I don't have much to report, but I wanted to keep you as informed as possible.

Five of the Seven Clan leaders have already arrived. Some have even brought along family. Lord Wallish and Ron Lord McDullun are the only two missing, but I suspect they will arrive shortly. Kato is currently out charming everyone with a hunt. I fear that he may be winning over even the more hesitant of the Clan leaders. However, I can tell that at least a couple are still very wary of joining forces with him. There is still hope. I have to believe that. Just like I believe in you.

I don't know what plans you and Ehren have crafted, but I am sure whatever you have come up with will be successful.

I will let you know as soon as possible when everyone will be together for you to come and make your appeal. You can do this.

Forever Yours,

Alak

I read the short note twice before passing it to Ehren, who nods when he's done, passing it back without a word. I can feel Bram's glare on my neck, but I don't bother to look at him.

Not much later, we leave the forest behind and cross into open fields. Being so exposed does little to calm my nerves. When we stop for lunch I can barely eat a thing. It doesn't help that I haven't released any magic, and I can feel it swarming inside me. Ehren watches me, his eyes full of concern, but I carefully avoid eye contact and brush him off when he asks how I'm doing. By the time we reach the end of the day, I feel overwhelmed and physically weak. We decide not to put up the tents tonight, and I make my bed as far from the others as I can. I close my eyes and turn away from everyone, curling into a ball. I'm so focused on keeping it together I don't even hear Ehren come over to me.

"Astra," he says gently, placing a hand on my side, causing me to jump slightly.

"I'm fine," I mumble, not bothering to look at him.

"You are not fine."

I curl into a tighter ball.

"Astra, please," he begs, his voice pained.

I will myself to turn over and look up at him. Worry lines his face.

"If this is too much to ask—" he begins, but I sit up, placing a finger over his lips to silence him.

"I will do anything for you."

Ehren's shoulders drop and he bows his head. "That's what terrifies me. Please, let me help you."

I'm not sure why, but tears burn my eyes.

"Oh, Ash," Ehren whispers, drawing me up into his arms.

I lean into his chest, grabbing his shirt in my fists as I let my tears flow freely. After a few minutes I pull back and look up at him.

"Talk to me," he says softly, brushing a stray lock of hair out of my face. "If you can't go when Alak asks, you don't have to. We will find another way. Alak will understand."

I swallow and nod. "I'm not afraid of convincing the Clans to go against Kato. Our plan is solid. It's more . . ." I pause, trying to make sense of what I feel enough to put it into words. "I haven't seen Kato since he left. It broke me that day, and I don't know what will happen, what I'll feel if —when that happens again. But I have to face him eventually, so I may as well do it now, before he can cause too much trouble for you, for us, for the kingdom. I really hate being separated from him. I hate being on different sides."

Ehren cradles me and gently kisses the top of my head. "I understand."

"And I feel like he's my responsibility, even though I know logically I have no control over his decisions," I mumble into Ehren's chest. "And if I don't do everything I can to make this right, I won't ever be able to forgive myself."

"Please know I don't expect you to bear this alone. I am here for you."

I nod and snuggle in closer. After a few moments in his arms, my worries fade a bit and I pull away with a sniff. Ehren smiles softly.

"Feel better?"

I nod and smile. "Yes. Thank you."

"Always." He takes a deep breath and glances over toward the others. "Why don't you come back over and join us? Eat something. Then I'll use the sleeping spell, and you can just relax for a few hours and sleep."

I exhale and nod. "All right."

I move my bedroll closer to everyone else while Ehren goes to get me food and prepare the spell ingredients. Cal is actually the one that delivers the food. It's only a bit of bread and cheese, but I accept it with a smile. I expect him to go back to his spot next to Makin, but instead he sits cross-legged next to me.

"Don't mind me," he says with a small smile. "I'm just going to sit and make sure you eat every bite."

I raise my eyebrows in question as I nibble the cheese.

"I've been there before," he explains, glancing away. "I've allowed stress and anxiety to overwhelm me to the point where I didn't eat." He looks back at me, soft understanding in his eyes. "So, I'm going to make sure you eat every meal."

I smile and whisper, "Thank you."

I eat quickly and quietly, Cal sitting beside me casually chatting. When I'm done, Cal gets up with a wink and settles back down next to Makin. Ehren approaches with the sleeping spell ready to go. I can feel Bram's steady, assessing gaze as Ehren kneels next to me. I can tell he wants to be near me, but he's respecting my boundaries.

"Ready?" Ehren asks.

I hesitate and look past him to Bram, meeting Bram's eyes with a small nod. His lips part and his eyes widen slightly. Before I can say anything, he's standing, gathering his bedroll in his arms. Ehren gives him the briefest glance as he settles down beside me. I offer Bram a slight smile and turn back to Ehren.

"Ready."

Ehren smiles and begins the spell. As it takes effect, I settle back onto my bedroll, the familiar comfort of Bram's arms encasing me.

The next morning, I awake to an even heavier cloud hanging over me. My nerves and uncertainty from yesterday have nothing on how I feel today. I know I need to release some of my magic, but I'm too afraid to let any of it go. True to his word, Cal makes sure I eat at least a few bites of breakfast before we start out.

All morning, I'm on high alert. Every small sound makes me jump, and I'm extremely jittery, unable to sit still atop my horse. I can feel the wary glances of my traveling companions, but I avoid making any direct eye contact. I can't handle their pity and concern today. When Felixe finally appears in my lap with a tattered scrap of paper in his mouth, it's almost a relief, though I'm disappointed when I see how short the hurriedly scribbled message is.

See you in one hour, love.
   — Alak

I take a deep, shuddering breath and look toward Ehren.

"I have one hour."

"What do you need me to do?" he asks without hesitation.

"I think I just need a few moments to get ready. To prepare."

Ehren gives me a knowing nod as he dismounts. Everyone else follows suit. Ehren leads the others a little way away so I can change. Before we left Gleador we sat down with the royal seamstress to create a dress fitting of my position. I quickly shed my travel clothes in favor of the dress. It's multiple layers of flowing material from the waist down in varying shades of purple and silver. The many layers hide several pockets. The top is a medium purple with a bone corset overlay. The bones are thin enough and arranged in a way that I'm not uncomfortable, but it forces me to hold myself straight while emphasizing my feminine curves.

Once I'm dressed, Sama braids my hair into a tight crown, leaving a few pieces of hair down to frame my face without hiding my scars. She carefully adds touches of kohl around my eyes, color on my cheek bones, and makes my lips blood red.

Next comes the crown. I'm not sure where Gleador's obsession with bones comes from, but they managed to craft a stunning and terrifying crown from six bones. They're all the same size with a slight curve, each end splitting into a "v." The tips of the bones are welded together with a circular gem centered perfect inside each diamond shape created by the bones. The crown fits tightly, perfectly formed to my head.

As I approach the others, who have settled on the ground to play a game of cards, all eyes turn to me.

"Well, damn," Makin says with a low whistle. "If they don't immediately bow in your presence, they're fools."

Nyco nods in agreement. Ehren stands and walks up to me, taking my hands in his.

"You look perfect." He leans in closer and lowers his voice. "You can still decide not to do this. The choice is yours. The choice will always be yours."

"I appreciate that, but I'm good. I'll be fine. I can do this."

Ehren drops my hands and takes a step back with a nod. "All right. Let's get the treaty."

I follow him over to his horse. He pulls a scroll tied with a golden ribbon from his pack. One of the other preparations we made before leaving Gleador was to draw up an official document with all the terms of an agreement between Ehren and the Clans, guaranteeing a free Athiedor. I reach out a trembling hand and take the treaty, sliding it carefully into one of my hidden pockets.

Ehren reaches back into his bag and pulls out gems. Just a small fortune from Gleador, but hopefully enough to get attention from the Clan leaders. I slip them into another pocket. I turn away from Ehren and carefully study the landscape around us. I know Felixe will help guide me to Alak, but I'll have to come back on my own. My eyes settle on Bram, who watches me with a steady gaze. His lips turn up at the corners into a smile and my heart flips. Cal draws my attention and offers me a similar smile and a gentle nod. Ehren places a comforting hand on my shoulder. Somehow, I think I'll be able to find my way back just fine.

When the hour is nearly up, I call to Felixe. He appears immediately on my shoulder. I feel instantly comforted, as if the swirling storm of magic has settled. I reach up to scratch his ears.

"You know where to take me, right?"

He replies with a sharp bark.

Ehren grins. "I guess that means 'yes.'"

I smile. "Let's hope so." I take a deep breath. "All right. Let's go."

Ehren fades from view as I'm pulled into a wisp. But this is different. I have less control, even though I can tell I'm being steered toward a specific place. I feel like I'm falling and floating at the same time, like I'm moving in slow motion. When I finally land on solid ground, it takes me moment to realize I've stopped wisping. I find myself in a narrow hallway constructed of smooth stone walls. A nearby window casts rays of light across my face. I creep to the corner and peer around. Not far off is a room, the wooden doors thrown wide, a glowing light flickering into the corridor. I catch bits of muffled conversations in thick accents floating from the room, but I can't quite make out what anyone is saying.

A servant bearing a tray of ale and drinking glasses shuffles down the hall, and I quickly duck out of sight before he can spot me.

"Ah! The ale has arrived!" Kato's voice booms over the conversations.

My heart stills. Everything about his voice is familiar. I'd almost forgotten what it sounded like. It's warm and charismatic. It's comforting. It's disarming. My stomach plummets as I remember he's my enemy in this.

I press against the wall and squeeze my eyes shut. I can't do this. I just . . . I can't. I can't face him. I can't go against him. Ehren will understand. Alak will understand. They'll support me.

I hear hurried footsteps in the corridor, and I take another peek, seeing the servant scurry away. The terrified expression on his face is concerning. What has my brother become? It's a distinct reminder of why I'm here. I can't let Kato gain more power. I have to stop him. I may be the only one who can.

I startle and duck back into hiding as someone else enters the corridor. This time it's a man, maybe ten years older than I, dressed in a sharp, green tunic, using a polished wooden cane to support his left leg with each step. He's easily one of the most attractive men I've ever seen. He pauses mere feet from the door and straightens his shirt in a nervous manner, inhaling deeply before releasing the breath slowly. He schools his features into a confident, cocky smile and strides into the room. I hear Kato's voice again, but this time it has less control over me.

"Welcome, Lord McDullun. We were beginning to wonder if you would be on time."

So *that's* Lord McDullun. From what Alak has said, he's a possible ally.

"I wouldn't miss it," comes the easy, natural reply.

"Well, then, let's begin," Kato replies.

I hear the heavy creak of the doors as they close. I wait a moment before leaving my secure hiding spot to make sure the doors have shut completely. I need to make a bold entrance. I need to get their attention and hold it. They're in support of Kato as much for his power as his promises, and I need to prove from the first moment I can match him in every way.

I walk toward the doors and pause outside. It's now or never. I straighten my shoulders and force my face into the most confident expression I can. I summon a small kernel of concentrated magic and flick it toward the doors. They fly open, slamming against the wall with a loud bang. Every eye turns toward me, wide with shock. I ignore the curious, frightened expressions of the Clan leaders and settle my gaze on Kato. He stands at the head of the table, opposite me. His expression goes from startled to furious in a flash. I feel his power roll out.

What are you doing here?

I nearly jump at his voice in head. It used to be such a common, normal thing but now . . .

I raise my chin and answer out loud with far more bravado than I actually feel.

"Hello, brother. It's been a while."

CHAPTER TWENTY-SIX

ALAK

With only an hour to prepare for the meeting everything feels chaotic and rushed, despite the fact we've known this was coming for well over a week. Kato's previous aggravation with Ronan has completely faded away into an overconfident swagger. I catch a few questioning glances from Lord Wallish, and I give as much of a reassuring smile as I can but avoid any opportunities for conversation. I know what he's wondering. He wants to know if I've found a way to stop Kato. And I have. At least, I think so.

I sink against the wall outside the room where we're set to meet and close my eyes, my heart racing. Did Astra get my message? Will she arrive in time? And if she does, will the Clans listen?

This is our last chance, but I have faith in Astra. She can do this. We can do this.

"Did you find more of the ale?" Kato's voice breaks through my thoughts.

I jump slightly and flash him a winning smile. "Of course!"

"Good," Kato smiles. "I know today we're just finalizing everything, but every little bit helps to make sure everything goes smoothly."

He struts past me into the room and looks around. His eyes scan every corner and he nods with satisfaction. High windows stretch along the back wall, filling the room with glowing light. At the head of the table is a large, ornate wooden chair that is just short of being a throne. Along the table are more chairs, though much simpler in design. There is no chair at the end opposite of where where Kato will sit. He wouldn't dare let anyone think they're his equal.

Kato strides across the room and settles into his seat, his eyes gleaming. He remains seated as the first few people start filling the room. The first to arrive are, of course, Niall, Caitlyn, Ian, Kayleigh, and Aine. Aine takes a seat directly to Kato's left when he makes it clear the seat to his right is for me. I'm honored, I suppose, but mostly terrified.

The Clan members arrive in groups, chatting with each other. Despite dragging their heirs and family members with them, the only people attending the meeting are the leaders themselves. I can't help but wonder if they're a little afraid of what might happen if something goes wrong. When Lord Wallish enters the room, he catches my gaze and I sit a little straighter, but neither of us dare to communicate more than that.

I feel a twinge of magic, which I at first attribute to Kato's rising frustration that Ronan is, once again, the only person missing but, I realize with a start, this magic is soft and gentle. It's not Kato's magic. I hide a smile.

"Ah! The ale has arrived!" Kato booms cheerfully.

I look toward the door as a servant stumbles into the room with a tray of the ale Kato requested. The Clan leaders clap the boy on the back as the ale quickly spreads around the table. As soon as the boy can, he scurries from the room back to the safety of the kitchen. Not long after, Ronan finally strides into the room. He meets Kato's glare with a cocky grin.

"Welcome, Lord McDullun. We were beginning to wonder if you would be on time," Kato says evenly.

Ronan tilts his head, his eyes twinkling in a way that I can tell unsettles Kato. "I wouldn't miss it."

Kato motions for Ronan to take his seat as he says, "Well, then, let's begin."

Kato makes a simple motion and the heavy doors to the room creak closed. I try to avoid the eyes of the Clan leaders, but I know several have shifted to me. They're waiting. Hell, I'm waiting. I can sense Astra. Or, at least, I think I can. Maybe it's wishful thinking. I reach toward the bond. I'm sure she's near. If only . . .

The doors fly open and a ripple of pure, raw magic courses over the room as Astra marches in, her head held high. The magic she sent out would be enough to bring any normal mortal to his knees, but she exudes pure power beyond magic. If the Clans were expecting her to be a small, nothing of girl, willing and ready to sit on the sidelines, they now know they were wrong. Very, very wrong.

Astra's features are like carved stone, fierce and sharp. They match well with the bone crown glittering atop her bone-white hair and her bone corset. Her curves are perfection, showing she is no girl, but a woman of power and position. I feel overwhelming pride, and it takes every ounce of self-control I possess not to rush to her side or fall prostrate at her feet.

I feel Kato's magic swell as the air around us heats. He's seething. I glance to him and see his lips tighten into a firm line as his hands clench into fists.

She meets Kato's gaze evenly and a wicked smile curls onto her lips. I doubt anyone in the room is breathing. I know I'm not.

"Hello, brother. It's been a while."

Kato tenses even more, but he's not the one to speak first.

"What are you doing here?" Aine hisses.

Astra's eyes snap to Aine and a cold look of pure hate flashes across Astra's face.

"I don't remember addressing you," Astra replies smoothly.

Aine narrows her eyes, refusing to back down. "And I don't remember you being invited."

Astra holds Aine's gaze for a moment before pulling her eyes away and giving a carefree shrug. "I go where I'm needed."

"You aren't need—" Aine starts, but Astra cuts her short.

"I don't care the slightest about you and your opinion."

Aine stiffens, and I bite my cheek to keep from smiling.

"Aine is correct," Kato says, barely containing his anger. "You are not needed nor are you welcome."

"That's a pity," Astra says, tilting her head innocently, "because I have a counteroffer that might interest some of the Clan leaders."

"A counteroffer?" Lord Kensdor chokes out, his voice strained.

Astra's features soften as she smiles her most enchanting

smile. Lord Kensdor noticeably relaxes under the warmth of her gaze.

"Yes. I bring a counteroffer from Prince Ehren himself and I"—she scans the room—"I suppose I need to get my own chair."

She sighs and carelessly flicks her hand to craft a chair. But it's not just any chair. It's made from her one-of-a-kind silver light and is far more ornate than Kato's own chair. Hers is a bloody throne, no question about it, and it's all I can do not to stand and applaud. The eyes of the leaders go wide at her easy display of magic and sneak looks at each other to share in the wonder. Astra pretends not to notice as she settles on her throne.

"Much better. Now, let's get straight to business, shall we?" She pulls out a scroll of paper tied with a golden ribbon from the folds of her dress and lays it on the table. "This is an official treaty from Prince Ehren ensuring the freedom of Athiedor as long as the Clans do not stand against him."

With a furrowed brow, Lord Dughlas leans across the table and plucks up the treaty. He unties the ribbon and immediately starts examining the contents.

"I do apologize that it is not written in Yallik. We were pressed for time with limited resources. We will draw up a second treaty in Yallik if you wish," Astra adds.

"What does it say?" Lord Loudain asks, leaning forward.

"I'm sure Lord Dughlas can confirm, but I will sum it up," Astra offers.

A few of the lords startle in their seats when they realize Astra knows who they are. I wonder how she knows, or if she just guessed. I bloody love her. She continues.

"Essentially, Ehren requires nothing of you except that

you not fight against his right to the throne. Once he is on the throne, Athiedor will be made free."

"I've already offered them a free Athiedor," Kato says tightly.

Astra meets his gaze. "But at what cost? How many soldiers must they sacrifice to your cause before they get their freedom?" Ronan and Lord Loudain shift in their seats, and a few others purposefully look away. "And how long before you betray them for your own purposes?"

Kato shoots from his chair. "How dare you! I would never go back on a treaty!"

Astra's eyes flash as she rises, pressing her palms against the surface of the table. "You promised to be by my side forever, and yet you betrayed me, your own flesh and blood, your twin. You betrayed your friends, who literally risked their lives for you. Why should these strangers be any different?"

No one in the room misses the raw emotion ringing in Astra's words as they strike their mark.

"*You* betrayed *me*!" Kato yells, flames flickering to life behind him. Several lords gasp and swear.

"Did I? Because as I recall, *you* left *me* after attacking me for not following you. This scar is courtesy of your own flames, is it not?" Astra counters, her voice perfectly level as she tilts her neck so the sunlight streaming in lights up her scar like liquid silver.

Kato's lips part and, for the briefest moment, regret flashes across his face, but it's quickly hidden beneath his façade of confidence.

"You chose non-magic people over me, putting us at risk. I made the logical choice, as did Alak." Kato nods to me and I want nothing more to shrink away.

Lord Dughlas pushes the treaty back and all eyes shift to him.

"Well," Lord Wallish prompts, "is it as she said?"

Lord Dughlas looks nervously toward Kato before nodding slowly. "Aye. Athiedor will be free as soon as Ehren is crowned, as long as we do not align with those who would keep him from his rightful throne."

"But Ehren doesn't have the throne right now. He's a prince without a kingdom," Lord O'Brick cuts in. "Surely he expects us to provide men to help him obtain the throne."

"Naturally, any assistance from the Clans would help Prince Ehren obtain the throne faster, and, therefore, help him to free Athiedor that much sooner," Astra concedes with a nod, "but we demand nothing. We will take what you willingly give. In return, you will be well compensated."

Lord O'Brick huffs. "Compensated? With what?"

Astra grins as she reaches into the folds of her dress and pulls out a handful of gems, which she tosses onto the table before settling back onto her throne. The gems catch the sunlight and rainbows cascade across the table. Lord Loudain gasps as he plucks one up.

"These . . . The worth here . . ." He shakes his head in disbelief, raising his wide eyes to Astra. "But how?"

"King Naimon of Gleador has signed a treaty of alliance with Prince Ehren in favor of Ehren ascending the throne. Gleador has thrown their financial support behind Ehren and is willing to fund any army and supplies needed to support our cause." She nods to the gems and adds, "You're all welcome to keep these. We have plenty more."

"But you'll need more than gems from Gleador and what supplies and men the Clans may provide," Lord Bashmore says, eyeing Astra steadily. "We have seen indisputable evidence of Kato's power, but yours is little more than rumor. You might be able to convince some people of your might with your conjuring of thrones and flicks of magic, but that won't win a war. Kato at least has power worthy of winning a war and battle skills."

Something flickers across Astra's face that I can't quite place, but it looks like pain. She lowers her eyes and bows her head as she takes a deep breath. When she raises her head with a jerk, her eyes are pure, liquid silver, shining like starlight. Her lips part as she holds out her right hand, palm up. The room begins to tremble. At first it's only slight, but the shaking grows until everything shudders with such great force it feels like the fortress might collapse around us. Terrified eyes shoot to Astra as she stands and slowly rises, hovering in the air as her skin begins to glow. She raises her other hand, palm up, and tendrils of silver starlight slither from her fingers and entwine themselves around the necks of everyone at the table. My own heart stills as one wraps around my own throat, tightening before loosening slightly. I feel a tender flicker of magic reach for my own, and I know that even in this state she recognizes me.

"What do you think—" Aine begins but she's cut short as Astra snaps her glowing eyes to meet Aine's.

"You really should be silent," Astra says, her voice reverberating with power.

She twists her hand and Aine's eyes go wide as silver stitches appear across her lips, sewing them shut. Ian cries out and leaps from his seat.

"Enough!" Astra yells, her voice vibrating across the room.

With another thrust of her hands everyone except Kato and the lords, myself included, are slammed against the back wall beneath the windows. I feel the breath knocked from my chest with the power of it. Her power tightens around us with a crushing force. After a moment it fades from me but, judging by the terror written on Kayleigh's face and the fury on Niall's, everyone else is still under her full power.

"Is that enough of a display?" Astra asks. "Perhaps a bit more?"

With a flash a woman no longer stands at the edge of table. Instead, a snarling silver wolf stands on the end of the table. All of the lords, except for a grinning Ronan, scramble away. Even my own heart races, and I feel relief when she turns back into her normal self, standing once again at the edge of the table. Slowly she draws most of her magic back. The room stops shaking and the tendrils of magic fade as her skin and eyes return to normal. Her magic holding us in place against the wall remains, however.

"You can't do this," Kato hisses, his own flames rising.

"Obviously, I can," Astra challenges. "But, to be entirely honest, I would rather not be on opposing sides, brother. You can sign the treaty, too. You can join us again."

Kato laughs, but there's nothing pleasant in it. "Never."

Astra sighs and lets her eyes travel around the table. "Do you see his true self? If he turns his back on his own twin, how can you truly believe he won't turn his back on you and your people if it suits his whims?" She meets their eyes one by one as she continues. "Can you tell me that every single person in your Clans has magic? Kato wants magic and magic alone to reign. Those without magic are nothing to him. They are expendable. Are you willing to sacrifice those people when a more peaceful option is available? Ehren will leave no one behind. Everyone is equal to him. He believes in magic and non-magic side-by-side."

"But can you lead an army, girl?" Lord O'Brick challenges.

Astra smiles. "I could, but I don't have to." Lord O'Brick scowls. "I have Captain Bramfield behind me, ready to lead an army of trained soldiers. I also have a prince on my side that is not only trained in battle by the best teachers possible, but also trained in the art of politics. If you read the treaty I brought, you'll see that Ehren has plans to make the freeing of Athiedor as seamless as possible. The lands of Athiedor currently belong to Callenian nobles. Ehren is already putting plans into place to make sure the treaty isn't challenged. Kato has no power over such things. He does not understand the complexities of ruling. Ehren, however, does."

Lord O'Brick glances to Lord Dughlas who gives him a conceding nod. "It's true. Prince Ehren has covered everything very efficiently. And the witnesses of the treaty are excellent choices, including King Naimon of Gleador himself."

More gasps and swears ripple around the table, and I beam with pride. I can't help it. But no one is looking at me, so I don't care. All eyes are shifting from Astra to Kato and back again.

"Well, then," Ronan says, a wide grin spreading across his face, "have you a quill, love? I'd like to sign this and be on my way."

"You wouldn't dare!" Kato roars.

Ronan meets Kato's eyes and his smile curls into something slightly more sinister and challenging. "Oh, but I do."

Kato screams and flames shoot down the table, but they're stopped fast and hard by blasts of cool air. I look down the table to discover Astra standing, palm out, her eyes focused on Kato. She meets his gaze as she pushes back his flames and casts a shield over the lords. She lifts her other hand in the air and twirls it, revealing a pen dripping with black ink.

"I believe this will suit your needs," she says, passing the quill to Ronan without taking her eyes off Kato.

Ronan plucks the quill from her fingers and signs with a flourish. When he's done, his eyes pass around the table as he holds the quill out.

"Who's next?" he asks.

Lord Wallish clears his throat, "I'll sign."

"We had a deal! You signed a treaty!" Kato snarls, his eyes flashing literal flames.

"Indeed," Lord Wallish muses as he takes the quill, flicking his eyes over the treaty before carefully adding his own signature. "That treaty was negated on multiple points today."

Once his name is clearly written below Ronan's, Lord Wallish looks toward Kato one last time before adding, "I believe I will be off now."

Lord Wallish wisps away and a murmur breaks out over the table. Kato slams his fist into the table, scanning the remaining lords.

"And which others of you will betray our alliance?" he spits. "My sister comes in claiming I will betray you with little to no proof, and yet you're all willing to betray me on her words alone."

All the lords save Ronan avoid Kato's gaze. For a moment, I fear we have failed. Two Clans will not be enough, but then Lord Loudain reaches for the quill, adding his name. Kato makes a sound somewhere between a choke and a growl.

"Sorry, mate," Lord Loudain says evenly as he completes his signature, "but I have to choose what is best for my Clan."

No sooner is his signature complete then he wisps away and Lord Bashmore is adding his name. One by one, each Clan leader follows suit, Lord Dughlas being the last to add his name. Before he signs he has the decency to look apologetic, though he doesn't say a word. Flames roll off Kato but Astra is keeping them perfectly contained with her shield. I can feel it taking a toll on her magic, but she remains cool and collected, giving each lord a grateful nod as they sign their names. Soon, only Ronan remains.

"Well," Ronan drawls, his eyes glinting with mischief as he scoots back from the table and pushes up with his cane. "This has been quite the experience. We really should do this again."

"You!" Kato yells, thrusting a finger in Ronan's direction. "This is your doing!"

Ronan laughs, and I find myself marveling at his confidence and swagger.

"I wish I had the sort of connections to pull this off, mate, but, alas, I do not. I am, however, pleased with the turn of events." Ronan turns and inclines his head toward Astra. "It was a grand pleasure to meet you, love. I hope we can get to know one another better in the future. Maybe bring that prince along with you."

Astra gives Ronan an earnest smile. "I hope that can be arranged."

With a roguish wink, Ronan wisps away.

"Are you happy now?" Kato demands, his eyes locking with Astra's.

Astra's shoulders drop and a shadow crosses her face as

her façade fades slightly. "No. As long as you and I are on different sides of this war, I cannot be happy."

The earnest pain tinging her words is like an arrow to my heart, but Kato seems mostly unaffected.

"Then join my side."

Astra shakes her head. "No, Kato. You may find it easy to fight against friends who have loyally defended you, and you may find it easy to steal a crown and kingdom to which you have no right, but I do not."

Kato scoffs. "Ehren doesn't deserve the crown or this kingdom. He only thinks he does because he was born to it. What has he done to keep his father from going after magic? Nothing! I have done more for the cause of magic than Ehren ever can, because he simply does not understand."

"You're wrong." Astra raises her chin and her eyes settle into an unforgiving glare. "Ehren loves his kingdom—every single person in it, no matter their magical status. He is striving to understand magic to the point where he can perform basic spells. Magic doesn't make you better than everyone else. How you treat people is what makes a leader great or horrible and, right now, dear brother, you would not make a good leader, let alone a great one."

Kato grinds his teeth before slamming both hands onto the table. The table dissolves into a pile of ash, but Astra barely reacts.

"Please, Kato, come back with me," Astra offers, extending her hand to Kato.

"No! I thought if I could show you my power, if I could gather an army, you would understand the power of magic, but you willingly stay ignorant. You claim you're loyal, but what about your loyalty to me? To Alak?"

I want to shrink into nothing as Astra lets her eyes fall on me for the first time. Her gaze is careful, controlled. I can't read anything in her eyes. I swallow hard as my heart races.

"Alak made his choice to betray me and, if he stands by it, then he is as dead to me as you will be if you choose to continue down this path."

Her words strike deep. She might as well have struck me physically. It would have hurt less. Even though I know she doesn't truly mean them, I react almost instinctively.

"Can't you see I can offer you more than Bram?" The words spill out before I can stop them. But since I've said them, I might as well say more. "We could be truly great together. I've seen what you're capable of. You know what I can do. Please, Astra—"

"Stop. Just . . . stop," Astra commands, her eyes closing for a brief moment before they flick open again. "If you really think I can be swayed by promises of power, you know nothing about me."

Something in her voice echoes real pain, and I wonder if I took it a step too far.

"And I suppose you don't care anything about the power your position as Court Sorceress has," Aine laughs. "You're such a hypocrite."

Astra's eyes flash silver and the room goes cold. "I accepted the position as a favor to Ehren because I care about him and I support him." She meets Kato's eyes again. "Please, Kato. After this, there's no going back. Come back and help Ehren. This whole 'magic only' power grab isn't you, and it won't end well."

Kato shakes his head. "You don't understand. I wish you could. I thought you might. He said . . . I hoped you might eventually see the things I do." Astra's face scrunches in confusion as Kato continues. "But I have plans I can't go back on. I still need you, Ash. I want you by my side as my equal, but I can't just stop. People without magic don't understand us. They'll try to manipulate us and control us if they're in charge."

"Ehren would never—"

"Maybe not now, but eventually he would. It's how it always happens. Magic and the magicless can never be equals. I know. He's told me."

Genuine concern floods Astra's face and her lips part as she studies her brother's face.

"Who?" she whispers. "Who said?"

Kato growls and runs a hand through his hair in frustration as he shakes his head. "No one. It—it doesn't matter." When he looks back up at Astra, his expression is hard and cruel again. "So, is this your final choice? You refuse to stand by me?"

Astra pauses, then nods once. "Yes."

"Then leave," Kato snarls. "And don't bother coming back. Next time we see one another, we will be true enemies."

"Kato," Astra says softly, her voice breaking as tears well in her eyes. I clench my hands by my side to keep from reaching toward her.

"Go!" Kato yells, throwing flames, but by the time they reach where Astra stood, she's gone, along with the treaty and all traces of her magic.

I suddenly feel empty and an ache fills my chest. It takes Kato a moment to react, but when he does he snaps into command mode.

"I want you to check every single room and drag any of the Clan leaders or their families that are still here back into this room to account for their actions!" he demands.

"And if they're gone?" Kayleigh asks hesitantly.

Kato grits his teeth. "And if they're gone, then good riddance. They'll soon regret turning their backs on me. Now GO!"

Without any further questions, we rush from the room but find exactly what we expect—every room has been vacated. Some rooms show that the occupants left in a hurry. They're left in scattered disarray with a few things left behind. Others look as if they've barely been used. I doubt Ronan even touched anything in his room. Feeling somewhat relieved, I make my way to my room. I opted for a small room far from the others and, right now, I'm glad of my dark corner of solitude. I slowly open the door with a sigh and step into my room. A single thin window casts a stream of light into the room, but most of the room is shrouded in shadows. As I go to close the door, I catch movement out of the corner of my eye. I immediately pull on my magic, ready to attack.

"It's just me," a quiet voice says.

I can barely breathe as Astra steps from the shadows into the ray of light.

"Astra," I whisper, my heart racing.

"Felixe showed me which room was yours," she says, motioning to where the Fae Fox lays curled up sleeping on my bed.

I quickly shut the door and lock it before turning back to her. Tears slide down her cheeks, and her eyes are swollen from crying. Gone is her façade of power and pretense. This is just Astra, raw and broken. My heart shatters.

"Those things I said before," she stumbles, looking down at her trembling hands clasped in front of her, "I didn't mean them."

"Come now, love," I mutter, crossing to her and taking

her hands in mine. "If you think I don't know that, you don't know me very well. I didn't mean my words either."

Her beautiful amethyst eyes lift to mine and a smile tugs at the corners of her mouth. I reach a hand to her face and wipe her tears away. She leans into my touch.

"Are you all right, love?" I ask, though the answer is obvious even before she shakes her head.

"I never expected to be on opposing sides of Kato. I was holding out hope, but now I don't know what to do," she admits, holding my gaze. "Do you have any idea who he was talking about?"

I shake my head. "I have no idea, but I will do my best to find out."

"So you're staying with Kato?"

I pause and bite my lip. I don't want to. I'm tired of pretending, tired of being so far from Astra.

"Do you want me to stay?"

"I'm not sure," she says slowly. "I—I miss you but—"

"But you need to know who Kato was talking about," I finish for her. She nods, and I catch the guilt flicker in her eyes. "Then I'll stay. Do what I can."

She almost looks disappointed, but she nods again and glances away.

"Shouldn't you be getting back to Ehren?"

She sighs. "I should. I just needed a moment to gather my thoughts and my energy."

"Can you wisp that far?" I ask, reaching out my Syphon senses to test her magic.

She smiles and lifts her hand. For the first time, I notice the bracelet. I trace my fingers along the glowing stone and inhale sharply as magic hums beneath my touch.

"A Syphon Stone?"

She nods and her smile widens slightly.

"That's how you shifted and had so much magic that easily and quickly without draining you entirely."

"Technically, I can shift on my own, but yes, Kai put some of his shifter magic in the stone, so I was able to shift into a wolf with less effort."

"Y-you can shift?" I'm missing so much and I bloody hate it.

"I can. I typically shift into a Fae Fox. On my own it's very draining, so I used Kai's wolf form instead since it was his magic."

"What else can you do?"

She shrugs. "I don't know. Whatever I need to. I have to learn new things to survive."

I scowl. "I don't like being apart from you. I want to be by your side." The confession tumbles out before I can stop it. "Every day we're apart, I feel like I'm dying inside."

Her eyebrows knit together for a moment, and I'm afraid I've said too much, said the wrong things. But then, in one swift movement, her lips meet mine. It takes me by surprise, but I eagerly return the kiss as soon as it registers. This kiss is different than any we've shared before. It's filled with a specific sort of need and longing. It's an admission. She presses into the kiss as I wrap my arms around her, drawing her closer. I need her closer. The kiss escalates and I realize we're heading toward the bed. I can't tell if it's her leading or me or if it's entirely mutual.

Someone drops something in the hall, and we jerk apart, reminded of where we are. We're both breathing heavily, and there's a fire in her eyes that sends a rush through me.

"You should go," I manage, my voice rough.

She nods but makes no move to leave. I want to pull her

back into the kiss, but I can hear the shuffle of footsteps in the hall. I reach out and lift the hand bearing her Syphon Stone.

"Can I add some of my magic?"

"Of course," she says, her own voice rough.

I let my finger glide along the stone, and it brightens as my magic transfers. It's a warm and welcoming feeling.

"Not too much," she whispers. "You may need your magic."

I give her a little more before pulling my hand back. I meet her gaze.

"And how about I give you a little magic more . . . directly?" I offer and she nods, absentmindedly tracing her tongue along her bottom lip.

I smile and lean forward, pressing my lips to hers, transferring my magic. I can sense her magic receiving mine eagerly. She pulls back after a few moments.

"Alak, I—"

"Alak," Ian's voice outside the door interrupts as he knocks.

I swear under my breath. "What?"

"Kato wants us in the meeting room immediately."

"I'll be there in a minute."

"He said—"

"I'll be there in a minute," I snap, my voice firm.

"Gods. Fine. Take too long, though, and it's yer own neck."

His footsteps fade down the hall as I turn my attention back to Astra.

"I need to go anyway," she says softly.

I trace a finger along her bottom lip.

"I love you. You know that, right?"

Her eyes widen slightly. "Alak—"

"You don't have to say anything," I add quickly, suddenly fearing her response, her rejection. "I just need you to know. I love you, Astra. I love you more than anything else or anyone else in this world."

More hurried footsteps rush down the hall, stopping outside my door accompanied by Kayleigh's voice.

"Alak, you better come quickly. Kato doesn't seem very happy or patient."

"I'm coming," I answer, looking at my door with a scowl. When I glance back at Astra, she's gone. Suddenly, it hurts to breathe.

"Are you coming?"

With a sigh, I unlock and open the door. I force a smile.

"Sure. Let's go meet our doom, shall we?"

CHAPTER TWENTY-SEVEN

ASTRA

My heart beats wildly in my chest as I wisp away from Alak. I know if I stay another moment, I won't be able to leave him. I'll either stay and risk myself, along with everyone else, or I'll insist he come back with me. Even as he fades from view, I feel like I've made the wrong choice. I'm just glad I don't have to witness his reaction when he realizes I'm gone.

He loves me. The thought takes my breath away and makes me feel light and free. But I can't focus on that right now.

My wisp brought me back just a little way away from Ehren and the rest of the camp so I can compose myself. I use a touch of magic—familiar, warm illusion magic—to erase any sign of the tears I've shed before wisping to the camp. Ehren stands off to the side, sparring with Cal while Makin and Nyco watch. He immediately pauses and turns to me, his gaze mingled with fear and anticipation. Bram rises from his seat, taking a single step in my direction before he freezes. The others watch me with bated breath but no one says a word. My magic is drained, and I'm feeling it, but I manage a smile.

"They signed it," I say, pulling the treaty out of one of my pockets.

Makin whoops and punches the air and Nyco claps as Cal grins from ear to ear. Sama bounces up and down whispering, "I knew it! I knew she would do it!" Bram beams with quiet pride, and even Kai smiles. Ehren looks as if a huge burden has been lifted.

"They signed it? They really signed it? All the Clans? All seven of them?" Ehren stumbles in disbelief.

My smile widens. "Every single one."

Ehren rushes to me and wraps his arms around me, lifting me into the air and spinning me around. My crown tumbles to the ground, but neither of us care. He laughs and I join him. When he sets me down, I feel breathless in a completely wonderful way. He presses his forehead to mine and closes his eyes.

"You and me, Ash, we're going to change the world," he whispers.

He pulls back and his sharp sea green eyes sparkle as they meet mine.

"Not to be a downer," Sama cuts in, "but I can sense Astra's magic, and it's quite low, other than what little she has stored in her stone."

Ehren tilts his head with a frown. "You should have said something."

I shrug. "It hadn't come up yet."

Ehren steps back and turns toward the others. "It's early, but we'll go ahead and make camp. Stay alert since it's still daylight."

"I don't want to put us at risk," I insist. "I can travel."

Ehren shakes his head firmly as he turns back to me. "Absolutely not." I open my mouth to protest but Ehren places a finger over my lips. "Shush. No arguing. Now, go rest."

He nods to where the others had been sitting. I shake my head at him but follow orders. As I sink down to the ground, I realize exactly how tired I am.

"Here," Cal's voice says from above me, and I look up to find him handing me a blanket.

I accept the blanket with a smile. "Thanks."

"I'll be back later to make sure you eat something," he replies with a wink.

I take a deep breath and nod. I settle onto the ground and bunch the blanket under my head like a pillow. I am a little surprised at how quickly I fall asleep. When I wake up, it's to the smell of food cooking over a crackling fire. The sun is starting to set and the world is covered in a golden glow. I still feel a bit tired, but I push into a sitting position.

"Feel better?" Bram asks gently from where he sits to my left.

"A bit," I say but my words are buried by a yawn. My cheeks tinge pink as Makin laughs.

"Looks like you might need a touch more sleep," Cal says with a smile, elbowing Makin.

"Maybe."

My body feels stiffer than usual, and I realize it's probably because I'm still wearing my elaborate dress.

"I might need to change, though, before I rest any more," I say, adjusting the corset.

"We set up your tent," Ehren replies, nodding behind me.

I twist around and locate my tent set up not far away.

With a grateful nod I stand, stretching, and make my way over to the tent. I find Sama inside sorting through her bag.

"You're awake," she greets me, smiling.

"Yeah, and I need to get out of this dress." I hesitate and then add, "Can you help me? I have a feeling it's not going to slip off easily."

Sama rises. "Of course! I can't believe you were able to get any sleep in it anyway."

With her help, I'm able to change into normal riding clothes quickly. They seem more comfortable than normal after that dress. I sigh with relief as I stuff the dress into my bag. Once I'm done, we both head back out to the fire. Cal is distributing plates of meat—rabbit maybe? I settle back on the ground next to Bram, and he smiles gently down at me. Cal hands me my plate, which I can't help but notice has a larger portion of meat than normal. I arch my eyebrows at him in question.

"You need to replenish your energy," he replies simply before leaving to take his seat between Makin and Ehren.

Nyco pulls out a stiff, relatively stale loaf of bread, and we pass it around the circle, each tearing off a piece. Makin adds a bottle of mead to the rounds. Something feels different, lighter tonight. We all have the taste of victory on our lips. It's a small victory in a much bigger war, but it's something we needed. Desperately.

Bram shifts and leans back on his palms, one of his arms stretching behind me. I automatically shift closer to him, eager for the comfort of the familiar. Ehren catches my gaze and lifts his eyebrows, his eye glinting with mischief as the corner of his lips twitch. I chuckle slightly and shake my head at him. He shrugs, turning his attention back to Nyco, who is telling the story of the first time he realized he could communicate with insects.

"They were everywhere, just staring at me," Nyco says, gesturing dramatically.

"Were you scared?" Sama asks, leaning forward, her eyes wide.

"I was more puzzled than anything," Nyco replies with a shrug. "When I asked what they were doing and they replied, I shit my pants."

Makin laughs so hard he starts choking on his food.

"You would," Ehren laughs.

Nyco laughs along with them. "I mean, really, would you have reacted any differently?"

"Can't say I would," Makin coughs.

"Sometimes, I wish I had regular magic, like on my own," Sama admits wistfully.

"You can borrow my magic anytime you want," Nyco says quickly and Sama cocks her head curiously. Red rises in his cheeks and he adds, "I mean, if bugs are your thing. You know."

"It's definitely interesting magic," Sama says softly, her own cheeks slightly pinker than normal.

"What was it like when you first shifted?" I cut in, looking over at Kai who sits to my right.

He gives a non-committal shrug. "I've lived in the Hundan Valley with magic for years. I'm not sure I actually remember the first time I shifted enough to share any details. From what I do remember, it was a freeing experience, like something I was always meant to do."

"Any particular good shifter stories you want to share?" Ehren asks.

Kai starts to shake his head, but then pauses, something that looks remarkably like a smile crossing his lips. "Well, there was this one time where I jumped from the middle of the waterfall as a wolf. Leyana—" His voice breaks for a moment, but he swallows and continues. "Leyana, my sister, told me I scared her to death. But I didn't care. It felt like flying."

Without thinking I reach over and place my hand on his, giving it a slight squeeze. He smiles at me in appreciation before I pull my hand back.

"I'm going to fly one day," Makin says dreamily.

Cal laughs. "And how will you manage that?"

Makin grins and shrugs. "No idea, but I'm going to find a way."

"Have I ever told you the story of when I pulled a prank on the princesses from Ascaria?"

"You didn't!" I gasp.

Ehren grins as Bram replies, "Yes, he did, and he nearly caused an international incident, almost killing a peace treaty with Ascaria."

"Oh, it wasn't *that* bad!" Ehren scoffs waving Bram off.

Makin leans forward eagerly. "I need to hear this story."

Bram rolls his eyes. "Don't encourage him."

"What's done is done," Ehren says before launching into his story.

I stifle another yawn and lean tiredly against Bram, who shifts so I can make myself more comfortable. At some point in the story, my exhaustion catches up with me and I drift off. I don't even realize I'm asleep at until I find myself standing on a battlefield surrounded by piles of the dead. Their bodies are all broken and contorted, their eyes milky white, staring at nothing. Blood drips from the corners of their mouths and their bodies are covered in scars. I stumble back, staring around in horror.

"You did this," says a woman's voice.

I spin around to find a young woman, not much older than me, clutching a young child against her shoulder.

"You killed my husband."

"No," I protest, backing away and tripping over a body behind me. "I would never . . ."

"My husband was a good man," the woman says. "He was just doing his job as a soldier, serving the rightful king, and you killed him."

Her accusations stab like cold metal.

"Please, I never meant to hurt anyone. I didn't have a choice!"

"There's always a choice," another voice says from behind me and I turn to find an older woman. "Your choice killed my son."

"And my husband."

"And my brother."

"And my father."

I squeeze my eyes shut and clamp my hands over my ears. "Stop! Please! I can't . . . I didn't want to kill anyone!"

A hand grabs my arm and I scream.

"Astra! Astra! Wake up!"

My eyes flicker open to Bram hovering above me. My throat is sore from screaming, sweat beads line my forehead, and my whole body is shaking. Bram breathes a sigh of relief, but his forehead remains knitted in concern. He helps me rise into a sitting position.

"Are you okay?" he asks, tenderly resting his hand on the small of my back.

I swallow and glance around to find everyone staring at

me, concern lining every face. I take a shuddering breath, unsure of what to say. In one smooth motion Ehren stands up and offers me his hand.

"Come on. Let's go."

I place my trembling hand in his, and he helps me to my feet. Ehren draws me to his side, wrapping a supportive arm around me as he leads me to his tent. I can feel eyes boring into my back, but I don't turn. When we duck behind the flap of Ehren's tent, I'm grateful I'm out of sight. Ehren slides his arm from around me, and I settle on the edge of his cot. It only takes him a few moments to prepare the spell. He kneels next to me, his eyes meeting mine.

"Are you okay?"

I take a deep breath and shake my head. "Not really, but I'm as okay as I can be."

Ehren nods. "I know what you mean. It's been a long day. It couldn't have been easy seeing Kato."

Tears start spilling unbidden down my cheeks. Ehren sets the spell aside and pulls me against him.

"It's okay. It's going to be okay," Ehren whispers, stroking my hair. "We'll find a way to get through this, you and I. We can do this."

I sob into his shoulder for moment before I pull back, wiping my tears with the back of my hand.

"Kato kept hinting that something bigger is coming, and he won't listen to reason. Alak is trying to help, but I don't know what he can really do. This isn't the Kato I know. Something has happened, but I don't know what. We've always fixed everything for each other and now . . . Maybe if I were stronger . . ."

Ehren grasps my hands firmly and meets my eyes. "It isn't your fault. At all. You understand?"

I nod weakly.

"And your dreams, I assume they're about the soldiers you've . . . taken care of?"

I nod again with a sniff.

"They're not your fault either. If anything, those deaths are on me."

"Ehren, no," I protest quietly.

Ehren smiles sadly. "My father sent them after me. Maybe if I hadn't run . . ."

Now it's my turn to grip his hands a bit tighter. "You didn't just run. You know that. And it's not like you had much of a choice."

His eyes swim with a deep sadness. "I hate every second of this, you know. We both have people in our lives that should be supporting us that have, instead, made themselves our enemies. You have Kato and I have my father." He sighs and shakes his head. "Anyway, how about we let you get some sleep?"

"Ehren," I say softly as he releases my hand to grab the spell mixture, "If you ever need to talk, I'm here. Like you said, we're in this together."

He smiles softly. "I know." He kisses my cheek. "Now, get comfortable."

I settle down on the cot and Ehren begins the ritual. He makes the mark on my head and whispers the words that make the world fade to a blissful dark.

CHAPTER TWENTY-EIGHT

ALAK

I expect to find Kato wild-eyed and furious, but he actually seems calm. Too calm. In some ways, that's far more terrifying. Even Aine seems unsettled, which is a bit of consolation. Once we're all in the room, Kato nods for us to take a seat and we comply with hesitation. He takes his seat where the head of the table would be had he not turned it to ash.

"Someone betrayed me," he says evenly, his eyes meeting each of ours in turn.

My gut twists, and I clench my teeth, forcing myself to look as innocent as possible. I don't dare look away from his penetrating gaze.

"I will find out who it was. I don't know if it was someone in this room or one of the lords, but when I find out, that person will regret the day he was born."

Well, trick's on him. I already regret the day I was born.

"Who even has contact with Astra?" I ask, hoping the slightly higher register of my voice doesn't betray me.

"I have no idea, but whoever it was can't hide much longer. Not with the allies I have," Kato assures me.

"What allies?" Niall asks hesitantly.

Kato's lips curl into a smile that sends shivers down my spine. "I'll save that reveal for another day. Let's just say, you won't want to be on any side but mine once they're revealed."

I do *not* like the sound of that.

Caitlyn meets my gaze from across the table and locks eyes with me. She doesn't say anything, but I know she knows I was the one who betrayed Kato. Somehow. I do my best to beg her to say silent without being obvious. She gives me an almost imperceptible nod before turning her attention back to Kato.

"Well, what now?" Aine asks.

"Now, we go back home and wait. We ready ourselves. And then, we take the crown."

I have the urge to get out of Kato's presence as quickly as possible, so when he dismisses us to gather our things to prepare to leave, I practically leap from my seat. I'm halfway to my room when Caitlyn catches up with me.

"Alak!"

I want to keep walking, but I stop. With a sigh, I turn to face her.

"Look—" I start but she cuts me off.

"I know," she says simply. "Did you forget I can read auras?"

Shite. I had forgotten that, actually.

"Please, Caitlin," I beg. "You can't—"

She shakes her head. "I won't." She glances around quickly before leaning closer and adding, "I don't like what's happening. I don't agree with any of this."

I scowl. "Then why are you going along with any of it?"

"For the same reason you are," she says with a shrug. When I scowl she adds, "For love. I love Niall with all my heart, and he supports Kato. I've tried to talk him down, but once he gets an idea in his head . . ." She sighs and shakes her head.

"Thank you for keeping my secret."

Her eyes meet mine. "I won't volunteer any information, but I'm no good at lying. If I'm asked directly, I'm not sure I can get away with a lie. I'll have to tell the truth."

I nod. "I understand."

I turn to leave, but she reaches out, placing her hand on my arm, stopping me.

"Does she know?"

"Know what?"

Caitlyn tilts her head and smiles slightly. "It seems like sometimes you aren't such a great liar yourself."

I glance away. "I don't know what you're talking about."

"Fine," she says, releasing my arm. "But you should tell her if she doesn't know already. Soul bonds are rare, and she deserves to know."

I don't say anything else as Caitlyn turns and walks away. I am in so much trouble, and I don't even know what to do next. But I can't run. I have to stay. I have to be useful.

Kato's lethal calm lasts the next few days. We leave early the next morning, and Kato takes up his place in Niall's house again. He meets in secret with people one on one. I anxiously await my turn. I catch up with Kayleigh after one of her meetings.

"What's Kato planning?" I press, but she only shakes her head. "Come on. You can tell me."

Kayleigh looks at me wide-eyed. "If you think I'm going

to tell you anything, you're crazy. If Kato wants you to know, he'll tell you."

She tries to walk away, but I place my hands on her shoulders and turn her to face me. I scan her face. She's worried. No, she's terrified.

"Kayleigh, what is it?" I ask, afraid of her answer.

She refuses to meet my eyes. "I—I can't." She finally looks up at me. "And even if I wanted to, I'm not sure what I can tell you. Kato is searching after answers in unusual places. And I . . . I just can't."

She jerks from my grasp and scurries away, and I'm too afraid to chase after her.

Even more upsetting than Kayleigh's reaction is the fact that Kato is constantly meeting with Fionn. The first time I see Fionn go in to see Kato, he looks terrified, and rightly so. When he leaves, he seems . . . vindicated. With each meeting he holds his head a little higher. On more than one occasion, he meets my eyes and grins in a way that makes me want to punch his fecking face.

The meeting that worries me the most, however, is when Kato meets with Caitlyn. This is the first time she's been with Kato without Niall. When she leaves, she practically runs away. She catches me watching her, and her lips part like she wants to say something, but instead she wisps away. I can't find her anywhere afterward.

That evening, Kato finally summons me. I push down my fears and saunter into the room with far more bravado than I feel. As soon as I walk through the door I sense the wrongness in the room. My magic recoils so sharply it's physically painful. Bile rises in my throat, but I force it back down. When my eyes meet Kato's he's different. His features are set and cold. I used to be able to see traces of Astra in his face. They looked different, but they had the same smile. They had the same sparkle in their eyes. They wore the same light expressions. Now, there is no trace of Astra left. There is nothing light or friendly. Even his eyes seem a deeper, darker shade of purple.

"What's happening?" I sputter as Kato's lips curl into feral smile.

"Why don't you tell me what's happening," Kato says, tilting his head. "After all, you seem to be the one holding the answers."

I shake my head, ignoring the fear swirling in my gut. "I don't know what you mean."

"Why don't we start with what you and Lord McDullun discussed?"

"I already told you," I reply a little sharper than I mean to. I soften my voice and continue, "We went over the pros of him joining your alliance, and then we talked about how hard it is to be in love."

"Hmm . . . ," Kato muses. "And that was all? No insurrections? Because it was quite evident that he went into that meeting knowing there would be an out."

I shake my head. "I didn't plan anything with him. Who knows what he did with his ten days."

Kato's eyes snap to mine and he growls, "You're lying."

"I-I'm not. I swear—"

"I know for a fact you are!"

I search through the last few weeks and try to think of anything I've done wrong. Then I remember Caitlyn. I start shaking my head vigorously.

"If it was Caitlyn that said something . . . She doesn't really know things. She guesses. Her magic isn't an exact art form."

I'm rambling defensively. I've lost this battle. I know I have. Kato just confirms it when he laughs.

"Believe it or not, she actually tried to cover for you." He leans forward in his seat. "I have someone who is much better at digging out the truth, though."

As he speaks, the feeling of wrongness grows, and I choke on my own magic. A figure steps into the room and my magic screams. While it stands like a man and has the overall body and general appearance of a man, the thing that stands before me is far from human. It stands a little too tall, stretching to at least seven feet and has a body covered in inky black scales. It wears black leather pants, but the rest of the body is fully exposed. Its hands end in long black talons, and, I notice as it steps closer, so do its feet. Its eyes are glowing yellow and have long slits for pupils. Leathery black wings are folded behind its back and a long, forked tongue flicks out from behind rows of jagged teeth as it licks its lips in amusement at my terror.

I scramble back, but I feel a force bear down on me, freezing me in place.

"What are you?" I ask, my voice hoarse with terror.

"What? Not who?" a gravelly voice chides in an accent so thick it doesn't even sound like he's speaking a human language at first. "Tsk. You humans are as rude as we remember."

Kato takes a step forward, grinning wickedly, his eyes flickering flames. "This is the ally I mentioned before. He's a Dragkonian."

My mind races with the horror stories I heard as child—tales so dreadful there was no way they were true. They were meant to fuel nightmares. No, this can't be real. Because if it is, I'm dead. The creature chuckles.

"Ah, I see my reputation does indeed precede me. My name, though you did not ask for it, is Akaash. Or, at least, that's the closest it is in your human tongue."

My eyes dart to Kato. "Why? Do you understand what this alliance means?"

"It means," Kato says with a shrug, "that going against me was a mistake."

"I suppose you want a bit of evidence of how he was contacting your sister?" Akaash offers.

Kato nods. "What can it hurt to have a little proof?"

With a feral grin, Akaash steps forward. I try to jerk away, but my actions are pointless. His magic holds me firm. He sighs and glances at Kato over his shoulder.

"This one seems to like struggling. I can hold him, but it would be much more fun if I could concentrate my energy on . . . other things. Where are the chains?" I jerk harder at his words. I try to wisp, screaming in pain as his magic digs in, tethering me tighter. He turns his eyes back to me and chuckles. "Nice try, but no one gets in or out of this room unless I allow it."

"Fionn," Kato calls.

I'm filled with more panic as Fionn steps into the room, smiling and holding metal cuffs in his hands. He quickly crosses the room. I try to pull away but instead find my arms being lifted against my will and there's nothing I can do to fight it. His grin growing, Fionn meets my eyes, revenge glowing in his stare, and he claps the cold stone over my wrists before securing them to a chain that's been embedded into the ground at my feet. My magic suddenly goes quiet. I feel like my air supply has been cut off. I collapse to the ground with a gasp, struggling to breathe. Even my heart seems like it's struggling to beat. Akaash looks down at me and tilts his head.

"Yes, it's quite painful sometimes to have your magic suddenly cut off, but you'll stabilize soon. In the meantime . . ."

He reaches out a clawed hand and closes it over my head, his claws digging into my scalp. I cry out, but the pain has only just begun. It's like his claws are reaching inside my head. Memories start rushing to the surface. A flash of Felixe, then Aine, then . . .

No. No. No. I push the memory of Astra at the masquerade away. Akaash chuckles and dives after the memory, cutting through my skull like a knife. He pulls up the memory, no matter how much I fight him. After that memory is his, more images involving Astra float to the surface. The last day we spoke alone before I left with Kato, all of our correspondence, her in my room after the meeting. When he finally releases me, I drop to the ground, gasping as blood slides from my temples down my cheeks.

"So, he is the one who betrayed me?" Kato asks coldly, standing above me and looking down with disdain.

"Oh, he's betrayed you deeply. He was never on your side," Akaash confirms.

"Bastard!" Kato yells, kicking my face with his boot.

Blood floods my mouth, my cheek under my left eye swelling immediately.

"Please, I can explain," I mumble.

He kicks me again, this time in the stomach. I double over, spitting blood.

"I have no need for your apologies," Kato says with a dismissive wave.

"He has a soul bond," Akaash offers and I scream a sharp, "No!"

Kato pauses. "A what?"

No. He can't know about that. Astra . . . No.

"Please," I beg.

"A soul bond," Akaash offers, deriving obvious pleasure from my distress. "It's not complete, but it's there nonetheless."

Kato looks down at me with renewed interest. "So, they *are* connected."

"Oh, indeed. If the bond were complete your sister would likely feel every bit of pain as this human. As it is, however, she will likely only feel some pain through a broken bond."

"But we could draw her here?" Kato muses and Akaash nods. "That would make it easier."

"Kato, no!" I plead, spitting blood on the floor. "No matter what, she's still your sister."

"She betrayed me!" Kato yells. "She is *nothing* to me now but a means to an end." He looks at Akaash. "Do what you need."

Akaash flashes a tooth-filled smile as his eyes glow. "Excellent."

He leans over and jerks me to my feet. I try to struggle, but it does no good. I have no magic and my body is weak. I'm not sure what exactly I expect but when he digs a claw into the flesh at the base of my spine, pain like I've never felt before ripples through my body. I scream as he carves into my flesh. When he's done he throws me to the ground and steps back.

"That's it?" Kato asks, disappointment ringing in his voice.

"That was merely insurance," Akaash replies, licking my blood from his claws. "Delicious," he purrs. "Now we have fun."

He stretches out his hand and black flames shoot out, wrapping around me. Pain radiates over my skin, and I want to die. In fact, I'm sure I am dying. Death would be a welcome release from this agony. I feel like my flesh is melting from my bones, but there is no real sign of damage. I start fading into unconsciousness. The flames stop and I feel a tug on my mind, forcing me back to full consciousness. I melt into the floor, gasping.

"It's no fun if you black out on me. I'll give you a moment."

My brain races. I have to stop him. I don't care if I die. Not really. Not that I want to die this way, but if Astra can even feel a tenth of this . . . I have to stop it.

"Kato," I choke out.

"No talking," Akaash snaps and the flames start again.

This time they're worse. Akaash has a hold on my consciousness, so I can't fade away in the slightest. I feel every moment. Uncontrollable tears stream down my cheeks as my skin starts to split in some spots, blood leaking to the floor. When he pauses again, I curl up on the floor. Everything hurts. I glance up and look at Kato, my vision blurred. He's looking down at me with disinterest. I catch Fionn's eyes. He looks horrified, but I know I have no help in him.

"My, my," Akaash mumbles. "She is taking her time. Maybe I underestimated how she feels about you. Or your bond is weaker than I thought. Either way, I think maybe we should increase this a bit."

I'm screaming before the flames even start. I feel like my

bones are being pulled through my skin, threatening to break. I *hear* some of them crack. The flames stop.

"Please, kill me," I beg, weeping. "I'm of no use to you."

Akaash looks like he's considering it, but then I feel it. Akaash notices it as well. A slight pull. A whisper of magic that's not my own. It's the bond. I try to push it away.

"Kill me!" I scream, crawling toward Akaash and Kato. "Just kill me!"

Akaash chuckles. "Now, why would I do that when my plan is clearly working?"

A circle of black flame surrounds me as the room shudders with magic. And then the worst thing possible happens—Astra appears.

CHAPTER TWENTY-NINE

The morning after my success with the Clans, everyone seems hesitant to get back on the road. They keep insisting we can wait longer if I need to rest. After I threaten to turn the next person who asks if I'm okay into a toad, they finally stop.

The giddy feeling from the previous night seems to have mostly faded. Everyone settles back into a more somber mood. I'm not sure if it has to do with my breakdown courtesy of my nightmare, or if everyone realizes how many more victories we'll need for Ehren to get on the throne. Whatever it is, the air feels heavy. It doesn't help that it's a gloomy, overcast day. The longer we sink into the gloom the harder it is to break free of its grasp.

That's when Makin starts singing. His voice is slightly off-key but relatively pleasant. At first, we all glare at him or, in Kai's case, outright ignore him, but after a while, we're caught up in it. He's singing mostly war ballads and soon Cal, who has an amazing voice, joins in, followed shortly by Nyco, who is equally talented, and eventually even Ehren.

"You're not going to sing?" I tease Bram, pulling up my horse next to his.

Bram smiles and shakes his head. "Not this time."

"Bram sounds like a dying cat when he sings," Ehren says with a grin.

Bram rolls his eyes. "I do not."

"Oh yeah?" Ehren challenges. "Then prove me wrong."

Bram pauses, listening to the others sing, then shakes his head. "I don't know this one."

"Liar!" Makin yells before launching into the next verse of a ballad.

"Come on, Bram," Ehren goads him, eye twinkling. "Join us."

Bram sighs. "Fine."

He hesitates for a moment and then joins in on the chorus. His voice is quite pleasant. It's not perfectly on key, but it's warm and comforting. I smile and he tries to hide his own smile.

When the song ends he glances over at Ehren. "Happy?"

Ehren grins. "Very."

They launch into another song, this one lead by Nyco. Bram doesn't sing this round, but he does hum along. When Makin starts the next song Cal cuts him short.

"You can't sing the Ballad of Ramsey in mixed company!" he chides, scowling. "There are ladies present!"

"I thought you liked songs about lovers," Ehren teases in a low, sultry voice that makes Cal blush a deep crimson from the tips of his ears all the way down his neck. Ehren's own cheeks tinge a barely noticeable pink as Makin glances between the two, smirking with unabashed delight shining in his eyes.

"Did you just call me a lady?" I cut in quickly. "I'm not exactly a lady."

"Neither am I," Sama adds, smiling playfully.

"See?" Makin replies, his grin returning.

Bram scowls. "That does not automatically make it an acceptable song for mixed company."

Makin rolls his eyes. "Fine."

The next song he chooses instead is actually one I know. Makin's eyes go wide with delight when I join in.

When the song ends Makin says, "I bet she knows the dirty one, too."

I throw my head back and laugh. "The naughty songs I know could curl your toes."

Makin flushes and looks delightfully intrigued. "Can you share one?"

"No," Bram says firmly and Ehren laughs. I just grin.

"You, sir, are no fun," Makin pouts.

"It is my job to keep you in line," Bram retorts, sitting straighter, a smile playing on his lips.

"Sama, why don't you share a song you know?" Nyco says carefully.

Sama turns bright red and shakes her head. "Oh, no. I can't sing. At all. And I don't think I know any songs anyway."

"Well, we could ask Kai, but I'm not sure wolves can sing," Nyco mumbles, looking down to where Kai's giant wolf form plods along beside our horses. Kai growls and I laugh.

Instead of forcing Kai into his human form to sing, they go back to singing war ballads with the occasional tale that borders on being inappropriate. The latter seems to bring Nyco, Makin, and Ehren the most glee. When we finally stop for the night, it's a welcome reprieve. We opt not to make a full camp, but we do light a fire to chase away the night's chill. I settle between Ehren and Bram. Ehren uses the spell so I can sleep.

The next few days settle into the same pattern. The boys take turns leading songs in an attempt to lighten the mood. When I know the words I sing along, Bram joining in on occasion.

One afternoon, we make a quick stop at a river where Ehren says the Isle of Naskein has requested he place a portal stone.

"Apparently, this water is enchanted," Ehren explains, staring skeptically at the water.

Sama dismounts her horse and leans down, letting water trickle over her fingers. She stands and wipes her hand on the side of her shirt.

"They're right. This water definitely has magical properties."

"Is it safe to drink?" Makin asks, eying the water.

Sama shrugs. "It should be."

Nyco jabs Makin with his elbow. "Try it. See what it does."

"Okay. Why not?" Makin says with a nod, kneeling next to the water.

"Why not?" Cal huffs with a scowl. "There are a thousand magical reasons why not."

Makin grins. "That's what makes it fun."

Before anyone else can voice any concerns, Makin leans over and scoops a handful of water to his lips and takes a sip. Nothing happens, but I feel a tingle of magical mischief in my fingertips. I can't resist. I slowly draw a bit of illusion magic and make Makin disappear. No one but me can see him.

"Makin!" Cal yells, looking around frantically.

"What? What happened?" Makin asks, looking down at his arms.

I cover my mouth with my hand to stifle my laugh. Sama, who must be able to sense my magic, meets my eyes and bites back a grin.

"You— You're gone!" Cal stutters, staring at the space where Makin stands.

"What do you mean 'gone'? I'm right here," Makin replies, brow furrowed in confusion as he gestures at himself.

"You're invisible," Nyco whispers in awe.

"I'm WHAT?" Makin cries.

He starts spitting like he can undo drinking the water, and I double over laughing. His gaze shoots to me, and he points in my direction.

"You're doing this!" he accuses, as Sama joins me.

"Sorry! Sorry!" I choke, tears leaking down my face as I withdraw the spell, and Makin appears to everyone again.

I wipe away tears as Makin grins, placing his hands on his hips.

"I didn't know you had it in you to be so mischievous. Well done," Makin says, giving me a nod of approval. "Well done."

"But the water *is* actually safe?" Nyco asks, casting a wary, side-eyed glance at the river.

I nod. "Yes, that was all me."

Seeming a little relieved, everyone stoops and refills their water skeins. They take a few hesitant sips, eyes darting toward me with each one, before they truly relax. While Ehren plants the stone, Sama motions me over to the water.

"I know you've already gone and done whatever it was you needed to with the magic you had stored in your Syphon Stone, but I thought it might not hurt to add a little water magic to the stone. You know, just in case," she explains.

I nod. "That's not a bad idea."

I don't add that I've been storing a little of my own magic in the stone the past couple of days. She makes quick work of transferring the magic, and I feel the stone surge with the power.

Once we are on our way again, we fall back into our pattern. Over the next couple of days, however, even the more inappropriate songs start to lose their luster. Ehren promises we are only a day or so away from Hounddale by his calculations, but we're tired of always being on high alert. We're all starting to get tense again, ready to know what the future has in store.

I'm riding a little way behind Bram, who is arguing with Makin over some detail from his last ballad when something feels off. At first, I don't think much of it. I chalk it up to being tired and general road weariness. But then a strange pain thrums in my head. I hiss and drop the reigns as my hands fly to my temples, my eyes squeezing shut. Ehren is the first to notice.

"Are you okay?" he asks, riding up next to me.

I open my eyes and nod, although the headache remains. "My head just hurts all of a sudden."

Bram twists in his saddle, his face etched in worry. "Do we need to stop?"

"No, I think—"

The pain intensifies and I nearly tumble from my horse. Ehren leaps from his and rushes to my side. I fall into his arms, allowing him to support me as Bram jumps off his horse, rushing over.

"I think I need a minute," I mumble.

Slowly, the pain starts subsiding. I shake my head in confusion. I feel like I should know what's wrong. It's familiar and strange all at the same time.

"Are you okay now?" Ehren asks, eyes flicking over my face.

I start to nod but an overwhelming pain sweeps over me, centering on my lower back. I scream and drop to my knees, clawing at the spot where the pain is radiating from.

"It's burning!" I scream, tears welling in my eyes.

Someone, I'm not sure who, lifts my dress enough to expose my lower back and traces a cool, calloused hand over the spot. Their touch should cause more pain, but it doesn't.

"There's nothing there," Kai's bewildered voice says. I hadn't even realized he had shifted.

The pain ceases and I take a shuddering breath, looking up at Ehren, my eyes wide with terror. Ehren looks to Sama.

"Is this magic? Can you sense anything?" he demands, his voice tinged with fear.

Sama steps forward hesitantly, licking her lips. She places her hands on my back where I had been clawing and jerks back with a hiss, clutching her hand to her chest.

"This is something very dark," she whispers, her eyes wide.

"What?" Bram demands.

Sama shakes her head. "I don't know." She scowls and adds, "It's not actually happening to her, but to someone else."

That's when it clicks. And I don't know how I know, but I know it all the same.

"Alak," I choke out. "It's Alak. Someone is hurting Alak."

"You can't know that," Bram objects.

"Felixe!" I cry.

Felixe pops immediately into view. He whines, his eyes even wider than normal.

"Is Alak in trouble?" I ask.

He whimpers and yips, spinning in a nervous circle.

"That doesn't mean—"

Bram's words are cut short by my scream. Pure pain ripples over my body. It's more intense than anything I've ever felt before. I can barely register anything else around me as I tumble forward into Ehren's arms. When the pain stops I gasp, wiping away tears with a trembling hand.

"I have to go to him," I whisper hoarsely, forcing myself to sit up. "If he's being tortured, it's because Kato found out. He's with Kato because of me. I have to go to him."

"Absolutely not," Bram says firmly, clenching his fists.

"It's probably a trap," Ehren adds.

More pain ripples over me, even more intense this time. I collapse against Ehren and squeeze his hand as I scream, my nails digging into his hand so hard they draw blood. When it stops, I'm crying. I don't even remember starting to cry.

"I have to go. If he's feeling this because of me, then—"

"You cannot go," Bram spits. "That is out of the question. Right, Ehren?"

I look up at Ehren who stares down at me, his face almost expressionless as he weighs the options in front of him.

"Right, Ehren?" Bram repeats with more force.

Ehren ignores Bram and locks eyes with me. "Astra, if something happens and you don't come back . . ."

"Would you be able to come back?" Kai asks evenly.

Before I can answer the pain returns. This time I feel

like my bones are breaking from the inside out. Ehren gathers me in his arms and holds me against his chest, whispering words in my ear I can't quite make out. I have to stop this. I have to get to Alak. I don't care if it's trap. I *have* to go. I'm the only one who can.

When the pain finally subsides, I consider Kai's question. I pull away from Ehren and look around at the faces watching me. I'm not sure where our physical location is on a map, but I know these people. I know I can find my way back. I nod.

"I can come back. I *will* come back. With Alak."

I struggle to stand, and Ehren helps me. Nyco strides forward and places his hand over my Syphon Stone.

"You may need this," he whispers. Before his hand is even completely gone from my wrist, Kai is adding his magic.

"You can't go," Bram cries, desperation thick in his voice. "Ehren, you can't let her go!"

Ehren shakes his head. "It's her decision."

I shoot him a thankful look as his eyes meet mine.

"Come back to me," he whispers, his voice breaking.

I nod and look to Felixe. I don't even have to say the words. He just appears on my shoulder. Without another thought, I pull on whatever binds me and Alak together. It feels strained, like it's buried, but it's there. With Felixe's help, I wisp away.

At first, it feels like before when Felixe lead me to Alak, but then I can sense it going wrong. There's a barrier that threatens to push me away. But I fight it, squeezing through. It feels like thousands of tiny needles scraping against my skin, but I manage it. The world is hazy when I first land, but everything comes into focus. I gasp when I see a barely recognizable Alak in a crumpled, bloody heap on the floor surrounded by a circle of black flames. He's broken and covered in so much blood I wonder for a panicked moment if he's even alive. Then, he shifts slightly and his eyes meet mine. My heart stops. He's alive, but barely.

"No," he says, choking on his own blood.

I take a step toward him, but a cold voice like gravel stops me in my tracks.

"Well, now, who do we have here?"

I spin and my breath catches at the creature standing next to my brother. He's a warrior. That much is obvious. His muscular torso is bare, save for the scales which cover his body like onyx armor. He stands straight and tall, like he's used to the powerful bowing and cowering before him. This realization makes me stand even straighter. He shifts, and I notice the wings folded on his back. My brain spins as I put the pieces together.

"You're a Dragkonian," I spit, disgust and fear swirling inside me.

The man, or creature, whatever he is, smiles. Or at least I think it's a smile. It's really more a flashing of his jagged teeth.

"You're quite the clever one," he says. "Much quicker than your lover over here."

I almost snap back that he's not my lover, but there's no point. This creature doesn't care about keeping his facts straight. Instead, I address my brother, who is staring at me with cold disinterest.

"How could you align with the Dragkonians? They're one of the most despicable races to ever exist."

Kato shrugs. "I needed allies. They needed allies. Our visions align. It's a good match."

"You're a fool!"

Kato's eyes flash. "No, Astra, you're the fool! That much is obvious. You didn't even hesitate to fall into our trap."

I refocus on Alak and rush to him. I send a quick flash of magic to dim the flames so I can kneel by his side. My magic doesn't hold the flames off, however, and they flicker back to life, trapping us both. I don't care. I gather Alak's head into my lap.

"What did they do to you?" I whisper, my voice barely controlled.

His swollen emerald-green eyes meet mine. "You shouldn't have come." His voice barely sounds human, it's so hoarse from screaming and drowned by the blood bubbling in his mouth.

I feel like I'm breaking in a different way now. It's a different type of pain, but it's a crushing pain all the same. I scan his body assessing his injuries. I doubt there's an inch of his body that isn't wounded in some way. There's so much blood, I can't even tell where one injury ends and the next one begins. It takes me a moment to notice the shackles on his wrists. I reach out to unlock them with my magic, but my magic dissolves against the stone. I try again to no avail. The creature laughs.

"You thought this would be an easy rescue mission, no?" he mocks with a sneer. "Those shackles are older than most of the world you know. They are unbreakable by magic."

I look back at the cuffs and notice the ancient symbols scratched onto them. He's right. My magic can't unlock them. But maybe, just maybe, a spell can. I reach into my memories and recall Ehren's unlocking spell he gave me before I went to meet the Clans. With a quick prayer to the gods, I reach into my stone and sort through the magic to find the spell. I concentrate and pull it to the surface. I call the spell forward as I place my hands on the cuffs. They open and I feel a rush of relief.

"Impossible!" the creature roars with such force the ground shakes.

Alak moans and something in me snaps. I gently set Alak to the side as I stand to my feet and meet the creature's stare.

"How?" he spits. "How did you do that?"

"I did it because you underestimated me."

I shoot a concentrated blast of magic his way. He dissolves the magic midair and retaliates, but I block it.

"If I didn't need you and your power to free my brethren, I would kill you right now, girl," he snarls.

I glance to my brother, but he doesn't even react. The Kato I knew is gone, but everything in me wants to get a rise out of him, to show *some* emotion.

"Is this who you were talking about? The 'he' in which you had so much faith?" I challenge.

Kato laughs. He *laughs*. And for the first time in my life I want to strike my brother with enough force to do some damage.

"This isn't who I was talking about the whole time, if you must know. I have many powerful allies."

The creature strikes again, and it takes a good portion of my energy to stop it. I quickly lean down and help Alak to his feet. I have to hold him up. He has no strength on his own. I can barely support his weight. I need to get him out of here now. I try to wisp, but nothing happens.

"There is no escape," the creature laughs.

"I got in, didn't I?"

He laughs again. "You got in because I wanted it to happen. I need your magic. I am not letting you out."

The flames encircling us stretch and lick the ceiling. I

glance around, desperate to find a way to escape. For the first time I notice Fionn hovering in the corner of the room. He meets my eyes with such a cold glare I know he will be of no help.

"Felixe," I whisper.

The Fae Fox disappeared when I broke through the barrier, but maybe he can return to help now. With some effort, Felixe appears on my shoulder. He's weaker than normal, but I can tell he still has magic. Alak mumbles something against my ear, but I can't make it out completely.

"What?" I whisper on the verge of panic.

"Take my magic," he says, only slightly clearer, his voice hoarse and garbled by blood.

"I can't. In your state it will kill you," I protest.

"It really matters not," the creature says with a carefree shrug. "I plan to kill him in a moment. And then probably you when I am done extracting what we require."

No. I can't die here. Ehren's broken face flashes into my mind. *Come back to me.* I promised him I would. I have to. I reach inside and pull every bit of magic I have. Alak senses me reaching for my magic and forces his into me with what little energy he has. I don't fight it. I embrace it. I reach into the well of power stored in the stone. I don't know if it's enough, but I have to try. I combine it all and thrust it forward with as much force as I can. I feel the barrier breaking down. I hear the Dragkonian say something to Kato, but I can't make out his words. I push harder and the barrier cracks. It's a small crack but it's enough for me to slip through with Alak and Felixe in tow. I feel myself spiraling into nothing and I focus. I focus on Ehren and Bram and how they make me feel safe and wanted. I focus on Makin's laugh and Cal's shy blush. I focus on Nyco's sheepish grin and Sama's caring touch. I focus on Kai's careful smile reserved for only a few. I focus and I find my way home.

My feet hit the ground and I manage to hold onto consciousness just long enough to know I made it. I see Ehren rushing toward me. I hear someone calling my name. Then, the world goes dark.

Part Three:
Together

CHAPTER THIRTY
ASTRA

I'm on a battlefield that seems to stretch on endlessly. There are no bodies like before, but the ground is soaked in so much blood the ground is like mud.

"You pushed yourself too far, you know," a voice says from behind.

Anger swells in me as I spin and find the dream version of myself standing behind me. She stands tall, draped in her purple cloak, the hood down. I open my mouth to snap back at her but pause. She's different. She still looks like me but at the same time, she's changing. Her features have altered slightly. They're sharper, longer. She holds herself differently.

"Who are you?" I whisper, noting every subtle difference.

She smiles. "I thought we already established this."

I shake my head, taking a step toward her. "No. You're not me."

She sighs. "You are correct. I am not entirely you, but I am a part of you."

"My power?"

She nods. "The source of it."

"What does that even mean?"

"Now is not the time to discuss it, but I'll have to tell you everything soon, I'm afraid. Much sooner than I anticipated."

Her eyes stare off, past me, unfocused.

"Because of the Dragkonian?"

"Yes. I thought we had more time."

Now I'm truly angry. "More time? We never know how much time we have for anything in this world. If you knew this was a possibility, you should have told me!"

Her eyes meet mine and everything in me stills. "You are correct, but you are just beginning to understand your powers. You still don't know what you're capable of. Too much information can be . . . intimidating."

"Alak almost died!" I yell, clenching my hands in fists at my sides. "He may be dead by now."

Alak. My head pounds and the world around me swims. I force myself to focus back on the other me.

"Is he alive?" I ask breathlessly, terrified of the answer.

She looks away. "I don't know." She lifts her eyes back to mine. "I don't see much of the mortal world. I am trapped here, in the in-between."

My chest feels heavy. "I need to get back. Can you help me?"

She nods, closing the distance between us. "I can. You are close enough to consciousness I can help guide you back to your world."

I set my mouth in a thin, firm line. "And next time I see you, will you actually tell me what I need to know?"

She smiles sadly. "I will."

I inhale and release the breath slowly. "Fine. Send me back."

She lifts a cold hand to my forehead and presses gently between my eyes. The world around me fades, and I feel like I'm falling.

My eyes flutter open. Everything hurts, and I struggle to think clearly. I can't remember where I am or what happened.

"You're awake!" a bright, young voice chirps.

With a groan, I raise my head and a familiar face leans over me. It's a young girl with long, dark hair and bright brown eyes.

"Hanna?" I croak, trying to make sense of the muddled memory.

A smile breaks across her face and her eyes light up. "You remember me?"

I nod and it hurts, making me grimace. Concern flashes in her eyes.

"You're supposed to be resting. Grandmother told me to give you a tonic when you woke up," Hanna replies, reaching for a nearby cup.

"A tonic?" I ask with a scowl.

I squeeze my eyes shut trying to piece everything together. I'm not in Honeyhallow. That much I know. This tent belongs to Ehren. I'm with Ehren. But how did Hanna get here?

"Yes," she continues. "Your body is still healing." She pauses and considers me for a moment before continuing, her face growing very serious. "You're really lucky I know a Seer, you know. Without him telling us we needed to be here, you probably would have died."

"What?"

She nods. "Pip saved me and Grandmother by warning us that the soldiers were coming. We've been wandering ever since, going wherever Pip thinks is best. And then he got a really strong premonition that we needed to be here. We're not great at wisping, but we were close enough that we felt the surge of your magic. It called to us. When we found you, you were unconscious." Her face pales. "I thought you both might be dead, and we were too late."

Both. Suddenly, I remember everything. I jerk up, my body screaming in protest.

"Alak!" I search her face, desperate for an answer. "Is he . . . ?"

I can't form the words. She glances away, unwilling to answer. Tears well in my eyes. I reach for her small hand and place mine on top. She lifts her eyes to mine.

"Please," I beg.

"He's . . . alive," she replies hesitantly. Overwhelming relief washes over me as I sink back onto the cot. "But . . ."

"But what?"

Hanna bites her lip and glances away. "But he was hurt really badly. He'll live, Grandmother says, but . . ." Her voice trails off and she shakes her head. "You'll see later, but right now you need to drink your tonic."

She holds the cup out to me, and I take it, shifting into a sitting position. I throw back the cup and down the sticky, bitter liquid. It's strong and the effects are almost instant. My head feels fuzzy and my tongue feels like cotton. I relax back onto the cot and let the tonic take effect.

At first I don't dream, but when I start to dream I find myself in a tomb. It's empty and I try desperately to find an exit, but I'm trapped. There's one door, but it's sealed tight. I bang my fists on the door.

"Let me out!" I cry.

"Too good to rest with your dead?" a voice says from behind me.

I turn and find a young man near my age. He's been dead for a while, his flesh rotting and sagging from his bones. His clothes are torn and bloody.

"Please," I beg, my voice shaking. "Just let me go."

"Why would we do that?" another voice says.

I spin to find a similar figure. I blink and the tomb fills with the living dead, their eyes fixed on me.

"I'm sorry!" I weep. "I didn't have a choice!"

"There's always a choice," the first body says, taking a step closer. "And you chose to fight and run instead of giving yourself over."

"How many of us have to die for your cause?" the second corpse asks.

I cover my face with my hands. "I—"

A hand grabs me and I scream. And I'm still screaming when I wake up.

"Astra?"

I turn and find Ehren sitting by my side. His expression is heavy, and it looks like he'd been asleep. I take a deep breath as he blinks down at me.

"Ehren?" I whisper.

"You're awake. Thank the gods," he sighs, relief flashing on his face. His brow furrows as his eyes scan me. "You were screaming. Are you okay?"

I force myself into a sitting position. I'm still a little sore, but I feel much better.

"It's just my normal nightmares. How long have I been out?"

Ehren glances toward the tent entrance where a thin strand of light shines through.

"Well," he muses, "it looks like it's morning and last night made a full two days since you left on your rescue mission."

It's been more than two days. A lot can happen in two days. I meet Ehren's eyes and silently ask the question I can't voice. Ehren glances away for a moment before meeting my gaze again.

"He's still asleep last I knew, but alive." I exhale and nod. "From what I understand, Healer Heora has been keeping him asleep with her magic and tonics so he can heal properly. But he'll have scars, she says."

"Scars?"

Ehren nods and then something in him breaks. He chokes back a sob and engulfs me in a tight hug. I wince slightly but lean into him. When he pulls back his cheeks are damp with tears.

"What is it?" I ask gently, scanning his face.

"I was terrified every moment you were gone," he confesses. "And then you reappeared and there was so much blood."

"It wasn't mine."

"I know. I know. But in that moment I didn't. I just saw you collapse and Alak . . . I thought for sure he was dead." Ehren's voice breaks, and I place my hand on his. He swallows and continues. "And then suddenly, there were these three people who just appeared. The older woman claimed she was a Healer, and I just handed you over to her without a second thought. Only after did I realize the risk I took."

"Bram would have recognized them," I offer and Ehren nods.

"Yes, he did. But if he hadn't . . . Astra, I would have never forgiven myself."

I reach out and wipe away his tears with gentle strokes. "I'm okay. You did the right thing."

Ehren forces a smile. "Thank the gods Fate was on our side." He pauses then asks, "Can you tell me what exactly happened? I had no idea Kato had that kind of power."

My face falls and my heart sinks. "It's worse than we thought."

"How much worse?"

"The worst it can possibly be."

I quickly fill Ehren in on Kato's new alliance with the Dragkonians. All color leeches from his face and he swears.

"How can we fight against that?" he asks, running a trembling hand through his hair.

"With the help of the gods, I suppose," I mumble, leaning against his chest.

He wraps his arms around me and holds me tightly for a moment. We both need the comfort. After a moment, I draw back and look up at Ehren.

"Can I see him?"

Ehren hesitates. "I think you're supposed to rest more."

"Please, Ehren?"

He sighs and offers me a weak smile. "Fine, but if Healer Heora asks, I protested more."

I laugh. "Deal."

Ehren helps me to my feet and I need to lean on him for support more than I expected as he guides me out of the tent. My eyes are still adjusting to the bright daylight as others rush over to me. Bram stands just out of reach, his face set in a concerned scowl.

"You're awake!" Makin says cheerfully.

"Thank the gods," Cal adds as I smile.

"It takes more than evil incarnate to bring me down," I reply as carefree as I can manage.

"You're still weak," Sama says, placing a hand on my arm.

I nod. "A bit, but I need to see Alak."

"Did you tell her?" Kai asks from where he surveys me from a couple yards away.

I look up at Ehren. "Tell me what?"

Ehren shakes his head. "I told you he would be scarred, but there's no preparing for it."

Fresh terror rises and part of me wants to run. I scan the group, but they're all avoiding my eyes, even Bram. I let Ehren guide me toward the other tent. As soon as I duck under the flap my eyes find Alak. He lies on a cot not far away. His shirt has been removed, his chest bare, covered in fresh, swollen scars. The scars swirl up over his neck onto his face. His cheeks are still swollen and much of his exposed skin is deep purple from bruising. With a tremorous breath, I sink down next to him, reaching out to touch one of the seven scars snaking across his face. A sob breaks out at the sight. Ehren stands by awkwardly, not knowing what to do.

"Why don't you allow us a few minutes?" a gentle voice says from the corner of the tent.

Ehren nods and ducks out as I turn my eyes to Healer Heora. She smiles, her eyes crinkling.

"Hello, child," she says gently, kneeling on Alak's other side with some effort. "As good as it is to see you up and about, you should be resting."

I shake my head and look back down at Alak.

"I couldn't rest without knowing . . ." I break off, lifting my eyes. "Will he be okay?"

Healer Heora sighs. "The magic that did this was very dark. It's much more than I ever thought I would have to fight. I did my best. He had many broken and shattered bones, but those were the easy parts to heal. Some of the outer wounds I could heal, but the dark magic used ensures they will leave scars."

My eyes focus on Alak's face as she continues.

"Many of the scars will fade over time so they're less noticeable, but they'll always be there. Especially the one on his back."

"His back?"

She nods grimly. With effort, she turns him on his side and I lean over. Bile rises in my throat as I look at the nasty symbol carved into his flesh.

"Wh-what is that?" I manage.

Healer Heora shrugs as she lays Alak back down. "I've never seen it before. Your young prince has been searching his books, but so far we haven't found an answer. It's nothing good, I can promise you that. My magic recoils from it."

She pushes up from the ground with a soft grunt and makes her way back over to the corner where she begins mixing things from her bag.

"Now, you need more sleep. I know you wanted to check on your friend, but your body needs to heal more. You exhausted your magic to a very dangerous point. You could have killed yourself."

"I had to."

She nods. "I understand, but now you need to rest."

I look down at Alak and take his hand in mine. "Can I stay here? With him?"

Healer Heora considers me for moment before she nods

once. "Fine. As long as you rest, I suppose it doesn't matter where you do it."

I lie down on the cot next to Alak, still holding his hand, but I'm careful not to press up against any of his wounds. I take the tonic without protest and slip into sleep.

I wake a few hours later very hungry. Healer Heora provides me a broth that soothes my aching throat. She looks tired, and I surmise it's because she's been healing Alak. More of his swelling is gone, and the scars don't look nearly as raw. After my broth, I lie next to Alak for a while, my fingers intertwined with his. Healer Heora doesn't insist I take a tonic, and I don't ask for one. I doze off and on for a couple hours before Ehren pops back in, insisting I need fresh air. Healer Heora approves, and I reluctantly allow myself to be led outside.

The sun is just starting to set and everyone is gathered around a fire eating. Cal hands me a plate of food. The idea of eating turns my stomach, but I take it anyway. I manage to nibble a little dinner while I listen to the conversations. My eyes fall on a gangly boy about thirteen years old sitting next to Hanna. I find out he's Pip, the Seer who helped save my life. His long, black hair hangs in his eyes, which he uses to his advantage to avoid eye contact with everyone except Hanna. Even when I try to thank him, he just shrugs.

"He makes Kai look like a cuddly bunny," Makin whispers, leaning toward me.

I laugh and nearly choke on my food while Kai, who sits at my feet in wolf form, growls.

"Have we been in the same spot this whole time?" I ask, glancing around to take in our surroundings.

Nyco nods. "Yep. I have my scouts on full alert."

"You have your *bugs* on full alert," Makin corrects with a shiver. "Just say bugs. We all know it's creepy crawlies."

Nyco scowls but Sama laughs lightly.

"I also have a few spells in place," Ehren adds. "They're helping to mask our location. I don't have many more of the supplies I need to maintain them, though, so hopefully we can move on soon."

"Once my magic is a little stronger I can help with that," I offer and Ehren nods.

"Make sure you give yourself plenty of time to recover. Don't push it."

Sama smiles at me. "I'm really glad you're okay."

Bram abruptly stands to his feet and storms away, mumbling something about checking the perimeter. I glance to Ehren and arch my eyebrows.

"Bram has been, uh, really struggling with, well, everything," Ehren admits, clearing his throat.

I stand and Ehren stands with me, but I shake my head. "Let me talk to him."

"Are you sure?"

I nod. "I'm sure."

Ehren sits back down as I follow Bram's path. The sun is mostly set now and the world outside our circle is covered in darkness. It's cooler than I expected, and I wrap my arms around my body as I step up next to Bram. He doesn't look down at me, but keeps his gaze fixed ahead.

"What's wrong?" I ask carefully.

He shakes his head and clenches his teeth. I place a hand on his arm, and he finally looks down at me. The gold flecks in his eyes shimmer in the moonlight and my heat skips a beat.

"You could have died. You almost did," he says, his voice so quiet I barely hear him.

"I had to save Alak."

"No, you didn't. You didn't have to go. You knew it was likely a trap and you went anyway."

"Was I supposed to let Alak die?"

Bram looks away. "Yes."

I'm slapping his face before I even realize what I'm doing. I jerk my hand back as he looks down at me in shock.

"I'm sorry," I say quickly. I scowl and shake my head. "You know what? No, I'm not. Not entirely. I am sorry I struck you. I shouldn't have physically lashed out, and I apologize for that, but it's time you get over yourself and move on."

His lips part like he has something to say, but I don't give him the chance.

"I know you blame Alak for Isabella, and I can understand that. I really do. But Alak is important to me and our cause. He risked his life in an attempt to bring Kato back. He helped us win over the Clans by obtaining valuable information. Now, thanks to his sacrifice, we know about the Dragkonians, and we wouldn't have that knowledge if not for Alak. He nearly died for us. The least I could do was save his life. And you know what? I would have done the same for you. Or Nyco. Or Makin. Or anyone one else."

"He did it for you," Bram says quietly. "I don't think Alak cares about anyone but himself and you. But you're right, I suppose." He looks back at me and I can see the pain in his eyes as he adds, "I will never forgive Alak. I can't. And if he hurts you or leads to your death, I will kill him. He makes you reckless."

I shake my head. "He doesn't make me anything."

"Yes he does," Bram insists. "You may not see it, but I do. You're different around him. In some ways, you're better, but he also feeds that dangerous side of you. The reckless side. If it weren't for him, you would still be safe. He *will* be the death of you."

"You mean," I spit, "if it weren't for him, I wouldn't understand my magic as well as I do? If it weren't for him, I wouldn't be Ehren's Court Sorceress?"

Bram looks away. "You would be safer. You would be mine and I would protect you."

"Fuck you," I snap, backing away.

Bram's eyes jerk to me. "What?"

"Fuck you!" I yell, furious. "I'm sick of this. I thought we were past this, but apparently you just can't move on."

Bram starts to speak, but I shake my head and storm away. Tears threaten to spill out as I approach the fire. Ehren shoots me a concerned glance, but I look away and duck into Alak's tent.

"Can I sleep in here tonight?" I ask Healer Heora, my voice trembling slightly.

She nods. "I'll prepare you a tonic."

Without a word I sink down onto the cot and bury my face against Alak's shoulder and I cry. Healer Heora approaches and rubs soothing circles on my back for a moment before handing me my tonic. I down it, eager for sleep, snuggling up against Alak.

"I need you to be okay," I whisper, giving his hand a gentle squeeze. "I need you to wake up."

With a sigh of pure exhaustion, I surrender to sleep.

CHAPTER THIRTY-ONE

ALAK

I'm drowning in my worst memories, the memories shifting into nightmares. I stare my father down from a hundred different angles, reliving the worst moments of my life. He yells and swears at me. He hits me. I fall again and again. He reminds me how worthless I am. I don't fight back. I can't. But then Astra appears.

The first time, I'm just a boy and she's just a girl. I didn't know Astra as a child, but I still recognize her. It's her amethyst eyes and her moonlight white hair.

"Stop hurting him!" she yells.

And my father turns to her with a snarling laugh, raising a broken bottle, ready to strike her.

"No!" I yell, lunging between them.

The bottle hits me and I fall. Astra rushes to my side. I look up at her and beg her to run, but she never does. Instead she offers me her hand and helps me stand.

"Together," she whispers.

Then, we both use magic to make my father vanish. As

soon as he's gone, the image resets. Each time it's slightly different. We're different ages. Sometimes it's a bottle, sometimes fists. Astra always appears and helps me stand, helps me feel strong.

Little by little the dreamworld seems to have less hold on me. I know because I'm starting to feel pain. Everything hurts. The more pain I feel, the more alert I become. When I'm able to finally force my eyes open, I think I must be dreaming. Inches from my face is Astra's. Her eyes are closed in sleep and her pink lips are parted slightly. Her white hair is spread out like spilt milk, a few strands falling across her face.

Every movement hurts, but I manage to shift and look around. I have no idea where I am. It's a small tent of some sort. There are a few bags and assorted items scattered around. The cot Astra and I are sharing fills the majority of the tent.

I settle back down and reach a tentative hand out and brush the hair from her face. I don't fully believe she's real until I can feel the warmth of her skin beneath my fingertips. She takes a deep breath and her eyes flutter open. I pull my hand back and tuck my arm under my head.

"Alak?" she asks, her voice still groggy with sleep. Her eyes suddenly widen and she jerks up into a sitting position. "You're awake!"

She looks around the otherwise empty tent. "I should get Healer Heora or Hanna or . . ."

I laugh and reach out and place my hand on hers, my muscles aching. "Just . . . stay." My voice is hoarse and raw.

She takes a deep breath and smiles, giving a short laugh. She lays back down, her face inches from mine. She reaches out her hand and traces her fingers across my face. It hurts, but at the same time it's comforting.

"Do they hurt?" she breathes.

I blink. "Do what hurt?"

I realize with a start that she's tracing actual wounds on my face. My lips part, and I knit my eyebrows in worry. What do I look like? Judging by the look on her face, it's not good.

"Am I terribly dreadful to look at?" I ask, trying to bury my true concern beneath my carefree attitude.

She leans forward and presses a kiss to my cheek. I quiver at her unexpected touch.

"You have a few scars. Healer Heora said they'll probably always be there, but they look much better today." She kisses me again, this time at the corner of my mouth. I inhale sharply as she kisses the other corner.

My body screams at me as I push forward, but I ignore the pain, pressing my lips against hers. I wrap my arms around her and pull her close. Everything hurts, but it's worth it as she leans into the kiss. After a moment she pulls back, tears brimming in her eyes.

"Is my kissing that bad, love?" I tease.

She laughs and shakes her head. "You're an idiot."

I smile. "I know, love."

Her smile fades and a shadow crosses her face. "I thought you were dead. I thought—"

She breaks out into a soft sob. I pull her close again, ignoring the pain. I caress her back and kiss her temple.

"I'm okay, love. Thanks to you." I draw back and look down at her. "Though, you shouldn't have come for me. If you had died—"

"But I didn't," she cuts in. She laughs bitterly and shakes her head again. "I guess we're both fools."

I laugh. "Maybe. I'll happily be a fool for you, though."

Her lips are on mine again, more eager this time. The warmth of her touch outweighs any pain I feel.

"Well, you seem to be feeling better," an amused voice interrupts.

I jerk back with a hiss of pain. I glance to the foot of the cot and find Ehren standing just inside the tent, looking down at us, arms crossed. His eyes sparkle mischievously.

"Morning." Astra grins, sitting up, her cheeks slightly pink.

"Well, Healer Heora asked me to check on you both, but I'm not exactly sure what to report."

Astra throws her pillow at Ehren and hits him square in the face. Ehren laughs and tosses the pillow back.

"Feel like breakfast?" he asks, his eyes switching between Astra and I.

"You should stay here and rest," Astra says, turning to me.

"Oh, I see," Ehren teases. "Kisses are fine but moving for food is off the table."

"Help me up, you oaf," Astra demands, holding out her hand.

Ehren takes it and helps her to her feet. Astra winces slightly and for the first time I remember that she did take some hits. She forces a smile.

"I'll bring you back some food," she says before leaving the tent with Ehren.

She's not the one to return, however. Instead, I'm greeted by a shy girl with long dark hair.

"Grandmother said I'm to let you eat, and then give you

another tonic so you can heal," she informs me, handing me a cup of warm broth.

I take a sip. It's salty but soothing.

"You're a Healer?"

The girl nods. "Healer in training, I suppose. My grandmother is the true Healer."

"You saved my life." It's not a question, but she nods anyway. "Thank you."

She shrugs. "It's what we do. Now drink this," she says, handing me a cup filled with a dark red liquid. After the broth, the tonic is so bitter it nearly makes me gag.

"That's disgusting," I choke.

She smiles. "Everyone says that."

The world around me starts to grow fuzzy. I try to fight it but after a few moments, I allow myself to sink into a dreamless sleep. The next time I wake up, it's night. My body feels much more relaxed, albeit a bit stiff and sore. I sit up and find I'm not alone, but it's not the girl in the tent this time. This woman is much older with kind eyes.

"How are you feeling?" she asks gently, offering me a smile.

"Like I was raised from the dead," I answer honestly and she chuckles.

"I heard you were a witty one."

I narrow my eyes. "You're not going to make me drink another dreadful tonic are you?"

She arches an eyebrow. "Not if you don't want one, but it might help."

I shake my head. "I want out of this bed. How long have I been here anyway?"

"Three days," she replies simply. She tilts her head and surveys me a moment. "Fine. I have bone broth for you to drink, and then, if you like, you may take a brief walk outside."

I nod, sensing there's no point in arguing with her. She offers me a bowl of warm brown liquid and I down it, not even realizing how hungry I was until it touches my lips. When the bowl is empty, I wipe my mouth with the back of my hand and hand her the bowl.

"Thank you."

I struggle to stand, all my muscles screaming in protest, but I manage with no help. I stumble outside. Not far from the tent is a crackling fire surrounded by people, most of whom I have no idea who they are. I recognize the tiny figure of the girl who helped me earlier. Next to her is a scrawny boy with shaggy hair not much older than she is. *Seer,* my magic whispers. I turn my attention to the girl sitting not far down from the Seer. She's got tanned skin and wears a blue headscarf. I startle at the magical void I find around her. It's as if she's drawing the magic in. *Syphon.* Makin and Cal I recognize. Makin laughs heartily while Cal shakes his head at whatever Makin is saying, a tight smile on his lips as if he's trying not to laugh. The boy sitting between the Syphon and Cal is new, too. I can't place his magic, but whatever it is makes my skin crawl. Astra, Ehren, and Bram are nowhere to be found.

"Hey! You're alive!" Makin cheers when he spots me approaching. Cal elbows him.

I grin. "I am. Not sure if that's a good thing considering how much everything hurts."

Makin laughs as does the young man with the odd magic. My eyes settle on him and he grins.

"Name's Nyco," he offers with a nod.

"Nice to meet ya," I reply, my accent a little thicker than usual.

"Want to have a seat? We still have a bit of rabbit left from dinner if you'd like some," Cal offers.

I shake my head. "Naw. I just had a delicious dinner of bone broth." I glance around. "Where's Astra?"

"She's in that tent, there," a voice with a thick Gleador accent cuts across the darkness beyond the fire.

My head snaps up to find the owner of the voice. He's tall and well-built with a scowl to rival Bram's. He's clearly a few years older than the majority of our party, but I doubt he cares. He seems like the kind of person who doesn't care about much. Magic pours off of him. *Shifter.* This must be Kai.

I realize he's pointing, and I follow his finger to a nearby tent, slightly larger than the rest. I give him a grateful nod. "Thanks."

Nyco opens his mouth like he wants to say something, but a sharp look from Kai has him snapping his mouth shut. I pause, cautiously curious, but brush it off and make my way to the tent. When I lift the flap I find Astra, but she's not alone. She's asleep, her head resting on Ehren's outstretched legs. Her hair spills over his lap and he's absentmindedly playing with a silky strand with one hand while the other turns a page in a book of spells. He looks up at me and a grin curls on his lips.

"May I help you?"

"I, uh, I was just looking for Astra," I fumble. "I didn't realize you'd be in here as well."

"This is my tent," Ehren says simply, meeting my eyes like a challenge.

"Oh," I mumble.

Of course. Just because she's not with Bram doesn't mean she'd automatically be mine. I've been away and Ehren is a prince. A damn good looking prince. Hell, even I've considered . . .

"It's not whatever you're thinking, I can assure you," Ehren adds, his eyes shining.

"It's not?" I ask stiffly.

He shakes his head. "No. Astra can't sleep as of late, and I have a way of helping her. But it leaves her defenseless, so she can't be left alone."

"Why can't she sleep?"

Ehren pauses, considering his answer before shaking his head. "Not my tale to tell. The point is, it's not what you think."

"So, she's sleeping?"

"Obviously." He grins. "And I, unfortunately, really need to leave. I have to check the spells around our perimeter and make sure they're still good before joining Bram for the night watch. Honestly, your arrival is almost a blessing. Can you stay with her while she sleeps?"

I clench my jaw. I feel like it's some cruel joke, like he's playing me. My face must be easy to read because he adds, "There's no real catch, I just—"

"What?" I say, snapping more than I mean to.

He's quiet for a moment before he finally says, "I need to know what really happened with Isabella. I need to know I can trust you. There's more to the story. I know there is. But I need to know. For peace of mind."

My heart stops as my eyes dart to Astra.

"Don't worry. She won't wake. She's under a spell," Ehren explains.

"She's . . . what?" My eyes widen as I take in her sleeping form. "Is that safe?"

Ehren stares at me steadily, something challenging in his gaze. "Of course it's safe. Do you really think I would put her at any risk?"

He sounds upset and rightly so, I suppose. "How does it work?"

Ehren waves me off. "I'll explain what I can in a minute, but first tell me about Isabella."

I close my eyes and shake my head. "I can't. Please, don't make me relive that." I open my eyes at look at Ehren dead on. "The day I found her dead was the worst day of my entire life."

Ehren's eyes widen. "What do you mean 'found her dead'? A maid found Isabella."

Shite. I swallow and turn away. I can't look at him.

"I . . ."

Where do I start?

"Well?" Ehren says, his voice suddenly cold and hard.

"For one, I loved her. I sincerely loved her. I was in love with her. I wanted to marry her. I intended to marry her. None of that was a lie." I look back up at Ehren, fighting back my tears. "For the record, I never had sex with her, and I did not take any money from anyone for sleeping with her."

Ehren scowls. "We heard that Dylan promised you one hundred markes if you seduced Isabella and at least one person witnessed you fleeing from her room."

I shake my head. "Look, mate, you can believe me or not. I don't care. No, that's a lie. I do care. And I cared that day when you and Bram immediately believed the rumors. I ran because I knew you wouldn't listen to reason. You wouldn't have believed a street urchin over a noble, no matter how friendly we were. Losing your friendship was almost as hard as losing Isabella. So, yeah, I ran. But I never seduced her for money. I never made her do anything she didn't want to do. In fact, I stopped her from doing things. People assumed, and you assumed right along with them. Yeah, I messed up and didn't handle everything right, but I was barely fifteen. I didn't expect her to kill herself. You have to believe at least that. I actually went to her that morning to apologize for running out on her. That's when I found her. I panicked and hid when the maid came in."

My accent grows thicker with every word as frustration swells in me. I can't help it.

"You were in the room when she was found?" Ehren asks quietly, his face pale.

I nod. "I—I saw you and Bram come in. It broke me. I couldn't stand to stay. I left from the balcony and ran straight to the stables. I rode until I couldn't handle it anymore and then . . ."

I stop, looking down. Ehren doesn't need to know what happened next. He doesn't care.

"And then you tried to kill yourself."

My head jerks up and my eyes shoot to his. "How . . . ?"

"I saw your scars." He bows his head.

I swallow and nod. "Someone saved me. At the time, I thought he was a crazy old man, but now I'm almost positive he was a Seer."

Ehren raises his head. "A Seer? What did he tell you?"

I take a deep breath. I've never told anyone what happened that night. No one knows. Ehren can sense my hesitation.

"You don't have to tell me," Ehren concedes. "I trust you."

"Thank you."

Ehren gently lifts Astra's head from his lap and stands slowly. "I'll find another place to sleep tonight when my shift is over. Feel free to make yourself comfortable. If anything happens, I know the counter spell to wake her. If not, she'll wake on her own in a few hours."

I take up his spot on the cot. He's almost through the door before I blurt out, "He told me about Astra."

Ehren spins back to face me, his eyebrows knit together. "What?"

"The Seer, he told me about Astra." I laugh and shake my head, turning away. "He promised me that if I chose to live, I would meet a girl who would accept and trust me for who I was, and that I would love her more than anything. I thought for sure he was crazy. I could never imagine loving anyone after Isabella, let alone loving someone more than her. All I had was a name, a vague promise, and a premonition involving the twins. But it was enough to keep me alive."

"So, all these years, you've been living in anticipation of meeting Astra." Ehren speaks so quietly I barely hear him.

I look up at him, a bitter smile on my lips, and nod. "Aye, mate. I was told she would need me, and that I would love her. I assumed that meant she would love me back, but Fate is a cruel bitch."

Ehren's face floods with sympathy. He opens his mouth to speak, but I shake my head. "No, don't pity me. I pity myself enough for the both of us."

"I wasn't going to pity you. Astra— Never mind. If there's anything you need me to do, let me know."

I arch an eyebrow. "What can you do about it?"

Ehren shrugs. "I don't know. But you were right. We were friends, and I want to be friends again, Alak. Astra is my very best friend and my confidant. I want her happy, and I think she would be very happy with you."

I freeze at his words. He offers me one last smile before he exits the tent. I settle down further on the cot, my body eager for more rest. I'm tempted to pull Astra closer, but my sore muscles really can't handle it. Instead I lie next to her, shoulder to shoulder, linking my fingers with hers. Despite sleeping most of the day, it doesn't take me long to drift off.

CHAPTER THIRTY-TWO

ALAK

I wake to find an extremely large wolf sleeping at the foot of my bed. I startle into an upright position, my body protesting. I blink several times, but, no, I'm not imagining the wolf. It shifts in its sleep and grumbles. I'm barely breathing.

"Don't mind Kai," Astra says in a soft, sleepy voice.

I turn my head slightly, keeping one eye on the wolf. "Right . . ."

She laughs and props her head up on her hand. "Wasn't Ehren here when I fell asleep? Where is he?"

"He had to help on night shift and check the barrier spells," I explain, trying very hard to pretend I'm perfectly fine with the wolf.

I finally manage to look away from Kai and realize Astra is watching me closely. I smile and lie back down. I reach for her and she snuggles against me. I wrap my arms around her, and she tucks her head under my chin. I inhale deeply, perfectly content. Neither of us speak. Slowly, our breathing harmonizes, and I can feel myself drifting back to sleep. That is, until I hear a deep growl. I start to jerk away, but Astra holds me tight.

"Shut up, Kai," she mumbles.

The wolf growls again, and I sit up, holding up my hands defensively, palms out toward the wolf that now stands on all fours, snarling at me.

"Fine! I'm getting up!"

I scramble from the bed as Astra swears. I turn and start digging through Ehren's bags to find a new shirt.

"One day Kai, I'm going to barge in on you and someone," Astra sighs.

"That will never happen, and you know it," a cold voice says.

I spin and find that a full-grown man now stands where the wolf stood moments before, his cold gray eyes locked on me.

"Maybe not," Astra concedes, throwing back her blanket and stretching, "but one day, I'll find your weak spot, you know."

Kai flashes a very wolf-like grin at Astra. "I look forward to it."

He looks back at me as I pull a shirt over my head. He takes a couple steps toward me and drapes his arm over my shoulder. I wince, but he acts like he doesn't notice.

"Why don't you and I go find some breakfast while Astra gets ready, eh?"

I nod in agreement. As if I would ever disagree with this man. Wolf form or no, he could beat me to a pulp without hesitation.

"I'll be out in a minute," Astra promises with a smile as I'm pulled out of the tent.

I find most everyone sitting around the edges of a smoldering fire.

"Did you enjoy your sleepover with Kai?" Makin teases, making Cal choke on his coffee.

"Yeah, it was blast," I say, eyeing Kai, who still has his arm around me.

Kai finally lets his arm slide away as he walks over and accepts a cup of coffee from the Syphon girl, who's studying me like she's trying to figure out a puzzle.

"Would you like some coffee?" she asks at length.

"That would be great, thanks," I reply, taking a seat next to Nyco to put distance between me and Kai.

"My name is Sama, by the way," she offers as she hands me coffee. She hesitates a moment before adding, "You're the Syphon that was traveling with them before, aren't you?"

I nod as I take a sip of coffee. It's very bitter, but it's good. "I am. And you're a Syphon, too."

"I've never met another Syphon," she admits, cocking her head as she examines me.

"His real talent is illusion magic," Ehren's voice says from behind me. I turn and look at him as he settles next to me. "Is that my shirt?"

"I woke up with a growling wolf at my feet. I grabbed the nearest shirt I could," I say and Ehren laughs.

"Yeah, understandable." Sama hands him a cup of coffee and he accepts it with a grateful nod. "Thank you." He takes a sip. "The liquid of the gods."

"You were supposed to come back after your fresh air," the Healer's voice cuts over the subtle chatter of the group.

I grimace and twist to face her. The woman is small and old but quite intimidating. She stands glaring at me, her hands on her hips.

"I, uh . . . ," I stumble.

She shakes her head and sighs. "Well, you didn't die overnight, so that's something."

"Was that a risk?" Nyco asks, eyes wide.

"Not necessarily," the Healer admits. "But never forget that death is a friendly foe that can approach you at any time, and being careless is a good way to invite him in. Now, come here, boy, and let me check you over."

She motions for me to stand, and I comply. I stand in front of her and she holds out her hand, palm forward, and closes her eyes. A soft golden glow surrounds her hand, and she moves it in front of me, tracing my body from head to toe. When she's done, the glow fades, and she opens her eyes with a satisfied nod.

"So, am I going to die?" I ask, my voice joking but real worry pressing at the back of mind.

"Not from these injuries," she says with a soft smile. "It seems that some special . . . bonds of magic can have extreme healing effects."

Her eyes meet mine, and I know without question what she means. I swallow and nod.

"Oh, is that coffee?" Astra asks, and I turn to see her approaching the others, grinning ear to ear.

She catches my eyes briefly before settling down where I had been sitting a few moments before. I can't help but smile. She accepts a cup of steaming coffee and takes a sip.

"Liquid of the gods," she mumbles.

"I literally *just* said that!" Ehren laughs.

She takes another sip and grins at him. There's a certain easiness between the two of them, and I can't help but feel a twinge of jealousy.

"Are we finally leaving today?" Bram's sharp voice cuts in. I turn to find him glaring at me with nothing short of hate.

"That's up to Healer Heora," Ehren replies with a shrug.

"You're all always so ready to push yourselves to the brink of death to get moving!" Healer Heora cries, throwing her hands in the air. I duck my head to hide a grin.

"So, that's a no?" Ehren asks, arching an eyebrow.

Healer Heora sighs. "It's up to Alak and Astra, but my recommendation is that they take it slowly. They are still healing."

My aching bones agree, but I can tell Bram really wants to get moving. They all do.

"I think I can manage," I say with a shrug.

"Me too," Astra agrees with a nod.

"Great!" Ehren declares clapping his hands together once. "Let's finish breakfast, pack everything up, and get on the road. If we leave now we can probably be to Hounddale by tomorrow afternoon."

Hounddale. Why does that sound so familiar? I notice something shine on Bram's face and it clicks. That's where he's from. Where Isabella was from. I try to bury my thoughts and busy myself by fiddling with the edge of my shirt.

"What about the horses?" Makin asks. "We don't have enough for everyone, even if we redistribute and leave supplies behind from the supply horses."

Ehren nods, chewing his bottom lip.

"What do you mean?" I ask, scowling. "Who else has joined besides me?"

"I'm afraid my granddaughter and I as well as our friend may have complicated things a bit," Healer Heora says with a guilty smile.

"Not at all," Ehren says firmly, standing quickly. "Your arrival saved lives. It was more than fortuitous. We will make whatever arrangements are necessary."

Everyone else nods in vigorous agreement before launching into a debate of how everything should work. The additional mouths to feed have depleted their food supply enough that the food storage isn't an issue. They decide to leave behind one of the smaller tents and more elaborate cots and supplies. The wealth, which, it turns out, is far more than even I suspected, is distributed evenly between the horses. It is decided that some will have to walk alongside the horses. The horses go to those who need them most—mainly anyone who went up against a Dragkonian in the past week, the elderly, and the young.

Once everything is packed away and everyone is situated, we start our journey. It's slow, but we make pretty good time. Though after about an hour, I'm regretting not asking for another day to heal. Everything hurts, and I'm vaguely aware of every injury I sustained. I glance over at Astra and try to read whether she's feeling any of the same. Her lips are pressed into a tight smile, but I can read her discomfort. And I'm not the only one noticing.

When we stop for a break, I practically fall off my horse. I collapse onto the grass, lying on my back and staring up at the bright blue autumn sky. After a moment Astra settles next to me, sitting cross-legged.

"Here," she says, offering me a long bronze leaf.

I prop myself up on my elbows and arch my eyebrows. "Are you offering me leaves? We don't have any food better than that?"

She laughs. "They're billweed," she explains. "It helps

with muscle aches and general pain. At least that's what Hanna said when she just made me eat some."

I pluck the leaf from Astra's hand and place it in my mouth and chew. It's not bad.

"Very leafy," I mumble, and she laughs again.

Gods. I missed that sound. I smile and lie back down, crossing my arms behind my head. Cal approaches and offers us bits of cheese and dried meat. Apparently, it's all we have to eat besides a bit of dried fruit. Rations are low. I feel a little guilty eating any of it.

The break is all too short, but by the time I'm climbing back on the horse, the billweed is working. I still hate riding the horse, but it's bearable. Makin breaks out into song a few minutes later. I don't know the words, but many of the others do. When he finishes, I teach them all a classic drinking song. By the end, even Hanna and Astra are joining in on the chorus. As Ehren leads the next song, I smile to myself. I forgot how much I missed having friends.

When we stop for the night, we opt not to set up tents since that will only be more work for us in the morning. The night is mostly warm, but we huddle around the fire anyway. We weren't able to find any animals to slaughter for dinner, so we finish off our rations, praying we can make it to our destination before we starve tomorrow. Astra casts a shield around us, insisting everyone can sleep and no one needs to be on watch. Bram and Kai refuse to listen and promise to stay up "just in case." Astra rolls her eyes and sets up her bedroll between me and Ehren.

"Do you need me to help you sleep?" Ehren asks softly.

Astra glances toward me, and then back to Ehren, and nods. "Maybe."

"Give me a minute," Ehren replies, stepping away to prepare whatever it is he needs to for her.

I reach out and link my fingers with Astra's, and she turns to me with a smile that doesn't quite reach her eyes.

"Can you tell me why you can't sleep?" I ask, my voice a low whisper.

Astra sighs and looks up at the night sky. At first I think she's not going to answer, but then she says softly, "Because the dead haunt my dreams." She turns her amethyst eyes back to mine, and I can read the distress there.

"The dead?" I ask and she nods.

"All the lives I've taken," she clarifies. "When I sleep without the spell, they show up, asking why I killed them for doing their jobs. And most of the time, they aren't alone. Their families, the ones they left behind, join them."

She takes a shuddering breath, and she looks back up at the sky. I tighten my grip on her hand.

"I have so much blood on my hands, Alak," she whispers, her voice breaking, my heart breaking along with it. "I'll probably have so much more on them before this is all said and done." She turns back to me, and I see the tears glistening in her eyes. When she speaks again, I can barely hear her. "Can you love someone like that?"

A sob catches in my own throat and I scoot closer to her and press my lips to her forehead. "Yes. Without a doubt."

Ehren clears his throat and I pull away as he kneels beside her. He places his finger in a spell mixture before tracing a symbol on Astra's forehead. She blinks a couple times and then, just like that, she's asleep. I look up at Ehren as he takes his place on her other side and gives me a nod. Tonight, it takes a little longer to fall asleep but, after a while, I manage.

Sleeping on the ground leaves me incredibly stiff and sore in the morning. Healer Heora notices immediately.

"Take this," she insists, holding out some leaves that look a lot like the ones I ate yesterday, but slightly greener.

I take them with a wink. "You're my favorite person this morning, Healer."

She makes a tutting sound and waves me off, but I catch her smile as she turns.

With the rations gone, there's no breakfast and no lunch. No food tends to make people irritable, and our traveling party is no exception. No one sings today; instead, we snap at each other for every tiny infraction. When the countryside starts turning into farms and fields, relief washes over us. We skirt around the actual town and head to the outer rim farms. Bram leads the way, coming to a sudden halt, staring off at the nearest farmhouse. Ehren steps to his side.

"That's it?" Ehren says, placing a hand on Bram's shoulder.

Bram nods. "It's been years."

I suddenly feel for Bram. I can't imagine coming home after all this time. My return to Athiedor was different. They were family, but not in quite the same way. To be able to see my mother again . . .

Bram takes a deep breath and leads the way, Kai shifting into his human form. I guess meeting people as a wolf doesn't always come off as friendly. As we approach the house, a young woman steps into the yard and my heart stops. It's Isabella. But no, Isabella is dead. This is her sister. Her younger sister, I realize. I blink, clearing my thoughts and notice the subtle differences between this girl and Isabella, but the similarity is still eerie.

"Are you okay?" Astra asks and I look over at her.

I try to force a smile but it doesn't take. "I'm fine."

The girl looks up at us and freezes before her mouth drops open.

"Mama!" the girl cries. "Mama! Come quick!"

An older woman rushes outside, wiping her hands on her apron.

"Someone better be dying, child," the woman scolds, scowling at her daughter.

The girl doesn't speak, pointing toward us in response. The scowl still holding, the woman looks toward us and Bram just watches, frozen to his spot. His mother's mouth drops open.

"Alexander?" she gasps.

Bram finally finds his legs and he rushes forward, running to his mother. She pulls him into a warm hug. When he pulls back she hits him square in the chest, and I choke back a laugh.

"How dare you not write your own mother these past few months?" she chides.

"I have been busy," he mumbles, red flooding his cheeks.

"Yes, I know," she continues, clucking her tongue. "We've seen the reward posters. I can imagine running from the king is a full-time job, but you could've at least let us know you weren't dead or captured. Do you have any idea how worried I've been?"

"I'm sorry, Ma'am," Ehren says, stepping forward. "I'm afraid that's a bit my fault."

The woman's gaze softens as she steps toward Ehren. She takes his face in her hands.

"You look like you're wasting away," she says, turning Ehren's head.

Ehren's eyes go wide and he blinks, using his most pathetic voice. "I haven't eaten all day."

"Oh, gods," Astra murmurs, rolling her eyes.

Mrs. Bramfield finally looks past Ehren and Bram and takes us all in. She sighs and drops her hands to her sides.

"I suppose you all need a bite to eat and a place to stay?" she asks, her eyes trailing over our group.

"We don't wish to be any trouble," Healer Heora says.

"No trouble at all," Mrs. Bramfield says with a wave. She turns to her daughter. "Diana, can you help these weary travelers find a place for their horses and then go out and fetch your brothers and father?"

The girl, Diana, nods and beckons for us to follow. Bram, Ehren, and everyone that is already walking head on inside while the rest of us dismount and follow Diana around the back of the house to tie our horses before going inside.

The house is warm, friendly, and smells like fresh baked bread and spices. We join the others around a long wooden table as Mrs. Bramfield divides out bread and cheese. Once we all have food, she settles in a rocking chair nearby and watches her son.

"So, can you share with your mother what you've been up to, Alexander?" she asks pointedly. "Last we heard, you were engaged to be married? Has that happened?"

Bram flushes a deep crimson, and he focuses very intently on the bread in his hands. Astra nearly chokes over her own bread and does a very good job of looking away.

"No, Mama," Bram mumbles. "That, uh, was only a cover for the king. There was never any real engagement."

I have never felt as sorry for anyone in my life as I feel for Bram in this moment. He lifts his eyes slightly and meets

Astra's before glancing away quickly. I want to shrink into nothing.

"I see," his mother drawls, but thankfully that's the end of her interrogation on the subject.

An older man with a thick brown beard and three young men swarm into the room behind Diana. Bram leaps from his seat and is greeted by his eager brothers. After a moment, we finally get our introductions. The young men are Lee, Christopher, and Mal. Christopher and Mal are married, but their wives are in town with their children for whatever reason. Diana seems particularly enthralled by Ehren's presence until I speak for the first time.

"You have an accent!" she swoons and my face goes red.

"Aye, that I do," I say slowly. I can feel Bram's cold eyes resting on me, willing my immediate demise.

"Alak has a way of charming everyone with that ridiculous accent," Astra laughs. "Thinks he's something special." She meets my eyes before leaning closer to Diana and adding with a grin, "He's not."

Ehren chokes on his drink as he tries to hide his smile. Bram still seems less than amused.

"I can't help I was raised in Athiedor," I mutter defensively.

"But you could at least try not to steal all the ladies' hearts," Makin cuts in with a grin. "Give the rest of us a fighting chance."

I shake my head, eager for a change of conversation. Mr. Bramfield is kind enough to give it to me.

"So, what brings you all here to our home?" he asks before adding quickly, "Not that you're unwelcome. Just under the current circumstances . . ."

"I understand if you would rather not house fugitives," Ehren says carefully, but Mrs. Bramfield cuts him off.

"Nonsense. I have no idea what's happening in that court but the stories . . ." She shakes her head. "You are all welcome in our house."

"Thank you," Ehren says earnestly, bowing his head. "We need a place to shelter while we evaluate what damage my father has done and come up with a plan. Hopefully, we won't impose long."

Mr. Bramfield nods, assessing the situation. "Very well."

Something about the way he says it makes it clear he isn't happy at all, but he's not one to say a word against the prince. Despite us having just eaten, Mrs. Bramfield insists on making us a proper meal. Astra, along with Healer Heora, offers to help her in the kitchen while I get pulled into conversations with Bram's brothers. It turns out Bram is the friendly brother and comes by his scowl honestly.

Shortly before dinner, Bram's brothers excuse themselves in favor of their own homes, promising to return later. Dinner is a simple vegetable stew, but it's delicious and filling. I try my best to avoid looking toward Diana. Every time I do, memories of Isabella swarm and smother me. It doesn't help that Diana now seems intent on getting me to talk as much as possible. After an hour of dodging her questions with clipped answers, I excuse myself, claiming I need fresh air. It's not a lie, really.

I step outside and take a deep breath of cool night air, closing my eyes.

"I know exactly how you feel," Ehren says quietly behind me.

He steps next to me and I look over at him. "I know it's not her but . . ."

Ehren nods, shoving his hands in his pockets and looking up at the stars. "I know. It's like a cruel trick."

I'm not sure what else to say but, somehow, knowing Ehren feels the same is comforting. I follow his gaze to the stars. They wink down and I smile. Suddenly, something feels wrong. I think for a moment maybe I've pushed myself too much, and I need to rest. A spot on my lower back surges with sudden pain. I cry out, grabbing Ehren's shoulder to keep upright. Ehren turns a worried gaze to me.

"What's wrong?" he asks, eyebrows knit in concern.

"My back," I gasp, reaching a hand back and pulling up my shirt.

Ehren leans over and swears. "Your scar—it's glowing," he murmurs in disbelief.

Pain surges again as the scar heats. I drop to my knees and place my forehead against the cold ground, my fingers digging into the soil.

"Alak!" Astra's voice cries as she rushes outside.

I turn quickly to tell her stand back, but when I open my mouth I can only cry out in pain. She rushes to my side, throwing her arm around my shoulders.

"What's happening?" she asks, her voice thick with fear.

All too soon, we have an answer. A couple yards in front of us a pillar of flames spirals up and Kato steps out. Astra lunges for him, shooting a ray of silver light. Kato blocks it with little effort, laughing. He feints to the right, but his left hand throws a dagger. I try to warn her, but it's too late. She dodges, but the dagger scrapes her arm, a thin red line of blood appearing.

"You missed," she hisses.

Kato stands back, crossing his arms. "Did I?"

"You . . ." She stops, her eyes going wide as she staggers. "Poison?"

Kato nods. "A special blend just for you. We wouldn't want your magic to interfere with my plans again."

"How did you find us?" Ehren demands, standing straight, muscles tense.

"My good friend Akaash carved a tracking rune on Alak here, knowing he would easily lead us to Astra once her magic had a chance to refill."

Astra gasps and falls to her knees. Ehren makes a move toward her, but Kato cuts him off with a blast of flame. The pain in my back subsides enough that I can stumble to my feet. I attack Kato with a burst of magic, but he laughs, warding off the attack.

"Don't insult me with your pathetic magic," he snarls. He turns his gaze back to Astra as she wavers. "Seems you're weak enough."

Kato takes a step toward Astra only to be cut off by a giant wolf leaping through the air. Kai's teeth lock onto Kato's arm, ripping the flesh. Kato's eyes flash as he throws Kai with terrible force to the ground. Kai yelps and struggles to rise. Bram is the next to leap from the shadows, swinging his sword. His blade clashes against one made of flame. Kato meets Bram, hit for hit, inching closer to Astra.

"Enough!" Kato roars. He vanishes and reappears standing over Astra, his sword across her throat. Bram freezes, and Kato's eyes gleam with nothing short of evil. "That's what I thought." He jerks Astra to her feet and winks at me before they vanish in a swirl of flame.

Bram rushes to the spot where they just stood.

"No! No! No!" he screams, his voice echoing through the night. His eyes flash up to mine. "This is your fault!"

He lunges toward me and his hands clasp around my throat. I don't fight back. At this moment, I'm inclined to let him kill me.

"Stop!" Ehren cries, trying to pry Bram's hands from my throat.

"No!" Bram yells. "I've wanted to kill him for years. I've had enough!"

"He may be our only link to where Kato took Astra," Ehren says, his voice heavy but even.

Bram growls and throws me to the ground. I gasp and reach a hand to my throat.

"I'll find her," I promise, my voice hoarse. "On my life, I will find her."

"What are you waiting for?" Bram demands. "Go get her!"

"No," Ehren says firmly, and Bram shoots him a lethal look.

"What do you mean, 'no'?"

"I mean," Ehren says calmly, "we need a plan. You can't just rush in expecting to save her. Astra barely made it out last time. Without her magic to help, Alak doesn't stand a chance."

I hate it but Ehren has a point. And it kills me.

"What do we do?" I ask. "We can't just let them have her."

Ehren shakes his head. "I don't know. I need to think."

"You don't have time to think!" Bram yells, throwing his hands in the air.

Ehren meets and holds Bram's gaze. He stands at his full height, and I see the prince and leader in him surface.

"What we don't have time for is rash mistakes. We need a plan."

CHAPTER THIRTY-THREE

My head spins as Kato jerks me to my feet. I want to fight against him, but I can't. I can't even put two thoughts together. I barely manage to lift my head as Kato whips flames around us to wisp me away. The last thing I see before I disappear is the panicked, near feral look of desperation on Alak's face.

When the flames fade, I have no idea where I am. I'm surrounded by walls of stone with no windows. Everything is lit by dozens of candles scattered throughout the room. In the center of the room is a long stone table. A table with chains and shackles. I try to pull from my brother's grasp but it's pointless.

"Kato, please," I gasp as he drags me toward the table.

"You had your chance to join me willingly," Kato says. "You chose another option, however, and now you must be by my side by force."

He thrusts me down on the table, and I don't have the energy to move let alone struggle. My hands are cuffed above my head, and I glimpse the same runes carved in these as were carved on the ones that held Alak days before. The moment they close around my wrists what little connection I still have with my magic snuffs out entirely. A sob breaks free as my feet are chained.

"Kato," I plead, my voice a quiet choke. "I am your sister. I am your twin. Look at me. Please."

For the first time since wisping me away, Kato meets my eyes. Something in him shifts, like a mask has been lifted. I see the true horror of what he's done register, and his eyes widen with panic. He starts to reach for me; then, as quickly as he changed, he's gone, replaced with a cold unfeeling expression that is nothing like the brother I know. All hope I have vanishes.

"I see she's ready to go." The voice of a Dragkonian cuts across the room as his heavy footsteps come closer. When he's by my side, he leans over my face and looks down at me, sneering. "Just try to get out of this one."

I spit in his face and he growls, striking my face. It stings and warm blood dribbles down my cheek, but I meet his gaze with every bit of defiance I can muster in my current state.

"You underestimated me once and you're doing it again," I reply through clenched teeth.

He chuckles and stands straighter. "You are a feisty one. I like that. I was planning on killing you when we were done draining all your magic, but I might save you for breeding instead."

The horror that ripples through me must be evident on my face because he chuckles again and traces a long talon down my face. I flinch away, which delights him even more.

"Yes. So many humans are pathetic and weak. They can't stand up to breeding but you"—his talon traces lower across the curve of my breast—"may be a good bitch for us."

I gasp with relief when he lifts his finger. "I'd rather die."

"That can be arranged."

I hear more footsteps and the creature turns to look toward the newcomer. I raise my head enough to see Fionn approaching, his eyes flashing with delight when he discovers me on the table. Kato steps toward him and takes the bowl he's carrying, placing it on a pedestal to the right of my head. I catch a glimpse of shimmering black liquid that smells like rotting flesh. I gag.

"Fionn here has also found his uses," the creature says, placing a hand on Fionn's shoulder. Fionn at least has the good sense to flinch in fear. "He is our little spell caster and potion master. This potion will help us drain your magic while retaining it for later use."

"Why?" I gasp. The effects of the shackles combined with the poison fumes are starting to quickly pull me under. "Why do you need my magic? You clearly have plenty of people willing to help you. Why me?"

The Dragkonian considers me for a moment, but answers despite his reservations. "You have very strong, raw magic. It is difficult to find magic like yours. Your twin has similar magic and was, therefore, able to free me. But the bastards that sealed our Isle were clever. They made it so that no one person could open our gates. Kato was able to crack the spell enough to release me, but my brethren are still trapped. With your magic, we can free my army."

My heart stops beating. Kato can't want this. He can't. No one can. An army of Dragkonians will destroy everyone and everything. But one glance to Kato shows he feels no fear.

"Now," the creature says, dipping a claw in the swirling liquid, "let's begin."

He lets a single drop of the liquid fall on my forehead. The second it touches my skin, I scream. I feel like everything inside me is being flipped inside out. A second drop hits and fire floods my veins. I vaguely hear someone mumble something and the next thing I know, everything goes dark and silent.

I'm alone, sitting on the edge of the table. The shackles and chains lie in a pile at the foot of the table. Standing a few feet away is a cloaked figure, her back to me.

"I need answers now," I demand.

Her shoulders drop and she sighs, turning to face me. The differences between us are clearer now. There's still a resemblance, but she's obviously not me anymore.

"Start with your name. Who are you?"

She smiles sadly. "I feel like you already know the answer to the that." She pauses and adds, "I am a physical representation of your magic—that was no lie. However, I am more, and you know who I am."

"You're Aoibhinn, aren't you?"

She nods. "I am."

"How did I end up with your power?"

She exhales slowly. "You have to understand, this was all supposed to be a solution to a problem. I told you last time, I don't have a real foothold in the physical world. There a a few things I can sense, largely tied to Alak, but I rely mostly upon your mind and your memories. I thought everything was working as it was planned."

I stand. "What was planned?"

She shakes her head and places a hand to her forehead. "I'm not even sure where to start."

I cross my arms. "The beginning is usually a good place."

"You're right. You know my story, or at least a version of

it that's survived the ages, but the essential details are correct. I was gifted by the gods with magic before I was born. I wasn't the first to be gifted, but magical humans were rare and far between at that time, though magical creatures and species existed. People feared me and locked me away for things beyond my control. When I finally escaped my imprisonment, I was tempted to lash out."

"But you didn't," I cut in. "You used your magic for good. Helping and healing."

She nods. "Yes. I can't say I never made any mistakes and that I only ever did good, but I strived to better the world. For years I succeeded, and I was content. But I stopped aging, and everyone I loved began to die." She lowers her head as sadness shimmers in her eyes. "I swore I'd never love. I focused even more on good deeds, but everything started to change when I met him."

"Who?"

She raises her eyes to mine. "Caedios."

My eyes widen. "The dark wizard?"

She glances away. "Yes. The first time I met him he was a young boy, taken in by a wizard friend. He was kind and gentle, but even then I could tell he was broken, shaped by his past. I found myself visiting him more and more and, as he grew older, we became close. As you know, the wizard was like a father to him and when he was murdered, Caedios snapped. He tried to reach out to me, but I didn't arrive in time, so he called to dark forces. When I arrived, Caedios was driven by blood and revenge."

"And you just let him continue his slaughter?" I ask with a scowl.

"No! Of course not! I reasoned with him, and I thought I

reached him for a while. He played the part well, and we grew very close."

"You were lovers."

She nods. "Yes. We soon discovered that he was no longer aging. It seemed like fate. I no longer had to be alone." She pauses then adds, quietly, "You have no idea the loneliness immortality brings with it. Not yet."

She lifts her eyes back to mine. "Eventually, I had to come to the realization that Caedios wasn't who I wanted him to be. He was too influenced by his dark magic. So we parted ways. For decades that was enough, but he grew too powerful. The gods that had granted me my power made me an offer. They would give me a weapon that could kill an immortal, and if I killed Caedios, they would allow me to enter their ranks as a goddess. I would no longer walk the earth alone. I accepted."

"And you did it," I say. "I saw a record of it. You slew him with a magical sword."

"Aye, I did. It was the hardest thing I ever had to do, but Caedios was cleverer than we gave him credit for. He used the darkest of magic to bind his soul to this world. He made it so he could be born again, this time with magic. The gods tried to undo it, but the best they could do was alter his magic and manipulate the details."

"What do you mean? What did they do?"

"They delayed his reincarnation and put into effect the process that would eventually separate magic from the human realm. They ensured that he would be reborn in a time where magic didn't exist. They also bound him so that only a piece of him—his magic-infused soul—could return. His magic would be placed in a new host, and I would be right alongside that host to help guide him and keep him from repeating his past sins."

"Wait," I interrupt with a scowl. "You're saying that Kato is possessed by the soul of Caedios?"

Aoibhinn nods slowly. "And I am bound to you in the same way, only your choices are entirely your own. The only way we could guarantee our powers would manifest together was to—"

"Be born as twins," I finish for her. I'm equally impressed and horrified. "Why didn't you tell me any of this before?"

"At first, I couldn't really remember. It's like all the time that passed was a long sleep. By the time I remembered all the details, it seemed like the plan worked. It wasn't until Kato was already too far gone that I realized the plan had failed."

I close my eyes, processing the information. "Is there any way to bring back the Kato I know?"

I open my eyes to find Aoibhinn watching me sadly. "I have no idea. At first, maybe, but now . . ." She shakes her head. "Every dark action and every dark thought drags him deeper, giving Caedios a stronger hold. As I communicate and influence you, Caedios does to Kato, but Caedios has more dark influence that allows him to have more control. I don't even know if your brother can truly exist anymore. He is likely a mere shell at this point."

I shake my head and turn away from her. "No. No. There has to be a way." I spin back to face her. "I have to save my brother!"

"If anyone can, it's you. But know it may not be possible. Be prepared for that possibility. And be prepared for the solution should you fail."

"The solution—" I break off as the pieces fall into place. I shake my head, fighting back tears. "I will *not* kill my brother. I—I can't."

Aoibhinn crosses the distance between us and places a gentle hand on my shoulder. "When the time comes, you may have no choice."

A tear breaks free as I shake my head harder. "No. I can never— No."

She sighs. "Let's pray you can save your brother, then." She pauses and glances up. "It's time for me to go. You're about to wake up. Stay strong, Astra. You can survive this. Just hold out. He's coming."

Aoibhinn disappears as I feel myself pulled into consciousness. Everything hurts. I slowly open my eyes, but the world is blurry and out of focus.

"See," Kato's voice says. "She's not dead."

"We need to allow her magic to replenish before we drain more," the creature says. "We can get more that way. Better to have more than necessary than not enough."

Kato sighs. "Fine." He glances toward me for a moment before he turns and walks away. "I'm going to get something to eat."

Kato leaves my line of vision and his footsteps fade. A tear slides down my cheek as I stare at the ceiling.

"Not so brave anymore, are you?" the creature snarls with pleasure. He steps closer. "I told you there would be no escape. I do not do well with losing, and I will not lose to you again."

He leaves the way Kato did and the lights snuff out once he's gone. I'm drowning in darkness, and I have no way of escape. For the first time, I feel truly without hope.

CHAPTER THIRTY-FOUR

ALAK

Ehren grabs his bags and locks himself in a room while the rest of us are expected to wait. Bram's family does the best they can to distract us, but there's no way to hide the unease in the room. Kai paces the room like an agitated animal before finally shifting and going outside to guard the farmhouse. I feel caged in the house and eventually go outside myself. I walk as far from the house as I can toward a barn at the back of the property. I pause outside and glance at my reflection in a rain bucket. It's the first time I've seen my face since receiving my newest scars. Seven jagged lines cut across my face at odd angles. They're thin enough that my features are clear beneath them, but my face is forever altered.

Akaash did this. Kato did this. And now they have Astra. I couldn't stop her from being taken. I failed. I fecking failed her. Again. Gods know what they'll do to her.

I scream and kick a wooden pail sitting on the ground so hard it splinters. I sink down onto the ground, leaning against the rain barrel, and pull my knees up against my chest. I lean forward, placing my head on my knees as the sobs break free. My entire body shakes from anger and frustration. I feel completely and entirely helpless.

"Get up."

I lift my eyes and find Bram glaring down at me.

"Go away," I mumble.

"Get up," he repeats with more force. When I don't move, he leans down and grabs my arm, jerking me to my feet.

"Feck off, mate!" I snap, yanking from his grasp.

"This is your fault, and you're going to take me to her now," Bram orders.

I shake my head. "Ehren's making a plan."

"Damn Ehren and his gods-forsaken plans! It is just as much his fault as yours that Astra is in this mess! He kept pushing her to use her power and now it has all backfired. I don't care about what he is planning. He has been locked in that room for hours. It is nearly dawn and every minute we waste could be another minute Astra suffers."

I give a bitter laugh. "You want nothing more than to rush in and save her, but you can't. You *can't.*"

"I can and I will."

I set my jaw, meeting his gaze. "Not without me you can't. And you hate that, don't you?"

His fist flies through the air and I barely manage to duck before it makes contact. I grab his arm to flip him, but he kicks my legs out from under me. I crash to the ground, my already sore muscles screaming. His next punch lands on my cheek, but I kick him off, scrambling to my feet. He swings and I dodge, punching up and knocking his chin. He steps back and spits blood. I expect him to come to his senses and back down but he doesn't. He's like a feral animal, cornered and looking for any way out.

"Look, mate," I say, holding my hands up defensively. "We can fight all night, but it won't bring her back. Trust me, I'd love to get in a few more punches. If we storm in without a way out, we're only killing ourselves and possibly her along with us."

Bram's shoulders drop, and he hangs his head. "I just—"

"I know," I say, taking a step toward him. "I know. Now, how about we head back to the house?"

Bram nods slowly and we begin making our way back to the house. We're nearly there when Ehren comes rushing out.

"There you are!" he cries, racing toward us.

"Do you have a plan?" I ask, scanning Ehren's face.

He nods and licks his lips. "I do." He reaches into his pocket and pulls out two glowing stones.

"Luvgim?" Bram asks, furrowing his brow. "How can that help?"

"Alak has a connection to Astra. According to Sama, they have a soul bond." Ehren glances to me for confirmation.

"I . . . yes. But it's incomplete," I confess, avoiding looking at Bram.

"Still," Ehren continues, "it's enough that you can find her no matter her location and get to her." I nod. "But getting to her does no good if you can't get back. That's where the Luvgim comes in. It will give an extra boost of magical energy and, since it can be used by someone with no magic, someone else can go with you as backup."

Ehren's eyes drift to Bram and he straightens. "How do I get it to work?"

"Well, that's the thing," Ehren says. "You don't really

have any magical training, so you don't really know how to use the Luvgim on your own. That's why I've been finding spells in my books I could tie to the stones, so you can access the necessary magic more easily. This gem"—he holds up the smaller of the stones—"has enough power to help you wisp along with Alak and back again with Astra in tow." He holds up the other. "This one contains a very strong and very ancient spell meant to break almost any barrier. Its effects will be momentary, so once you activate the spell you have only a second to leave. Don't use it until you are completely ready. If you use it too soon, you'll be trapped."

"I don't know that it will be enough," I admit. "You weren't there. Akaash—the Dragkonian—is extremely powerful. We'll have to fight our way out. My magic won't be enough, even with whatever help the Luvgim can give Bram."

Ehren nods. "I know. That's why we also have these."

He holds up two objects. It takes me a moment to realize he has Astra's Syphon Stone bracelet. I snatch it from his hands.

"How did you get this?" I demand.

"Pip apparently told Hanna that Astra might be separated from us, unable to access her magic. When Hanna warned Astra, she left it in their care so we would have it to help get her back."

"That little twit," Bram growls. "He knew? And he let her be taken?"

I admit, I'm angry at this fact, too, but Bram looks like he would literally kill Pip right here and now. Ehren holds up a hand.

"Stand down," Ehren commands firmly. "He didn't really know anything. He just had a vague feeling. Hanna told me he also senses a link between this Syphon Stone and her return."

"So we get Astra back?" I ask, barely daring to hope.

Ehren meets my eyes. "It's a possibility. In this stone, I put the spell Astra used last time to unlock the spelled shackles, but a touch stronger. The stone also holds a very strong attack spell." Ehren pauses and holds up a ring, which I realize also has a small Syphon Stone. "I also added a defense and shield spell to my ring. They're not as strong, and they may not do much against such a powerful dark creature, but it should do something, possibly giving you a chance at escape."

Ehren looks from me to Bram, worry and determination in his eyes. "Do you understand? I know it's not much, but it's all we have. This is our one chance."

"Got it," Bram says, holding out his hand. "I can do it." I clear my throat and he glances at me, adding stiffly, "*We* can do it."

Ehren drops the Luvgim stones in Bram's open hand and offers me the bracelet and ring. I slip them on. Ehren takes a step back and eyes us.

"You two will truly have to work together. You realize that, right? Any divide between you and everything falls apart."

Bram studies me for a moment but finally nods.

"For Astra, whatever it takes," Bram says and I nod in agreement.

"All right. Good luck," Ehren replies with a nod. "Bring her back safe." He pauses and smiles, though it's stiff and forced. "And try not to die yourselves."

"On my life, Astra will return," I swear.

Bram exhales and turns to me. "So, how do we do this?"

He's nervous and unsure. Somehow, this helps me feel steadier. I extend my hand to him. He scowls at my hand. I roll my eyes.

"Take my hand if I'm to guide you," I instruct. He lifts his hand but hesitates. "Weren't you the one complaining about how limited time is?"

With a grunt he grabs my hand. I swallow, nerves swelling in my stomach. We're really doing this.

"Okay, now, I'm not sure how the Luvgim works, but usually with magic, contact is key."

He sticks his other hand in his pocket, and I feel the surge of magic the moment he brushes against the Luvgim. It's magic is unlike anything else I've encountered. I close my eyes and roll my neck as I adjust to the magic, careful not to Syphon it away.

"What now?" Bram prompts, shifting uneasily.

I open my eyes and Bram startles.

"Your eyes are glowing," he mumbles.

"Must be the effects of the Luvgim," I reply. I glance around. "Felixe?"

Felixe appears on my shoulder, and I reach up a hand and stroke his head. He looks up at me with wide, terrified eyes.

"Can you take me to her?" I ask.

Felixe replies with a low whine. Felixe is scared. Not just for himself, but for me and Astra.

"We'll be fine, okay?" I promise, stroking him again. "I have to get to her, though. You can help, right?"

Felixe holds my gaze for a moment before replying with a short yip.

I release a long breath and look over at Bram. "Let's do this."

I close my eyes and concentrate on the incomplete bond. With Felixe channeling my magic it's easier, but the bond is so faint. Too faint. But at least it's still there. That means she's not dead. I pull on the bond and let my magic do the rest. Even taking Bram along with me, it's like slicing a hot knife through butter. Until I reach the end destination. There's a barrier. A strong one. I feel Felixe's magic surge as we push through. The barrier is meant to keep out people like me and Bram, but Felixe has a power all his own. It hurts like hell as we pass through, but it works.

We land hard, falling to the ground. I feel the loss of magical connection as Bram's hand pulls from mine. I can't sense Felixe at all. I stumble to my feet. Everything is dark. At first I'm afraid my sight has been affected until I turn and notice a low, dark glow not far away. I breathe a sigh of relief. At least I'm not blind. I summon a touch of magic and form a ball of soft glowing white light in my palms. It's nowhere near what Astra could do, but it's enough to see by. As my eyes adjust, I gasp. Lying not far away, next to the dim dark glow, is Astra, chained to a table.

"Astra!" Bram cries rushing past me.

It takes me a moment to find my feet but when I do, I follow him. He leans over her and presses his head to her chest.

"Sh-she's alive, isn't she?" I ask, terrified of the answer.

I can feel the bond. She has to be alive. But it's not enough to keep me from panicking.

Bram rises slowly and looks at me grimly.

"She's alive," I say firmly.

"Barely," he admits, and I breathe a sigh of relief and reach out to her.

She's cold. Too cold. I scan her body. She has shackles on her hands and feet.

"We need to go. We'll be discovered soon."

Bram nods. "Unlock her shackles and I'll carry her."

I open my mouth to argue, but we don't have time. My body is still recovering from my last encounter with Kato and Akaash, and I'm not sure how well I can stand a fight against them should they appear. I nod and draw from the magic in the stone on my wrist. I close my eyes and sort through the stored spells. I find the right one, pulling it to the surface. The shackles click open, and I open my eyes. Bram doesn't hesitate, immediately scooping her up.

"Now, now," Akaash's voice cuts through the darkness.

I spin as candles flicker to life all around us, revealing Akaash standing in the corner of the room with Kato by his side. I summon swirling attack magic around my fingertips, but I know I don't stand a chance against Akaash and his dark magic.

"I don't like when when people take what belong to me."

"Astra doesn't belong to you," I spit. I glance over my shoulder at Bram. "Get her out of here."

Bram's lips part as he considers what I've said. He has the Luvgim. He can get her out, but he shakes his head. "We're all making it out of here."

I shake my head as Akaash laughs.

"You are all so optimistic. It is refreshing in a way. Being locked up for centuries has been boring. At least you humans are entertaining with your level of stupidity." He strides toward us, Kato following. He stops a few feet away with a snarl as I cast a simple attack spell from the ring. "You'll die for that."

"Try me," I reply.

I take a step backward toward Bram. We have to be touching to wisp together. Akaash notices my movement and throws up a barrier of black fire between us. My magic recoils and flickers out. My body flinches in the memory of what that fire can do. Akaash flashes his teeth and takes another step toward me.

"There will be no escaping this time, Syphon. You will die today. And when I am done with your prized female, I will make her mine, and kill her after she births my offspring."

Every bit of self-preservation in me vanishes at his words. I don't care if I die. I glance back at Bram and Astra through the wall of black flame. My resolve shatters. I won't make it out alive. And that's okay. I smile. Today I die, but it's for a worthy cause. I straighten and stand at my full height and look dead into Akaash's glowing eyes.

"You should really stop underestimating us."

I unleash the attack spell Ehren put in Astra's stone, and it's enough to knock Akaash back several feet. I maintain the blast and throw up the shield spell around Bram and Astra.

"Get her out of here!" I yell over my shoulder.

I turn my focus back to Akaash as his magic responds to the attack. I throw in as much of my magic as I can and extend the power of the spell, my body shaking with the effort. It takes all my focus, and I hope Bram listened to me. I feel the shudder of powerful magic from behind me, and I know he's released the magic meant to break the barrier. All hopes of escape sink within me. I prepare to surrender the last of my power to a final attack when I feel a hand grasp my shoulder, pulling me into a dark void.

We're spinning, weightless and wandering. I can sense a hand on my shoulder, and I struggle to organize what magic I have left. We tumble from the void and plummet to the ground. I land face first, fresh soil filling my mouth. I'm weak and every inch of my body trembles with the effort it takes not to slip into unconsciousness, but I force myself up with my palms, spitting out the mud in my mouth. I hear coughing from behind me and turn my head as Bram rises to his feet, Astra in his arms. His eyes find mine. I try to stand but I can't. The best I can do is make it to my knees and even that's a struggle. My heart stops as I stare at Astra, limp in Bram's arms. If she's dead because Bram tried to save me, too . . .

"What did you do?" I yell, my head pounding. "You were supposed to get her and leave. You were supposed to . . ." My voice catches and ends in a sob.

"She's alive," Bram says, "but she won't be for long. We need a Healer."

I look around. We're in a forest nowhere near Hounddale. I shake my head. "Where are we?"

Bram scans our surroundings. "I don't know. I can't . . . I don't know how to wisp. I just pulled us out."

I release a sigh and sink back down to a sitting position. It's all I can do not to collapse entirely. Bram eyes me with concern.

"Are you okay?"

I shake my head and run a trembling hand through my hair. "No. I'm not. I'm almost completely drained. I was ready to die. I didn't think I'd need my energy." I look up at Bram. "We need a miracle."

Felixe appears a few feet away, and he looks from me to Astra. He yips and spins, wanting me to follow him. I try to rise but I can't. I drop to the ground and fight back a sob. I raise my eyes to Felixe with desperation. He wisps to me and presses his forehead against mine. I feel the slight transfer of magic. It's not much, but I manage to rise to my feet. I'm still unsteady, but I stumble after Felixe.

"Where are you going?" Bram calls after me.

"No idea," I call over my shoulder.

He follows with no more questions as we stagger through the woods after the glowing Fae Fox. I'm wondering how much longer I can last when the woods around us shift. I feel like the ground slides from underneath my feet and the air grows thinner. The trees are the same, but different somehow. Everything is sharper, cleaner, brighter. I wonder if my exhaustion is creating a delusion, but when I look back at Bram, he's staring around in confused wonder.

"What . . . ?" Bram starts to ask, but he trails off as his eyes focus on something behind me and go wide.

I spin and see the most magnificent person I've ever laid my eyes on. He's tall and lean, draped in silk and sheer fabrics. His shimmering skin is paler than moonlight and his eyes are like blue crystals. A crown of silver thorns sits on top of his long silver-blue hair and pointed ears peek out beneath the thorns. His proportions are perfect and he's heartbreakingly handsome. He takes a step toward me, his pale lips parting as he speaks. But it's not words I hear at first. It's music—music that reaches inside me and warms me in a way I never thought possible. But slowly, the music translates to words.

"Why are you in the forest of the Fae?"

Despite the delicate sound of the words, I can read the threat behind them. My mother told me stories of the Fae when I was a child. They are as fierce and deadly as they are beautiful and kind. What side of the Fae you see depends on how you honor them. I drop to my knees and bow my head, my heart racing.

"Please, we meant no offense," I manage, my voice cracking. I raise my eyes but stay bowed. "We managed to escape a very evil enemy and had no idea where we were. Felixe, my familiar, guided us here. We seek asylum a-and help. M-my friend requires healing."

"Can you help us?" Bram says behind me.

I clench my eyes shut and pray the Fae doesn't see his question as insolence. I look back up at the Fae as he considers Bram and Astra behind me. At length, he nods once. I breathe a sigh of relief.

"Rise," he says to me and I use what little energy I have to obey his command. "Follow me."

He turns and walks away. His movements are like liquid, and he traverses the forest like wind. It's nearly impossible to keep up with him as he weaves in and out of the trees, but by some miracle we manage. He pauses outside a large cluster of trees growing so close they are intertwined. He ducks through a small gap and we follow.

The sight that greets us steals my breath, and I stare around in awe. At first I think we've simply walked into another grove of trees, but after a moment I realize that the trees are actually dwellings, growing from the ground and twisting toward the sky above. More Fae wander about, moving as gracefully as our guide. A few of them immediately notice our presence, and I can feel their wary eyes tracking us as we move along the uneven path.

Our Fae guide leads us to one of the dwellings and motions for us to step inside. We comply, marveling at the spacious room we find. A fire sits in a hearth at the far end of the room, giving the room a soft, warm glow. A Fae woman stands next to the fire, her long silvery lavender hair woven in a braid that almost reaches the ground. At first glance she looks young, but when I look into her eyes I can tell she's lived many lifetimes.

She turns her attention to the Fae as he enters behind us and says something in their musical language. This time it doesn't translate, but I don't need a translation to know that she's not happy with humans being brought into her home. Her and the male Fae go back and forth for a few moments. When the woman's eyes finally settle on Astra she nods and motions for Bram to lay her on a bed carved—no, growing—in the wall. Bram obeys without hesitation.

She steps toward Astra and runs a careful hand over Astra's face before jerking her hand away. Her eyes lift to mine and her nostrils flare.

"This girl has been affected by very dark magic," she hisses, her words finally translating to my ears.

"It's not our magic," I say quickly, a little more defensively than I mean to so I add a soft, "Ma'am."

She raises her chin and looks from me to Bram and back to me.

"Tell me what happened, then."

My words tumble out. I'm not even entirely sure what I say, but Bram stands beside me, nodding along, so whatever I'm saying must make sense. When I finish the woman nods with satisfaction.

"We knew the Dragkonians were stirring. We could feel their evil. Whatever they needed this girl for, it cannot be good. I will heal the girl, but it will take time to restore her."

"We can wait," Bram says hurriedly.

The woman looks up at Bram. "Indeed." She tilts her head. "You have no magic of your own."

Bram nods stiffly. "You are correct."

She looks to me as I stagger slightly. "And your magic is nearly drained." I nod and she motions to the bed on which Astra is laid. "Rest."

I arch my eyebrows. "On the same bed?"

The woman looks puzzled. "Do you see another bed? If you wish to rest, this is the place to do it. Besides, sharing a soul bond, albeit an incomplete bond, I would think you would want to be as close as possible. It will help you both to heal more quickly."

Unable to form a reason not to, and to avoid Bram's harsh look, I climb into bed beside Astra and wrap my arms around her. Bram tenses. The woman ignores him and stretches her palms over Astra, her magic glowing a soft blue.

"This is the second time someone has mentioned the soul bond," Bram says stiffly. "What is it? Are they soul mates?"

The woman scoffs in disgust, shaking her head, but doesn't stop her magic. "You humans truly know so little about magic. Soul mates are a human notion that belittles the idea of a soul bond. A soul bond is the most sacred and blessed of natural magic. To lower it to human standards of emotions is abominable." Bram's face flushes a deep red. "They are rare amongst humans but common amongst the Fae, so perhaps that is where your misunderstanding lies. A soul bond exists only between two Fae, or, in your case, humans, who have a connection deeper than anything else. Their magic is meant to be one, together. They each use their own magic, but when they work together there is little that can stand against them." The woman pauses thoughtfully, "Though, such compatibility in magic would create compatibility in other ways, I suppose. For Fae that is not an issue. We don't let our emotions invade our decisions as much as humans. We live our lives by instinct."

"So, she is free to love who she wishes?" Bram presses.

The woman snaps her head around to glare at Bram. He shrinks back as I hide a smile. "Do you wish to badger me with questions, or do you wish for me to heal your friend?"

Bram inclines his head, taking a step back. "I am sorry for my insolence."

The woman makes a tutting sound, but I can tell Bram has won her over a little.

"Elidyr, why don't you find this young human male some food and a place to rest?" she instructs.

The male who led us here bows. "Of course."

He motions for Bram to follow him. Bram hesitates and fixes his gaze on me and Astra.

"Nuala will care for your friends. Do not fear. Now come."

With a sigh of resignation, Bram complies. I realize after he leaves that a weight of sorts has been lifted from me, but I'm not sure exactly what.

"Now," Nuala mumbles, resuming her healing, "I can work. Lie back and rest. No evil can reach you here."

I close my eyes and rest my head against Astra's shoulder. She's already starting to warm. I let the soothing magic and the comfort of safety lull me to sleep.

CHAPTER THIRTY-FIVE

ALAK

I have no idea how long I sleep, but when I wake, I feel more rested than I have in years. It takes me a moment to recall where I am. When I remember, I snap my eyes open and turn to look at Astra. She's snuggled against me, a soft warm glow on her cheeks. Her chest rises evenly with each breath. Relief floods over me.

"Yes, you'll both live," Nuala's voice says.

I lift my head and find her sitting next to the fire in a chair, her hands weaving something out of thin branches.

I clear my throat. "Thank you. For everything."

She shrugs, her eyes still focusing on the work in her hands.

I lick my lips and glance around. "Bram, my, uh, friend that I arrived with, where is he?"

She looks up at me. "He's safe."

I nod. "I am sure. I just—"

"He is with Elidyr." She looks back to her work. "You are welcome to leave and find him. Your bond-mate is safe here with me."

I ease from the bed, careful not to disturb Astra. She shifts slightly but doesn't wake. I stretch and roll my neck. I feel stiff, but the aches that plagued me for the last few days are gone. I start to walk toward the door.

"Do you plan on enacting the soul bond?" the woman asks, stopping me in my tracks.

I don't turn to face her as I reply, "It's up to Astra."

"Hard for her to decide if you won't tell her."

I turn and find her eyes on me. "It's complicated."

She shakes her head and gives me a knowing smile. "It is not. You should not let fear keep you from doing what is best. Sometimes, it is worth the risk to take the leap. It might be terrifying at first but, in the end, the advantages far outweigh the concerns." She pauses thoughtfully before adding, "The Fae bonding ceremony is far superior to the human ceremony. Perhaps, if you can make up your petty human mind, you can leave fully bonded."

I stare at her as I consider her words. I realize that I want nothing more than to complete the bond. I'm terrified at the thought, yes, but suddenly the idea of a completed bond is appealing.

"Now, go find your companion," she mumbles, waving me off. "I have more important things to do than discuss the problems of stubborn humans."

With a nod, I duck outside. The Fae are much busier than they were when I arrived earlier. Judging by the sunlight filtering down through the leaves above, it's early afternoon. I make my way through the clearing, the eyes of the Fae following me. I have no idea where I'm going, but I'm a little too intimidated to ask anyone for help. I'm relieved when a Fae with bright pink hair calls out to me.

"Human!" she calls, beckoning to me. "I can take you to your friend if you're tired of wandering aimlessly."

"I would appreciate it," I say, inclining my head.

She grins and there's something a little unsettling about it. It's probably largely due to the fact that her teeth are just a little more pointed than human teeth, like sharpened bone spears.

"There's no need to be as formal with me. My brother is a bit intense, as is my mother, but I am fascinated by humans and am thrilled to have you in my presence. You can call me Hycis."

She extends her hand to me, and I accept it cautiously.

"I won't bite you," she laughs. Then her blue eyes spark with mischief as she purrs, "Unless you want me to bite you."

"Hycis!" Elidyr snaps, stepping out from the doorway of the closest dwelling.

Hycis rolls her eyes and looks at her brother. "I was just getting to know the human."

Elidyr shakes his head and scowls. "The human boy has no interest in your advances. His interest lies with the human girl."

Hycis looks back at me, tilting her head as she takes me in. She bites her bottom lip seductively as her eyes meet mine. I swallow as color rises in my cheeks.

"Perhaps the human boy wants more than a simple human girl."

"Alak," I choke out and she arches her eyebrows. "This human's name is Alak. And, as remarkably alluring as you are, I confess I have no interest in you."

It's a half-truth. She's a stunning creature and part of me would willingly be led to her bed without hesitation. But, thank the gods, part of me is reasonable enough to recognize the danger she poses and to remember who I truly love.

Elidyr laughs as Hycis scowls and pouts, crossing her arms. "I thought humans would be more fun."

"You have much to learn of the human realm, sister," Elidyr says before turning his attention to me. "Come inside."

This dwelling is much like the one I just left, but it's obviously a home meant for multiple people. There is one main room with two rooms off to the side and a spiraling staircase growing into the room at the back, leading up to additional levels. I scan the room as Bram comes out from one of the side rooms.

"Oh, you're not dead," he says blandly as a way of greeting.

I flash him a smile. "It takes more than that to kill me."

Bram cocks an eyebrow. "Pity."

Elidyr glances between us before turning to his sister.

"Let's allow our human guests to chat for a bit on their own," he suggests, placing his hand on Hycis's shoulder.

She looks like she wants to protest but allows herself to be led outside anyway. Once they're gone, I turn back to Bram.

"So, how's the magical forest?"

A smile tugs at the corner of Bram's mouth, but he manages to contain it.

"It is very different here. The Fae aren't overly friendly."

"Ah, so your type of people," I tease. He looks less than amused, so I grin.

"They've been kind enough the last couple of days, but I'm ready to return to the human realm. Hopefully, we can—"

"Wait," I cut him off with a wave of my hand. "How long have we been here?"

Bram's eyes meet mine. "They didn't tell you when you woke up?" I shake my head. "Three days. You have been out for three full days."

I feel like the ground has been pulled out from under me, and I stumble forward. Bram instinctively catches me.

"Are you all right? Do you need me to take you back to the Healer?"

I shake my head. "I just need to sit."

Bram helps me to a chair and I collapse into it, raking a hand through my hair.

"So," I say slowly, "it's been three days?"

Bram nods. "Yes. According to the Fae you were both nearly dead. They marveled at the fact you were able to stand." He studies me for a moment. "You were going to sacrifice yourself, weren't you?"

I look up and meet his eyes. Brown eyes with flecks of gold. I wince and look away.

"I was," I admit. "Why did you save me? You risked everything to save me."

"I was going to leave you but . . ." He trails off.

I look back up at him. "But what?"

"But, as much as I hate it, I know what you mean to Astra. I also knew you would never leave me behind, and I could not let you sacrifice yourself. The wall of fire fell when the Dragkonian focused his attack on you, so there was no reason for me not to take you with us."

I consider his words and nod slowly. "Thank you."

He coughs and looks away. "It was nothing."

The air is awkward between us, and I'm grateful when

Elidyr renters the room, a tray of food in his hands. He sets the food in front of me.

"I figured you could use some nourishment."

I look up at him and narrow my eyes. I remember enough from the stories my mother told me as a child to know that some Faerie food can trap you and alter your mind.

"Is this food safe for a human to eat?"

"That food is perfectly fine," Hycis says, stepping into the room, a half-eaten piece of fruit in her hand. "We're saving the really enchanting food for later."

Her eyes sparkle with mischief as she takes a bite of her fruit.

Elidyr sighs. "It is safe."

My stomach grumbles as I realize that I'm actually starving. I dive into the plate of food. The fruit is unlike any I've ever had. It's almost unnaturally sweet. The bread is so soft it practically falls apart in my hands. I shovel the food down, Bram watching me with disdain. When I'm done, Hycis pulls me to my feet.

"Now that you're not going to collapse from hunger, I will show you around."

Part of me wants to return to check on Astra, but my curiosity gets the best of me. I allow myself to be led outside, Bram following behind a few steps. Hycis introduces me to a variety of Fae, most of whom assess me with wary eyes, but a few seem eager to meet me. I'm almost surprised to see Fae children, though I'm not sure why. They have to reproduce, I suppose.

We spend most of the afternoon exploring the village and settle next to a trickling river. I'm lost in the wonder of the water when I hear Hycis gasp. I look over at her, puzzled, but her gaze is fixed beyond me. I glance to Bram who sits to her right, and he's staring openmouthed past me as well, his face bright. I turn and everything in me warms and lightens. Astra is being led toward us on the arm of a handsome Fae with long, dark green hair and copper skin. Astra's dressed in a long, flowing Fae dress that makes her look like she's floating. Her hair is down, and on her head sits a simple crown of branches and flowers. Her eyes lift to mine and her lips part into a smile. I realize I'm standing, though I don't remember doing so. My legs move almost independently as I rush toward her. She pulls from the Fae and meets me halfway, crashing into me with such force I almost tumble to the ground. I wrap my arms around her and hold her close. I close my eyes and rest my chin on her head.

"You're alive," I whisper, my voice trembling. Tears spill from my eyes as I tighten my grasp. "You're alive."

She pulls back slightly, and I open my eyes and look down at her. Tears rim her amethyst eyes as she stares into my soul.

"You saved me," she whispers, her voice quivering slightly. "You shouldn't have, but you did. You came for me."

I smile. "I thought it was only fair since you rescued me first."

She chokes on a laugh. "I suppose."

Bram clears his throat, and I pull away from Astra, leaving only one arm looped around her as I turn to Bram.

I lean down and whisper in her ear, "Bram helped a bit."

"A bit?" Bram laughs. "I saved your sorry ass." His eyes meet Astra's and his features soften. "I am glad you're okay."

"Thank you," she says, smiling.

"I must say," Hycis cuts in, "you're pretty attractive for a human."

Astra laughs a full, hearty laugh. I think I might be glowing now. Is this what happiness feels like? Gods. No wonder people like to be happy.

"Thank you," Astra replies, smiling, "but there's no way my beauty can ever compare to yours."

Hycis flashes her teeth in a grin. "Well, human, if you think flattery will win you my respect and devotion, you are quite right." She crosses over to us and loops her arm through Astra's. "Let's get you some food."

"Oh, gods yes," Astra gasps. "I'm starving."

Hycis guides us to the center of the Fae village where a long table is laden with food of every kind. Astra's eyes go wide as she takes in the spread.

"I can eat any of this?" she asks in awe.

"I would not eat anything that glows or sparkles," the green-haired male says. Until that moment I hadn't realized he followed us. "And avoid the Faerie wine if you want to keep your sense."

"You're no fun, Fenian," Hycis mumbles as Astra nods and carefully assesses the selection of food before choosing a plum-like fruit and taking a bite. Her eyes roll back in delight and she moans slightly. My heart quickens.

"This is amazing," she mumbles in awe.

I clear my throat and reach past her and choose a small purple berry. I pop it in my mouth and have to resist reacting the same way she did.

"It's all delicious." I pluck up more berries, popping some in my mouth and offering one to Astra.

She grins and opens her mouth. I nearly choke on my own berries as I swallow. I place the berry in her mouth, my fingers brushing her lips ever so slightly. Heat rushes through my body as I jerk my hand back.

Hycis grunts something that sounds a lot like "Humans."

I turn away and glance at Bram. He's watching us with lethal calm, but if Astra notices, she doesn't acknowledge him. Instead, she starts filling a plate. The rest of us follow suit and we settle down on twisting roots off to the side to enjoy our food. The conversation is light and carefree. I only halfway pay attention, my eyes trained on Astra. Everything feels like a dream. I'm afraid that if I look away for too long everything will disappear.

I'm barely listening to the conversation when someone mentions the soul bond. I snap to attention, sitting straighter.

"What soul bond?" Astra asks, knitting her brows and glancing toward me in confusion.

I take a deep breath and release it slowly, trying to form an answer, but nothing is coming out. I blink at her in wide-eyed horror, my brain scrambling for something—anything—I can say.

"You don't know of the bond?" Fenian asks, looking from Astra to me.

Astra slowly shakes her head as she watches me, waiting for my answer. Trapped. I'm bloody trapped.

"I, well, I . . . ," I fumble, avoiding Astra's prying gaze.

"He knows," Bram supplies for me.

I shoot him the deadliest glare I can before shifting my eyes to meet Astra's.

"I know about it. Yes," I finally concede.

Hurt flashes across her face, but she hides it quickly and turns her attention back to Fenian.

"What does the bond mean?" she asks carefully.

Her hands are clasped so tightly in her lap her knuckles are white. I fight the urge to reach out to take them, forcing myself to look up at Fenian, my mind and heart racing.

"What do you know of soul bonds?" he asks steadily.

"I'm afraid I've never heard of a soul bond, despite all my studies," Astra confesses, her cheeks pink.

Fenian shifts his assessing eyes to mine and I sigh.

"I don't know much. Just that the bond connects two people and their magic in a . . . unique way. Binds them together."

Fenian nods. "In the simplest terms you are correct, but the soul bond is much more. What do you know of Fae magic?"

This time, Astra has an answer.

"Fae magic is from the earth. It's all natural magic. Fae can possess multiple forms of magic at once, unlike humans who can typically only possess so much at one time and are skilled in only one or two forms of specific magic."

Fenian nods again. "Yes. Humans have partial magic. You simply cannot contain the type of magic possessed by the Fae. Your magic stems from gifts, some from the Fae, some from the gods, and some from the Earth herself."

"Half the human gods are Fae," Hycis mumbles under her breath, and Fenian doesn't bother to correct her.

"But even among the Fae, few are able to possess a full realm of magic. Instead, we share magic through soul bonds. While not every Fae is soul-bonded, most are. It is a sacred bond that binds us to our partners, allowing us not only to increase our own magic but also to support our bond-mate, even across great distances. We are attuned to everything they feel. We are connected."

Fenian places a fist over his heart and closes his eyes, breathing deeply. Elidyr mimics the motion in a way that makes me think they must be bonded themselves.

"The bond is sacred and precious. Bond-mates' first

instincts are to protect one another, and they will die to do so," Elidyr adds.

I sense Bram look my way, but I purposefully keep my eyes fixed on Fenian.

"So," Astra says slowly, processing his words. "A soul bond is a way of allowing two people to share their magic?"

Fenian nods. "In essence, yes. With humans, the circle of magic is often still incomplete, but it does increase your magic's stamina as well as your abilities. I can sense the power behind your magic. It is as close to Fae magic as any human I have known in my six-hundred years. If you complete a bond ceremony and embrace the soul bond, you will be stronger than some Fae. This is perhaps why you did not recognize the bond for what it was. Your magic was drowning out the bond. It is not uncommon for the weaker of the two bond-mates to recognize the pull of the bond first."

Astra's lips part as she looks at me, and I can no longer keep my gaze away. I try to read her expression, but it's so many emotions mingled together I can't quite sort them all out.

"You knew the bond existed?"

I nod.

"And you didn't say anything?"

Betrayal. That emotion is definitely betrayal. I wince.

"Aye, love," I whisper.

She holds my gaze, though she speaks to Fenian, "And this bond, it creates . . . feelings that one would not normally have if the bond did not otherwise exist?"

I swallow as panic swells through me. I press my hands firmly against the ground to keep them from shaking. I'm barely breathing as I wait for Fenian's response. Her eyes do not leave mine as Fenian answers.

"While the Fae are not without emotions, we process them differently than humans," he says carefully. "However, a soul bond does not create new emotions or feelings"—he spits the word "feelings" like it disgusts him—"but it can enhance or heighten any emotions or ties that already exist. It creates an ease between the two bond-mates, instilling trust and devotion."

She pulls her eyes from mine at last, and I sink away from her, ashamed.

"You mentioned a ceremony?" she asks, and Fenian nods. "What does the ceremony entail?"

Fenian shakes his head. "I'm afraid I cannot share the exact details as they vary from soul bond to soul bond, but it involves a complex intertwining of spirits. What you feel now is only the surface of what a true bond would feel like if you completed the ceremony and embraced the bond. I can only imagine what sort of power you would be able to wield should you bond."

Astra nods and stands abruptly. "I need a moment."

She rushes away, but I find myself frozen to my spot, watching her disappear into the twist of nearby saplings.

"You should probably go after her," Hycis says, eyeing me.

"I don't know what to say."

Hycis shrugs. "Then don't say anything. Listen."

I nod, stumbling to my feet. I push past Bram and follow the path Astra took. It doesn't take me long to find her. She stands with her back toward me, leaning on a thin tree.

"I'm sorry," I finally manage.

"Were you ever going to say anything?" she asks, not bothering to turn around.

"Of course I was. I just didn't know how to tell you."

She spins to face me, tears glistening in her eyes. "How long have you known?"

I shake my head. "Not that long. Not really. I—I suspected it early on when Felixe took a liking to you. It's very rare for a familiar to be so at ease with someone besides his Master. The more Felixe connected with you, the more I was positive he wasn't just my familiar alone, but yours as well. A soul bond is one of the only reasons two people might share a familiar. But even then, I wasn't really sure. I thought maybe he was just drawn to your pure and powerful magic. The bond itself was so new and unformed. I convinced myself I was reading into everything that made me think it existed. I put it to the test when I left with Kato and used Felixe to correspond between us. I think, at that point, I knew for sure, but I still managed to talk myself down. When I escaped Aine, Felixe bringing me to your side, and I saw you for the first time in weeks, I no longer had any doubts. I knew."

"Then why didn't you tell me?"

She's hurt. And it's killing me. I feel like she's sliding from my grasp, and I don't know what to say to fix it. I'm drowning.

"Because," I huff in frustration, throwing my hands in the air. "Because I'm a fool and an idiot. I was afraid it would change things between us. I didn't understand it, and it terrified me. It still does. I was already in love with you by the time I fully realized or admitted it to myself. I wanted you to love me for me, not because of a bond." She takes a step toward me, but I keep rambling. "And I didn't know how to tell you. I thought surely you must feel some part of the bond, but you didn't say anything. You gave no indication. I didn't know where to start. I couldn't do it in a letter, could I, love? Something like this can't just be jotted down on parchment and sent off. It's something you do in person, face to face, but we were apart. That was my fault, I know. I almost told you after the meeting with the Clans. Gods, love, I wanted to tell you, but the time wasn't right. The time was never bloody right."

I'm yelling now, and I know it. But I can't control it. Everything I've been bottling up for months is spilling out, and I don't know how to stop it. She's slowly closing the distance between us.

"I know I messed up. It's what I'm best at. It's probably my greatest talent. Believe me, I know. But I love you, Astra. I love you with every bit that I am, and I will die for you. I almost did die for you. More than once. And I will risk my life over and over again for you. By enacting the bond, you might feel that same way. You might be willing to die for me, and I can't handle that. So maybe, just maybe, I kept the bond a secret for that reason as well. Because, while I want you to return my feelings, while I want you to love me like I love you, I'm terrified of what that means, of what you might risk."

I stop to gasp for breath. I didn't even realize I started crying until she lifts a gentle hand to brush away a tear. I place my hand over hers and press it against my cheek, yearning for her touch.

"You're such a fool, Alak Dunne," she says softly, "if you never noticed, I feel the same way about you already. I suppose my own daring rescue wasn't enough. What should I try next?"

Her lips curl into a delicate smile and no force in the world could hold me back from pulling her into my arms. I'm not sure if she kisses me first or if I kiss her—it's such a mutual action. I lift her, holding her flush against me as we kiss, barely taking time to breathe. When I set her down, she steps back, her eyes shining.

"Alak," she says, her voice barely above a whisper.

"Yes, love?" I ask, my eyes searching her face in a desperate attempt to read her thoughts.

She takes a deep breath. "I love you."

My heart stops and I find it hard to breathe. The entire world has slowed. I blink, afraid I'll suddenly wake up and find this all a dream.

"What?" I ask, breathless.

"I love you," she repeats.

I lift a shaky hand to my lips and can't hide my grin as her words take hold. "Say it again. Please."

Relief washes over her as she laughs and shakes her head at me. "I love you, Alak Dunne."

I lift both hands, palms together, and press them to my lips. A tear slides free, but this is a tear of pure and utter happiness, of relief.

She lifts her hand, wiping the tear away. "What's wrong?" Her forehead knits with worry. "Did I say some-thing wrong?"

I laugh, looping my arms around her waist. "Nothing. There is absolutely nothing wrong in the world at this moment. Do you have any idea how long I have waited to hear those words come from your lips?"

She smiles. "I love you."

I lower my lips to hers and allow them to linger only for a moment before I draw back. I look down into her mesmeriz-ing, amethyst eyes and brush a stray strand of hair out of her face before gently tracing a finger down her cheek.

"I love you, too, Astra."

I press my forehead to hers, closing my eyes. Our breaths are matched, and I have a feeling her heart is racing nearly as quickly as my own. I want this moment to last forever.

"Do you have any idea how much I love you?" I whisper. "I love you so much it hurts, and I never thought I would ever get to hear you say those words. A piece of me still believes I don't deserve you."

"Alak—" She pulls back, looking up at me, almost alarmed.

I stop her short with another kiss. This one filled with years of longing, leaving us both breathless. I pull her tight against my body, yearning for her to be near. She surrenders completely, arching into my touch. My magic reaches out for hers, and it rises up to meet me. Everything feels like it's finally falling into place. The world may be going to hell, but we have each other and, in this moment, that's all that matters.

But, as with anything in my life, nothing good lasts forever. She pulls back, breathing heavy and looks up at me, swollen lips curling into a contented smile. Doubt rises in me, and I can't keep it from shadowing my face. I pull back, releasing her as I turn away.

"You do realize that everything you're feeling could simply be the soul bond. You may not actually love me at all," I say, my voice rough and raw.

She laughs, light and free. I turn to her, confusion swelling. She reaches out and takes my hands into her own.

"You said you wanted me to love you of my own accord, and that you thought I might be aware of the bond to some extent," she says, her voice quiet but steady.

I nod against my own will. "Aye, love."

"But you heard the Fae. The bond doesn't create emotions."

"No," I say quickly, "but it does enhance them."

She takes a few steps away and each step feels like a dagger directly to my heart. She studies me for a moment, and I barely dare to breathe as she weighs the decision in front of us.

"So, what bits of what I feel are the bond and what bits are true emotion?" she ponders more to herself than to me. She meets my eyes and I can see the scholarly contemplation there. "I trusted you against all reason. Bram, who had risked his life for me already and whom I loved, warned me against you, and I trusted you anyway. I met you alone in the dark of night when you were nothing but a stranger and, somehow, I was never really worried. I knew I would be safe with you. I was drawn to you. That was the bond."

I swallow and nod. "Aye, love. I believe it was. I was drawn to you in the same way. I almost avoided you because of Bram and our history, but I couldn't. At first, I thought it was just because my Syphon powers were drawn to your magic, but now I realize that was my magic recognizing the bond."

She nods slowly, processing. "I was engaged to Bram when you kissed me in my room after the ball."

I inhale sharply, opening and closing my mouth several times as I consider my words. "I have no defense for that beyond the fact that I had been burying how I felt about you for some time at that point, and the pure relief that you were okay overwhelmed me. But, if I recall correctly, you kissed me first."

She nods and smiles, but the smile quickly fades. "But was my reaction due to heightened feelings because of the bond or because I was actually developing real feelings for you? And when you saved my life in Athiedor, what I felt that morning after toward you, was that my magic responding to yours? That's what you're worried about, isn't it? That everything has been the bond and nothing more?"

My heart stops. "You—you felt something in Athiedor?"

She opens her mouth momentarily before snapping it shut and shaking her head. She sinks to the ground and places her head in her hands.

"I don't even know how to process this," she whispers.

I kneel down next to her and place a finger under her chin, gently lifting her face to mine.

"Look, love. I know it's a lot to sort through. I've been sorting through it for months, and I still don't understand it. I love you. I'll always love you, and I don't believe it's the bond that makes me feel that way. But, if you decide not to complete the bond, I understand. It can be as much of a burden as blessing."

She smiles and something in me lifts.

"I want to do the ceremony," she says quietly.

"You do?" I ask breathlessly.

She nods. "From what Fenian said, our bond may be one way to beat Kato."

Of course. She doesn't want the bond for what it means to me. She's too logical for that.

"And," she adds, looking away, "even if it confuses me, I want to be closer to you. I don't care if my emotions are heightened by the bond. I know what's in my heart." She looks back up at me, her eyes shining like stars. "I love you, Alak. I've tried to deny it and push away the feelings, but I love you."

Relief washes over me. "You're sure?"

She laughs again and nods. "Most definitely. And the reason I know it's not just because of the bond is because it isn't only your magic I'm drawn to. I see your eyes every time I close mine, and I long for the comfort of your touch. I love your laugh and that ridiculous accent." I laugh and she continues, stroking my cheek. "I love you. Every bit of you, scars and all."

I can't hide my grin. "Well, I think you might be a little insane to love someone like me, love, but I'm not going to push you away." I take a deep breath and my next words are barely above a whisper. "I love you, Astra, and I want nothing more than to complete our bond."

Her name is a prayer on my lips, and as I say it her face glows. She holds my gaze for a moment and then her lips are pressed to mine. This kiss is different. It's pure. It's holy. I long for her and she longs for me. I barely dare to breathe. All I want is Astra, and all she wants in return is me.

A snapping branch breaks into our moment, and she jerks back, her eyes searching the woods around us. It takes my mind a second longer to adjust.

"Oh, I . . ."

Bram stands at the edge of the trees not far away. His eyes are locked on Astra, lips parted. I think he would look less wounded if he had a physical dagger sticking in his chest. He fights to control his features, and he's not entirely unsuccessful, but I know him too well for him to hide the evident pain. I know Astra can sense it as well.

"Bram," she whispers, rising and taking a tentative step in his direction.

He startles and shakes his head, forcing a smile. "We were just wondering, uh, where you went and if, uh, you were okay. I see you are."

He turns abruptly and Astra takes a few steps after him. She turns and looks at me, guilty desperation written all over her face.

"Go." I offer her a smile and nod. "I'll catch up."

"Thank you." She mouths the words more than actually says them before she disappears into the trees after Bram.

I stand, frozen in a trance, staring at the trees. Then, everything sinks in and happiness and hope surge in my chest. I feel like I may burst. Laughter rips from me, tears of overwhelming joy streaking down my cheeks. She loves me. She really, truly loves me. It takes me several minutes to reel everything in and, even once I manage to stand, I can't hide my smile.

CHAPTER THIRTY-SIX

ASTRA

It takes me several minutes to collect my thoughts. My emotions are a swirling abyss, and I can't make sense of anything. For a moment, I envy the Fae and their lack of human emotions. But no, in reality, I am thankful for everything I feel, because no matter how confusing or how much it hurts, emotions—true heartfelt emotions—are what separate humans from other species. We feel in ways they can't. And while those feelings may make us weak in the eyes of those like the Fae, and they may baffle and confound us, in the end they make us stronger in a way that even the Fae in all their magical might cannot understand.

I grapple with everything that has happened in the past few days. Kato is all but lost to me, but Alak is closer than he's ever been. The idea of the soul bond explains so much, but in itself is a terrifying concept. To think of tying myself to someone, of intertwining our fates so thoroughly, is a lot to take in. It's a crushing amount of responsibility. And yet I've never wanted something so much in my entire life. I want to be with Alak. I know this now. I've tried to deny it, but now I never want to leave his side.

When I return to where the others are gathered, I pause, looking for Bram, but he didn't return. I sigh and scan the trees behind me. I have no idea where he could be, but I have to find him. It takes several minutes of pointless wandering, but I eventually locate him. He sits on the ground, leaning against a tree, eyes closed and cheeks damp with tears. My heart stills as guilt overwhelms me. As I approach, his eyes snap open and flick to me. I stand straighter, calm and composed, wearing the mask of confidence I've leaned to wear well.

"Are you all right?" I ask, even though the answer is obvious.

He attempts a smile and fails. He takes a deep breath, looking away. "I will survive."

I swallow. I'm tempted to leave him in peace, but instead I sink down next to him and rest my head on his shoulder. He tenses.

"What are you doing?" he snaps.

I look up at him, but he refuses to look at me, his gaze fixed ahead. I can't blame him.

"I'm sorry." The words are pathetic and lacking, but they're all I have to offer. "Do you want me to leave you alone?"

He sighs and shakes his head. "No." He finally forces his gaze to me, meeting my eyes. "I should hate you, I suppose, but I want you near me. Always. I doubt that will change any time soon."

My breath catches. "Bram, I—"

He laughs bitterly, looking straight ahead again. "I know,

I know. I saw." He squeezes his eyes shut, shaking his head. "On second thought, give me a few more minutes alone."

I consider arguing, though I know it would be pointless. He deserves time away from me. I nod and rise, brushing grass and leaves from my dress. I walk away but pause after a few steps, glancing over my shoulder at Bram.

"It may not be worth much, but I did love you. I still do, really. I always will. I just . . ."

I let the words go unspoken, but he knows what I want to say. He keeps his eyes closed, nodding. With a sigh, I rejoin the others.

Alak has returned, and I settle next to him. He smiles down at me, and I lean against him as he wraps his arm behind me. The curious and amused eyes of our Fae companions are impossible to ignore.

I turn to the Fae, eager for a distraction. "Are you aware of what is happening beyond your borders?"

They exchange quick glances before the blue-haired male—Elidyr, I believe his name is—answers with a sharp nod. "We have heard whisperings along with what news you brought when you arrived."

"So you know the Dragkonians will soon be free and will reign in terror once again?"

They exchange glances once more.

"We knew that attempts were being made to free more of them, but the task is not easy. It would take an overwhelming amount of cunning and magic to lift the shield we helped to put in place," Fenian replies.

"The Dragkonians are an abomination and an insult to Fae," Hycis spits.

"My brother has already succeeded in freeing one of the Dragkonians from the Isle of Atroxmorte," I reply.

"That should not have been possible," Fenian says, his voice even. "How he managed to accomplish such a task is unnerving, to say the least."

"It's true, nonetheless," Alak says, shifting. "I saw Akaash myself."

I'm not sure exactly what the Fae say next, but I can only imagine it's some sort of swear. They mumble amongst themselves for a moment before Fenian addresses us carefully.

"The Dragkonians were made from Fae magic."

"Stolen magic," Hycis cuts in angrily. "The Fae were tricked and manipulated."

Fenian nods and continues calmly. "True enough. But stolen magic or no, we feel some of the burden of the tragedies they caused in the human realm. When some of the greatest human sorcerers came to us requesting aid, we did what we could. We bound the evil creatures to their own Isle of ash and magma, sealing them in with powerful magic. If your brother has indeed managed to free even one Dragkonian, well, the fate of the human realm is once again in danger."

"Can you help us?" Bram asks, walking up behind me.

It takes all my willpower not to turn and look at him. He settles down next to me, giving me several inches of space.

"Yes and no," Elidyr replies. "During that age, we could pass more freely between our realm and the mortal realm. It was easier for our greatest warriors to aid the calls of men. But our worlds have been separated for too long. When magic faded in your realm, we were cut off."

"But you found us and brought us here," Bram presses. "You have some access."

Elidyr nods. "Some, but it is not nearly enough. We also cannot step from our realm for more than a few minutes without certain protections in place. To imprison the Dragkonians again would require time we do not have."

"In what way can you help?" Alak cuts in.

"Bellyon berries," Hycis replies and our eyes turn to her. "They're a plant that only grows here in the Fae lands. They are a deadly poison to Fae and, since the Dragkonians share some of our . . . heritage, they are affected the same way. The tiniest bit of juice from a ripe berry is most often fatal."

"Do you have these berries here?" Bram asks eagerly.

"Yes," Fenian replies, "but they are not yet ripe. They have only begun to bloom and will not be ripe for months."

Bram's face falls.

"And the berries are no good if they're not fully ripe?" I ask, searching for any bit of hope.

"Well, the current state of the berries may possibly cause some minor harm or discomfort, but nothing that will last or kill," Hycis says with a shrug. "You are welcome to take a few with you as a precaution, but until they are fully ripe, they won't be of much use."

"How will we get the berries when they are ripe if it is difficult to cross between realms?" I ask.

"We will find a way," Elidyr says firmly. "We have no desire for the Dragkonians to wreak their terror on any race or species. When the berries ripen, we will get them to you. This I swear."

"In the meantime," Fenian jumps in, "you can secure your soul bond. Doing so may give you a fighting chance until the berries are ready."

"We are willing to complete the ceremony," I say.

Alak straightens and looks at me with a sense of longing. Bram shifts and looks away.

"Very well. The ceremony works best at sunset and

sunrise. It is nearly sunset now. If we hurry, the ceremony can be completed tonight."

I inhale sharply. I wasn't expecting it to happen so soon. I only found out about the soul bond minutes ago. I glance to Alak. He nods and gives a half shrug. As I meet his eyes, I know without a doubt this is something I want to do. I look back to Fenian.

"Let's do it tonight."

Fenian stands in one smooth movement. "I will go find Master Halzar and have him prepare."

Hycis looks over at me, tilting her head like she's examining an interesting painting. "I suppose we should get you ready."

"What exactly do I need to do to get ready? Can't I just do the ceremony like this?"

Hycis flashes her teeth in a grin as she rises. "Absolutely not! Something as sacred as a bond ceremony requires preparation! You must be washed and cleaned of the earth."

I glance to Elidyr and he nods, somewhat reluctantly. "My sister speaks the truth. But our time is limited, so we must make haste." His eyes shift to Alak. "If you will permit me, I would be willing to assist you with your preparations." He looks over at Bram and adds, "You, of course, are welcome to join us as well, though you will not be permitted to view the ceremony."

Alak and I exchange a quick look before he rises, shaking his head. "Whatever you say, mate."

With a satisfied nod, Elidyr beckons for Alak to follow him. Bram looks less than pleased, but rises, scowling even deeper than usual. Alak takes a few steps forward before turning to look at me over his shoulder. My heart skips a beat as his eyes meet mine.

"I guess I'll see you later, love," he says, his voice rough with emotion.

I can only manage a small smile before he turns and disappears into the trees with Bram and Elidyr. Once they're gone, Hycis swoops toward me, extending her hand.

"Well, are you ready or not?"

I eye her hand for a moment. Sudden nerves swell in me, and my stomach turns. I place my hand in hers, and she pulls me to my feet with more strength than I thought possible for someone her size. I suppose the many stories and legends I've read of the Fae and their superior abilities are true.

She glides through the forest with the grace of a deer while I trip along behind her. We wind our way along the outer edges of the village, but she pauses once to speak to two Fae woman—one with long golden-yellow hair that does nothing to help her overly pale complexion, and the other with deep violet curls perfectly complimenting her dark brown skin. They eye me with interest and delight as they converse rapidly in their musical Fae tongue. They nod, agreeing to whatever Hycis is saying before they hurry off, glancing back at me over their shoulders.

"Ina and Rynia have agreed to assist us," Hycis explains as we turn and continue on our path.

I nod and follow without a word, despite the fact that a thousand questions swirl through my mind.

We finally come to a halt in a grove of weeping willow trees, their long branches dripping to the ground, wafting in the evening breeze. With a grin, Hycis steps forward and draws back the curtain of branches, revealing a steaming hot spring. Hycis steps through the opening and I follow, the curtain falling closed behind us, giving a semblance of privacy.

I gravitate toward the warmth and notice a few Fae spread out, unashamed of their nakedness as they laugh and talk, moving through the warm water, steam curling around them. Color rises in my cheeks. With a nervous glance, I peer around. At least all the Fae seem to be female.

"The males have another spring they prefer to use," Hycis says as if she can read my thoughts. Her lips turn up into a wicked grin as she adds, "And, of course, there is an additional spring for anyone to use and a fourth for carnal activities."

My blush deepens as she laughs.

"Well, we don't have much time, so perhaps you should disrobe?" she suggests, motioning me forward.

I take a hesitant step toward the hot spring and slip out of my Fae dress. A couple of the Fae females glance my way, more out of curiosity than anything. I happily wade into the water, eager to hide from their prying eyes. I sigh as the water wraps around me like a warm hug. It soothes my muscles and comforts me.

I've only been in the water for a few moments when the golden-haired Fae enters the glade, a few vials in her hand and something draped over her arm. Hycis grins at her before turning to me.

"Ina brought some of our sacred oils for you to use. Do you require our assistance, or—"

"I can do it myself," I cut Hycis off, reaching for the vials.

Hycis shrugs and passes them off to me. "A little will go a long way."

I don't hesitate to quickly use the oils, afraid that if I take too long Hycis or Ina will help me regardless of my protests. I open the first vial and a sweet scent of floral and wood greet me. The second vial smells like rain and roses. They make my skin feel like flower petals and my hair soft as silk. When I slink from the water, Hycis waves her hand, using a quick burst of magic to dry me. Ina offers me the robe draped over arm, and I quickly wrap myself in it.

Without a word, Hycis and Ina turn and stride away, expecting me to follow. We take a winding, roundabout way to the Fae homes, entering what appears to be the back door of a dwelling. The purple-haired Fae woman sits at a table, smiling gently as we enter the room.

"My name is Rynia," she says, rising to hand Hycis a thin fold of fabric. "It's a pleasure to meet you."

I nod, prepared to introduce myself, but Hycis cuts me off, thrusting the fabric toward me. "Put this on."

Puzzled, I take the fabric from Hycis and realize with a shock of horror it's a dress. Only calling it a dress seems generous, seeing as how there is very little to it. The fabric itself is nearly entirely sheer and will do little to hide my body. I might as well be naked. I look up at Hycis, eyes wide.

Ina laughs. "I heard humans were ashamed of their bodies, but I did not expect this much of a reaction."

I scowl as Rynia looks at me with empathy. "There is no need to be ashamed. In ceremonies such as the soul bond ceremony it is necessary to be connected with the earth and air. There should be as little between you and them as possible. This dress is a sacred symbol of the bond we have with the earth, the giver of our powers and the granter of bonds."

I swallow and nod, looking back at the dress in my hands. I hesitate only a moment longer before dropping my robe to the ground and slipping the dress over my head. Two thin straps over my shoulders hold up the iridescent fabric, which dips low, barely covering my breasts. As I suspected, the material does little to conceal my body beneath, every curve evident.

"Now, we need to fix your hair," Hycis says, eyeing me.

"I know what might help," Ina says, leaving the room with a flourish.

Hycis motions for me to take a seat, and she and Rynia begin weaving my hair into braids. Rynia braids a crown around the top of my head while Hycis weaves in smaller braids throughout my hair, leaving most of it to hang loose. Ina returns with several small flowers and incorporates them into the braids. When they're done, all three Fae women stand back and take me in.

"She cleans up nicely for a human." Ina grins.

Rynia smiles softly. "You look lovely."

I manage a weak smile. "Thank you."

"Now," Hycis says, clapping her hands together once, "we need to get you to your soul bond ceremony."

I expect Hycis to lead me outside, but instead she leans forward, grabbing my hands. Before I understand what she's doing, the room with Ina and Rynia is gone and we're standing outside. I blink and look around. To my left I see long willow branches hanging down but, unlike those surrounding the hot spring, these leaves are silver, sparkling and glimmering in the evening light. I look at Hycis and she's watching me with a strangely somber expression.

"What?"

She takes a deep breath before answering. "The soul bond ceremony is one of our most sacred ceremonies, even among the Fae. Few humans have ever had this privilege throughout our entire history."

I weigh her words and nod. "I am grateful for the opportunity."

She nods, glancing toward the silver curtain. "All you need to do is enter the glade. Master Halzar will guide you from here." She pauses. "If you do not come out, it has been an honor and a privilege meeting you."

I want to ask what she means, but she's gone in a blink. With a sigh, I turn toward the curtain of silver leaves. I can feel the pull of magic calling to me from the glade. I take a deep breath and step inside.

The glade is an open circular area surrounded by curtains of silver willow branches. Thick, bright green grass covers the forest floor, sprinkled with small, vibrant flowers. At the opposite end of the glade is an arch of twisting vines growing from the earth. Beneath the arch, standing behind a stone pedestal bearing a large, round stone basin, is a Fae man. Of all of the Fae I've seen, he is the first I immediately think of as being older. It's not his long silvery hair or beard. It's not even in the reverent way he holds himself or the flowing silver robes he wears. It's something about his eyes. They swim deeper than any I've ever seen, displaying more than mere centuries of wisdom.

"You must be Astra," he says, offering me a kind smile.

I nod and he motions for me to take my place on his right next to the pedestal. My stomach twists and turns with nerves as I cross the magical glade. No sooner have I taken my place on the left of the basin than Alak enters the glade. I feel him through his magic before I see him. I raise my eyes to meet his, my heart beating wildly. He's shirtless, all his scars, new and old, clearly visible. The loose-fitting pants he wears seem to be made of the same material as my dress. I flush deeply as I take in all of him. Alak attempts one of his carefree grins, but his own nerves weaken the smile as he takes his place across from me on the other side of the pedestal.

Master Halzar looks between us. "Before we proceed, I must ask you to take heed. Once we begin, the ceremony cannot be halted and once completed the bond will be permanent. There is no way to break the bond in this life once sealed."

I stare into Alak's eyes and something in me stirs.

"We understand," Alak replies, holding my gaze.

Out of the corner of my eye, I see Master Halzar nod.

"You should also know that the ceremony is not entirely benign. It is as much a test as anything. If you fail to pass, the bond will not be secured, resulting in madness, at best, and, at worst, death."

I tear my eyes from Alak and look at Master Halzar. "Death?"

He gives me a grave nod. "Yes. Death. It is relatively rare among the Fae, but possible. Even more so among humans."

I swallow and look back at Alak. I see the concern in his eyes as he watches me. But it's not concern for himself. No, I can see he would willingly die for a chance to complete the bond. His concern is for me. The thought warms me.

"We don't have—" Alak begins, but I cut him off with a smile.

"I accept the risk."

Alak stills, relief washing over his features. His eyes smile as he replies, "I also accept the risk."

Master Halzar nods. "Very well. We shall begin."

He speaks in a language that sounds even more ancient than the Fae we've already heard. It rises around us, a song on the air. I hold Alak's eyes as my magic reaches for his and his for mine. They weave together, and I can barely distinguish one from the other.

"Now you must swear to one another," Master Halzar says after our magic combines. "Repeat after me: I give my soul and being to be tied forevermore, bonded for life and the worlds beyond."

The words grace my tongue as I stare into Alak's eyes. When he speaks the same words, my heart soars.

Master Halzar reaches into his robes and withdraws a dagger, the blade made of diamond and the golden hilt lined with blood-red rubies.

"The bond must be bound through blood." He hands me the dagger. "Cut your hand and allow the blood to drop into the basin, committing your bond in blood and soul."

I hold the dagger for only a moment before I slice my palm. I barely register the pain as the red blooms against my pale skin. I hold my hand over the basin and squeeze it into a fist, the thick red sliding down the side.

"With my blood I commit my soul."

Master Halzar nods and I pass the dagger to Alak. He takes it, his hand brushing mine, sending shivers through me.

"With my blood I commit my soul," he says as the dagger slides across his palm.

Master Halzar takes the dagger and begins chanting in ancient Fae, his voice growing louder as the drops of mine and Alak's blood slowly slide toward each other. When they finally meet, magic surges up with a blast, the world disappearing in a flash of silver light.

CHAPTER THIRTY-SEVEN

ALAK

All I can see is blackness. Everywhere. Nothing but cold black. The glade is gone. Master Halzar is gone. Astra is gone. Astra.

I look around in confusion. Is this what is supposed to happen? Did something go wrong? Am I dead? No, I can't be dead. But if I'm not dead, where am I? And where is Astra?

"Alak," a soft voice says in a thick Athiedor accent.

My heart stops as I turn and find a woman standing behind me. She has long red hair and bright emerald eyes. She smiles softly and I go weak.

"Mum?" I whisper, my voice breaking. She looks exactly how I remember her.

"Yes, my dear boy," she whispers. "I only have a moment, so I need you to listen."

I take an unsteady breath and nod. She smiles sadly.

"Do you know where you are?"

I shake my head.

"You're in the in-between. You have to fight through to complete the bond."

The bond. Seeing my mother almost completely wiped it from my mind.

"Face your fears. Follow your magic. You can do it, my strong, brave boy."

"What do you mean?" I ask, trying to wrap my mind around what's happening.

"I'm sorry, but I can't say more." She glances over her shoulder like she's heard something before looking back at me. "I have to go. Be strong."

I reach toward her, my hand trembling, ready to beg her to stay, but she's gone before I can get the words out.

"Mum!" I yell, racing toward where she just stood. "Don't go! Don't leave me again!"

"Too late, boy," a voice snarls from behind me.

I spin to face my father staggering toward me, a bottle of mead in his hand.

"No," I sputter, shaking my head. "No, you're dead."

He laughs and takes a swig from the bottle, smacking his lips. "Thanks to you I am, but that's the thing about the dead, boy—we don't always stay dead."

He laughs and it echoes around me like a hundred ghosts. Suddenly I feel ten years old again, small and help-less, an old, familiar panic filling my chest.

"You're as worthless today as you were a decade ago," my father slurs, staggering closer.

I clench my fists by my side. "I'm not worthless."

He huffs. "Tell that to your mother." He motions behind me and I spin around. My mother lies on a bed, her red hair spilling over a pillow, her eyes open but unseeing.

"Mum?" I choke out.

"Couldn't even help your own mother," my father says, stepping behind me. "All you had to do was care for her. She only needed medicine. She could have lived. You failed her."

I spin to face him. "I was a boy!" I spit. "A child!"

He waves me off. "Child or no, you failed her. You killed your mother through negligence."

"No!" I scream. "No!"

I swing at my father, but he disappears, his laugh echoing from behind me. I spin and find him a few feet away. I charge again, but he vanishes.

"You'll never be able to get rid of me," he says, behind me once again.

When I turn to face him, he's drinking from the bottle. He sees me watching and offers it to me. "Want a sip to drown your sorrows?"

I shake my head, tightening my clenched hands. He shrugs and takes another gulp.

"More for me I suppose. Though you're sure to follow in my footsteps, eventually. My blood runs in your veins."

"No," I spit. "I'm nothing like you and I never will be. I refuse to be anything even resembling you."

He chokes on his mead he laughs so hard. "You really think you're that much better than me, boy? Why? Because of your mother? She's dead. You killed her."

I shake my head, but he continues.

"Because of Astra? Like you deserve her. She doesn't know half of your past. Do you really think she'll accept you once she knows everything? Hardly. Besides, you'll fail her eventually, just like you've failed everyone else. You constantly let everyone in your life down."

"You're wrong," I whisper. He laughs. I step toward him, straightening my shoulders and say again, louder this time, "You're wrong."

I stop in front of him, but I don't strike him. I stand tall and stare directly into his eyes, jaw set in defiance.

"I learned from my mistakes. Astra loves me, scars and all. I love her, and she loves me. That's enough."

My father smiles but doesn't speak. His eyes look past me as a soft voice says, "What about me Alak? Don't you love me?"

I still and turn slowly. Isabella stands behind me, blinking her big, brown eyes.

"Isabella," I breathe, stepping toward her.

A smile plays on her lips as she tilts her head. "You love me, right, Alak?"

I nod, reaching forward and taking her hands in mine. They're smaller than I remember. And softer. I trace my thumb across her knuckles as I look deeply into her gold-speckled eyes.

"Then why did you kill me?"

Her words send shivers over my spine.

"I didn't kill you, Isabella."

"But you did. Don't you know I died of a broken heart?"

My eyes go wide as she pulls her hands from mine and takes a step back. Blood drips from her wrists as she watches me.

"No. Stop. Please, stop," I cry, but I can't reach out to her. I'm frozen in place. "Isabella, no."

"Why didn't you love me, Alak?" she asks, her eyes glassy. "You failed me."

"I did love you, Isabella. I will always love you," I whisper hoarsely.

"Do you love me more than Astra?"

Her question stills my soul.

"No." The word tumbles out, but she doesn't react. "I

feel stronger love for Astra, stronger than anything I've ever felt, but that doesn't make my love for you any less significant."

She watches me and my eyes glance back down to her wrists. They still bleed, the blood puddling around her feet. Bile rises in my throat, and I feel light-headed and dizzy at the sight.

"Poor Astra," Isabella murmurs. "She'll soon find how shallow and worthless your love is."

I open my mouth to speak, but Bram's voice yells from behind me.

"You killed my sister!"

I turn to face him and find his sword point barely an inch from my face. I back away slowly.

"I didn't. You don't know the whole story." I glance back over my shoulder, but Isabella is gone. I look back at Bram and meet his eyes—the same gods-damned, gold-speckled brown eyes. "I didn't kill your sister. I swear."

"Do you swear on your life?" he asks, pushing the blade against my neck.

I swallow slowly. "I swear on my life that I never wished ill intent toward your sister. You don't know what happened."

"But I do," Ehren says, stepping from the shadows behind Bram. "I know the story."

I nod slightly, the point of Bram's sword threatening to break through my skin. "Yes, you know."

"And yet," Ehren says, meeting my eyes, "I still don't trust you."

My heart sinks. "Please, Ehren . . ."

"Enough!" Bram yells. "Today, I finally get justice."

Ehren nods in agreement.

"Please," I plead. "Think about Astra."

"Oh, we are," Ehren says with a nod. "That's why we plan on destroying you before you destroy her."

I stumble away from Bram's blade, ready to run. But when I turn, Bram is there. I spin. He's everywhere, duplicated a hundred times over. I close my eyes, squeezing them shut as tight as I can.

"It's not real," I whisper to myself. "It's not real."

"Alak!" Astra's voice breaks through my thoughts.

I snap my eyes open. I'm alone again.

"Astra!" I yell as I take off running.

"Alak!" she says again, her voice an echo sounding from far away.

I take a deep breath. The bond. This is all about the bond. I pause, reaching inside and finding my magic. I search for the bond and find a whisper of it. Hope rushes over me as I pull on it, and I feel it strengthen. The darkness around me fades into a snow-covered forest. The trees are coated in ice, their branches stretching toward a gray sky. Snow crunches beneath my feet as I stride forward, searching for Astra. She must be here somewhere.

"As if it would be that easy."

I freeze and turn slowly to face Kato.

"My sister is stronger than you. You're weak. You're nothing. It's ridiculous you even remotely think you're a match for her," he mocks.

"We love each other," I say, struggling to keep my voice even. "We have a soul bond, and that's stronger than any bond you have with her."

Kato laughs. "I am her *twin*. We share a unique bond unclaimed by anyone else in the world. You cannot override that! In the end, she will choose me over you."

"You're wrong."

Kato arches an eyebrow. "Are you so sure about that? How well do you actually know my sister?"

"I know her well enough."

"You think you do, but the reality is you barely know her at all. You're in love with the idea of her. You yearn so badly to be wanted, to feel needed, you're willing to blindly accept her. You do realize that you're binding yourself to her for all eternity?"

I nod. "I know what I'm doing. I'm aware that Astra isn't perfect, and I sure as hell know I'm not perfect. I love her all the same. I'm willing to go through life with her by my side, fully bonded."

"You know she'll never die, right?" My eyes widen, betraying my surprise and Kato grins. "She possesses the spirit of Aoibhinn and will live an immortal life. When you die, you will sever the bond, leaving her behind to live out her days alone and broken. How much more selfish could you be?"

"You're lying," I say, but something inside my chest tells me it's true.

Kato gives me a pitying look. "Poor, mortal human boy, so lost and broken. Finally feeling wanted, only to discover that, once again, he's fallen short."

I lunge forward, throwing magic toward Kato, but he only wisps away, laughing.

"You're a coward!" I yell, turning around. His eyes flash. "You're hiding behind your own insecurities, trying to make my pain outweigh yours, but it won't work. I may not be the strongest or brightest, but I don't need to be. I am who I am meant to be, and that's enough for Astra."

Saying the words aloud lifts a weight I didn't even realize

had been pushing down on me. I take a step forward, confidence surging through me. Kato eyes me for a moment before shrugging.

"Fine. If that doesn't bother you, maybe this will."

He vanishes, replaced by Akaash. Akaash meets my eyes and my blood runs cold. Just being in his presence brings back the flashes of pain I felt under his torture. I expect him to unleash his flames and am rattled when Astra appears by his side.

No, not Astra. Not the real Astra. This Astra is an empty shell meant to mock me. Her amethyst eyes are dead. Akaash wraps an arm around her, pulling her close and she arches eagerly into his touch. Even though I know it's not real, fury surges through me.

"My precious pet," Akaash purrs, lowering his lips to Astra's as he runs an eager hand over her body.

"My love," Astra says in return.

"No," I whisper. I close my eyes for a moment, shaking my head. "Astra would never do that. Never."

"But she would kiss me."

I open my eyes to find that Astra is now wrapped in Bram's arms, her eyes locked on his face with admiration. My heart sinks as a familiar ache fills my chest. Bram grins and leans down, his lips falling on hers. I should look way, but I can't. When Bram pulls back, his eyes meet mine once again, this time in challenge.

"She wants to be with me, you know. Not you."

I drop my shoulders. "I never meant to take her from you. I will always let her love whom she will. I will never hold her back from loving you. If she had truly chosen you, I would have let her go."

The confession tumbles out, every word of it true.

"I love Astra," I continue. "I will love her until the day I die, but I will never force her to be with me or to be someone she is not."

My eyes match Bram's and hold. The illusion shimmers, and he fades away. I'm alone.

"Alak!" Astra's voice echoes around me, closer this time.

"Astra!" I yell back, reaching out with my magic. "Astra!"

My magic propels me forward as I race through the trees, following the trail of magic as it grows stronger. My feet slide underneath me, and I realize I've run onto a frozen lake. I see movement below the ice a few feet away. I rush over and brush away the snow. Astra's face appears beneath the frozen water. Her eyes lock on mine as her hair floats out around her. Panic overwhelms me as I pound against the ice with all my strength. It doesn't even begin to crack.

"No!" I cry, pounding harder.

Is that what Master Halzar meant by death? Will Astra drown in icy water before my eyes? No. I can't let that happen. I won't let that happen. I strike the ice again and again to no avail.

"The bond. Use the bond," my mother's voice whispers in my ear.

I take a deep breath, closing my eyes. This close, the bond is immediately accessible. It takes hold and the ice begins to crack. I strike the ice again and break through. With a gasp, Astra breaks above the surface of the water and I reach toward her.

CHAPTER THIRTY-EIGHT

ASTRA

A snow-covered landscape stretches around me, reaching on endlessly. I'm not surprised when Aoibhinn appears in front me.

"What are you doing here?" I ask, my voice sharp. "And where is Alak?"

She smiles wryly. "And here I was thinking the two of us got along like sisters."

"Sisters fight. Why are you here? Rather, why am I here, and where am I?"

"The in-between," she says simply. "You have to face your fears before you can complete the bond."

"My fears?"

She nods. "Yes. And if you fail, you will be forever lost in this world."

Her words strike me and I falter slightly. I glance around with a scowl.

"Is Alak here?"

She shrugs. "I guess that's for you to find out."

I open my mouth to retort, but she disappears before I

can get another word out. I growl in frustration and look around, trying to figure out what to do next. I need to find Alak and complete the bond.

"When you were born, I knew you would inevitably disappoint me," a voice says behind me.

I turn and find my mother standing a couple yards away, watching me.

"Mama?"

"I never asked for twins, you know. It wasn't supposed to be possible," she says, her voice steady as she shakes her head at me. "And then you were born, tiny and weak. Kato was stronger. He'll always be stronger than you."

"I can be just as strong as Kato," I say, my voice barely more than a whisper.

My mother huffs. "You really think so? I don't."

Her words feel like a slap in the face, and I falter, stumbling back a step.

"You never said—"

"I'm sorry. Was I supposed to tell you up front that you were a disappointment? Your father finally found a way to make you useful, and you screwed it up." Her words bite and I fight back tears. "Do you know how much debt we have? You could have alleviated some of that debt, but you couldn't even agree to a simple marriage."

She shakes her head in disappointment as I choke back tears.

"You couldn't have expected me to marry Marco," I manage. "He was horrible, Mama."

"No less than you deserve," my father says behind me. I spin to face him. His cruel eyes scan me in disgust. "You've always thought you were better than us. Spending all your time with Mara, like you deserved everything she had.

You're still reaching for things beyond your grasp. Court Sorceress? Really? Do you think that makes you special? You're nothing."

A tear breaks free and slides down my cheek.

"No. I . . ."

My words fade off. I don't know what to say. He's not wrong. Not really. He shakes his head.

"As I expected. You've traveled the world, and you're still little more than a pathetic dreamer. Alak deserves better."

Alak's name spurs something inside me, and I stand straighter.

"Alak loves me in spite of everything. He doesn't care about you or my past."

"You're a means to an end for him," my father replies, waving me off. "He's always wanted a position of importance, and you have it. You don't deserve that position or his affection."

"You're wrong."

"Am I? Was he really worth abandoning your family?"

I shake my head, clenching my hands by my side. "I didn't abandon you. *You* abandoned *me*."

"What about me?" a quiet voice says from behind me. My blood chills as I turn to face Mara. "I have never been anything but a good friend. You just left me."

"I wrote you," I say weakly.

"Once. You wrote me once out of obligation, and you never replied to the letter I sent you. I told you our village was falling apart, and you didn't even care."

"I care," I whisper, but she doesn't act like she hears me.

"People are dying, and you don't even seem to notice. You keep right on following the prince in an effort to take over a kingdom that doesn't even want you. You turned your back on Kato. I never thought you would do that."

"Kato is different, Mara," I plead. "You have to see that. He's not the same Kato you knew."

"But do you really want to destroy him?"

I shake my head and take a step toward her. "No. I don't want any of this division."

"Then why do you keep fighting? You're just spurring him on. It's your fault he went to the Dragkonians. If you had stayed by his side, you could have brought him to see reason."

"No, you can't know that."

But even as I say the words, I feel the reality of Mara's accusation crash around me. I squeeze my eyes shut.

"She's right, you know," Kato says.

My eyes snap open. Kato now stands where Mara stood moments ago. He grins at me, but it's not his normal smile. This one is cruel and unfeeling.

"You have always been able to balance me. When you refused to come with me, I had to fill that void."

"No, you can't put that on me," I say, anger rising in me.

"Why not? It's the truth. And are you really doing any better on your own? Just look."

He points behind me and I turn. Behind me the once-empty landscape has turned into blood-soaked snow. I gasp and take a step back, bumping into someone. I turn around and find a little girl no more than five or six years old. She looks up at me with sad blue eyes.

"Are you the one that killed my daddy?"

I stare at her as guilt overwhelms me.

"He was a soldier for the king. Did you kill him?"

"I . . ." No more words come.

"Are you really any better than me?" Kato asks, drawing my eyes back to him. Akaash appears beside him. "Than us?"

"I don't do dark magic," I manage. "I only defend myself and my friends. All wars have casualties. I try to keep them to a minimum, but those people came after us."

Kato considers me for a moment. "Believe that if you will. I suppose Alak won't mind being bonded to a killer. After all, he is a killer himself."

His words sting, but they remind me of my purpose here. I need to find Alak. I take a step back, searching wildly.

"Alak!" my voice sounds lost over the snow.

"Astra!" Alak's voice echoes back, faint and far way.

My heart leaps as I race away from Kato.

"Alak!"

"Astra!"

A hand grabs my arm and jerks me back. I gasp and spin around, coming face to face with Ehren's father, the king of Callenia.

"Do you know how much trouble you've caused?" he snarls.

I yank from his grasp, stumbling back. "I haven't caused anything."

"So you're denying it was you and your gods-forsaken brother who brought magic back? You didn't turn my own son against me?"

I shake my head. "Anything that turned Ehren against you was your own doing."

He laughs, but there's no joy in it. "Foolish girl. Ehren would never have defied me if it hadn't been for you. It's because of you that he ran. Because of you I had to send my soldiers after him. Because of you they're dead. Everything is because of you."

I take a shaky breath, tears threatening to break free again.

"No, that's not true. It can't be."

"And if you keep up this charade and grasp for power, you'll kill my son. Is that what you want? Some friend you are."

I shake my head. "No. I will protect Ehren with my life."

The king arches his eyebrow and looks behind me. "You're too late."

My heart seizes and I spin. I'm in a forest. From the nearest tree hang six bodies. A scream catches in my throat as I recognize the broken bodies of Ehren, Makin, Cal, Sama, Nyco, and Kai.

"It's okay," Bram says, making me turn.

Relief washes over me at the sight of him. I rush into his arms, and he holds me firmly. He brushes my hair from my face.

"See, I'll always be here for you, no matter how many times you break my heart."

His words make me jerk back. Wait. This isn't right. I look up at him and he smiles cruelly.

"That's right, Astra. You will always come back to me. You don't really love Alak. It is just the bond, and you know it. You have been manipulated by forces beyond your control."

I pull from his arms, shaking my head. "No, you're wrong. I love him. I love Alak."

Bram laughs. "You can lie to yourself all you want, but we both know it's not true. One day, you'll wake up and realize it was all the bond. The bond he lied to you about. People that love you don't tell lies. They don't keep truth hidden. He doesn't love you, and you don't love him. Not really."

I play his words over in my head, stepping away.

"You're wrong."

Bram rolls his eyes, and it gives me strength. I laugh and he frowns.

"You're wrong. I don't love Alak because of the bond. The bond is something else entirely. I can feel it and all the pieces that tie us together. I can sense the trust and emotions tangled up in the bond. But the way I feel about Alak isn't just the bond—it's more. It's things the bond can't touch."

I smile as the pieces finally fit together, any reservations I've had falling away.

"I love him because he sees me. He doesn't care about my magic or how I look or what I can do. He loves me for being me and nothing more. He doesn't care that I'm a nothing girl from a nothing town. He doesn't care that I'm a Court Sorceress. He just cares about *me*. In return, I love him for who he is. He's broken and scarred. He's always been there for me, no matter what, and he always will be. Not because he has to, but because he wants to. He's never failed me or let me down. He always fights for me.

"I love his smile, his kind heart, his accent, the mischievous twinkle in his eyes. I love every single thing about him. Even if we didn't have the soul bond, I would still choose him."

I grin and close my eyes, reaching out with my magic. I can feel him. I open my eyes and race over the snow.

"Alak!" I laugh.

"Astra!" his voice calls back. He's close. So close. "Astra!"

I run toward his voice, expecting him to appear at any moment. The ground beneath me shifts as I'm pulled under ice cold water. I struggle, but I can't swim. Even if I could, it would do little good. I'm trapped under a sheet of ice. Panic threatens to take over.

Then I see him. Alak is above me on the other side, looking down. His eyes are open wide with panic as he pounds against the surface above me. I reach up and press my palms against the ice, hoping the pressure may break me free, but it does nothing.

Alak is yelling my name and clawing at the ice. I'm more distressed by his panic than by drowning. If I die, then I die, but I can't stand the thought of him being hurt in any way. I reach out with my magic, searching for our bond. His magic finds mine at the same time, and I feel a surge. The ice begins to crack and I break free, Alak pulling me from the water.

I gasp, air filling my lungs, but it's not the icy air I'm expecting. I'm back in the clearing, laying on a bed of grass. I blink in disbelief and sit up, attempting to orient myself. I glance down at my palm and am startled to find the cut from earlier has already healed.

"Astra," Alak's voice calls hoarsely to me.

I look over and scramble across the distance between us. I have a need to be with him. Our magic fills the air around us with more power than I've ever felt before. I can sense every piece of Alak as I'm drawn into his arms.

"You're okay," he whispers, his voice and hands shaking. "You're okay."

I pull back and look into his eyes, brimmed with tears of relief.

"I'm okay," I say, pressing my lips to his. I can taste his desire.

Someone clears their throat, and we jerk back and look

up. Master Halzar stands above us, smiling. Alak stands, pulling me up with him. For the first time since waking up, I realize it's night.

"How long were we out?" I ask.

Master Halzar replies, "You were in the in-between nearly three hours. Not very long considering the amount of time these bonds can take to mold together. Your bond must be very strong indeed." His eyes shift between us before he continues. "Over the next few hours, perhaps even days, your bond will be strong and raw as your bodies adjust. Eventually, it will settle and became as simple and normal as breathing."

"So, we won't always feel this . . ." I search for the word.

Alak completes the thought for me. "Passionate?"

Master Halzar's lips twitch with amusement. "Not always. The ebb and flow of your bond will be unique to you. Sometimes, you may be overwhelmed by emotion or magic. You will find a way forward, together."

He pauses before adding. "The bond ceremony is one of the most sacred and intimate ceremonies among Fae or human. While physical consummation is not a requirement, many bond-mates often choose to seal the bond in such a way."

My heart races as I try very hard not to look into Alak's eyes. He shifts next to me but doesn't move away. If anything, he moves closer.

"In case you choose to follow this path, I have made arrangements."

He motions to the ground behind him, and I notice a pile of soft blankets. I wonder if they've been there the entire time, but I simply didn't notice them before now. I swallow and glance at Alak out of the corner of my eye.

"Even if you choose not to be as intimate, you may remain here for the night. No one will bother you, I can assure you." He clears his throat and glances quickly at each of us before bowing his head. "I bid you goodnight."

After he disappears, the glade is too quiet. I slowly turn to face Alak. He takes both my hands into his and looks deeply into my eyes. I can feel his emotions stirring, headed by desire.

"We don't have to . . . ," he starts, running his thumb over my knuckles.

I take a slow breath and glance toward the blankets.

"Astra, I'm serious. We don't have to," Alak insists. "Just being bonded to you is more than I could ever ask for. If we never—"

"I want to," I whisper, cutting him off.

"What?" he asks, his voice barely audible, genuine bewilderment flashing across his face.

I look up at him, my heart thrumming wildly inside my chest, threatening to break free. "I want to."

I feel his rush of desire through the bond as a smile spreads across his face.

"Are you sure?"

I smile and nod. "Yes. I just . . ." I glance away.

"You what, love?" he asks, voice laced with tenderness.

I look back at him. "I've never . . ."

"Oh." Realization washes over him as color rises into his cheeks. "*Oh*. That's fine, love. I don't expect a thing of you. I only want whatever you're willing to give. Nothing more. And we can stop at any time should you change your mind."

My breath catches in my throat as I lean forward and press my lips to his. He returns the kiss with more heat than I expect, and I'm instantly swept away. I want more. I *need* more. I pull him toward the blankets, and we settle on the ground, our kiss growing more and more intense. My head reels, and I can barely think. All I can do is feel. I'm swimming in a sea of desire.

My teeth catch his bottom lip and he moans, moving into me. His hands slide up underneath my dress, exploring my body as my hands run over his, tracing his scars and smooth muscles. I half expect him to pull back at any moment, but he doesn't. He pushes forward, casting his pants to the side. He slips the dress from my body and looks down at me, his lips parting as he stares at me in awe.

"Gods," he whispers, breathless. "You're beautiful."

Tears fill my eyes as I look up at him. "I love you."

He smiles and leans forward, brushing his lips across mine, sending shivers down my spine.

"I love you, too, Astra." His lips press to my neck and I gasp. I can feel him grin against my skin as his lips roam across my body. I arch into his touch craving more.

"Please," I gasp, desire overwhelming me. "Please."

I don't even need to finish my request. Alak meets my eyes with a roguish smile, mischief twinkling in his eyes. "You sure, love? I can leave you be if—"

I hit him playfully and he laughs. "So be it, love." He lays down, his body hovering a mere breath above mine, leaning his head in so his lips brush my ear as he whispers, "I am yours to command."

I barely have time to register his words before the world shifts as he presses into me. I cry out and arch into him. Together, we move as one. We share one breath, one heartbeat. No one and nothing exists beyond us.

But it's more than just our bodies. Our magic is fused as one. It sweeps through us, allowing me to not only feel every sensation cascading over my own body but also everything he feels as well. It echoes around us, a driving force adding an intensity to every motion.

The heat rises in me until I can't go any higher. Our magic bursts free as everything rushes together in culmination, swarming the glade with a burst of light and power. Alak looks down at me, breathing hard, drenched in sweat, pure and utter joy and satisfaction shining on his face. He collapses on the blankets next to me, and I fold into his chest. I'm exhausted, yet I've never felt so alive.

Together our breath steadies. Alak holds me close. We don't need to speak. We are beyond words. The world is perfect in this moment. Slowly, we drift into sleep, intertwined as one.

CHAPTER THIRTY-NINE

ALAK

I wake in a dream that has become reality. Astra rests in my arms, her hair spilling across my bare chest. I scarcely breathe, not wanting to disturb her. She's so peaceful. Our bond is still strong, pulsing between us, but some of the initial intensity has faded.

Astra shifts, her head brushing the bottom of my chin. I tilt my head, kissing her forehead. She sighs softly as her eyes flutter open. She looks up at me, still covered in the haze of sleep.

"Morning, love," I whisper, not bothering to hide my grin.

She blinks at me a moment before a smile spreads across her lips as she dips her head, snuggling closer. I notice a slight tinge of pink in her cheeks and laugh.

"Come now, love, you're not ashamed of me already?" I tease, though true insecurity and worry hide beneath my words.

She laughs, the sound a sweet comfort on its own, and raises up so she can look down into my eyes. "You caught me,

Alak Dunne. I only needed one quick roll with you in a Fae glade to tire of you."

She grins and I wrap my arms around her, flipping her onto her back. She squeals and looks up at me, grinning.

"Now what are you going to do?" she purrs, biting her lip.

Desire rushes through me as I match her wicked grin. "Well," I muse, "I was thinking something like this."

I lean in and press my lips to hers. It's meant to be a simple kiss and nothing more, but I soon realize that nothing is simple between us anymore. She winds her fingers into my hair, pulling me against her, and I oblige. The kisses quickly become hungry, filled with need. Each little caress and gentle touch only escalates things further until our bodies and magic are once again flawlessly intertwined as one.

Last night, everything was slow and deliberate—a discovery of something new and wonderful. This morning, everything is fueled by intense desire, lust mingling with love, want mingling with need.

By the time we're done, I'm more than satiated and breathless. Astra sighs with contentment, snuggling against me.

"I wish we could stay here like this all day," she murmurs.

"Who says we can't?" I grin.

She giggles and traces her hand absentmindedly in circles on my chest.

"We should probably already be headed back to meet everyone else. They'll soon notice we're missing."

"So?" I say, kissing the tip of her nose. "Let them miss us."

She raises her lips and we begin kissing again. Astra

stops, though, before we can push it further. She fumbles in the blankets until she finds her dress, sliding it over her head. She stands and looks down with dismay. I fold an arm behind my head and grin up at her.

"What's the matter, love?"

She scowls, pinching at the fabric. "This dress doesn't conceal much."

"I think it suits you," I tease and she laughs.

"You might not mind, but I can't walk around the Fae village in this. I didn't mind as much last night because no one was really around, but this morning . . ."

I rise, nodding. As much as I might enjoy the view, it's not one I want to share. A quick check of the blankets reveals that, while a couple of the blankets were less than perfect thanks to our . . . activities, one remains mostly unsoiled. I drape it around Astra's shoulders and use a little illusion magic to add extra coverage. I quickly pull on my pants, not caring in the slightest who enjoys my view. She slips her hand into mine as we make our way back through the village.

I'm not entirely sure where we need to go, but somehow we find the correct dwelling. Elidyr and Hycis are seated at the table, munching on fresh fruit. When we enter, their eyes fall on us with interest. Hycis grins with uncontrollable glee.

"Well, how does it feel to be bonded?"

Astra blushes, and I give her hand a squeeze.

"It feels complete," I answer for us both.

Astra nods, looking up at me. "Yes, complete."

"I remember those days," Hycis says with a sigh and a far-off look.

"You're bonded?" Astra asks with guarded curiosity.

Hycis's eyes shine. "Yes. You met my bond-mate last night. Rynia."

Astra gasps and grins. "I had no idea!'

Hycis shrugs. "It's common enough among Fae. We've been bonded for nearly two hundred years now. Most days the bond is as simple and necessary as breathing. Other days, there's the needing and wanting."

Her eyes watch us for our reaction, and she grins when we oblige, color rising on our cheeks.

"Did you participate in the typical post-ceremony activities?" she asks pointedly, arching her eyebrows with interest.

"Hycis," Elidyr scolds her, his tone sharp. "There is no need to be crude."

She grunts and shrugs. "It wasn't merely for curiosity's sake, though I am rather curious." Her eyes fall on Astra whose face is bright red. "Astra may like to clean up a bit and perhaps take a preventive tonic."

It takes me a moment to understand Hycis's meaning, but I can feel Astra react immediately.

"Oh, yes. Please," Astra mumbles.

Hycis rises from the table. "Well then, follow me. We'll take care of everything and get you ready for the day."

"We are close to finding a path back to the human world near your traveling companions," Elidyr cuts in, "so you may wish to dress in your own garments."

Astra gives him a nod of thanks as Hycis ushers her away. As soon as she's out of my sight, my heart physically aches. I have to fight every instinct to go after her. When I finally tear my gaze away from the door, I find Elidyr watching me.

"It will get easier," he says evenly. "Being apart."

"I don't think I want it to get easier," I confess with a sigh.

The corners of Elidyr's mouth turn up slightly. "Some

parts will never fade. Fenian and I have been bonded 300 years and there isn't a day I do not . . . desire him."

Elidyr shifts uncomfortably in his seat before changing the subject. "You might as well ready yourself while you wait. Follow me."

I make quick work of washing up and dressing, eager to get back to Astra. When I'm done, however, I find Bram, not Astra, seated at the table. He eyes me with equal disdain as I take a seat. I reach to the center of the table and select a piece of fruit.

"So," Bram says, slowly as I take a bite, "I suppose you took care of everything."

I choke on my breakfast, coughing violently. He frowns, clearly missing how his words could be taken. I take a deep breath and clear my throat.

"Um, yes. We are bonded, if that's what you mean."

Bram nods. "I see."

He glances away, and I feel a surge of guilt, remembering the Bram from the dream world.

"You know, I never meant to take her away from you."

Bram meets my eyes with a cold glare, his jaw set, but he doesn't speak. I refuse to back down from his gaze.

"We were friends once. Can't we be again?" I offer, attempting a smile.

Bram sighs and shakes his head. "How—after everything you have done to me, everything you have destroyed—can you believe that we could ever be friends?"

Something in me sinks at his words.

"Bram. I—"

I look up with a jolt as I sense Astra's magic enter the room. I don't even remember standing, but I'm on my feet, drawn to her. She smiles, making her way to my side just as eagerly. She intertwines her fingers with mine and looks up at me, her eyes bright. I lean down and brush my lips against hers.

"I missed you," I whisper.

"I missed you, too," she replies, pink tinging her pale cheeks.

"Gods," Bram mutters under his breath.

Astra's eyes go wide as she peers past me to where Bram sits at the table, watching us with obvious disgust. Hycis laughs and brushes past us.

"Don't worry," she says, plopping into the chair next to Bram, "for most bond-mates the outward shows of affection diminish relatively quickly."

"Yes, for Hycis and Rynia it was a brief 50 years," Elidyr says, coming inside with Fenian close behind.

Bram looks a little pale and nauseous at the prospect as Hycis laughs.

"Please, brother! As if you two were any better! I had to move out!"

I glance over at Astra and expect to find her face bright red, but instead she seems fixated on the conversation, observing with the eyes of a scholar. I smile.

"Well, I promise to at least try to be less obnoxious," I swear with a grin.

"I don't," Astra says, her voice thick with mischief. Bram's eyes widen. And she adds, "Sometimes I rather enjoy causing trouble."

Hycis bursts out in rich laughter, and I can't help but chuckle. Astra grins.

"I see Alak has already started to rub off on you," Bram groans, but he can't hide his smile.

"In more ways than one," Hycis mutters under her

breath with a wicked grin, making Bram scowl with confusion.

"Anyway," I cut in quickly before Bram can work it out. "What is the plan for today?"

"Actually," Fenian says, stepping forward, "that's why I am here. We have found a place near your companions where our two realms meet. Once you are prepared, I will lead the way."

Bram stands. "Let's go now."

"There are a few things you should take with you," Elidyr says, nodding to Hycis.

Hycis nods and rises, disappearing into one of the rooms. When she returns, she holds a small brown bag and something wrapped in a piece of cloth. She holds the pouch out to Bram.

"These are a few of the Bellyon berries," Hycis explains as Bram spills a few solid, round berries into his palm. They shimmer green with a slight blush. "They aren't ripe enough to kill a Dragkonian, but the berries should weaken them."

She holds out the second item to Astra who accepts it, pulling her hand from mine. She peels back the cloth.

"My bracelet! And Ehren's ring!" Astra cries, her eyes going wide at the Syphon jewelry in her hand, the stones themselves pulsing with a white light.

Hycis nods. "We filled them with Fae magic, the only magic that can truly stand against a Dragkonian. Your newly bonded magic will be powerful, but volatile. Until you learn to wield it to its full advantage, your best chance against a Dragkonian is pure Fae magic."

Astra nods, sliding the bracelet onto her wrist and slipping Ehren's ring into her pocket.

"Well, I suppose we should get the humans on their way," Fenian says with a curt nod.

Astra knots her fingers back into mine as we follow Fenian outside. Elidyr and Hycis trail along behind us, stopping at the edge of the Fae village.

"It was an honor to meet you. I hope we'll soon meet again in your human world," Hycis says with a grin.

Elidyr nods. "Yes, while unexpected it was not altogether unpleasant."

"Careful brother," Hycis laughs, elbowing Elidyr, "or they might think you actually like them."

Elidyr rolls his eyes and Hycis grins.

"Thank you for your hospitality," Astra says. "And for all your help."

The Fae nod in response.

"We should make haste," Fenian insists, motioning for us to follow.

With one last parting nod, we follow him through the Fae woods. He moves swiftly and we struggle to keep up. When he stops abruptly, we nearly crash into him. He turns to us, his face grim.

"You need only continue walking and you will find your companions," Fenian says, his voice steady. "Be aware that time does not pass the same in our realms."

"Wait," Bram says, stepping forward. "What do you mean?"

"When our realms were side-by-side centuries ago, one could pass between them and the days and hours would match. Now, time passes differently and inconsistently. A day in one realm may be hours or weeks in the other. I cannot tell how much time you have been gone."

"So we could have been gone for weeks?" Astra asks, her face pale.

Fenian nods. "I pray you will arrive back in time to stop the evil from spreading, but you should be prepared for anything."

I feel worry surge from Astra through our bond, and it does nothing to qualm my own nerves.

"Farewell," Fenian says, motioning for us to step forward.

We comply and, after a few steps, I feel a shimmer of magic prickle across my skin. The world goes dull and everything seems out of focus for a minute as we adjust to the human realm. When we turn around, the world of Fae is gone.

Bram scowls as he looks around.

"This isn't right," he mumbles. "There are no forests around Hounddale."

"Well, you heard Fenian, mate. We don't know how much time has passed. Maybe they had to move on."

Bram nods. He and Astra exchange a worried look. I squeeze Astra's hand, trying to comfort her as best I can. Since there's little hope in worrying and fretting, we move forward. The minutes tick by and we wait with anxious breath for an impending disaster. The closest we come, however, is a giant wolf with gray eyes.

CHAPTER FORTY

ASTRA

I immediately recognize Kai's wolf form when he leaps out at us, snarling. He pauses and blinks, shifting into his human form. His mouth drops open as his eyes meet mine.

"You're alive," he whispers, his voice as quiet as the wind.

For a moment, he stands there, blinking, as if I could fade from existence at any moment. Then he's rushing forward, gathering me in his arms. I release Alak's hand for the first time in nearly an hour and wrap my arms around Kai. When he pulls away, tears shine in his eyes.

"We thought you were dead," he explains, letting his eyes travel to Bram and Alak. "When you didn't return—"

"How long have we been gone?" Bram cuts in, everything about him tense.

None of us dare breathe while we wait for Kai to answer.

"Eight days. You left just over eight days ago."

"Shite," Alak mutters as Bram swears.

The color leeches from my face, not daring to contemplate the amount of evil Kato could master in that amount of time. Kai eyes us warily.

"Why? What do you know?"

We all exchange a look before I reply, "It would be easier to tell everyone at once."

Kai nods. "Camp is not far. Follow me."

Kai remains in his human form as he leads us to the camp, glancing over his shoulder at regular intervals at us like we could vanish at any moment. We step into the clearing and find the tents set up with a small fire burning in the center. Hanna and Pip sit cross-legged by the fire, facing each other as they play a dice game. Sama and Nyco stand talking at the end opposite us. Sama is the first to notice our arrival. She looks over with a causal glance, but her eyes go wide followed by a sharp gasp when she sees it's more than Kai returning.

"What?" Nyco asks, following her gaze. When he sees us he curses.

Hanna just stares at us wide-eyed murmuring, "You were right, Pip. You were right."

The flap on the largest tent lifts, and Ehren steps out.

"What's going—"

His words are cut short when his eyes fall on us. His cheery façade falls away as a sob breaks from his lips. He recovers more quickly than Kai did, rushing to me. He squeezes me so tightly I can barely breathe, but I don't protest in the slightest.

"I am never letting you out of my sight again," he whispers, holding me firmly. He pulls back and looks down at me in wonder. "Gods, I honestly thought I'd never see you again."

Bram takes a step forward, and Ehren's eyes fall on his

friend. He releases me and reaches for Bram, wrapping him in a backslapping hug.

"And you, how dare you go off on a death-defying adventure without me and not return immediately?"

Bram chuckles as Alak clears his throat. Ehren grins wickedly, reaching for Alak.

"I even missed you, you crazy fool," Ehren confesses, planting a ridiculously sloppy kiss on Alak's cheek as he embraces him.

Alak laughs, its warmth flowing through me. Ehren steps back, taking us in, grinning as the others approach, including Healer Heora who has just stepped from her tent.

"Why aren't you in Hounddale?" Bram asks, and Ehren's face falls. "And where are Cal and Makin?"

"Cal and Makin are out scouting the area. We had to leave Hounddale a few days ago because someone alerted nearby soldiers of our location. We barely escaped," Ehren explains.

"Surely my family didn't—" Bram starts but Ehren cuts him off with a wave.

"I have no reason to believe your family had any part in it. If they did, it was unintentional. They were very hospitable to us in the time you were away." Ehren's face grows serious as he shifts his gaze between the three of us. "You have no idea how worried and distressed we were when you didn't return. I thought I had sent you to your deaths."

I meet Ehren's eyes and smile softly. "But we're okay," I assure him, reaching for his hand and giving it a small squeeze. "We're okay."

Ehren returns my smile but it's weak. The worry he's felt the past several days still shines in his eyes.

"Where exactly are we now if not Hounddale?" Alak asks, drawing our attention.

I step away from Ehren and slide my hand back into Alak's. He relaxes, shifting closer to me so our arms brush.

"Well, we refused to give up hope you would all return and didn't want to travel too far from Hounddale, so we took cover in the nearest forest," Ehren replies. "We're in Greenwake Wood, roughly a two-day ride from Embervein."

"Gods in heaven above," Makin's voice cuts in.

I look past Ehren as Makin and Cal enter the camp several yards away, their eyes wide. I grin as Makin rushes toward us, Cal close behind.

"You're alive," Makin says in wonder. "You're alive."

"Are you hurt at all?" Cal asks, his eyes scanning us for any sign of injury.

I smile. "Not anymore. The Fae healed us."

"The Fae?" Sama breathes, eyes wide with wonder. "You met the Fae?"

I nod. "Yes, a lot has happened in the last few days." I meet Ehren's eyes as my face falls. "And not all the news we bring is good."

Sama watches me closely, her eyes squinted as if she's trying to solve an intricate puzzle. She gasps as she looks from me to Alak.

"The bond," she whispers. "You completed the bond."

Ehren turns to me, eyebrows raised. "The soul bond?"

"What?" I ask, frowning as I turn to Alak who meets my eyes with sheepish guilt. "Did literally everyone else know about the soul bond besides me?"

Alak glances away. "Well, love, you see, the thing is . . . there were, um . . . the circumstances . . ."

"If it helps," Ehren jumps in, "I only found out the night you were taken."

I narrow my eyes at Alak who is doing his best to look innocent.

"I suppose that helps some."

Alak leans down and plants a kiss on my cheek. "The part that matters is that we're bonded now and that I love you."

I smile and raise my lips to his. "I suppose."

"Dear gods," Ehren mutters, "please don't tell me you two will be all over each other all the time now saying things like that. I don't know if I can handle it."

I laugh and shake my head. "We won't."

Alak grins and releases my hand in favor of wrapping his arm around me and pulling flush against his side.

"I, however, make no such promise," Alak says with a wink.

"I hate to break the levity of the moment," Bram says, clearing his throat. "We may not have much time before the world goes to hell."

"Bram is right," I add grimly. "We really should start toward Embervein as soon as possible, and we may already be too late."

Ehren eyes me with concern as we fill him and the others in on everything that has happened. We pack up the camp as we talk. I share all the details of Kato and Akaash's plans to use my magic to unlock Atroxmorte, including the fact that he's under the dark influence of Caedios. Bram takes over, describing their daring rescue and escape into the land of Fae, with Alak concluding the final details of our bond and promises from the Fae for future support. I give Ehren back his ring and explain how it is filled with Fae magic.

By the time everyone is caught up, we're ready to leave. Before fleeing Hounddale, Ehren was able to secure additional horses and supplies, so no one has to walk, though Kai prefers to stay in his wolf form. It had still been mid-morning when we left the Fae realm, but it's just after noon here, dark falling after only a few hours of riding. We don't stop right away, however, but continue pressing forward until exhaustion takes hold.

When we do stop, we don't set up camp. We share a few bites of the available rations before huddling together on the ground to sleep. Alak cradles me in his arms, and I dissolve into our bond, craving its warmth and comfort. Even with the bond's gentle caress, it's difficult to sleep. I doubt any of us are able to sleep more than a couple hours each. We're all up before dawn, ready to resume our journey.

We ride fast and hard all day, not even bothering to stop to eat. None of us have an appetite, anyway. When we finally spot the outline of Embervein rising in the distance, some of the tension leaves Ehren's body. It's impossible to know for sure from this distance, but it looks like we may have made it in time.

Our relief is short-lived, however. Within the hour, I feel a surge of dark magic approaching. Alak can sense it as well. We exchange a wary glance, which doesn't go unnoticed. Before Ehren can ask, he has his answer. In the distance, a dark cloud approaches, moving through the sky at an impossible pace. We pause in our riding and gape up at the sky. Bile rises in my throat as I realize it's not a cloud we see, but a formation of at least a hundred Dragkonians headed directly to Embervein.

Ehren spurs his horse forward, pushing her as fast as she can go. We race toward Embervein, but we all know we won't make it. We're still at least fifteen minutes away when the Dragkonians descend into the city. Ehren presses on for a minute before coming to an abrupt halt, twisting to face me, his eyes wide and manic.

"Wisp me in," he pleads. "Take me into Embervein."

"Ehren," Bram says, his voice strained and quiet, "it's probably too late."

"No," Ehren insists, shaking his head. "I have to—I have to at least get Winnie out. And my mother. I have to try. I *have* to."

I take a deep breath. I know there's no point in arguing with him. He won't take no for an answer. I nod slowly.

"Okay."

Alak starts. "You're going to go straight into the fray?"

I look over at him and nod. "I can take everyone with me. I've wisped everyone before."

Alak shakes his head firmly. "No, you'll need as much of your magic as possible to fight and get people out. You take Ehren and get Winnie. We'll follow behind and join when we can."

I nod. "We'll need a place to meet and send survivors who are unable to evacuate completely."

Ehren nods, calming as he formulates a plan. "You're right." He lifts his eyes to Bram. "Take Healer Heora, Hanna, Pip, and Sama and set up a camp in the forest in the clearing nearest the river. We will send the weak and wounded there."

"Ehren, I am not letting you leap into battle without me by your side!" Bram shouts. "Are you insane?"

"Captain Bramfield," Ehren commands, sitting straighter, his voice cold, "your prince is giving you a direct order. You will follow it." His shoulders sink slightly as he adds, "I need to send people to someone I trust."

Bram sighs and nods, clenching his jaw. I jump from my horse and reach up to Ehren.

"We shouldn't waste more time."

Ehren nods and takes my hand. I glance back at Alak. I can see the worry lining his face, but he gives me a nod. He knows I'll see him again. I concentrate and pull my magic forward, wisping Ehren and I directly into the castle.

The palace is already in complete chaos. People run and scream, the air thick with the scent of fear.

"Find Winnie and my mother," Ehren commands, racing down the hall in the opposite direction.

I nod and weave through the halls. I'm closest to Cadewynn's room, so I start there. I'm not surprised to find it vacant. I'm rushing down a corridor away from her room when a young man nearly plows into me. He jumps back, his hand on his sword. I recognize his uniform as the one worn by Ehren's Guard, the soldier recognizing me a moment later.

"Mistress Astra?" he asks. "Does this mean Prince Ehren has returned?"

I nod. "His orders are to evacuate everyone. Anyone who can't travel far is to find Captain Bramfield in the woods." The Guard nods, ready to follow orders. "I need to find Princess Cadewynn. Do you know where she is?"

The Guard nods again. "Princess Cadewynn is in a hidden room below the library with those she managed to gather and hide before the attack ensued."

Of course. I should have known. I thank the Guard as he rushes off to fulfill his prince's orders. I wisp directly into the library room. It's dimly lit by a handful of candles. A couple dozen people are huddled together, their wary, terrified eyes turning to me when I appear. I raise a small orb of silver light, illuminating the room.

"Astra?" Cadewynn cries, rising from the center of the crowd. She blinks a couple times in disbelief before rushing to me and throwing her arms around my neck. "I knew you would come."

"Is my traitor son with you?" a cold voice asks from behind Cadewynn.

The queen stands, tall and regal, a dark shadow against my orb of light. Her face is set in a stone-cold glare of hate as she eyes me. I nod.

"Ehren is here. He sent me to find you, Your Majesty, and get you to safety."

The queen sniffs with disgust. "I don't need you or your magic."

My blood boils at her tone. I step away from Cadewynn toward the queen, holding my head high.

"Pardon me, Your Majesty," I spit, "but I beg to differ. Your kingdom is under assault from a very dark and dangerous foe. Without magic, it will fall and you with it. You may not like me, and you may not trust me, but I don't care. I love and respect your son, and I will follow him to the edge of the world. I will defend his honor and fight in his name. You can loathe me all you want, Your Majesty, but you will not speak ill of Ehren. Not when he risked his life to return to save you and Princess Cadewynn."

The queen holds my gaze, her eyes flashing with pure loathing, but she doesn't speak.

"Now," I say, turning my attention to the refugees huddled around us, "Captain Bramfield is setting up a camp in the forest for anyone who needs a place to run. I will use my magic to send you there. If you are able, it would be wise to continue and get as far away from Embervein as possible, immediately."

Heads bob in agreement.

"I want to help you," Cadewynn says, placing her hand on my arm. "These are my people as well. Let me fight to save them."

I meet her eyes and read her earnestness, but I shake my head.

"You've already saved all these people. Ehren will never leave the palace if he thinks you're even remotely in danger. You'll be safer in the woods. Your people will need you there. They'll need a friendly face and a leader until Ehren can join you."

Cadewynn considers my words and gives a short nod. I look at the group of people around me and take a deep breath. I reach out my magic and wisp them all away. My magic jolts with the effort it takes, but I still have plenty left in addition to the magic pulsing in my Syphon Stone.

I wisp from the library room and begin to search in earnest for Ehren. The mayhem has only increased. The Dragkonians are inside the castle walls. Human defenses mean nothing against them. Bodies litter the halls, the air reeking of blood. I stumble through the corridors, wisping away what people I can find. I send a blast of Fae magic, dispersing a group of Dragkonians attacking a handful of servants. They shoot me looks of gratitude before scrambling away.

I find Ehren with his father in the throne room. Ehren and King Betron stand facing one other, swords drawn. I hover near the door, not wanting to invade where I'm not yet needed. I curl magic around my fingers, ready to rush to Ehren's aid.

"You betrayed your kingdom!" King Betron yells, pointing his sword at Ehren. "You ran like a coward. This is your fault."

"I'm trying to save my kingdom!" Ehren cries. "Please, trust me! Come with me!"

The king snarls and takes a step back. "As if I would trust you! I know you've been gathering allies to rise against me. All these years I thought you didn't want the throne. Turns out you were merely biding your time, waiting until it suited you to overthrow me and steal the kingdom."

Ehren looks like he's been slapped across the face as he stutters, "No, I never—"

The king lunges forward, swinging his sword. Ehren blocks him and pushes his father back. Hurt shines in his eyes.

"I don't want the throne like this! I don't want it at all! I just want my people to be able to live in peace, no matter their magical status. I will fight for my people and my kingdom."

"If you don't want the kingdom, I'll be happy to take it off your hands."

Kato appears, sitting on the throne. He leans forward, grinning wickedly, his eyes gleaming. The king spins to face Kato, nothing short of hate in his eyes. I rush into the throne room, a sword of silver light forming in my hand.

"Get out of my kingdom!" the king roars.

Kato laughs and wisps from the throne, reappearing mere feet in front of the king, a fire sword in his hand. "Why don't you make me?"

"Stop!" I yell as the king makes to raise his sword.

"Ah, sister," Kato drawls. "I was wondering when you would rush in to try to save everyone."

"This isn't you," I plead. "Please, stop this nonsense."

"I never pull out of a game I'm winning," Kato replies, turning his attention back to the king. "So, how about we finish? Winner gets the kingdom?"

Kato lunges forward with his sword, but the king blocks it. I rush forward, but Kato stops me short, surrounding himself and the king with a wall of flames. I'm blocked and unable to even wisp inside the circle. Ehren and I are forced to watch as the king engages Kato in battle.

It quickly becomes evident that Ehren's ability to sword-fight is natural talent inherited from his father. King Betron's movements are nearly flawless, but Kato is still better. We watch with bated breath as the king dodges blow after blow, making a few strikes of his own. Kato seems agitated with how well the king fights, clearly expecting to win easier.

"To hell with fighting fair," Kato murmurs before disappearing.

He reappears behind the king, driving his sword through the king's back, directly through his heart. A scream catches in my throat as Ehren's cleaves the air. Kato withdraws his sword from the king's body and it disappears. The king falls, his crown tumbling from his head. Kato leans down and scoops up the crown, placing it on his head. He lowers the wall of flames and turns to face Ehren, a cruel grin on his face. Ehren's breath is ragged as he faces Kato, his hand tightening on the hilt of his sword.

"What do you think?" Kato addresses Ehren, gesturing to the crown on his head. "Do I look like a king?"

Ehren screams and charges forward, swinging wildly. Kato laughs, wisping out of Ehren's reach.

"You're pathetic," Kato snarls. "You'll never be a match for me."

Ehren looks at Kato, a broken shell of his normal self. His eyes drift to his father's fallen body, and I see something in him shatter. I step forward.

"I'm a match for you, though," I say, raising my sword.

Kato cocks his head and surveys me. "Perhaps."

I race forward. Kato meets my blow right before it strikes him, conjuring his own sword at the last moment. My actions draw his attention away from Ehren who rushes to his father's side. Kato tries to wisp, but I block his magic and force him to face me.

"You'll never be able to kill me," Kato spits. "You're too soft."

"I have no desire to kill you," I admit, holding his gaze, "but I will, if you force my hand."

Kato responds by charging at me. I dodge and swing my sword, his catching mine just as it hits its mark. He wisps away to another part of the room and I follow. My magic surges, and I realize Alak has arrived on the palace grounds. Kato must notice, his face twisting into a scowl, but it doesn't dissuade his next attack. Round and round the throne room we go, willing to fight to the death. Kato is so fixed on me he doesn't notice Ehren behind him until almost too late. Ehren lands a firm blow, slashing Kato's face before he can block it. Kato growls, blood pouring from the wound, and lashes out with magic, knocking Ehren back. I throw a quick shield around Ehren, blocking Kato's next blow.

"You need to go," I say to Ehren. He looks at me, a mere ghost of his former self, his eyes hollow. "Your people need you alive. Your sister and mother are safe. I will send you to them."

I expect Ehren to argue, but he surrenders with a sharp nod. He's given up. I swallow and wisp him away. Kato spins to face me.

"You will lose this war. You should have joined my side," he says, meeting my eyes.

"I would rather lose in the name of doing what's right than win on the side of evil," I reply, holding my chin high.

"You're a fool, Astra," Kato spits. "A damn fool."

He lunges forward, but I wisp from the room into a nearby corridor. I can't hold it together much longer if I continue to face him.

I make my way through the castle, following the tug of the soul bond. I round a corner and find a group of the king's soldiers fighting a cluster of Dragkonians. I draw from my Fae power and strike, the Dragkonians fleeing the magic. The head soldier turns to me.

"Gather everyone you can and evacuate the castle," I command.

"Who are you to make demands of me?" the man sneers. "I follow the king and the king alone."

His words strike a match in me. I stand to my full height, shoulders straight and head held high. I meet the man's defiant gaze.

"My name is Astra Downs and I am the Court Sorceress under Prince Ehren, ordained by the Order of Naskein." I let my gaze drift to the other soldiers, making eye contact with them one at a time as I continue. "The king is dead, but the prince lives. I am his equal and his voice. You will heed me or face the consequences. Choose now if you will follow your prince or a fallen king. My brother, Kato, sits on the throne, supported by evil. Your prince is good and kind, and he will be king. So choose, but do so quickly. You don't have time to make the wrong choice."

The soldiers blink back at me for a moment.

"I will serve the prince," one of the soldiers says, bowing his head.

Several others add their voices in agreement, their commander eventually bowing his head as well.

"We will serve the prince," he grumbles.

"Good. Then obey his orders and evacuate the city. Go."

Without another moment of hesitation, they comply. Weariness rushes over me as I continue my path to Alak. I step outside and stare out over the courtyard that lies just inside the castle gates. Alak and the others have arrived, but the courtyard is little more than a battlefield.

My heart races, and all I can smell is blood. I close my eyes, trying to clear my head, but they shoot open again when I hear a screech and feel the flap of wings. More Dragkonians have landed.

Nyco takes a stand at the far end of the courtyard, flanked by a few wide-eyed soldiers. It's hard to tell from this far away exactly what kind of insect he's commanding, but he has a swarm of them acting as a shield between him and the closest Dragkonian. Cal and Makin fight side-by-side at the opposite end, clearing a safe path for a string of people fleeing the castle. I conjure my twin swords and join the battle.

Each blow seems to make the Dragkonians a little more wary, but they know they have the upper hand. They are striking faster and faster, leaving a trail of wounded in their wake. A round-faced woman with graying hair is assisted by a younger boy and girl in hooded apprentice cloaks as she makes her way around to the wounded, medical supplies in hand. It's obvious by their tense shoulders they're nervous and terrified, but their faces are set in determination as they help as many people as they can.

We're losing. More Dragkonians join the attack, bringing with them the smell of blood and death. I consider using another blast of Fae energy, but my supply is very low. I only have enough for a couple more attacks. And with as many Dragkonians are already on the ground, a shield will do nothing. We have to get out while we still can.

"Everyone"—I yell, as loudly as I can—"leave the castle and city! Now!"

A few eyes turn toward me, weighing me, judging if my words should be heeded.

"The king has fallen. His throne has been stolen," I cry out with as much authority as I can muster. "The prince lives. Those who require aid may receive it in the forest. Everyone else needs to evacuate as far as you can. Now, go!"

My words take hold and most of those fighting begin hastily heading from the courtyard. Several soldiers hold their ground, guarding those that are weaponless as they run. Nyco wisps away, taking someone with him. Using some of my own energy, I reach out and wisp away some of the wounded who are unable to rise, along with the healers. It takes more of my magic than I anticipated, and I stagger backward, a hand catching my arm.

"You need to leave, too, love," Alak says firmly as I look up into his serious green eyes. My magic must be truly weak if I didn't even sense how close Alak was.

I nod weakly, glancing at those that remain. "I will." I turn back to Alak. "Take anyone you can. I'll be right behind you."

Alak arches an eyebrow. "I'm not leaving you."

"Don't be stupid," I argue. "We don't have time. Just go."

I feel his hesitancy shoot down the bond. I weave my fingers into his and look into his eyes. "I promise. I'll be right behind you."

He sighs and gives my hand a squeeze. "Fine."

He hesitates only a moment before stepping away and reaches out his hand to a couple people nearby. I recognize one as the stable boy, Peter.

"I can get you out of here," Alak says evenly.

Peter studies Alak for a moment before nodding and taking his hand. They blink away. I turn my attention back to the courtyard. Most of the living have fled. Only a handful of soldiers—Cal and Makin among them—and the dead remain. Cal must sense my gaze, and he turns his eyes to meet mine. I can see the exhaustion on every line of his face. The nearest Dragkonian notices Cal's distraction and swoops in, his talon claws stretched in front of him.

Time slows. Cal slowly starts to turn his head back to his attacker, but he reacts all too late. His sword is lowered, and he's too drained to raise it quickly enough. Makin, however, has his sword drawn. He half-dives and half-charges between the attacking Dragkonian and Cal, knocking Cal to the ground as the Dragkonian's claws dig into his chest. Makin's eyes go wide as the Dragkonian snarls in delight and digs his talons deeper into Makin's flesh before pulling away. Makin's blood shines against his black scales as he clutches Makin's heart. Makin's body collapses into Cal's arms, his blood soaking them both. His eyes are wide but unseeing and blood leaks from the corner of his mouth. Cal's wail of agony shatters the air as he clutches Makin's limp body.

Something in me finally reacts, and I pull out the little Fae magic I have left, blasting the Dragkonian away and throwing up a shield over Cal and— Over Cal. The Dragkonian looks furious but flies away. My chest aches as I look back at Cal. I race across the courtyard, my legs trembling beneath me.

"Wake up," Cal cries, shaking Makin's body. "Please, I need you. Wake up!"

He shifts, lifting Makin up, and buries his head against Makin's shoulder, sobs racking his body. He doesn't seem to care or notice that his own clothes and skin are now drenched with Makin's blood.

"Please," he begs, his voice trembling and broken. "Don't leave me. You promised. You promised you'd be there for me, no matter what."

I feel shattered. I can't handle it. I reach out and lightly touch Cal's shoulder, wisping him away with Makin, but I don't go with him. Not yet.

I turn back to the courtyard. It's in shambles, the perfect symbol of a fallen kingdom. Blood and bodies cover the ground as the Dragkonians screech their victory from the sky. For the first time, I feel truly hopeless.

Something tugs at me, and it takes me a moment to realize it's the soul bond. I release a shuddering breath and wisp away to the woods. The sight that greets me isn't much better than the one I leave.

CHAPTER FORTY-ONE

ASTRA

Bodies are strewn everywhere, and the air is filled with the mingled scents of blood and earth. My heart is heavy as I survey the damages of war. Alak's eyes find me across the clearing, and I meet his gaze. He's exhausted and worn, but he's helping where he can. My own magic is far too drained to help, but I stumble forward, clinging to consciousness best I can. I kneel down next to Healer Ileora who is trying to heal a wounded servant with a large gash across his chest.

"How can I help?" I ask.

She raises her eyes to me. "You, child, have already done your part. You need to rest."

I shake my head. "No. I will not rest when there is work to be done."

My body betrays me as I falter back. Healer Ileora sighs and pulls a vial from her nearby bag. She offers it to me.

"One drop, maybe two," she says, her voice even. "But no magic. Not until you've had time to heal naturally."

I nod and accept the vial, putting a drop on my tongue. I

recognize the bitter oil as my magic responds. It begins refilling, not enough that I can use it, but enough that it takes the tip off my exhaustion. I hand the vial back to Healer Heora, and she gives me jobs to do.

I drift between aiding Healer Heora, Hanna, and the court healers, assisting them however they need. I tear strips of cloth into bandages and help to bind wounds. Following careful instructions, I mix salves and ointments to help refill our dwindling supply. I clean wounds and bandages and make people comfortable. I hold hands of those who cry out in pain as their wounds are bound, healed, and sewn. But those are the easy jobs. The emotional jobs are harder.

I wrap my arms around a young woman, weeping as she watches the life drain from her best friend. I distract a young noble from the recent death of his friend as the court healer seals his wounds. But the hardest is when I rock a young girl, no more than five, in my lap, singing her a lullaby as she falls into the permanent throes of sleep, her wounds too many and great to heal. I turn off my emotions to deal, determined to focus and help.

I work until there are no more tasks for me to complete. Night has fallen and several bonfires light the dark woods. Some sort of magic surrounds us, protecting and hiding us from Kato and his evil army. I turn my weary eyes to Healer Heora who gives me a tired nod.

"Rest," she commands, her voice little more than a whisper. "Rest and tomorrow we begin again."

I'm too tired and drained—emotionally and physically— to argue. I make my way to one of the bonfires where food has been set up. I see Alak a little way off surrounded by a group of children. Half of them have fallen asleep, but the others are fixed in rapt attention as he performs some of his more basic magic tricks. He meets my eyes and offers me a small smile. I return it and take a few bites of bread. After a moment of consideration, I grab another piece of bread and stand. There is more work to be done. Work that I alone can do.

I travel along the outside of the camp, searching, until I find Cal leaning against a tree, Makin's body stretched out at his feet. I approach slowly and almost turn away when I see Cal's eyes are closed. His head turns toward me, and he opens his eyes, swollen and bloodshot. I offer him a weak smile.

"I can leave you alone if you need to sleep."

He shakes his head and sits up a little, leaning his head back against the trunk of the tree. "I don't mind the company."

I sink down next to him and offer him the bread. "You need to eat."

He takes the bread but makes no move to eat it. He just stares off at nothing.

"You know," he says after a moment, "Makin would have loved this." He shakes his head. "If he could have chosen his death, he would have chosen this. Maybe not this exactly, but going out in the blaze of glory, in a heated battle."

A sob breaks free and Cal discards the bread, putting his head in his hands.

"It should have been me," he moans. "It should have been me!"

He screams and grabs a nearby rock from the ground, throwing it as hard as he can. He screams again and claws his hands down his face. His anguish strikes my heart, and I fight back tears. I reach and place a gentle hand on his shoulder.

"Tell me about him. How did you meet?"

Cal lowers his hands and meets my eyes, something flickering in their dark brown depths. I place the bread back in his hands as he sighs.

"He came from another town. I think he told you that," Cal begins, absentmindedly tearing a corner of the bread. "He was so determined to be part of Ehren's Guard. He practiced so hard to rise through the ranks, but he kept falling short of the tests required to even be considered for the Guard." He takes a bite of the bread and chews for a moment before continuing.

"Ehren and Bram used to have us go watch the soldiers who were trying to become members of his Guard and keep an eye on those with the most potential. I noticed Makin right away, not just because of skill, but because of his fervor. Everyone else's determination paled in comparison to his. And even when he failed, when he fell short, he never let it keep him down. I couldn't help but be drawn to him.

"One day I found him practicing alone after a full day of regular training. I stood on the sidelines, just watching like I always did, but this time he called out to me. He told me . . ." Cal pauses to laugh and shake his head. "He told me that he preferred to meet his stalkers up close, so if I was going to stalk him on a regular basis he might as well know my name."

He laughs again and takes another bite of bread. I smile encouragingly and he continues.

"I introduced myself and found myself volunteering to help him train. We started spending every afternoon together. At first, it was all centered on the training, but little by little we opened up to each other.

"He told me about his first kiss and the girl he left behind to pursue his dream of being on Ehren's Guard. And he spoke affectionately of his sister, who loved to bake and create delicious concoctions. He shared stories of the mischief he and his brother caused in their small town. In return, I shared little pieces of myself. We grew quite close."

Cal stops and eats for several seconds, and I wonder if he's done, but he looks over at me and forces a smile that doesn't go to his eyes.

"I remember the day Makin finally passed the tests necessary to be considered a true Guard candidate. He was so proud. *I* was proud. We went to the Gilded Goblet to celebrate. While we were there, one of the soldiers who had been denied the Guardship approached us. He told Makin that he should stay away from me because I only sought the comforts of men."

Cal shifts uncomfortably, but I only nod. He swallows and looks away, a hint of a smile on his lips.

"Makin punched the guy's face and told him he didn't care. I was the best friend he ever had other than his brother, and he wasn't going to let something as ridiculous as who I kiss get in the way of that. No one said anything to him or me again.

"A couple weeks later, when he made the Guard, we went out and celebrated again. I got a bit drunk and I kissed him. Makin jumped back, and I stumbled away, apologizing. I was so ashamed. I avoided him for days. He found me outside one night and begged me to be his friend again. He apologized over and over again, pleading with me to forgive him. I was confused at first. I thought I had been in the wrong and that he would want nothing to do with me. He told me that he simply didn't feel that way toward me, and he wasn't sure he ever could, but I was too great a friend to lose. He told me that he would always support me, and he would be there for me, if I would let him.

"Makin was always like that, you know—supporting me, no matter what. He is— *was* always there for me." His voice breaks and looks back at me, a tear sliding down his cheek. "How am I supposed to go on in life without him? How do I put this behind me?"

My heart breaks looking into his eyes. I reach out and grab his hand, giving it a gentle squeeze.

"I don't think you can," I admit, my voice quiet. "I don't think you're supposed to completely move on. He was piece of your life, a piece of your heart. You can't just heal from that. You have to learn how to deal with it in whatever way you can so you can live your life." I hesitate before continuing, weighing my words. "Makin saved your life. He wanted you to live. So, live for him."

Cal's lips part as another sob breaks free, but he nods and glances to the body at his feet.

"You're right. You're right. Makin would want me to live. And I will. Just, not yet. Soon, but not yet."

"I think that's all Makin would expect. Take your time."

He looks back at me as I stand, offering me a sad nod.

"You should get some rest," I say.

"I will. I . . . I think I need another minute alone."

I nod and leave Cal to his thoughts. I'm wandering through the camp, headed toward the largest tent in search of Ehren when Alak wraps his arms around me. I lean back into his touch as he presses a kiss to my temple.

"You need sleep, love," he murmurs.

I nod and wrap my arms over his. "I'll sleep soon. I need to find Ehren first."

"Promise?"

I turn around in Alak's arms and look up at him. "I promise."

He presses his lips to mine, and I feel his exhaustion full force. He releases me with a sigh and turns to leave.

"Don't be long, love."

I smile and nod. Once he's gone, I make my way to Ehren's tent, but it's not him I find inside. Cadewynn lays sprawled across the bed, her mother next to her. A Guard jolts awake in the corner of the tent. I recognize him as the Guard I spoke to earlier when searching for Cadewynn.

"Mistress Astra," he says, his voice groggy.

"I'm sorry to bother you," I apologize. "I'm looking for Ehren."

"He's not here," the Guard says. "I think he went to check the spells protecting the borders. That's what he said last I saw him, anyway."

I nod and thank the Guard. I step back out into the night and send out a touch of magic, searching for Ehren. It doesn't take me long to locate him. I follow the trail and discover him at the far end of the camp, bending down over a small smoking pile of herbs, whispering a spell. He hears me approaching and glances up, his eyes red and swollen. He stands as I near him.

"Protection spell?" I ask, nodding toward the magic.

He nods. "I'm just reinforcing the barrier. No point in escaping the palace if we all die here."

His voice is flat and lifeless. He meets my eyes, his last bit of resolve vanishing. He takes shuddering breath.

"I failed, Astra. I failed my mother, my sister, my Guard, my kingdom, m-my father . . ." His voice breaks as he shakes his head. "My father told me I failed the kingdom by abandoning it, and he was right. I left and everything fell apart. I wasn't here to defend the city. I failed him. I failed everyone. The kingdom fell because of me!" He clenches his fists in anguish as tears stream uncontrollably down his cheeks. "My own mother won't look me in the eye. She blames me for my father's death and she's right. She's right, Astra. My father is dead because of me! Makin, my own Guard, my friend, is *DEAD*! Who's next? Who will I kill next?"

I feel a crack in the dam holding back my emotions as a tear breaks free.

"No, Ehren," I say, reaching out and taking his hands in mine. "You didn't fail the kingdom. You may have saved the kingdom." He shakes his head and looks away, but I continue. "You secured an ally in the Order of Naskein. You procured funds from Gleador and the potential promise of more support. You won over your discarded half-sister and gained her trust. If you had stayed here, you wouldn't have accomplished any of that. If anyone is to blame, it's me."

Ehren's eyes meet mine as my own tears spill free in full force, all the emotions I've been holding in pouring out.

"No, Astra. No."

I shake my head, cutting him off before he can attempt to console me, to drive away my own surging guilt. "Kato is *my* brother, *my* twin. I have known him my entire life. I should have noticed that he was changing, that he was different. But I didn't. I was too focused on myself. By the time I realized something was wrong, he was too far gone. He's a murderer. *He* killed your father, not you. And that's my fault. I am sorry! I am so sorry, Ehren. I failed you. And I need to stop him or he'll kill more. I—"

I break off as Ehren pulls me into a tight embrace. I cling to him, my tears soaking his bloodstained clothes. I don't know how long we stay there, weeping, holding each other as tightly as we can. I'm not even sure who is comforting whom.

We just need each other. When Ehren finally draws back, he looks down at me, brushing a stray lock of hair from my face.

"I don't blame you, Ash," he says, his voice low and quiet. "It's not your fault. Kato is his own person. You can't control what he does."

"Then you can't blame yourself, either."

Ehren nods and steps back, raking a hand through his hair as he scans the trees around us.

"What do we do now?" He drops his gaze to me. "I suppose the cowardly prince runs again."

I shake my head. "You were never a coward. Don't you dare think like that for a single second. Now? You do what you do best. You make a plan."

Ehren nods. "A plan." He swallows and nods, licking his lips. "A plan. I can do that."

I can see the gears in his head turning as a plan forms. He paces back and forth in front of me.

"First, we need to get out of this forest. Anyone who can needs to leave tomorrow. We work on getting everyone else out as soon as possible."

I nod. "I agree."

"Then, I'll reach out to any and every ally we have. I'll find support. I'll create support. We'll go somewhere safe and construct a plan. We'll get Winnie and my mother to safety where Kato can't reach them. I'll vet my father's soldiers and find which will be loyal to me." He pauses and turns to me, a smile curling on his lips, though it doesn't hold its normal levity. "I heard, by the way, about your little speech to my father's men. It seems you put them in their place, Court Sorceress."

I can't help but smile a little in return. "Well, I wasn't going to let them get away with disrespecting you."

Ehren smiles, but it fades quickly. "There's so much to do and figure out."

I nod. "And we'll figure it out together. You're not alone in this, Ehren. But now, you need sleep. We both do."

He waves me off. "In a bit."

"Ehren," I say firmly.

"There's one last border spell I need to check, but I'll come after I'm done."

I arch an eyebrow.

"I promise."

"Fine," I concede. "But if you're not resting soon, I will come find you and drag you to a cot. I don't care if you're the prince and rightful king."

His smile seems more genuine as he says, "I won't break my promise."

I leave Ehren to his spellwork and wander back into the camp. Things have settled a bit. The wounded still moan and many of the refugees toss and turn, but it's otherwise quiet. I scan the crowd and spot Hanna and Pip curled up together near one of the bonfires. I suspect Healer Heora is resting inside the healing tent. Nyco is also fast asleep, Sama sprawled across his chest. I realize with a sense of satisfaction that Cal lies not far from them, though I doubt he's sleeping yet. I suspect Bram and Kai will be up most of the night, patrolling the edges of the camp in constant surveillance despite the spells and wards protecting us.

I feel a pull on the soul bond and direct my attention to Alak. He's sitting at the far end next to a fire. I make way my over to him and settle on the ground next to him.

"Everything okay, love?" he asks, tracing a gentle hand across my tear-stained cheek.

I take a deep breath and shake my head. "No. Not really, but I'm managing."

He nods and lies down, drawing me down with him. He kisses the top of my head as I snuggle against him. I'm almost asleep when I sense Ehren approaching. I lift my eyes to him, and he offers me a weak smile. I shift in Alak's arms so I can face Ehren as he lies down next to us.

"As promised," he whispers, meeting my eyes.

I smile and reach out my hand, grabbing his. He squeezes my hand in response and closes his eyes. I take a deep breath and follow suit. We need rest. Who knows what tomorrow will bring? At least we will have each other.

EPILOGUE

EHREN

My kingdom is in shambles, under the rule of a cruel and misplaced king who stole my throne. But I have a plan. A plan to reclaim my crown and restore peace throughout my kingdom.

The first part of the plan is getting all the refugees of Embervein to safety. It takes the better part of a week, but we accomplish the task. Astra works with the Healers to take care of the more severe wounds, and the magic wielders help to wisp as many people away as possible. There are several servants and soldiers with no place to go, so they will join us as we travel to the Summer Palace.

It was Winnie's idea to use the Summer Palace. She's quite clever and while I do wish she could be safely stored away, I'm glad she's by my side for now. We haven't gone to the palace in years, but I spent summers there as a child and know the path there well enough. It's a smaller castle a little further north, but well-fortified and more easily defended. We can go there while we regroup and wait for word from our allies.

I write letters to all our allies, begging for their help. I lay out the situation, holding nothing back. I send my fastest Guards, and even some of my father's soldiers, to deliver our message. We need help or the continent will soon be in the throes of dark magic.

Winnie and my mother will go on to Gleador, out of the direct reach of Kato. Winnie isn't happy about it, but she understands. I can't lose anyone else. I can't even look at Cal without feeling the overwhelming guilt of Makin's death. Honestly, I can't look at anyone without feeling guilt, though Astra assures me that no one in our party blames me. I can still blame myself.

I feel this guilt the strongest on the day we burn the dead. Some of the dead have people there to mourn them, others do not. Some are nameless faces. Sama helps to take down descriptions and names of all those who lost their lives so their families can be contacted. With so many bodies, a grave is impossible, so we burn them, their ashes riding in the smoke to the gods above.

We burn them, save for one. Cal digs the grave, allowing no one to help him. He stands alone, a solitary figure over a mound a dirt. When he falls to his knees, the others rush to his side. I cannot. I watch from several yards away, the weight of Makin's death too much for me to bear. Cal's loss is too great, and I can't stand the thought of how much he must despise me. I've utterly failed him in the worst way. I long to comfort him, but I'm sure I'm the last person he needs at his side. He's always been my most loyal Guard and friend after Bram, but now I've surely driven him away. That thought alone leaves a cold void in my chest.

My kingdom has fallen and everything and everyone I love are at risk. I can't give up, but I struggle to fight. Doubt and feelings of inadequacy cloud my thoughts like a dark shroud. I have to remind myself that I'm not alone. I have Astra, and therefore Alak. I have Bram and what remains of my Guard. I have allies and I have magic. I only hope it will be enough to save us before we lose everything.

May the gods hear our prayers and give us the strength we need to fight the coming dark days ahead.

ACKNOWLEDGMENTS

I would like to say a special thanks to you, the reader. If this book is in your hands, I wrote it for you. You are the reason I write and the reason this book comes to life. Sure, I wrote the words, but without you, it's just ink on paper. You breathe fresh life into my story and it's because of you this book came to be.

I also can't leave without thanking my earliest readers: Shanti, Megan, and Lana. You all put up with the story in its toughest stages and helped to mold it into the story that exists today.

Special thanks goes to my editor, Andi. I'm really glad you know how commas work. Honestly, I think all the comma rules are made up, and without your help the world would know how bad I am at using commas.

Before I take a bow and go chug some coffee to prepare for the next project, I need to thank my family, as cliché as that may be. My mom has always been one of my greatest cheerleaders. She never let me think I couldn't be a writer. In fact, she always fed my dream. My husband is always supportive of my writing dream and even puts up with all my art demands. Even my kids encourage the writing process. Honestly, we're all a great team of dreamers.

EXTENDED AUTHOR NOTE

This book contains some of the following elements that may prove sensitive for some readers:

Mentions of Suicide

This is a continuation of the previously mentioned suicide and suicide attempts discussed in the first book. No suicide attempts are performed on the page. (Chapter Thirty-One)

Sexual Assault

Sexual assault of a male character is attempted by a female character at the very end of Chapter Ten. She fails in her attempt. Potential sexual assault is also hinted at as a possibility in Chapter Thirty-Three. No sexual assault is actually completed.

PTSD & Past Trauma

This is a reoccurring thing throughout the book as Astra

struggles with the guilt of having to kill off attacking enemies to survive and Alak battles with his past. These events reach a climax in Chapters Thirty-Seven and Thirty-Eight when the characters are forced to confront their deepest fears and insecurities.

Grief

Several characters grieve throughout the book as they relive previous traumas and experience new ones. This grief is especially strong in the final chapters and prologue.

About the Author

Amber D. Lewis is a new adult fantasy author with a Bachelor's Degree in Publishing. She currently lives in Taylors, SC with her husband and three kids. When she's not reading or writing books, you'll probably find her wandering the aisles of Target.

The Fire and Starlight Saga is Amber's first series, though she has several more in the works.

facebook.com/amberdlewisofficialauthorpage

instagram.com/mugshots_n_bookthoughts

twitter.com/ADLewis_Author

bookbub.com/profile/amber d lewis

goodreads.com/crymeariversong11